ALSO BY SHANNON WORK

Now I See You
Everything To Lose
The Killing Storm
Murder in the San Juans
Death in a Harsh Land

ECHOES
IN THE
DARK

A NOVEL

SHANNON WORK

This is a work of fiction. Names, characters, businesses, organizations, places, events and incidents are either products of the author's imagination or are used fictitiously. Any resemblance to actual persons, living or dead, or actual events is entirely coincidental.

COPYRIGHT © 2025 by Shannon Work
All rights reserved.

No part of this publication may be reproduced, distributed, or transmitted in any form or by any means, including photocopying, recording, or other electronic or mechanical methods, without the prior written permission of the publisher, except in the case of brief quotations embodied in critical reviews and certain other noncommercial uses permitted by copyright law.

ISBN: 979-8-9869376-5-6 (paperback)
ISBN: 979-8-9869376-7-0 (large print paperback)
ISBN: 979-8-9869376-6-3 (eBook)

www.shannonwork.com

"Each day we are becoming a creature of splendid glory or one of unthinkable horror."
C.S. Lewis

CHAPTER 1

Monday, August 26

"There are ghosts in gold mines, you know?" Benny said, propping his foot on a rock to tie his shoe.

"Ain't so." Colby poked at the ground with a tree branch he used as a walking stick.

"Are too," Benny replied. "They're called Tommyknockers."

"Tommyknockers? I ate there once. It's a restaurant in Idaho Springs."

"Not *that* Tommyknockers, you idiot. Tommyknockers, as in ghosts. They scare miners. Play tricks on them. Sometimes they'll even kill a man." Benny dropped his foot to the ground and fell back in step with his two companions.

It was the second week of sixth grade, and the trio was already playing hooky. By midmorning, they were two thousand feet above Telluride and climbing higher. The boys had spent their summer vacation exploring the mountains around town. They had illegally entered several abandoned mines and, despite a couple of close calls, had lived to brag to their friends about it.

Colby, the Tommyknocker skeptic, shook his mop of blond hair. "Well, I think you're lyin'."

"Am not."

"He's telling the truth," said Noah, the self-proclaimed

group leader. "But if you two don't stop jawing, we'll never get there."

Benny scrambled up the rocky hillside to catch up. "And where is *there*, exactly?"

"Only the coolest mine in the San Juans," Noah replied.

"What makes it so cool?"

"You'll see."

"It's getting cold," Colby complained.

Benny agreed, wrapping his arms around himself and rubbing.

The three picked their way up the forested slopes, fording creeks and crossing dangerous scree fields, large swaths of broken rock. They lunched near the top of a waterfall, staying clear of its chilly mist, which boiled below.

Twenty minutes later, with the lunch trash stowed securely in their backpacks, they set out again.

"How much farther?" Colby asked a while later, stopping to lean on his walking stick.

Benny pulled up beside him and propped his hands on his knees, catching his breath and spilling his sizable belly over the waistband of his shorts. "Yeah, Noah, are we there yet?"

Noah searched the gray cliffs above them until he spotted a series of granite formations lined up along the mountain's summit. "We're almost there," he said, pointing. "See the rocks? The ones that look like fingers pointing at the sky?"

"I can't see nothin' for shivering to death," Colby complained.

Benny straightened and let his gaze follow Noah's outstretched arm. "I see 'em."

"It's through those rocks somewhere."

"What is?" Colby asked.

"The mine."

Benny sighed. Their destination was still so far away. And to make matters worse, there was no trail and the terrain was nearly vertical. Although Benny wanted to turn back, he would never admit it. Noah would tease him again about being fat. He turned to Colby, hoping he'd complain about the mine being too far. Everyone knew Colby complained about everything, but he just followed Noah up the mountain. Benny rolled his eyes and started after his companions.

It took another half hour of climbing to reach the gap in the ridgeline that led to Shudder Basin and an hour of searching before the boys finally found the mine's entrance. They stopped well short of their destination, studying the gaping black hole from a distance. A massive iron door bolted to solid rock stood open. Although the day was overcast, a single ray of sunshine illuminated the entrance as if beckoning them inside.

Colby rubbed his eyes and gazed hard at the mine. "Looks creepy."

They heard a faint noise somewhere in front of them.

"What was that?" Benny asked.

Noah took a second to answer. "Sounded like a rock."

"I think something broke in the mine," Benny said, straining to see into the darkness. "Like a timber or something."

"Nah, sounded like a rock," Noah repeated.

A crow squawked overhead, and the boys flinched.

The three stood a while longer.

"You girls chicken?" Noah asked, breaking the silence.

Colby squeezed his walking stick. "Doesn't look safe to me."

"None of them are safe," Noah replied, trying to sound more confident than he was. "That's the adventure of it."

Benny squinted. "There's something written over the entrance."

"It's a sign," Colby said.

"I see it's a sign, you idiot. But what does it say?"

"Probably to keep out."

Noah started forward. "If you're scared, you can stay here. But I'm going to check it out."

Benny hesitated. "There's probably Tommyknockers in there."

Colby shook his head as he fell into step behind Noah. "If there *are* any Tommyknocker in there—and I'm not sayin' I believe in 'em—but if there are, then they're probably gonna kill us."

"Would you two girls shut up?" Noah whispered over his shoulder. "Everyone knows Tommyknockers don't mess with kids."

"Says who?" Benny asked, catching up.

"Says everybody who knows anything, you idiot."

The trio slowed as they got closer.

"The Judas Mine." Colby read the faded lettering aloud. "Never heard of it."

"I have," Benny replied. "It's haunted."

"You're lyin'."

"Am not. That's what I heard."

"You're sayin' there's Tommyknockers in there?"

"They didn't say Tommyknockers, you idiot," Benny said. "They said *ghosts*. Everyone knows they're different."

"Well, I've never heard of the Judas Mine," Colby said again.

"Will you two shut up?" Noah said, sounding brave. "I never knew of it either until I heard that famous treasure hunter talking about it at the cafe."

"The loud guy with all the teeth?" Colby asked.

"Yeah, that's him." Noah stopped and stared into the darkness.

"His name's Eli something," Benny said, pulling up beside him. "My parents were talking about him. He's been on TV."

"Whatever his name is, he was telling somebody there's a ton of gold still in there." Noah jerked his chin at the entrance.

"Gold?" Colby answered, squinting into the darkness. "That would be awesome."

Benny took his friend's arm. "Unless there's ghosts in there, too."

Colby turned and whacked him with the stick.

The three stood a second longer, then advanced slowly, Benny and Colby letting Noah take the lead. A rush of frigid air greeted them as they stepped into the dark. Having explored other mines, they had expected the drop in temperature. But they hadn't expected what they saw when their eyes adjusted to the drop in light.

All three pulled up just inside the entrance and froze.

"What's that?" Colby whispered.

"You mean, *who's* that?" Noah replied.

A man lay sprawled face down between the old rail tracks on the mine's dirt floor, a dozen or so feet from the entrance.

Benny felt his stomach lurch, but he took a step closer. "Is he dead?"

Still staring, Noah shook his head slowly. "I don't know."

"You think Tommyknockers got him?" Colby asked, stepping cautiously around the others. "Hey, mister." He reached out with the walking stick and poked the man's shoulder. "Are you alright?" There was no movement.

Benny took a step back and swallowed. "Doesn't look alright to me."

"He's not breathing," Noah said and pointed. "Guys, look at his back."

A small red bloom had stained the man's shirt below his left shoulder.

"He's been stabbed." Benny gagged, then covered his mouth with a hand.

"Or shot," Colby said.

A bat suddenly emerged from somewhere deep within the mountain. It flew erratically past the boys and out through the entrance. The trio shrieked in unison, their screams echoing in the darkness as they turned to flee.

CHAPTER 2

Wednesday, September 18

JACK MARTIN LOOKED over the one-room cabin that had been his home for the previous three months—two hundred square feet, enclosed by stacked log walls and a planked wood roof. Against one wall was a single metal cot that Jack had never used. A small reading table was pushed against another. There was only one chair and no electricity. The floor was dirt.

Living in the cabin hadn't been easy, but Jack was going to miss it. It had been one hell of a summer.

"I think that's everything," he said, stuffing the last of their provisions into his backpack.

"What about the dogs?" Otto asked.

Otto Finn was a lively octogenarian and Jack's neighbor at the campground in Telluride. He had spent every summer for the last fifty years at the high-altitude camp where the two men now packed to leave.

After returning from a trip to Texas several months earlier, Jack discovered that Otto had left for the mountains, taking the dogs with him. But he located the cabin using a GPS tracker he'd secretly slipped onto Crockett's collar before leaving Telluride.

The two men and their dogs had spent the summer over twelve thousand feet above town in a shallow basin hidden by rock outcroppings, the dogs chasing marmots and pikas and lolling in the grass, the men digging and picking their way through a maze of underground tunnels in Otto's mine.

The mine's location was a well-guarded secret, and Otto took several opportunities over the summer to mention he'd never had a visitor. Jack couldn't tell if the old man was put out with him for being there or if he enjoyed the company.

"The dogs are loaded and ready to go," Jack said. He tossed the backpack over his shoulders and glanced around the room a final time.

"I'll be out in a minute." Otto was carefully arranging his few remaining cigarettes in a small tin can. A canvas duffel bag was on the ground at his feet.

Jack stepped out of the cabin and into the morning cold and was immediately met by two excited dogs—one brown and one red. Both had modified rucksacks strapped to their backs. Hiking the summer's spoils out of the mountain required a team effort, and Jack had the feeling the dogs sensed it when he'd loaded the packs onto them ten minutes earlier. Neither had protested for long and eventually accepted the added weight as inevitable. Jack had been careful not to overload them, secretly storing some of what Otto had designated for the dogs in his own backpack. The added weight didn't dampen the dogs' enthusiasm. They danced at Jack's feet, wagging their tails, anticipating the next adventure.

Otto emerged from the cabin and turned to lash the door shut with a leather strap.

Jack took a moment to look over the setting that had become so familiar and caught a glimpse of the golden soil tailings that spilled from the entrance to the mine. He looked past the cabin and across the high alpine meadow. The wildflowers that had blanketed the slopes a month earlier were gone, replaced by a layer of frost covering grass, which was now dormant. Pockets of snow in the jagged peaks above them were already several feet deep. The mornings were growing colder, and Jack knew it was time to go. He let his gaze linger a moment longer, then turned to follow the old man out of the mountains.

There was no trail, and Jack thought the route Otto used to descend seemed illogical and circuitous but suspected it was done on purpose to conceal the way back if Jack were ever inclined to find it again.

Reaching town took a fraction of the time it had taken Jack to hike to the mine in June. Despite their dubious route, they were back at the campground by nightfall.

Jack was surprised by how much in Telluride had changed since he'd left. The summer crowds were gone, and the aspen trees were showing their fall colors. The grass around his Airstream trailer and Otto's army surplus tent had grown knee-high.

The men removed the rucksacks from the dogs and stowed them inside the tent.

Jack sifted through the contents of his backpack and handed Otto several drawstring sacks. "I think that's it," he said.

Otto nodded. "I've got a man coming to pick it all up in the morning. He'll take it and weigh it. I should have your cut by lunchtime." He brushed dried aspen leaves from the seat of a folding chair and sat. The day's journey had him understandably weary.

Both men watched as the dogs, now free of their loads, rolled in the grass that lined the creek bordering the campground.

After a few minutes, Jack held out a hand, and as his friend shook it, he said, "Thank you for the best few months I've had in a long time."

A smile creased Otto's weathered face. "It was a fine summer."

His speech had slowed, and Jack realized that since they'd gotten back to the campground, he had used the cane to walk.

It was as if, by leaving the mountains, he had aged decades in a matter of minutes.

Jack understood why. Returning to town was a letdown after his time in the mountains, disconnected from the distractions of humanity and technology. He had spent months working with his hands, pulling treasure from an unyielding mountain and communing not with people but with nature. When the two men weren't working deep inside the bowels of the mountain, they'd sat in the grass, watching elk graze across the steep slopes of the basin. Marmots and pika were always scurrying about, causing excitement as the dogs clambered to catch them. And Jack would miss the bears—a large cinnamon-colored mama and her two cubs that were always nearby.

The pull of the mountains was strong. Otto had felt it for a lifetime. Now Jack felt it, too.

It didn't matter that he wasn't expecting his cut of the summer's spoils to amount to much. They hadn't mined gold or even silver, but chunks of rock mixed with clusters of a particular stone. "Rhodochrosite," Otto called it. "It's a mineral."

The stones were pretty, mined from the mountain in shades of red and pink, but they couldn't be worth much. For decades Otto had let locals think he mined for gold, and before they'd left the mountains, he'd sworn Jack to secrecy that it wasn't.

It was hard to believe that finding the pink stone was how the old man made a living, but somehow, it was. And Jack was hopeful that whatever his share amounted to, it would be enough that he could stay in Telluride for a few more months before heading back to Texas.

"Come on, Crockett, let's go," he called to the brown dog. "You can play with Red tomorrow." Crockett reluctantly followed him to the Airstream.

As Jack approached the trailer, he noticed a small piece

of paper taped to the front door. It had wrinkled and curled at the edges, clearly having been there for some time. He pulled it free and unfolded it.

Jack—Call or come see me as soon as you're back in town. It's urgent.

It was signed by Tony Burns, the county sheriff.

Remembering the cell phone he hadn't used in months, Jack fished it from his backpack and turned it on and thought it was a miracle when he saw a sliver of battery power left. The phone pinged with a flurry of messages just before it died. But it was enough time to see that a majority of the messages were left by the sheriff's office. From the texts and the condition of the note taped to the trailer door, it was apparent Tony Burns had been trying to reach him for some time.

Jack frowned, wondering what had happened.

CHAPTER 3

JACK UNLOCKED THE door and laid his keys and the note from the sheriff on the tiny kitchen counter, then quickly glanced over the trailer's contents and was satisfied everything was as he had left it in June.

He went to check the time on his phone, and remembering the battery was dead, he glanced through the window and saw the sun sliding toward the horizon. It would probably be somewhere between six thirty and seven o'clock. If he was lucky, Pandora Cafe would still be open. The only thing that sounded better than a hot shower and a warm bed was a good meal.

He grabbed his keys from the counter, leaving the note. Whatever Tony wanted could wait.

"You hungry?" Jack asked Crockett.

The dog wagged its tail.

"Me too. Come on."

When they reached the cafe, it was open but not busy. Jack chose his favorite table, the one in front of the river-rock fireplace, and sat facing the door. Crockett settled on the wood floor and rested his head on the toe of one of Jack's boots.

The night was cool, but the gas logs were unlit. A few more weeks would change everything. The weather would turn cold, warranting the heat of a fire. Crowds in town and at the cafe would swell with tourists. Jack had been in Telluride long enough to recognize the ebbs and flows of the seasons. Although he loved the slower months, late spring and fall, when town was left mostly to the locals, he also enjoyed the peak seasons. The commotion that came with the tourists who flooded the small valley in summer and winter was exhilarating.

After missing most of the summer crowd while spending months in the mountains with only Otto and the dogs, he found that he was looking forward to the chaos of the upcoming winter—tourists traipsing through town carting skis and snowboards, the ruckus when all the restaurants and bars swelled with noisy patrons until well into the night. Telluride would morph from a sleepy mountain town into a bustling tourist destination practically overnight.

He glanced over the small crowd in the cafe, nodding at a handful of locals he recognized. A young waitress was clearing a table near the front. What was her name? It took a moment, but he remembered it was Casey. But he was disappointed there was no sign of Judith Hadley, the cafe's owner. Then the kitchen door swung open and she appeared carrying plates of food. She said something to the cook over her shoulder and laughed.

She wore a plaid dress Jack had seen her wear a hundred times and a burlap apron cinched around her waist. There was something different about her cropped gray hair—maybe she had cut it—but everything else was the same.

Jack smiled, watching her, and realized how much he had missed her. Although he'd known Judith for only a few months, she was like family. And Jack liked to imagine she resembled the mother he'd never known.

Judith set the plates on a nearby table, tucked the tray under her arm, and exchanged a few words with the diners. When she looked up and noticed Jack watching, her smile grew wider and she immediately came over.

"If you hadn't been sitting at your usual table, I might

not have recognized you," she said, setting the tray down and reaching out her arms. "Give me a hug, stranger."

Jack stood and happily obliged. "It's good to see you," he said, releasing her from the hug.

"Look at you." She held him at arm's length. "A real mountain man."

Jack stroked his beard self-consciously. He hadn't seen his reflection in months, but he knew his hair had grown well past its usual shoulder length. And his beard, usually short and neat, had also grown long over the summer.

"You look like one of those singers with ZZ Top," she teased. "Only more handsome." She bent to pet Crockett.

"We just got back in town."

Judith nodded at his chair. "Well, sit back down," she said, untying her apron. "I want to hear all about it." She took an empty chair at the table and motioned for Casey, who quickly came over.

Jack ordered a bowl of chicken and dumplings and spent the next several minutes regaling Judith with stories of living in the mountains and working with Otto in the mine, careful not to mention the pink stones. As he talked, Judith sat on the edge of the seat, listening.

When he was done, she leaned closer and dropped her voice. "I can't believe you've actually seen it. After all these years, I think you're the only one." She sat back, thinking. "I bet the old coot made you promise never to tell anyone where it is."

Jack sat quiet. Although Otto had insisted he never divulge the mine's location, Jack wasn't sure he could find the way back even if he wanted to.

Judith laughed. "I knew it," she said, watching him. After a while, she came forward in the chair, shaking her head. "Oh no. Don't tell me."

"Tell you what?"

"I should have expected it to happen."

"Expected what?"

"I can see it in your eyes. You've gone and caught gold fever."

Jack chuckled. "Not hardly," he said, remembering Otto's secret pink stones.

Judith took a pencil from behind her ear and tapped the eraser on the table. "It's a real thing, you know."

"What is?"

"Gold fever. We don't see much of it around here anymore, but there was a lot of it back in the sixties and seventies. Men being consumed by their obsession with gold—forgetting about their families and their jobs. The fever can drive a man crazy." She pointed the pencil at him. "So, you be careful, Jack Martin. Make sure you don't catch it."

"I won't," Jack said, holding up his hands. "I promise." His last case had slipped her mind. Because of his trip to Texas early that summer, Jack knew all too well how the hunt for gold could drive men mad.

"If you say so," Judith said. "But by the looks of you, I'm not sure I believe it."

When Jack finished his meal, he wiped his mouth with a napkin and leaned back in the chair. "I can honestly say that was the best meal I've had in months."

Judith was still sitting with him. "Well, I would hope so," she said, "after living off Otto's elk jerky and beans for three months." She paused a moment with a somber look on her face.

"Listen," she said. "I didn't want to mention it earlier and ruin your meal, but the sheriff's been looking for you."

"I had a note from Tony when I got back, saying to call him. But my phone's dead."

"You can use mine. Someone from his office has been in here every day looking for you."

Jack was surprised. "Do you know what they want?"

"I have a guess." She paused before she continued. "There's been a murder."

CHAPTER 4

JACK WASN'T SURE why a murder in San Miguel County necessitated him contacting the sheriff—unless it was someone Jack knew. Names and faces suddenly flashed through his mind.

"Buckley?" he asked. Buckley Bailey was Texas's former governor and a friend of his. God knew Buckley had his share of enemies.

Judith shook her head. "No, not Buckley."

Jack was relieved for a moment, then felt a knot catch in his throat. "Not Lea?"

Judith reached her hands across the table and laid them over his. "No, Jack, not Lea."

Jack let out the breath he'd been holding. He had rescued Lea Scotsman from the clutches of a murderer only a few months earlier. She was older than Jack but beautiful. And she still haunted his sleep from time to time. Jack pushed the memories aside.

"I don't think you knew him," Judith said, releasing Jack's hands. "He was a local boy. I say *boy*, but he was really a man. Probably going on forty. I've just known him so long."

"Who was he?"

The front door swung open, and a rush of cold night air flooded the cafe. Jack looked up as Deputy Kim O'Connor stepped inside. She was pretty. Nearing forty, with a small, birdlike frame. Her red hair was tied up in a ponytail—the only way Jack had ever seen her wear it.

He had worked with her on a search and rescue mission months earlier. And although the deputy was merely an acquaintance, Jack had seen enough to know that her petite stature and fiery red ponytail belied what a serious lawman she was.

She let the door fall closed behind her and scanned the room. When her eyes met Jack's, she was surprised, then her face relaxed with a look of relief. She made a beeline for his table.

"You're back."

Jack stood to shake her hand. "Deputy."

She said hello to Judith, then nodded at an empty chair at the table.

"Please," Jack said, indicating for her to sit. She did, then turned a cool eye on him. Something about her demeanor was off.

"We need you to come into the office," she said. "I know it's late, but Sheriff Burns wants to talk to you as soon as possible."

"Is it about the murder?"

Kim stole a nervous glance at Judith, then answered him. "It is."

"Who was killed?"

"A man by the name of Dylan Montgomery."

"I don't know him."

"There's no reason for you to, but Tony would like to talk to you anyway." When Jack didn't reply, her face tensed. "It's important. He needs your help."

Jack could tell from her expression that Dylan Montgomery's death was more than a run-of-the-mill murder—a jealous husband or a bar fight between fools. Something about it had upset the sheriff enough to reach out to him. And although Jack had a good working relationship with Tony Burns, it was unusual for a lawman to ask a civilian for help.

Jack was intrigued. "I'll come by in the morning."

Kim glanced down at the empty bowl in front of him. "Looks like you're finished."

Jack frowned. "You want me to come now?"

She nodded. "I'll call Tony. He'll want to know you're back." She got up from the table. "I'll meet you outside."

Jack watched her walk out of the cafe, then wiped his hands on his napkin, pushed his chair back from the table, and got up. "I guess I'll be going," he told Judith. "We can finish our conversation tomorrow."

He started to dig into his pocket for his wallet, but Judith waved her hand.

"This one's on me," she said, putting her apron back on. "I told you to come see me as soon as you got back to town, and you kept your end of the bargain." She started for the kitchen. "But you come back tomorrow, you hear? I've got a few more questions about the mine."

Town mother or town gossip—Jack wasn't sure which, but he didn't care. He would come back to the cafe the next day—for the company as well as for the food. And he was positive Judith would pump him for information. But not about Otto's mine. About his meeting with Tony Burns.

Jack smiled and shook his head. "Come on, Crockett. Let's go see the sheriff."

When the deputy saw them step outside, she ended a call and stuck her phone into her pocket. "My cruiser is just down the street."

Jack fell into step with her, Crockett close on their heels. Night had fallen, the streetlamps casting pools of light among the shadows. There was an ominous chill in the air, a harbinger of the coming winter.

Out of habit, Jack scanned their surroundings and noticed that a handful of restaurants and bars were the only establishments still open. A few locals still milled about in the dark. Was he imagining it, or were they stealing glances as he and the deputy walked toward her Tahoe? The murder had the town on edge.

Although Jack noticed the handful of people turn to look, he never saw the young girl watching from around a corner—or the little man gawking at him nervously through the dark window of the bank.

CHAPTER 5

TED HAWTHORNE WATCHED through the window of Telluride Bank & Trust as the deputy's Tahoe pulled away from the curb and started out of town. He had been locking up the bank when he noticed Jack Martin on the sidewalk.

Luckily, he had already shut the lights off, keeping the detective from seeing him. At least that's what Ted hoped.

He turned from the window, nervously adjusting the bow tie at his neck. He smoothed his oiled hair over his tall forehead and realized his hands were shaking. He quickly clasped them together and squeezed, trying to make them stop. But it was no use. Still trembling, they were now both slick with pomade.

Damn detective.

When he hadn't seen the detective for several months, Ted was sure he had left town. So why was he back?

Wondering about it made the jumpy banker even more nervous. Then it dawned on him—he was back because of Dylan Montgomery's murder.

Ted felt his heart race and pulled a pill bottle from the pocket of his slacks but struggled to open it.

"Come on, dammit," he said, fighting the childproof cap with trembling fingers. When his glasses slid down his nose, he pushed them back into place, transferring pomade onto their wire frames.

Of course Dylan's murder was why Jack Martin was back.

It made sense. It was why he was with that redheaded woman deputy.

Giving up on the pills, he stuffed the bottle into his pocket and scurried around the bank, checking and rechecking that the cash drawers, his private office, and the safe were all locked. It was his OCD—he had already checked that everything was locked. But seeing that detective again had him in a tizzy.

Ted snatched his keys from the teller counter and walked to the front door. He laid a hand on the dead bolt but stopped to check the sidewalk. When he was satisfied there was no threat of imminent danger, he unlocked the door and stepped outside, then immediately pivoted to relock it.

Instead of turning for home, he stood on the sidewalk to think, staring in the direction the deputy's Tahoe had disappeared over the horizon.

Dylan was dead, complicating things enough already. But now the detective was back in town. It could be a problem.

But Ted vowed not to let it be.

He drew himself up as tall as he could, threw back his narrow shoulders, and took in a deep breath, feeling his shirt tighten across his chest before releasing the air in slow, jerky puffs. He was a god, he was a king, he told himself—just like the self-help book said to do. And he wasn't going to let some bumpkin detective from Texas ruin anything.

He took his cell phone from his pocket and flipped it open, its small screen illuminating his face in the dark.

There was one man who could make all of his problems go away.

CHAPTER 6

When Kim pulled her Tahoe into the parking lot of the San Miguel County Sheriff's Office, Jack was surprised to see the place buzzing with activity. The sun was long gone, but there was more than a typical skeleton crew working the night shift. Something had law enforcement buzzing, and Jack suspected it was the murder.

Sheriff Tony Burns was at his desk and looked up as Jack walked in. "Where in the hell have you been?" Despite his harsh tone, the sheriff seemed more relieved than annoyed.

"Hello, Tony." Jack took an empty chair in front of the desk.

Burns motioned for Kim to take the other. He shuffled some papers and then set them aside. "You don't answer your phone. I thought I was going to have to shine a bat light into the clouds to get your attention."

"I've been—"

"In the mountains." Burns waved him off. "I know." There were dark circles under his eyes, and he slumped over the desk like a man on the verge of defeat. He laid his palms down in front of him. "Listen, Jack, I need your help."

Jack rested a boot on his opposite knee, wondering what was coming next. "What can I do for you?"

"There's been a murder."

"I heard."

Burns raised his eyebrows, glancing at the deputy.

"I didn't tell him, sir," Kim said. "He already knew."

"I became aware of the murder before Deputy O'Connor arrived at the cafe."

"The cafe?" Burns frowned, then relaxed his brows and nodded. "Of course. Judith Hadley."

"I would have found out anyway." Jack felt the need to defend his friend. "I'm guessing the murder has been the talk of the town."

"How much do you know?"

"Hardly anything."

"Then let me fill you in." Burns leaned his weight back in his chair, causing it to tilt. "The deceased is Dylan Montgomery, aged thirty-nine. Found by three Telluride juveniles on Monday, August twenty-sixth, in a mine called the Judas, located in Shudder Basin. Blunt-force trauma wound to the back of his head that wasn't fatal. Gunshot wound just below his left shoulder blade that was. Went clear through him, exiting near his naval. Coroner confirmed the death occurred within a couple of hours of the body being found. But due to the humidity and temperature in the mine, he can't estimate it any more precisely than that."

Jack interrupted. "Should I be taking notes?"

Tony Burns shook his head. "No need. If you agree to help, I'll give you the report. And I'll pay you." He let that sink in before he continued. "The deceased is from Denver but lived most of his adult life in and around Telluride. Owned the mine he was found dead in. No family. Not many friends, but plenty of acquaintances. And except for a disorderly conduct back in '07, no priors."

"Not many friends?"

"He's lived here a long time. Cordial with locals, but no regular drinking buddies. Kept to himself, mostly."

"Suspects?"

The sheriff shrugged, and Jack knew the source of his

anxiety. Three weeks and no suspects. He knew from experience, a case like this could drive a lawman mad.

"Anyone in town could have killed him," Kim interjected.

Jack looked at Burns. "That bad?"

The sheriff grimaced. "I'm afraid so."

"What about a possible motive?"

"Other than people generally not liking the guy? Nothing."

"Ouch," Jack replied.

"You're damn right, ouch," Burns echoed, coming forward in his chair. "And that's where you come in."

Jack still didn't understand. "How so?"

Burns exhaled a long breath. "Are you a licensed private detective in the state of Colorado?"

"No." Although Jack had solved several murder cases in the state after resigning from the Aspen Police Department, technically he had done it illegally. "I don't have a license."

The sheriff nodded. "We can take care of that." He leaned over and scribbled something on a notepad. "I'm going to be frank with you, Jack. We've hit a brick wall with this one, and I could use your help. As a private detective, you can do things I can't do—I'll leave it at that. And Telski is already breathing down my neck to get this thing wrapped up before the start of ski season."

Jack knew that Telski was the company that ran the ski resort, which also happened to be the largest employer in town.

"How can I help?" Jack asked and, for the first time since he'd walked into the office, saw the muscles in Burns's face relax.

"You can talk to the locals. We haven't been able to get much out of them. Could be easier for an outsider. But I want you to keep in touch with Deputy O'Connor. I've put her in charge of the *official* investigation. You two will work separately but together. But keep it to yourself. No sense in letting people know you're investigating this in an official capacity. They'd likely just clam up, and we'd be back to square one."

"You mentioned a wound to the back of his head."

Burns gathered up the papers on his desk. "Probably insignificant. Hitting your noggin on a cross timber or the ceiling of a dark mine is a regular occurrence for these guys. Plus, the coroner said the alcohol in his blood put him over the legal limit. He could have fallen over and hit his head because he was drunk."

Jack nodded. "Then let's talk about the gunshot wound. What do you know about the weapon?"

"Coroner pulled scraps of a nine-millimeter slug out of him, but there was no weapon recovered at the scene."

Jack thought out loud. "The murder occurred three weeks ago—the end of August."

"That's right."

"So there were still a good number of summer tourists in town."

Knowing where Jack was going with the line of questioning, Kim spoke up. "But a tourist wouldn't have been carrying a nine-millimeter."

"Or been that high up in the basin," Burns added. "For now we've ruled tourists out."

Jack agreed with the logic. "Did the victim own a gun?"

"He did," the deputy answered. "A nine-millimeter. But we failed to locate it in a search of the deceased's home."

Meaning the victim was likely shot with his own gun, a common occurrence in homicides. The Montgomery case just got more complicated—and more interesting.

"So, how about it, Jack?" Burns asked. "Can you help us?"

Jack rolled the question around in his mind as he gazed through the office window to where a full moon hung in the night sky. He was exhausted. Back in town for only a couple of hours and already hit with the prospect of hunting down another murderer.

But this time he would get paid for it.

He thought about the dead man in the mine and the locals keeping secrets from law enforcement, refusing to cooperate with the official investigation. Finding out who was responsible for the murder wouldn't be easy.

Jack felt his pulse quicken. He turned his attention from the window, looked back at the sheriff, and said, "I'll do it."

CHAPTER 7

Harriet Hughes stood at the kitchen sink with her bloody finger in her mouth, looking through the window where the view of Ingram Falls would have been if it were still daylight. Although it was dark out, a half-moon and a million stars had the mountains in silhouette on the horizon.

Both of Harriet's hips had been replaced a decade earlier. Her knees were going out, and her hearing was beginning to wane. But her eyesight was as sharp as ever. And no matter the time of day, she never tired of admiring her view.

A native of Telluride, she loved the mountains, having spent countless nights camping in them when she was younger. But that was ages ago. Now she often stood at her window and dreamed, fondly recalling memories of a placid childhood.

The back door suddenly opened, and a young girl burst into the kitchen, scratching her right arm and trying to catch her breath.

Harriet glanced at the knife in the bottom of the sink, then quickly hid her bloody finger in her apron. "Abby, it's long past dark. And if I've told you once, I've told you—"

"I saw that famous detective," the girl said between breaths, pushing strands of auburn hair out of her eyes. The ponytail Harriet had meticulously helped her with that morning was barely recognizable.

"Shoes?" Harriet pointed at her feet.

At twelve, the girl was small, her thrift-shop clothes hanging off her bony shoulders. But her gray eyes were large—some would say too large, especially for her thin face covered in freckles. In three or four years, Harriet would show her how to hide the freckles with makeup.

Abby kicked off her shoes and placed them neatly beside the back door.

Harriet sighed. "Now, who was it that you saw, dear?"

"That famous detective," Abby said, throwing her hands in the air. "He was walking down Main Street!"

The detective? Harriet nervously massaged her finger with the apron.

Abby noticed the blood and came forward, taking the wrinkled hand in her own. "Harriet, what happened?" She looked up, her large eyes filled with concern.

Harriet pulled her hand away and waved off the girl's question. "It's just a little cut," she said, taking Abby by the shoulders and steering her to the table. "Now calm down and tell me properly who you saw."

Before Abby's bottom hit the chair, she was talking again. "That detective! The one who found old Ms. Fremont—"

"The detective from Texas?" Harriet felt her mouth go dry.

The girl's head bobbed. "Yeah, that one. The detective who found old Ms. Fremont dead. I saw him."

Harriet dropped her hands to her lap, thoughts of the bloody finger long gone. *What's his name?* She pictured him in her mind—tall, dark, and handsome. She remembered the confident swagger and the cowboy boots that had the local girls all abuzz when he came to Telluride almost a year earlier. But she had heard he'd left town. Why was he back?

"Where was he, again?"

"On Main Street. He was walking with that pretty police lady with red hair. They were talking, then they got into her truck and drove away." She pulled up her right sleeve and scratched at her arm.

"Don't do that," Harriet scolded her. "It's a bad habit."

"But it itches."

Harriet's mind was already somewhere else. *Police lady with red hair?* It would have been Kim O'Connor. This was an unfortunate turn of events, and there were people Harriet needed to talk to.

She leaned across the table and dropped her voice, trying to calm the excited girl. "Now, take a minute to catch your breath. This is important, Abby. What were they talking about?"

The girl pulled her head back, pretending to be surprised by the question. "Well, I didn't hear nothing. I wasn't about to spy on a police lady."

At first Harriet didn't believe her. Abby had been living with her for a year, so Harriet was well aware of Abby's proclivity for eavesdropping. She'd found out the hard way. And although she'd vowed to be more careful around the girl in the future, the damage had already been done.

"You didn't hear a single thing they were saying?" she asked, dropping a skeptical gaze on the freckled face staring up at her.

Abby shook her head. "Pinkie promise, Harriet." She hooked her little fingers together and then pulled them apart. "Honest."

Harriet studied her for a moment and decided she was telling the truth. She got up from the table. "I made chicken spaghetti earlier—"

"Yay!" Abby's arms shot up.

"For the Davises," Harriet finished saying and saw the girl's face drop. "Mrs. Davis had her baby today. I wanted to take the casserole to them tomorrow. If you're ever home at a decent hour, you could eat dinner with the rest of us."

Abby pouted, swinging a leg back and forth under the chair.

Harriet's stern expression softened a bit. "But I made a second portion for us." The leg stopped swinging. "Mr. Eli and I ate it hours ago, but I made a plate for you. It's keeping warm in the oven."

"Thank you!" Abby said, leaping to her feet.

Harriet took the knife from the sink and slipped it into the cutlery block. "Try to keep the noise down. I don't want you disturbing Mr. Eli again."

"I won't," Abby promised. She was rooting around in a drawer and pulled out a hot pad.

Harriet did a quick survey of the room. "I've already cleaned the kitchen, so I expect it to look like this when I come down in the morning."

"It will," Abby said, setting the plate on the table. "Pinkie promise again."

Harriet locked the back door. "And be sure to turn off the lights when you're done. I'll see you in the morning." She smiled, watching the girl push her hair from her face as she ate. "Good night, Abby."

"Good night, Harriet," Abby mumbled through a mouthful of food.

Harriet watched her take another bite, then took the stairs to her bedroom, her old knees aching with each step. But what nagged at her more than the arthritis was wondering why the detective from Texas was back in Telluride.

CHAPTER 8

Thursday, September 19

JACK WOKE THE following day and couldn't remember having had a better night's sleep. Although the Airstream's wafer-thin mattress wasn't luxurious, it was a far cry from the dirt floor of Otto's cabin, which he'd slept on for months. He would miss the mountains, but for the time being he was happy to be back in town.

He had left the window open, and the cold morning air was redolent of frying bacon. Crockett leapt off the bed and waited patiently at the trailer door, wanting out. Jack pulled on a clean pair of jeans, grabbed his jacket, and the two headed for the smell of food.

"Good morning," Otto said, looking up from a tabletop griddle as Jack approached. He took a slice of bacon from a plate and tossed it to Crockett. The dog gobbled it down in a single bite, then ran to join Red hunting chipmunks along the riverbank.

"Morning." Jack took a seat at the picnic table and dragged a hand down his face.

Otto flipped several slices of bacon and stacked others on the plate. "Up late last night?"

Jack knew that the old man was fishing for information. The night before, after his trip to the sheriff's office, Kim had brought him back to the trailer. Although Jack hadn't noticed, it would have been in character for Otto to poke his head outside the tent when he heard a vehicle approach. Not much happened in the campground that Otto Finn didn't know about.

"I saw Tony Burns last night."

"The sheriff?"

"There was a murder a few weeks ago."

"I heard." Otto flipped more bacon. "But what does that have to do with you?"

"Keep it between us, but Tony wants me to look into it."

Otto stacked more bacon on the plate, letting the subject drop.

Jack watched him cook for a while. "Can I ask you something?"

"It's a free country."

"What is it about finding gold that drives some men crazy?"

"How much time do you have?"

"Give me the CliffsNotes version."

"The what?"

"Never mind," Jack said. "I remember reading about the gold rush in school. How men came from all over the country, obsessed with finding it. *Pikes Peak or Bust.*"

Otto scoffed and shook his head. "Leave it to a bunch of greenhorn Yankees to get the geography wrong."

"What do you mean?"

"The rush was along Clear Creek. If they went to Pike's Peak, they missed it to the south by a hundred miles."

"The first miners panned Clear Creek?" Jack knew the river. It was just west of Denver.

Otto nodded.

Jack thought of the dark tunnels and shafts he had spent months inside, searching for rhodochrosite. Panning for gold in a shallow river seemed more appealing. "So, what sent the early miners underground?"

"Once the gold was depleted in the creeks and rivers,

prospectors followed the veins to the source. That's when they started hard rock mining."

After spending his summer in the mountains, Jack's interest in mining had grown, and he found he was enjoying the history lesson. The two men sat in comfortable silence, Otto stirring the bacon and Jack watching the dogs play.

After a while, Jack asked, "What do you know about the Judas Mine?"

"Besides those boys finding a dead man in it three weeks ago?"

"Besides that."

"Well, for starters, its registered name is Budnick, not Judas. The original claim holders were two cousins—friends of my great-grandpappy." He took a second to continue. "The Judas is on an extension of the great Smuggler Vein."

"What's that?"

"Only the very reason you and I are sitting here today." Otto set the last of the bacon on the plate and switched off the griddle, then sat back in his chair. "Main vein runs up both sides of the box canyon and over the top of the north ridge. The Judas is just to the east of it."

"Is it a gold mine?"

"Gold and silver. Profitable back in its day." Otto gestured at the plate of bacon.

Jack reached over and took two slices from the top. "Is it still in operation?"

"I hear the dead man was poking around up there, but I don't know why. The Smuggler Vein played out in the seventies."

"Then why do you think he was up there?"

Otto shrugged. "Beats me. Maybe pulling out what's left. Couldn't be enough to pay the bills though, I reckon."

Jack knew that Dylan Montgomery had owned the Judas Mine, but it wasn't clear if the location of the murder was significant or merely a coincidence. He wanted to see the scene of the crime and was grateful Kim had offered to take him. He checked the time on his phone. The deputy would be there in an hour to pick him up.

The night before, on the way back to the campground, she had lamented the size of their list of potential suspects, admitting they had been unable to narrow it down. "Could be practically anyone in town," she'd said. But Jack pointed out that not everyone would have known when Montgomery would be at the mine.

It was early in his investigation, but Jack didn't believe for a minute that the murder was random. Montgomery's killer would be someone the victim knew.

"If I remember correctly," Otto said, "the Judas is one of the few mines in these parts that's still got its old rail system fully intact. I wouldn't mind seeing it. You need someone to get you up there?"

"I'm going later this morning."

Otto nodded. "That pretty deputy taking you?"

So he had been watching, Jack realized. The old guy was a sly one. "As a matter of fact, she'll be here in an hour," he said.

Otto struggled to stand, bracing his hands on the picnic table. He grabbed a slice of bacon and took a bite. "I almost forgot," he said, shuffling toward the tent. "I took care of some business yesterday, and I got something for you."

Jack watched Otto disappear into the tent, then turned his attention to the dogs. They had abandoned the hunt for chipmunks and had treed a squirrel. Red was on two legs, his front paws braced against the trunk. Crockett stood beside him, wagging his tail. The creek gurgled and flowed just beyond the dogs, sunlight glinting off the water. By the time Otto reappeared, the scene had nearly lulled Jack to sleep.

"What's this?" he asked, taking an envelope from Otto's outstretched hand.

"Your cut."

"Cut of what?" Jack was surprised by the weight of the envelope. He opened it and ran a thumb over the large stack of bills. His eyes bulged when he realized that what he thought were twenties were actually hundreds. "Otto, what's this?"

"Like I said. It's your cut."

Jack didn't count the money, but a rough estimate put the total somewhere in the tens of thousands. For a moment he didn't know what to say. How could the bags of rocks they had carted out of the mountains in backpacks and strapped to the dogs have been worth so much?

He looked up from the envelope. "What did you say the pink rocks were called?"

Otto chuckled. "Rhodochrosite."

Rhodochrosite? Jack had never heard of it before the summer. *A mystery rock*, he thought, and made a mental note to google it later. Otto obviously had a buyer for the stuff in town. But Jack had been around the secretive old miner long enough to know better than to ask.

He felt the heft of the envelope in his hand and shook his head. It was too much. "Otto, I can't—"

"You can. And you will," Otto insisted. "It's not up for discussion." The tone of his voice indicated the subject was closed.

Jack stared up at the mountains and did a quick calculation. When he added the unexpected windfall to the money remaining in his savings, he realized he would be able to stay in Telluride for at least another year. Something inside him stirred. It meant he could put off going back to Texas and getting a job. But even more important, it meant he'd be able to work the mine with Otto another summer.

He looked at his old friend and nodded. "Thank you."

"You're welcome." Otto chewed on a slice of bacon. "Now, tell me something. How are you gonna go about finding that killer?"

CHAPTER 9

ELI WREN OPENED the door to Telluride Bank & Trust and stepped inside. "My name is Butch Cassidy, and I'm here to rob the place!" he boomed.

His voice echoed off the pressed-tin ceiling soaring overhead, causing Ted Hawthorne to flinch. The bank president apologized to a customer and approached Wren. "Eli, please keep it down," he whispered. "It's bad for business."

Eli slapped the banker on the shoulder and laughed. "Lighten up, Ted. It's called a joke." He jerked a thumb toward the door. "Hell, you've got a plaque on the front of the building advertising Cassidy held up the place."

"That was a long time ago." Ted adjusted the bow tie at his neck, ran his hand over his slicked hair, and glanced back at his customers.

Ted knew that people thought he looked more like a nerdy college professor than a bank president. It stung, but he'd gotten used to it. In contrast, Eli had spent two decades working on Wall Street and was now a famous treasure hunter with magazine covers and a Netflix documentary. The two men couldn't have been more different.

Ted cleared his throat. "What can I do for you, Eli?"

"I've got another deposit." Eli pulled a canvas drawstring pouch from his pocket, and Ted eyed the bag curiously.

The first time Eli walked into the bank, Ted had known instantly who the man was. Although Ted had never spent a night in the mountains and could count on one hand how many times he'd ventured into the forest, he was an avid adventure fan—as long as that adventure was in a book or documented on film. He had read dozens of stories about Eli in places like *National Geographic* magazine and seen shows about him on networks like the Discovery Channel. And he had read Eli's autobiography, which had been published several years earlier.

Ted could quote Eli's most significant finds from memory, including the discovery of the *Santa León*, a Spanish galleon laden with gold and sunk off the coast of Trinidad. He had memorized even the most obscure details of his other expeditions, as well, including one where Eli had found the lost treasure of Mexican pirate Fermín Mundaca in a remote cave on the island of Isla Mujeres.

For years Ted had lived vicariously through stories of Eli's escapades of international wine, women, and treasure. And then, one day, the adventure hunter had come to Telluride in the flesh.

When Eli stepped into the bank months earlier and asked for a safe deposit box, Ted had been starstruck, peppering him with questions. He discovered Eli was searching for a legendary lost vein of gold in the San Juan Mountains. Ted sat with rapt attention as the treasure hunter outlined his plans for finding the fabled offshoot of the great Smuggler Vein, which was believed to have played out a hundred years earlier. Though he was skeptical of the gold's existence, Ted was still intoxicated by Eli's charisma.

For the last several months, Eli turned up at the bank once or twice a week like clockwork, requesting access to his safe deposit box. He would come dressed in fancy cargo pants and a long-sleeve shirt, dusty from a day spent in the mountains. The banker would watch as he pulled the same worn drawstring bag from his pocket and unloaded rock samples into the box. Eli was tight-lipped about what he'd found in the mountains, but Ted doubted it was gold.

Ted stood at the threshold to the vault and watched as Eli slid the drawer shut and locked it, then dropped the key into his pocket.

When he turned around, he smiled, exposing a mouth of movie-star teeth in his tan face. "There's gold in them thar hills, my good man. Gold. And I aim to find it."

Eli's enthusiasm could be infectious. Ted felt a surge of adrenaline before he remembered how many times he'd heard the treasure hunter say it before. Eli Wren and his declarations of gold were starting to become tiresome. But as long as he paid the monthly fee for the box, the banker wouldn't complain.

Eli slapped Ted on the shoulder as he strolled toward the front of the bank. "I've got big plans for this old mining town," he said over his shoulder. "Big plans."

Ted stood at the front door, watching Eli swagger down the street. Maybe there was still gold in the mountains above Telluride—maybe there wasn't. Either way, it didn't matter.

Ted let a smile slowly curl his lips, confident that no one knew he had grandiose plans of his own already set in motion.

CHAPTER 10

It was nearly eleven o'clock when Deputy Kim O'Connor finally arrived at the campground. "We had a rollover on Black Bear Pass," she said as Jack got into the Tahoe. "Sorry, I'm late."

"Everyone alright?" Jack almost hated to ask. He had seen Black Bear Pass from a distance and knew from Otto that the narrow gravel road was consistently named the most dangerous in Colorado. Calling the sequence of precarious high-mountain switchbacks a "road" was using the term loosely.

"Luckily, the passenger was out of the Jeep at the time, trying to help navigate a turn," Kim explained. "The driver went over but was ejected almost immediately. He's been airlifted to Grand Junction. It will take a while, but he'll be okay."

Jack thought about the remote location of the Judas Mine and wondered whether the journey would be anything like driving over Black Bear Pass. "What's the road like to Shudder Basin?"

Kim turned out of the campground onto Main Street. "Don't worry," she said. "It's not easy, but it's nowhere near as bad as Black Bear."

Jack sighed in relief.

"But I thought we could stop in Ridgway for lunch first," the deputy said.

"We go through Ridgway?" Jack thought it seemed out of their way.

"Unless you want to *hike* up to the mine," she said. "Which takes a good three hours. If you don't have access to an ATV, the best way to get up there is from the other side of the mountains."

"Too steep to drive from Telluride?"

"There's no road. We have to drive around the mountains to Ouray. There's an old freighter trail just outside of town people use to get there."

Jack didn't like the sound of the word "trail." The road wasn't going to be good. He hadn't realized the Judas would be so difficult to reach, then remembered how remote Otto's mine was.

"We'll be gone most of the day," Kim said. "So, I thought we'd stop and eat first. If that's all right with you."

There was a hint of resentment in her voice, but Jack ignored it. "Lunch sounds great."

Ridgway was a cow town and an old railroad stop on the flats on the western slope of the Rockies. The Uncompahgre River, a tributary of the great Gunnison River flowed nearby.

While they lunched at True Grit Cafe, Jack admired the plethora of John Wayne memorabilia that covered the walls. A plaque on the wall revealed scenes from Wayne's movie *True Grit* that were filmed in and around town. Jack had seen the flick half a dozen times, but now had the sudden urge to rewatch it.

Kim filled him in on details of the case as they ate. For an investigation that was now over three weeks old, the information was surprisingly thin. The absence of a murder weapon and a list of suspects was disappointing. Jack knew they had their work cut out for them. And to make matters worse, despite fighting it valiantly, the deputy's body language was screaming that she resented Jack being involved.

At a junction in the highway, Kim turned south and

headed back into the heart of the San Juan Mountains. They drove the next several miles in silence.

When they neared Ouray, Jack saw a sign referring to it as the Switzerland of America. He glanced up the road at the small town in the distance with snow-capped peaks soaring directly above it on three sides and agreed. It was beautiful.

A couple of miles from town, Kim turned off the highway onto a gravel road that bisected a large tract of land being advertised for sale. Jack read the sign and discovered the property included a house. After a few minutes, a small building nestled in a grove of pines on the lower mountain slopes came into view. It had white clapboard siding and a green shingle roof and looked like something out of a storybook.

Kim noticed him studying it. "It doesn't cost anything to dream, does it?"

"No, it doesn't," Jack said, still looking wistfully at the setting.

"It's small. But around here, it still probably costs a fortune."

A few miles farther, the gravel road disintegrated into little more than a wide trail. It was easy to imagine mule trains weaving back and forth, hauling supplies to the mines high above them.

The Tahoe bounced precariously, occasionally skirting the edge of steep overhangs, as Kim maneuvered the four-wheel-drive higher. Jack was impressed by how calm and controlled the deputy seemed. One wrong move and it would all be over; not even search and rescue would be able to help them. Twice, they broke through the tree line only to dip below it again as the road weaved higher into the mountains.

Jack had the window down and breathed in the cold air, trying to calm his nerves. When he thought the trip couldn't get any worse, Kim stopped the Tahoe and killed the ignition.

"This is as far as we go without an ATV or Jeep."

Jack's gaze swept the rugged terrain. Mine tailings riddled

the slopes around them, spilling down the mountainside like golden veils. He had learned from Otto that these mounds of crushed rock were waste piles, material left over after target minerals like gold and silver were extracted.

"The Judas is just around that bend in the ridge," Kim said, pointing into the distance. "Shudder Basin's below those peaks."

Hidden from view, the basin was still some distance away. Jack realized that, despite how far they had driven, getting to the mine would require an arduous climb.

He got out of the Tahoe and stood staring up at the basin. The sky above it was dark, with menacing clouds casting the mountains in eerie shadows. Despite having recently spent months off the grid in Otto's mine, Jack felt an inexplicable sense of dread.

What was it about the Judas?

He glanced at his feet and was grateful he'd opted for hiking boots that morning. It had been a last-minute decision. He took in a deep breath, steeling himself for what could lie ahead.

"It's about twenty minutes from here," Kim said, pulling two water bottles from the back seat and stuffing them into a backpack. Jack insisted on carrying it, which seemed to thaw her chilly demeanor a bit.

The two set out, with the deputy leading the way. They followed a faint trail that soon plunged them into a thick forest. For ten minutes there was nothing to see but trees. When the trail finally emerged on the far side, the views were stunning.

Jack stopped to take it all in, letting his gaze sweep across the mountains, where great swaths of grass fanned out before them. They crossed a brook that trickled from somewhere high above, and Jack resisted the urge to stop and feel the clear water.

He looked up and saw nothing familiar about the rocky

peaks. They were somewhere above Telluride, but the town was nowhere in sight. It was as if they had entered a magical forest and emerged into another world.

"Where are we?" he asked, almost in a daze.

"Shudder Basin." Kim stood beside him. "It's overcast today, but it's breathtaking, isn't it?"

Jack nodded in silence. Then the sight of a tiny human far below startled him. "Look," he said, pointing.

Kim pulled binoculars from the bag on his back and focused on the figure. Jack heard her sigh.

"That's Abby."

"Who?"

"Abby Mercer," she said. "A local girl. She's always in the mountains. Although she's only supposed to be up here on the weekends now that summer is over. She's cut school again." She handed the binoculars to Jack, shaking her head. "Her guardian is a friend of mine. I'll have to let her know."

"That's a schoolgirl?" Jack asked. "This far up?" She was wearing shorts and a gray hoodie that shielded her face. He watched the retreating figure until she disappeared into the trees below. "Is she safe up here alone?"

Kim scoffed. "We joke that Abby's part mountain goat." She shook her head again. "At least she's headed back down. Hopefully she's on her way home—or to school."

Jack handed Kim the binoculars, wondering what it would have been like to grow up in the mountains, and felt a surge of envy. He was sure it would be a far cry from his childhood on the gritty streets of Baton Rouge.

The two set out again, skirting a gorge that dropped a thousand feet below. The way to the mine was beautiful but deadly. After several minutes, the trail forked, and Kim took the path that climbed higher.

"What's that way?" Jack asked, stopping to study the alternate trail.

"It leads to Butch Corbin's place."

Jack saw a trace of smoke curling skyward in the distance. "Someone lives up here?"

Kim was climbing again. "He's got a cabin just around the bend there," she answered over her shoulder.

"Does he live alone?"

"He does."

Jack watched the trickle of smoke dissipate into the thin mountain air, then turned and followed the deputy higher.

Ten minutes later, just below a wall of gray cliffs, a gaping black void like an empty eye socket came into view. Something inside Jack urged him to stay away. But he continued forward, each step feeling strangely heavier than the last, as if something was trying to hold him back.

As they got closer to the Judas, the mountains above the basin seemed to close in on them. Was it claustrophobia? But he'd spent days working inside Otto's mine without any problems. Something about this basin and this mine felt different. He tried shaking off the ridiculous feeling as he followed the deputy.

When Kim reached the entrance, she unclipped a flashlight from her belt and switched it on, the beam of light slashing through the darkness.

As Jack stepped closer, cold air from inside the mountain washed over him like a chilled breath. He glanced up at the crudely painted sign above the entrance and shivered, then took his first step into the Judas Mine.

CHAPTER 11

Jack stopped just inside the mine's entrance, letting his eyes adjust to the dark. The cold, moist air quickly dampened the exposed skin on his arms and face. It wouldn't take long for it to seep through his clothes.

Kim swept the beam of light over the rock walls and ceiling. The main shaft was narrow, but it widened as it went deeper into the mountain. A rivulet of water trickled down the wall to their right, adding to a pool of water that ran lazily alongside one of the old steel rails back toward the entrance. There was more moisture farther inside, where large sections of the wall were covered with a dark, shiny slime.

Jack took another step and sank into sticky mud. His boot, now waterlogged, made a sucking sound as he pulled it free. He watched the footprint behind him fill with the oozing sludge.

The Judas was nothing like Otto's mine. Everything in the Judas was wet. The stale, frigid air smelled of mold and rotting wood. It would be a miserable place to work.

"What was the victim doing here when he was murdered?"

Kim pivoted, briefly blinding Jack with the beam of light before lowering it to her side. "All indications are that Dylan was mining. He's got drills and tools scattered all over the place, in different tunnels."

Jack couldn't believe it. "He was working in here?"

"We found records of him recently purchasing more supplies."

Jack poked at a spot of decay on a large cross timber, then wiped his hand on his jeans. The web of support beams that crisscrossed the walls and ceiling looked like they were on the verge of collapse. He couldn't imagine spending more than a few minutes inside.

"It's safer than it appears," Kim said. "We had it inspected before we did an extensive search. The body was here." She pointed to a spot roughly fifteen feet from the entrance. "But we searched the whole place."

"Who did the safety inspection?"

"Colorado Division of Reclamation, Mining, and Safety. Believe it or not, except for a couple locations farther inside, this place is structurally sound. We had personnel combing through all the tunnels and shafts in here for days."

"Find anything?"

"Not much. A couple of spent nine-millimeter casings, one slug inside the mine, but that's about it."

"*Two* casings?"

Kim nodded. "But he was hit only once."

Jack looked down at his boots, visible in the indirect light from the flashlight. They were both covered in mud. He raised his right knee and watched sludge immediately fill the void where his boot had been. "I guess there was no footprint evidence."

"None. We found signs of foot traffic outside the mine, but nothing identifiable. By the time we got here, the scene had already been compromised."

"The boys who found the body?"

The deputy nodded.

Jack asked Kim to slowly sweep the walls with the flashlight as he took mental notes of the scene. But there wasn't much to see.

On the way back to Ouray, the Tahoe bounced and shifted on the gravel road as Kim drove down the mountain.

Jack wanted to know more about the missing murder weapon. "Why would the victim have had a gun up here?"

She was surprised by the question. "Why *wouldn't* he? is more like it. You don't have to spend long up here to run into a bear or a mountain lion."

"A nine-millimeter isn't going to kill a bear."

"No, but it'll scare it off," she replied. "And it's easier to carry a pistol than a long gun. Plus, he had Butch Corbin for a neighbor. There's a reason locals call him Crazy Corbin."

Jack remembered the smoke he'd seen from the fork in the trail. "What's Corbin's story?"

"He's lived up here for as long as I can remember—cantankerous old coot. I can't think of anyone who likes him. Keeps to himself mainly. Comes to town only a couple times a year for supplies."

"How old is he?"

"Early seventies, I think. But who knows?"

"What's he doing up there?"

"He works the Crystal Lake Mine."

"By himself?"

"Butch doesn't like company."

Jack thought about it a moment. "Was he interviewed as a possible suspect?"

Kim took her eyes off the road long enough to scowl at him. "Yes," she said. "Of course we interviewed him." Her voice was clipped.

Although Jack hadn't intended to, he'd hit a nerve suggesting they hadn't done a thorough investigation. An awkward silence fell between them. The deputy had been chilly since the night before when she came to the cafe, and it was wearing on him.

After several minutes, she spoke. "Listen, Jack. You might think we're just some small-town sheriff's office, but we're still professional." Her grip on the steering wheel tightened. "We know what we're doing. We've just hit a snag—"

"I wasn't trying to imply anything of the sort. But if I'm going to help, I need to know everything about the case that you do—and then some. I get the feeling you don't want me working on this."

Kim was silent a moment, then sighed. "Listen, this case has everyone on edge. And you might have been a hotshot investigator with the FBI, but don't think for a minute that we're not good at our jobs, too."

So that was what this was all about, Jack thought. Interagency rivalry. An old-fashioned territorial dispute between law enforcement—Jack had seen it too many times to count. Although the deputy was competent, she was young. And she probably had little to no experience working with an outsider. But Jack knew he would have to tread lightly.

"I've seen you do your job," Jack said. "I know that you're a more-than-capable investigator. And I think that if we work *together*, we can solve this case." He let it sink in. "Now, I'd be grateful for any information you have that might get me up to speed on what you already know."

It seemed to work. He saw her face soften.

After waiting a few more seconds, he asked, "So, what's Corbin's alibi?"

"He doesn't have one. He was in the basin at the time of the shooting but claims he was working in his mine that morning."

Jack thought about it. An eccentric loner in the mountains only a short distance away from the murder. Could a dispute between the neighbors have turned deadly?

"What was his relationship with the victim like?"

"We asked Butch. He didn't have much to say about it, but he doesn't like anybody."

"Any guns registered to him?"

"Butch?"

"Yeah."

"A 1950 Winchester Model 12."

A shotgun that would take down a bear if needed, Jack noted. "What about handguns?" He was thinking about the nine-millimeter slug shot through Dylan Montgomery.

The deputy shook her head. "No. Just the Winchester. We searched his cabin but didn't find anything except the shotgun and a slew of knives."

But Corbin could have owned an unregistered firearm. Not being in possession of a registered nine-millimeter wouldn't rule him out.

"What about a list of people in the mountains that day?"

"That would be an impossible list to compile. There were probably dozens of people in the mountains that day. But all the way up here?" She shook her head. "The only person we know who's been in Shudder Basin in the last couple months besides Abby—the girl we just saw—is Eli Wren. But he's got an alibi for the day of the murder." She shrugged.

"He's the only one?"

She nodded. "But there could have been others we don't know about. You saw how remote it is."

Eli Wren. Jack thought the name sounded familiar and wondered why. "Who is he?"

"That famous explorer," Kim said. "The treasure hunter. He's been in town all summer."

Jack remembered watching a documentary several years earlier that detailed Wren's discovery of a sunken ship in the Caribbean.

The Tahoe bounced over a large rock, jolting the passenger-side tires precariously close to the road's edge. Jack threw a hand on the dash, bracing himself, then looked over the side and saw that it would have been a thousand-foot drop. The deputy hadn't flinched.

He took a moment to catch his breath, then asked, "What's Wren doing in Telluride?"

"Looking for gold."

"In Shudder Basin?"

"There and other places, I guess." Kim shrugged. "We know he's been up in Marshall Basin and around Ajax, too."

"But he wasn't near the Judas on the morning of the murder?"

"That's what he says. He came to us voluntarily after he found out what happened and said he'd been up there the week before but not on the day of the murder. A couple of hikers claimed to have run into him that morning. They weren't anywhere near Shudder Basin."

"And you believe him?"

Kim shrugged again. "We have no reason not to. Besides, his type doesn't typically go around committing murder. High-profiled millionaire treasure hunter? What's the motive?"

Gold, maybe, Jack thought. He thought of Dylan Montgomery's recent purchase of mining equipment and had a sudden urge to explore the Judas Mine further.

"Anyone else working in Shudder Basin besides Montgomery and Corbin?" he asked.

"Nobody that we know of."

Jack studied the deputy's profile. Her frigid demeanor had thawed a bit, but she hadn't exactly warmed up to him. There was something he needed her to do but was unsure how she would react to the request.

He waited until after she cleared the last switchback and began the easy descent to the highway, then turned to her and asked.

CHAPTER 12

"W E SHOULDN'T BE here," Kim said, pulling yellow crime scene tape off the doorframe and unlocking the back door.

Jack followed her inside and was immediately overwhelmed by the stench of trash. They were in a small dark kitchen. He flipped on the overhead light and was shocked by the mess. There were dirty dishes and garbage everywhere. Empty aluminum cans and beer bottles fought for space on the countertop. The sink was filled with an assortment of pans and dishes blotched with a mysterious green fuzz. An overflowing trash bin had vomited crumpled soda cans, used napkins, and an empty pizza box.

Jack ventured farther into the kitchen, his boots sticking to the floor as he stepped over a discarded box of Frosted Flakes. A cabinet door was left open, and he recoiled at the sight of a dead mouse amid the dust and grime that covered a set of mismatched glasses and plastic cups.

"Don't look at *me*," Kim said when he turned to her. "We found it this way." The deputy stood just inside the doorway, refusing to advance farther.

"Is the rest of the house like this?"

"I'm afraid so."

Jack was tempted to turn and abandon his search. Dylan Montgomery's home was as disgusting as any he'd ever seen. But he needed to learn more about the victim and asked to see the rest of the house.

"Help yourself," the deputy said. "I've spent too much time in here already. I'll wait outside." She stepped back over the threshold and left the door open.

Jack didn't know where to start. He was looking for anything to explain why someone would want Dylan dead.

He pushed an empty whiskey bottle out of the way with the toe of his boot, then stepped into the living room. Sunlight filtered through the threadbare curtains, illuminating the small space. An exposed bulb with a pull string hung from the ceiling above him, but he left the light off.

A stained green carpet covered the floor, a tattered recliner and love seat were arranged in front of a television atop a flimsy TV tray. Jack scanned the wood-paneled walls but saw nothing—not a family photograph or diploma, no posters or artwork—nothing indicating what had interested Dylan or what had been important to him.

There were two bedrooms off a small hallway. Jack peered into the shared bath and felt his stomach lurch. The pedestal sink and enamel tub were both ringed in the same black mildew that outlined the white tiles on the floor. He noticed the toilet was missing a lid and didn't dare look. Instead, he opened the mirrored medicine cabinet above the sink and found a bottle of ibuprofen, an old razor, and a toothbrush. A small black comb lay on the floor at his feet.

The larger of the two bedrooms had a simple double bed made with a single sheet and a dingy plaid comforter tossed on top. A quick check underneath revealed a pair of sneakers and a half-empty bottle of whiskey. Jack looked in the closet but found nothing unusual.

Dylan Montgomery was not only a slob but an enigma.

So far there was nothing in the house, no photos of family or friends, no books or reading materials, no knickknacks, nothing personal to provide a clue who the victim had been or why someone had wanted him dead.

Who lives like this? Jack wondered.

In the smaller bedroom, a cot was shoved against the wall, indicating Dylan might have had an occasional visitor.

Jack saw the deputy through the window. She stood outside waiting, and he made a note to ask her about Dylan's friends. Surely someone who knew the victim could shed some light on what made him tick.

Jack turned and saw a flimsy card table and chair pushed against the wall behind him. A ledger and a mason jar filled with an assortment of pens and pencils sat on top. He flipped through the ledger, studying the rows of numbers scribbled in a disorderly fashion, and realized it was a crude attempt at a budget. Jack ran his finger down the line of expenses: mortgage, utilities, food—all the usuals. But there was no entry for income. And from the dates listed, it was apparent Dylan had abandoned his attempt at budgeting months earlier.

Jack quickly scanned the rest of the pages, saw they were blank, and shut the book. Only then did he take notice of what hung on the wall over the desk. He would have expected a beer poster or a pinup in a bikini, but the only thing Dylan had hung on any of the walls in his house was a map of the San Juan Mountains. Framed in cheap black plastic, the map was large and well used, smudged in several places, with creases evident under the glass. Someone had drawn a small circle in red, marking a location high above Telluride. Jack squinted and leaned in, realizing the location marked was the Judas Mine.

He studied the map, wondering about its significance, then thumped on the plastic frame and ran a hand down its side. On a whim, he pulled it away from the wall and saw that it was hung on a simple thumbtack pushed into the sheetrock.

He started to lower it but noticed something taped to the back. Curious, he carefully lifted the map off the wall and turned it around, then set it on the floor. Upon closer inspection, he saw that the object taped to the back was a key attached to a cardboard tag.

He peeled it from the frame and studied it in his palm. The key was a distinctive type used for safe deposit boxes and had the Roman numeral 16 engraved on its bow. Jack flipped over the tag and noticed the faded logo of Telluride Bank & Trust. Memories of the bank's irascible owner came rushing back.

Ted Hawthorne had been a suspect in the death of a local congressman several months earlier. And although the cantankerous banker was innocent of murder, he was unethical.

Jack ran a thumb over the bank's logo, wondering what the existence of the key meant. Dylan had hidden it behind the map. But why?

The existence of the safe deposit box had Jack curious. He closed his fist over the key, pressing its hard ridges into his palm. Whoever had searched the house had missed it. He glanced through the window at the deputy and watched her for a moment, debating what to do next. Then, as he walked calmly from the room, he slid the key into his pocket.

CHAPTER 13

Jack climbed into the Tahoe. They were in Lawson, a neighborhood just over two miles down valley from Telluride.

"See anything interesting?" the deputy asked.

"The victim wasn't much for decoration, was he?"

Kim scoffed, starting the engine. "You noticed."

"Tony mentioned something about friends." Jack buckled his seat belt. "I need a list of his closest ones."

She pulled away from the house. "Dylan's lived here for as long as I can remember. Practically everyone in town knows him, but I can't think of anyone I'd call his *friend*."

"No one?" Jack hoped the deputy wasn't stonewalling him.

"You might start with Sean Sullivan. He probably knew Dylan as good as anyone. Well, aside from Vanessa Graham."

"Who is he?"

Kim turned onto the highway in the direction of town. "Sean was an acquaintance. He owns a small stake in the mine."

"The Judas?"

"Yeah."

Jack was surprised to discover Dylan had a partner. "Was Sullivan interviewed after the murder?"

Kim turned in her seat, leveling a cool stare, and Jack knew he'd made the same mistake again.

"Of course we interviewed him," she said. A few beats

of awkward silence passed before she continued. "Sean and Dylan weren't friends in the typical sense, but he tolerated Dylan better than most. In fact, Sean went with us to the mine after the boys got back to town and reported what they saw. We were both at the cafe when I got the call. He heard me talking to dispatch and offered to help locate the mine."

"Did he work in it with Dylan?"

She shook her head. "No. Sean's a bartender at Earl's Tavern."

"The place down the street from the cafe?" Jack remembered seeing it but had never stopped in.

"That's it."

"What was their relationship like?"

"Dylan and Sean's?" She thought about it a moment. "I'd say friendly, but not running buddies or anything. Dylan never could keep any of those for long. But they'd hang out occasionally. I'd see them together at the Buck now and then."

"The Buck" was local speak for the Last Dollar Saloon.

So, Dyan Montgomery and Sean Sullivan were occasional drinking buddies, but how did the unlikely pair end up as partners in a mine?

Jack asked, "Sullivan knew the way to the Judas?"

"He did. He'd been up there a couple of times. Dylan was always trying to get him interested in helping, but Sean never wanted any part of it. Although I'm sure he would have been happy to partake in any future proceeds if Dylan had found gold. But no such luck. There never is."

"Why be a partner if he isn't interested in mining?"

Kim shrugged. "You'll have to ask him that yourself."

Jack intended to. "Who's the woman you mentioned?"

"Vanessa Graham. Dylan's old girlfriend. They broke up years ago. It wasn't pretty, but they still kept in touch."

The deputy slowed as she drove through town, stopping at several intersections to let people cross the street. Colorado state law gives pedestrians the right-of-way, forcing drivers to slow down—a law Jack liked. It was a nice change of pace coming from the fast, mean streets of Houston, where pedestrians lived life on the edge.

Jack glanced through the windows of Telluride Bank & Trust as they passed and felt for the safe deposit box key hidden in his pocket. After another block, he said, "You can let me out here."

"Are you sure? I can take you to the campground."

"No. Here's good. I have a couple of errands to run."

When Kim looked at him skeptically, Jack suspected she knew he was keeping something from her. But she pulled to the curb and stopped.

"Thanks for the tour of the crime scene," Jack said, getting out of the Tahoe. "And for letting me get a look inside the victim's house."

"Sure thing. Just remember what Tony said and keep me posted on what you find."

Jack watched her make an illegal U-turn and head out of town toward the sheriff's office. He took several steps toward the campground, then glanced over his shoulder. When the Tahoe disappeared over the rise, he turned and began walking in the opposite direction.

Before he would call it a day, there was a cranky little banker he wanted to talk to.

CHAPTER 14

Jack pulled open the door to Telluride Bank & Trust and stepped inside.

A stout woman looked up from helping a customer. "I'll be with you in a second, honey. Just have a seat."

Jack settled into an antique leather chair in the bank's small lobby. He was in no hurry and wasn't sure Ted Hawthorne was even there. In fact, it would be convenient if he wasn't. Jack had an uncanny knack for getting information out of unsuspecting subordinates—especially women.

He crossed an ankle over the opposite knee and picked at his hiking boot, the sides still caked in mud from the mine. Now back in town, he wished he were wearing cowboy boots instead. Projecting the image of a serious detective was next to impossible dressed in hiking gear. His Red Wings would've given him a more commanding presence. Plus, he knew from experience that women liked his cowboy boots.

He studied the woman behind the counter as she counted a stack of bills while chewing gum. She was middle-aged, with a beehive hairdo that reminded him of his grandmother's. Her green polyester pantsuit was tight around her torso.

When she finished counting, she squared the bills and stuffed them into an envelope.

"See you next week, Charlie," she said, handing the envelope across the counter to a customer. She seemed friendly enough.

Jack stood up, nodded at the man as he left, and approached the counter.

The woman looked up and smiled. "Sorry about the wait, honey. We're technically closed, but how can I help you?"

Jack stole a glance at the woman's name tag. "Wanda, is it?"

Still smacking the gum, she grinned wider. "My mama named me Wanda, but, honey, you can call me whatever you like."

"I need to speak with Ted Hawthorne if he's available."

Wanda quit chewing for a second. "You look mighty familiar. Do I know you?"

"I don't think so."

"No, I do." She rested an elbow on the counter and shook a long red nail at him. "I wouldn't forget a face like yours."

Jack shook his head and grinned. "And if we had met, I'm sure I would remember."

Her eyes flashed with amusement, and she pushed off the counter. "Now, don't go flirting with me, honey. You're liable to get more than you bargain for." She started for the back of the building, swinging her wide hips from side to side.

"Tell me your name, honey," she called over her shoulder. "I'll let Ted know you're here."

"The name's Jack Martin."

Wanda froze, then pivoted back. "I knew you looked familiar. You're that detective, aren't you?" she asked, wagging a finger.

"I'm sorry to bother you after hours."

She waved off the apology. "Honey, you can bother me anytime."

Jack felt his cheeks flush.

A few minutes later, Ted Hawthorne emerged from an office in the back, running a hand over his pomaded hair. He walked erect, squeezing every quarter inch out of his small frame, and was nervous as hell. Just the way Jack wanted him.

"Good night, Ted." Wanda snatched a purse from under the counter and started for the door. "And a very good night to you, Mr. Famous Detective."

The two men waited for her to leave.

When she was gone, Hawthorne was the first to speak. "As you can see, Mr. Martin, I'm afraid we're closed. But if you'd like to come back, we open tomorrow at—"

"I have a few questions. It won't take long."

Hawthorne glanced at his watch, trying to appear busy.

Jack took a step closer. "I understand Dylan Montgomery did business with you."

The banker froze for a second, then lifted his chin, regaining his composure. "I'm sorry, but I'm bound by a fiduciary duty not to divulge who is or is not a client of Telluride Bank & Trust."

Jack wasn't in the mood. "Dylan Montgomery is dead. That means he's no longer a client."

Hawthorne blinked. "Well, I still can't—"

"Yes, you can. Unless you've got something to hide." Jack stuck his hands on his hips, letting the statement hang for a moment. He didn't like Ted Hawthorne and enjoyed watching him squirm.

"I don't have anything to hide. And if you're here to accuse me of murder again, you can just—"

"I'm not accusing you of murder. I just want to know what kind of business Dylan had with the bank."

Hawthorne stared defiantly for a moment, then thought better of it. His chest deflated, and he sighed. "Exactly what is it that you want to know?"

"What kind of business did he have with you?"

"Meaning what?"

"Meaning savings accounts, checking accounts, loans."

Jack felt the key in his pocket. He wasn't ready to ask about the safe deposit box—not yet.

Hawthorne pushed his glasses up higher on his nose. "Dylan had a checking account, but it's tied up in probate with his other assets. They probably will be for some time."

"Did he have money?"

Hawthorne frowned. "I won't give you a balance, if that's what you're asking."

"I don't need a balance. I just want to know the general state of his finances."

Hawthorne drew up again, hooking his thumbs under the lapels of his tweed jacket. "I can't tell you that."

"What *can* you tell me?"

"Only that Dylan was a customer. And now, if you'll excuse me...As I've already mentioned, we're closed."

"Did he have any debts?"

"I can't tell you that."

"Car loans?"

The banker wouldn't answer, but shifted nervously on his feet.

Jack was growing frustrated. "Investment accounts, CDs?"

Hawthorne swallowed but glared defiantly. Jack wanted to punch the little man. Instead, the two traded stares for what seemed like an eternity.

Jack waited for him to blink, then gave up and turned for the door. "I'll be back, Ted."

On the sidewalk, Jack started for the campground and heard Hawthorne lock the door behind him.

The encounter had been infuriating, but what Jack hadn't expected was to discover that the shifty banker was hiding something.

CHAPTER 15

OTTO FINN WAS sitting on a tarp spread along the riverbank at the edge of the campsite, whittling an aspen branch and letting the shavings fall to the ground between his knees.

Jack dropped down next to him. "Can I ask you something?"

"It's a free country," Otto replied without looking up.

"Do you ever go up to Shudder Basin?"

"Not if I can help it."

"What's wrong with it?"

"Shudder is the coldest spot in the San Juans. Might be the coldest spot in the Rockies."

"Is that the only reason you don't like it?"

Otto paused his whittling long enough for Jack to know there was more to the story. But the question went unanswered.

Jack had sensed something dark about the high mountain basin. It wasn't only because the surrounding ridge blocked most of the day's sun. Or that the location was unusually remote. It was something darker. It gave him an uneasy feeling of dread or foreboding, but Jack couldn't put his finger on what exactly it was.

"What do you know about Butch Corbin?" he asked.

"Not much."

"I understand he lives up there alone. That can't be easy."

"Butch is an interesting fellow."

"How so?"

"Hard to explain."

"Can you try?" Talking to Otto was sometimes like pulling teeth. "I can give you an example."

Jack waited for him to continue.

"Butch sleeps with a hunting knife and a Bible. He says it's to be ready for anything—natural or supernatural." Otto shook his head.

"Is he violent?"

"Not unless he needs to be."

"And he lives alone?"

"He does."

"How does he earn a living?"

"Lives off his mine. Same as I do."

Jack remembered the months of living in the mountains, the long summer days spent in the middle of nowhere with only Otto and the dogs. He had loved it, but he'd had company.

"Does Corbin come to town in winter?"

Otto shook his head. "Not that I know of."

Jack thought about Corbin as he watched the dogs play in the river. Month after month alone in the frozen basin—a place that was cold even in summer. He shuddered to think what complete isolation could do to a man. He watched Red wrestle a stick away from Crockett. Maybe Corbin had a dog.

After a while he asked, "What is it about mining that grabs ahold of some men by the throat?"

Otto's hands went still. "I can't say that I know."

"What drew *you* to it?"

"Mining?" He pulled at his long gray beard. "It's just what Finns always did, I guess." He laid the stick on the tarp and folded his pocketknife. A nostalgic haze had washed over his wrinkled face. "My pa's granddaddy moved out here in 1859, ten years after the strike in California. Men came from all over the world." He was animated as he spoke, remembering.

"Colorado's gold rush might not be as famous—everyone's heard of the forty-niners—but our rush dwarfed theirs."

"How so?" Jack had learned of the gold rushes in California and Alaska in school, but didn't remember hearing about Colorado.

"Way more men came to Colorado—and not just miners. Legitimate businessmen and outlaws, too. Granddaddy said it was a wild free-for-all in those days—lynchings, men killing each other over claims. There were even a handful of duels." He took a moment, remembering. "The country was in a depression in fifty-nine. Broken men poured into the Rockies dreaming of riches. Some found it. But most didn't."

"Why keep at it, then?" Jack asked. "Is it the thrill of the search?"

"Partly."

"But gold fever drives some men crazy."

Otto nodded in agreement. "I've known a few. Lost everything they had—money, family. Some even lost their lives. The key is to keep the fever in check. Not let it ruin you." He unfolded the pocketknife and pointed it at Jack. "One of the best tips my pa gave me was to never spend more than you make."

"So how'd you find *your* mine?" Jack asked.

"Passed down."

"From your father?"

Otto nodded. "And his father before that. Like most of 'em in these parts."

"What do you mean?"

He was whittling again but stopped to pull at his beard. "Prospectors tend to be a territorial bunch. If there was a son, claims were passed down in the family."

"And if there was a daughter?" Jack asked, half teasing his old friend.

Otto looked stumped by the question. It took him a

moment to answer. "Well, I guess a daughter could work a mine, too. Not that I ever heard of one doin' it."

Jack sat back and thought about everything Otto had said about gold fever. After months of working the old man's mine, he was beginning to understand. It wasn't just about getting rich, but about the hunt and the thrill of the find. Although it wasn't gold he and Otto had wrestled from the stubborn clutches of the mine, but rhodochrosite, Jack had still felt the fever firsthand.

But Otto had said it himself—the unrelenting quest for gold could lead some men to violence and others to ruin.

Jack's thoughts turned again to Butch Corbin, a man willing to spend his life in complete solitude, working alone in the dark in a frozen basin so far from civilization.

The thin ribbon of smoke rising from Corbin's cabin indicated he lived not far from the Judas.

Jack wondered if the basin had gotten too crowded. Or could Corbin have his eye on Dylan Montgomery's mine?

CHAPTER 16

Friday, September 20

Jack was up early the following day, eager to learn more about Shudder Basin and its only known resident, the reclusive Butch Corbin. But first, he needed breakfast.

He opened the door to Pandora Cafe and was happy to find his usual table unoccupied. As he crossed the room, he scanned the faces of the small early-morning crowd and nodded at a couple of locals he recognized.

Judith came over, taking a pencil from behind her ear. "Morning, Jack. What can I get you?"

"Colorado breakfast."

"You're hungry." She scribbled the order on her order pad.

"I am."

"Big plans today?"

"Maybe. What time does the museum open?"

"I think they open at ten." She frowned. "Why?"

"Otto mentioned they have a map I might like to have a look at."

"Now you've got me curious. What kind of map?"

"It shows all the mines around Telluride."

A man at an adjacent table turned to face Jack. "I know it," he said. He was alone, wearing a starched green fishing shirt and khaki cargo pants—both with expensive logos. An assortment of papers and notebooks was spread across the table in front of him.

"That map will show most of the mines in the area," the man continued. "But not all of them. There isn't one in existence that's completely accurate."

Judith tore Jack's order from the pad. "I'll get this in and grab you a coffee." She started for the kitchen.

The man in the green shirt was still watching him. "What exactly are you looking for?" he asked.

"The mines in Shudder Basin."

The man raised his brows. "That's a pretty remote area," he said. "But I happen to know it. Maybe I can help."

Jack studied him. There was something familiar about the guy—the shock of gray hair, the tan face, and his large white teeth. "Do I know you?"

"Eli Wren." He reached out a hand, and Jack shook it.

"The treasure hunter?"

"In the flesh and at your service. And you are?"

"Jack Martin."

It took a second, and then recognition registered on the treasure hunter's face. "Of course," he said, shaking a finger. "Telluride's famous detective. I thought maybe I'd run into you this summer. Heard you were up in the mountains somewhere. Judith said you were her best customer, so I was surprised when I didn't see you in here. You just get back into town?" Wren had an easy way of talking and a cheerful disposition.

Jack let his guard down a bit. "We got back Wednesday night."

Wren nodded. "Well, God bless you for staying up there so long. I'm in the mountains nearly every day, but I like a warm bed at night." He chuckled. "I do everything I can to avoid camping in the elements. I'm too old for that now."

Despite Wren being at least fifteen years older than him,

Jack understood. He was still stiff from sleeping on the dirt floor of Otto's cabin. "Yeah, I know what you mean."

Wren threw an arm over the top of an adjacent chair. "So, what do you want to know about Shudder Basin? Ask away."

Jack hesitated, but found he liked the treasure hunter. "I'm curious how many mines there are up there."

"Two." Wren hadn't hesitated. "The Crystal Lake and the Judas."

"The Crystal Lake must belong to Butch Corbin."

"It does."

"Have you met him?"

"Who? Crazy Corbin? Unfortunately, I have."

Kim O'Connor had used the same nickname.

"That bad?" Jack asked.

"That bad and *then* some. I'd love to get a look inside the Crystal Lake, but the old coot won't let me anywhere near it. I've been up there twice, and both times the crazy bastard threatened to shoot me for trespassing."

Jack thought of the nine-millimeter slug found at the murder scene. "What kind of gun did he have?"

"A shotgun. The man's a giant—like coming upon a grizzly. Crazy as a mad hatter, too." He tapped his temple with an index finger. "There's a reason the locals call him Crazy Corbin. You ever see Leonardo DiCaprio in that movie *The Revenant*? He was the mountain man attacked by a bear and then sleeps in a dead horse carcass? Probably smelled like rotting fish."

"Yeah, I saw it."

"Well, *that's* Crazy Butch Corbin. He even wears an old bison hide similar to something DiCaprio wears in the movie, if you can believe it."

Jack suspected the flamboyant treasure hunter was prone to exaggeration. He would have to meet Corbin for himself to believe it.

Judith reappeared and set a large plate of food on the table in front of him. "The Colorado breakfast." It was Jack's favorite. "Eggs, bacon, sausage, potatoes, and a side of fruit. I threw in a fresh biscuit for good measure."

"Thank you, Judith."

For the next half hour, as Jack ate, Eli Wren regaled him with stories of adventures in the Caribbean and the Andes. When Jack asked what he was doing in Telluride, he pulled a map from the assortment of papers in front of him and unfolded it.

"It's here, I tell you," Wren insisted, stabbing a finger at a location high above town. "The lost spur of the great Smuggler Vein. It could be my largest find yet."

"You really think there's still that much gold up there?"

"I *know* there is. It's just a matter of locating the lost vein. But I'll find it. And when I do, we'll bring in a ground crew, hire a handful of locals, and we'll dig it out. Hey—maybe you'd like to help. Judith said you were working a mine this summer. You're experienced now. A man of your physical stature—you'd be a huge asset on my team." Wren was grinning from ear to ear, flashing the bathtub-white teeth. "How about it?"

Jack was beginning to think gold fever was on the verge of becoming pandemic. He remembered the men he'd met only a few months earlier in Texas searching for Emperor Maximilian's gold. What was up with the obsession with lost treasure? he wondered.

Judith appeared and began clearing the table. Jack had intended to ask her that morning about Dylan Montgomery. As the beloved town gossip, she knew almost everything that went on in Telluride. But for some reason, Jack was reluctant to bring up the murder with the famous treasure hunter within earshot.

CHAPTER 17

When Jack left the cafe, he took the corner at Main Street and Fir and started the climb for the Telluride Historical Museum. Judith had said it would be at the top of Fir at a dead end.

"I was born there," she'd said. When he looked at her funny, she added, "The building was the town hospital until 1962. It wasn't a museum until several years later."

Eli Wren was still at the cafe when Jack left, his table littered with maps and reports. He had insisted on showing Jack several of them, confident he was on the verge of locating the fabled lost vein of gold. Despite being famous, and ridiculously wealthy, Wren was likable. But he was also a bit of a nut.

Jack glanced down at his cowboy boots. The climb up the sidewalk had his Red Wings rubbing at his heels, so he stopped for a second to relieve the pain—and to catch his breath. The museum was still a block away. It was two-story, clad in red sandstone native to the area, with a porch that ran the length of the front, its wooden balusters painted a complementary shade of red. Although the building was level, the street in front ran at an angle, dropping to the east, making the foundation on the right side appear to float several feet off grade, giving it a sort of fun house vibe.

A friendly woman in her seventies greeted Jack from behind the counter when he stepped inside. She was dressed in period garb, an old-fashioned dress with a high collar and ruffles at the cuffs of the sleeves, and her gray hair was twisted into a bun piled high atop her head.

The woman's smile drooped when Jack mentioned he was only there to see the map. "Go up the stairs and take a left," she said. "You'll find it."

Upstairs was a cluster of small rooms. Jack went into the first one on the left and weaved through exhibits displaying old mining equipment and rock samples. He stopped at a black-and-white photo on one of the walls of a group of miners near the turn of the century. Their faces were lean but surprisingly jovial despite the brutal circumstances in which they worked. Jack remembered the stories Otto had told about his great-grandfather being forced to spend hours underground breathing polluted air, sometimes not seeing sunshine for days.

After glancing at a few more photographs, Jack turned his attention to a glass case that held samples of ore taken from area mines. Minerals like gold, silver, and pyrite were encrusted in rocks of various sizes. Some also included minerals like copper and galena, but none were mixed with rhodochrosite. Jack wondered if anyone knew about Otto's secret pink stones.

When he found the map, Jack was surprised by how large it was. But its enormous size was out of necessity. The mines around Telluride were an elaborate honeycomb of tunnels and shafts. The print on the map was tiny—a maze of names and hatch marks, this way and that, tumbling one over the other.

Using his index finger, Jack traced a line from town to spots high in the mountains until he located Shudder Basin. He knew the Judas and Crystal Lake Mines were in close proximity but was shocked by what the map revealed.

The entrance to the Judas was east of Crystal Lake and quite a bit higher. But the tunnels of the two mines seemed to overlap. From the map, it appeared the deceased Dylan Montgomery and Crazy Butch Corbin had been mining on top of each other. Jack was more determined than ever to meet the man.

He took his phone from his pocket and snapped a photo of the map, focusing on the section that included Shudder Basin.

As he descended the stairs, the woman at the register looked up, "Did you find what you were looking for?"

"I did. Thank you."

"Care to see any of our other exhibits while you're here?" she asked hopefully.

It was early fall, and the museum was quiet. Jack realized he was the only visitor. The woman was friendly, and he was suddenly hit with a stab of guilt for not showing more interest in her museum. But he had things to do.

"I'll come back," he said. "I promise." He stopped at the door. "Can I ask you something?"

The woman's face brightened. "Of course."

"Have you ever heard of the Judas Mine?"

"Why, sure. Everyone around here has. There's a lot of history behind it."

Next Jack asked about the Crystal Lake Mine, and a shadow crossed her face.

"I went to school with Butch Corbin," she said. "His mine is of no historical significance."

"What makes the Judas special?"

"Well, for one, 'Judas' isn't its registered name. It's really the Budnick Mine—named after two cousins, Lon and Edgar Budnick. They fought on separate sides of the Civil War but became partners later. They should have known it wouldn't work out. Edgar accused Lon of high-grading—that's stealing in mining terminology—and Lon challenged him to a duel. Both were known to be stubborn. Well, they ended up killing each other down in Pandora. Shot each other dead in the middle of the street." She shook her head. "And darned if those investigating the duel didn't find out afterward that they'd *both* been stealing from each other."

"A duel?" Jack remembered Otto mentioning them.

"Yep. Shot each other dead. Just down Main Street past the cemetery. In fact, they're buried there side by side."

"So that's how the mine got its nickname."

The woman shrugged.

"The story of Judas Iscariot," Jack said. "He betrayed Jesus." When the woman looked at him funny, he added, "My grandparents had me in church every Sunday."

The woman shrugged again. "Maybe that's why. I don't know. But locals have called it the Judas ever since."

"What happened to it after the duel?"

"It was auctioned off."

"To Dylan's ancestors?"

"No, not Dylan's," she said. "To his wife's."

His wife? This was the first Jack had heard of the victim being married. He wondered why neither Tony Burns nor Kim O'Connor had mentioned it.

"Do you happen to know her name?"

"Whose?"

"Dylan Montgomery's widow?"

Her expression turned glum. "It was Cindy."

"What do you mean *was*?"

"Well," the woman said, "she's dead."

CHAPTER 18

As Jack walked toward Main Street, he tried calling Kim. When she didn't answer, he left a message. He wanted to know why in the hell he hadn't been told Dylan Montgomery was married. The woman at the museum had clammed up when Jack asked about Cindy, and he wanted to know why.

As Jack neared the corner, he heard the rumble of a motorcycle and looked up in time to see it cruise past. He watched as it passed Pandora Cafe and turned into an alley next to Earl's Tavern.

He had seen the bike before—an early-model Yamaha needing muffler work. The rider was a local—thirtysomething with an average build and sandy-blond hair. Jack had seen him dozens of times. The guy never wore a helmet—a good way to get killed on narrow mountain roads prone to rock and mud slides.

Jack had never met him, but when the guy emerged from around the corner of the bar and unlocked the front door, he suddenly wanted to.

A few minutes later, Jack stepped inside Earl's Tavern and took a moment to let his eyes adjust.

The tavern was windowless and dark, with wood-paneled walls that matched the planked floor. The overhead lighting was low and warm, reflecting off the mirror behind the bar. An assortment of neon signs hung around the room, still unlit.

"We don't open for another hour, but how can I help you?" The blond man was stowing boxes of liquor under the bar.

"Sean Sullivan?"

"You found him. What can I do for you?" He set the last box on the floor and reached out a hand.

Jack stepped closer and shook it. "My name's Jack Martin."

"The detective?"

"That's right."

"I've heard of you." He pulled a rag from somewhere below and set it on the counter. "We all have. I figured I'd run into you eventually. It's nice to finally meet you. Can I offer you a drink?"

Jack pulled out a stool and sat. "No, but thank you. I was hoping to ask you a couple of questions."

Jack could tell Sullivan was surprised by the request.

"I understand you were partners with Dylan Montgomery in his mine."

"Ah, now I get it." Sullivan was wiping down the bar but stopped. "You're helping the sheriff."

"Mind if I ask you a few questions?"

"Not at all." He was wiping again.

"I understand you own a minority interest in the Judas."

"I wish I didn't. That thing is cursed."

Jack thought of the Budnick cousins and their duel. "Cursed?"

"Yep. You couldn't pay me to step inside that thing again."

"But you own part of it."

"Not by choice." He sighed. "Now I'm stuck with it. Nobody's going to want to buy me out after what happened to Dylan."

"How did you get to be part owner?"

Sullivan chuckled. "I was an idiot." When Jack frowned, he added, "It's a long story."

Jack leaned back and hooked the heels of his boots on the stool's lowest rung. "I've got time."

Sullivan eyed him warily, then set the rag aside. "It came into my possession by way of a bet."

"A bet?" Jack had heard of people winning some weird things—comic books, horses, even a tractor—but never a share in a gold mine.

"Yeah, a *bad* bet. And not mine." Sullivan shook his head. "I was an idiot to lend him the money, but Dylan said it was only temporary, that he'd pay me back. That was almost five years ago." He pulled a stool from under the bar and sat. "You sure you want to hear the whole story?"

When Jack nodded, he continued.

"We were both at the casino outside Cortez—the Ute Mountain Casino, I think it was. I found out later that Dylan was a regular. Anyway, we ended up at the same poker table. I didn't know him, but he was betting big—and *losing* big. I was having better luck. So, when he ran out of chips, he asked me to stake him."

"You lent a stranger money?"

"I refused at first, but he kept pressing. It wasn't much—a couple hundred dollars. He promised me an interest in a mine as collateral. At first I thought he was kidding. Then some damned old Indian sitting at the table with us vouched for him and said he was legit. Another regular, and I could tell they knew each other." Sullivan ran his palms over the bar as he talked. "Anyway, this Indian makes Dylan out to be some hotshot gold miner. I thought, what the hell."

"And you lent him the money."

"Handed him a short stack of my chips. The idiot goes and puts it all on the roulette table. Loses the whole stack at once. That damn Indian laughed his fool head off." Sullivan shook his head and chuckled. "At least I had a witness. Nobody would believe it if I hadn't."

"So you ended up with a share of the mine."

"Unfortunately."

"What are you going to do with it?"

Sullivan looked up hopefully. "You want it?"

Jack held up his hands. "No. But thank you."

Sullivan's face dropped, and he sighed again. "Dylan was always trying to get me to go up there with him. He needed help working it, but that's not my gig. These old mines around here are death traps." He paused a moment. "You ever been in one?"

Jack mentioned he had.

Sullivan shook his head. "Then you know how claustrophobic they are. Especially that one," he added, referring to the Judas. "Like I said, that thing is cursed."

CHAPTER 19

The grass in the cemetery had yellowed and swayed in the fall wind. Jack sat on the ground a few feet from the concrete that bordered the two graves. They were side by side, outlined separately but also joined as one. Not husband and wife, but cousins. On the left was Lon Budnick. On the right, Edgar.

When Jack left Earl's Tavern, he had intended to return to the campground. But at the last second he'd changed his mind and continued walking until he'd reached the Lone Tree Cemetery. He had climbed the hill among the headstones to the spot where the woman at the museum said the Budnick cousins were buried.

Sitting alone in the grass, Jack wasn't sure what had compelled him to visit the dead men, but figured their graves were as good a place as any to sit and think.

The sun was high, but the fall wind chilled him. He sat on the cold ground, mindlessly digging his fingertips into the damp soil, and thought about what he had learned.

Before his murder, Dylan Montgomery had been preceded in death by a wife who, for some reason, people were reluctant to talk about.

Jack pulled his phone from his pocket, saw Kim still hadn't returned his call, and laid it on the grass beside him. Then, for the umpteenth time, he read the inscription in the concrete at the foot of the graves before him.

Whereupon blood betrays, wounds fester forever.

Jack thought about the cousins who had killed each other not far from where they now lay. The two men had fought on opposite sides of the Civil War but later reunited. After moving to the Rockies, they had ended up partners in a gold mine.

Jack wondered what had led them to murder. Had things been amicable at first, and then old resentments reared their head because of the war? Or was the motive more straightforward—just plain old-fashioned greed, cousins stealing from each other.

Jack had no living relatives of his own, but he couldn't fathom the rage it took to kill family. Or the insanity.

Could the mine be cursed, as Sean Sullivan had suggested?

But the sheriff said Dylan didn't have family in Telluride. Which meant that whoever had killed him was either a psychopath roaming the mountains or someone Dylan knew with an axe to grind. Jack had a strong feeling it was the latter.

He leaned forward and brushed dried aspen leaves from the concrete bordering the Budnick graves, cold and pitted from a century of snow and wind. He turned and looked to the end of the canyon, where Ingram Falls fell from the peaks above. And his thoughts turned to Butch Corbin. Before Jack had left the bar, Sullivan told him that Corbin had threatened Dylan on several occasions, but Dylan had never taken the threats seriously. Maybe he should have.

Jack's gaze slid north of the falls, where a winding gravel road led up to Marshall Basin. Shudder Basin and the Judas Mine would be high above it, hidden in the uppermost regions of the San Juans.

Who besides Crazy Corbin and the boys who'd found Dylan had also been up there that morning?

Could it have been Eli Wren? The eccentric treasure hunter had admitted to being in the basin several times. Although he had an alibi, could he have been up there the morning of the murder?

Jack's cell phone rang, breaking him from his thoughts. He picked it up from the grass and glanced at the caller ID.

"Kim, thanks for the callback," he said, hiding his annoyance at the delay. "I have a question about Dylan Mont—"

"Jack, we got a call," she interrupted. "A waiter at the Beaumont Hotel in Ouray saw Dylan in the restaurant the morning he died. There was another man with him."

"Why is he just now reporting it?"

"He came across the story of the murder in an old copy of the *Denver Post* today and recognized Dylan from the photograph."

"Did he get the name of the second guy?"

"No. And we had the manager of the restaurant go through the old tickets, but they must have paid in cash."

"I want to talk to him."

"Come into the office. We'll call him back together."

"No. I want to talk to him in person."

There was silence on the other end of the line for a second. "Alright," she said, "but I want to be there, too. I'll pick you up first thing in the morning. We'll go together."

"Why not now?" It was their first promising clue.

"It can't be today. The guy's on his way back from Denver at our request. He won't be in Ouray until late tonight. I'll pick you up in the morning. But you said you had a question for me?"

"No one told me Montgomery had a wife."

"She died years ago. We didn't think it mattered."

"Maybe, maybe not. The problem is, I needed to know." The silence was tense. "If I'm going to help on this case, I need full disclosure."

"We just didn't think it mattered. Cindy's been dead for over ten years."

"You knew her?"

"I did."

"What happened?"

For a while the line went silent again. "It's a long story."

"I've got time," Jack said, wondering why in the hell everyone seemed reluctant to talk about the victim's dead wife. He heard the deputy sigh through the phone.

"There was a fire. Cindy didn't get out in time." She spoke with a hint of sadness. "Listen, it's an hour to Ouray. We can talk about this in the morning. I'll give you the whole story."

They agreed on a time to meet and ended the call.

Jack pushed himself off the ground, brushed the grass from his jeans, and stuck the phone back in his pocket. After a last look at the Budnick graves, he started down the hill toward the campground.

The turquoise sky was cloudless, no hint of a coming storm, but there was something electric in the air. For the first time since learning about the murder, Jack thought he was on the verge of getting answers.

CHAPTER 20

Saturday, September 21

Deputy Kim O'Connor made the roundabout outside Telluride and headed out of town. "The guy's name is Spencer Troutman," she said. "Probably one of the last people to see Dylan alive before he was murdered."

Jack watched her clench and relax her hands on the steering wheel. The tendons in her neck were taut. She was nervous.

"First murder case as the lead investigator?" he asked.

She glanced at him without replying. After another few hundred feet, she slumped back in her seat. "Is it that obvious?"

"We all start somewhere," Jack said, trying to reassure her.

"Even you, Mr. Famous Detective?"

There was a cool edge to her voice, but Jack laughed. "Even me."

"Tell me about it."

"About what?"

"*Your* first murder case."

It was Jack's turn to tense. He felt a spot in his chest tighten, remembering his grandparents, dead in their bed in Baton Rouge. It had been decades, but the memory was still raw. Although he had been in high school at the time and not involved in the investigation, their murders had profoundly influenced the trajectory of his life.

It was the last thing he wanted to talk about.

"Tell me about Troutman," he said, changing the subject. "What do you know about this guy?"

Kim spent the next several minutes navigating the narrow highway and filling Jack in on what little she knew.

Troutman had waited tables at the historic Beaumont Hotel in Ouray for the last two years. A background check revealed nothing except a few traffic violations. Born and raised in Denver, graduated from a local junior college, and waited tables in Wheat Ridge before moving to Ouray. "The guy seems clean," she said.

At a lull in the conversation, Jack said, "Now, tell me about Cindy Montgomery."

They had reached the spot where the highway dead-ended in Placerville. Kim checked both ways, then turned right. She was still hesitant to talk about the dead woman, which piqued Jack's interest even more.

The deputy picked up speed and kept her eyes on the highway when she finally spoke. "Cindy was ahead of me in school, but we had a couple of classes together. She was one of the friendly older girls—pretty, but nice. Really took an interest in people. If she sensed something was wrong, she would ask you how you were doing. That kind of person, you know? Anyway, we became friends. Not close friends, but friends. I guess you could say that I looked up to her. After graduation, she went off to school—Boulder, I think—but met Dylan one summer vacation and never went back. An unlucky turn of events, in retrospect."

"What happened to her?"

"She died in the fire. It was twelve years ago, just before spring break. They had property up on the mesa outside Sawpit. She was home alone. Dylan was probably up in the mine—he was always up there. Anyway, the neighbors saw the smoke and called the fire department."

"Was there an investigation?"

Kim slowed the Tahoe, letting an elk cross the road. "The fire marshal handled the investigation. It started in the kitchen—they think it was a candle. Cindy had them all over the place. They found her upstairs in the bedroom. It looked like she had tried to get out but didn't make it. Her body was next to an upstairs window."

"How old was she at the time?"

"Probably twenty-eight, I'd guess."

"Any disabilities?"

Kim glanced at him, frowning. "Like what?"

"A mobility issue," Jack said. "Or a mental disability that might have made it difficult for her to get out."

Kim shook her head. "No. She was diabetic, but otherwise completely healthy, as far as I know. The fire marshal's report said she was probably asleep when it started, and it could have been too late to use the stairs when she realized what was going on. By that time the house could have been filled with smoke and she couldn't open the window." She shrugged, looking sad.

Jack wasn't sure what to make of it. Healthy adults usually made it out of house fires—especially young ones. Maybe being diabetic had somehow contributed.

"It was a horrible tragedy," Kim continued. "Everyone who knew her loved her."

"Including her husband?"

"Dylan?" She worked the steering wheel with her hands again. "Yeah, Dylan loved her. He was devastated after Cindy died. A lot of us were worried he might hurt himself." She paused, remembering. "The whole town turned out for her funeral." It was obviously difficult for her to talk about.

"I'm sorry," Jack said, and she nodded. But he wasn't

finished with the conversation. "You mentioned Dylan had a girlfriend around that time. Vanessa something?"

"Vanessa Graham." Kim shook her head. "But that wasn't until after the fire."

Jack committed the name to memory.

They spent the next several minutes in silence. Jack wanted to know more about the fire and Dylan's relationship with his deceased wife, but he let the subject drop.

When they reached Ouray, Jack was surprised to see the streets crowded with tourists, unlike Telluride, which was quiet in September. Then again, Telluride was smaller and more difficult to get to.

Rows of shops and restaurants lined both sides of the street. The Beaumont Hotel loomed large at the far end of town. It was an elaborate redbrick and stone building that rose three stories, with a corner tower that rose four. Topped with a slate mansard roof, it was an imposing Victorian-era structure.

Kim found a parking spot along the curb. "How do you want to handle this?"

"What do you mean?" Without waiting for an answer, Jack got out of the Tahoe and shut the door.

Kim came around the vehicle. "Well, since I'm with the sheriff's office, I think I should take the lead in questioning him." Her tense jaw belied her attempt to appear confident.

Jack wasn't in the mood for territorial posturing but needed to stay in the good graces of her boss. "Let's play it by ear," he said, then took the steps to the hotel and held the front door open for her.

The lobby was magnificent. A massive oak staircase dominated the center of the three-story reception area. Glass skylights soared overhead. Jack felt dizzy looking up at them and dropped his gaze to the plush carpeting beneath his boots, where a complex design of leaves and flowers was woven into a field of crimson. The room was a throwback to the turn of the century, and Jack loved it.

Spencer Troutman was sitting in an elaborate Victorian chair and rose to greet them. He wore green skinny jeans and a white silky shirt, the top few buttons left open to reveal a chain laid over a tuft of dark hair. It was clearly the waiter's day off.

"Exquisite, isn't it?" Troutman said, looking over the lobby. "Opened in 1887. Considered the finest hotel on the western slope back in its heyday." He talked with flamboyant flourishes of his hands. "Theodore Roosevelt and King Leopold of Belgium both stayed here. Can you imagine? Royalty all the way out here?"

Jack didn't care a lick about some old European king but was impressed by the mention of Roosevelt.

Troutman was still talking about the hotel. He was twentysomething with a flair for the dramatic and wore Gucci loafers, which Jack wondered how he afforded on a waiter's salary.

"But you guys didn't come here to talk about our fair Beaumont. Let's find somewhere more private," Troutman said, glancing over his shoulder. "These old walls have ears."

Jack and Kim followed him outside, and the three settled on a pair of benches facing the street.

Kim was the first to speak. "Thank you for cutting your weekend short and coming back to answer our questions." She cleared her throat. "Now, if you could recount the order of events on the morning in question regarding your contact with the deceased."

The waiter tilted his head sideways and frowned.

Jack jumped in. "Tell us about the morning you saw Dylan Montgomery."

"That's the day he was murdered, wasn't it? I knew it when I saw his photograph in the newspaper. Mother saved it for me. She's always trying to get me to move back to Denver.

But why would I do that with all the smog? Just look at this cerulean sky." He threw his hands in the air. "Anyhoo, Mother called me about the murder the second she read about it in the paper. I told her I was just fine, and if I was going to be murdered anywhere, I'd want it to be in Ouray, not Denver. She didn't think that was very funny."

Troutman paused to catch his breath. "Anyhoo, she saved the paper for my visit, and when I saw that poor man's photo, I knew it was him!"

"That's when you called the sheriff's office to report it?" Kim asked.

"It was. I knew immediately that I had a civic duty to my fellow man to help find who would commit such a hellacious crime."

Jack was growing impatient. "You saw a second man with Dylan?"

"I did. Talk, dark, and mysterious. Like some malevolent spirit manifested in—"

"Did you happen to get his name?" Jack asked.

"No." Troutman looked disappointed.

"What was his approximate age?"

"The murdered man or his companion?"

"His companion."

"Well, I would say fifty or so. But I'm not exactly sure. So many men get Botox and fillers nowadays, it's hard to tell some—"

"Approximately how tall was he?"

The waiter put his hand on his chin, thinking. "Probably a good three or four inches taller than me in his cowboy boots. So, maybe around six one, six two. He was sitting, so it was hard to tell. But he was fit." Troutman wagged a finger. "But not too bulky."

Jack nodded. "Facial hair?"

"Yes!" The waiter's eyes grew wide. "A beard." He

pointed a finger at Jack. "Full, like yours. Not as long, though, but thick."

Jack pulled at his beard subconsciously. He still hadn't trimmed it since being back from the mountains. "What color was it?"

"Black, like his hair."

So there it was. A tall, lean, maybe fifty something, with black hair and beard. But no name.

"Like his Jeep," Troutman added. "I remember now. His hair and his beard were the same color as his Jeep. He drove a black Rubicon. Fancy new one with all the bells and whistles. With an orange and blue license plate that gave it a bit of flair." Troutman pursed his lips. "But he was a lousy tipper. That's why I looked to see what kind of car he got into. Wealthy tourists are some of the worst tippers. In fact—"

"Did they split the bill?"

"No. The dark man paid. I remember because their conversation seemed heated. All of a sudden, he stood up and put cash on the table and left."

Jack thought about it a moment. The mystery man had paid for what was likely Dylan Montgomery's last meal following a tense conversation. Who was he? And what was his relationship to the victim?

"Had you ever seen Dylan in here before?" Jack asked.

"Never," the waiter said, wrinkling his nose in disapproval. "He wasn't the type who would dine here regularly. A bit shabby, if you know what I mean."

Troutman was eccentric but credible. Jack spent the next several minutes asking additional questions. Kim threw one or two in, trying to remain relevant. But Troutman knew nothing else of significance. He hadn't heard their conversation or knew where either man went when they left the restaurant. Presumably, Dylan had gone up to the Judas Mine. But where had the mystery man gone?

Kim thanked the waiter for his time and told him they

would be in touch. But before they left, she pulled a sheet of paper from her pocket and unfolded it.

"One last question," she said. "In order to confirm the validity of your statement, is this the same man you witnessed dining in the hotel that morning?"

It was a photograph of Dylan, different from the one published in the *Denver Post*.

Troutman glanced at the photo and nodded. "Yeah, that's him. I'm sure of it."

CHAPTER 21

"In order to confirm the validity of your statement?" Jack teased the deputy as they drove out of Ouray.

Kim grimaced. "Too much?"

"Too much, too official, too formal. Whatever you want to call it." He laid his arm on the open window of the Tahoe.

When it came to homicide investigations, the deputy was green, but she was a good cop. And for some reason, Jack felt compelled to help her get better.

"You'll learn that the best way to get information out of people is to put them at ease," he said. "Among other things, that means not talking to them like you're about to grade their English paper."

She sighed, embarrassed.

He added, "You'll also find that people often know more than they first admit." As they approached the gravel road that led to Shudder Basin, he said, "Turn here."

"Why?"

"I want to meet Corbin."

Kim hesitated, then swung the Tahoe off the highway at the For Sale sign.

Jack squinted into the distance at the small white house. Grass had grown up around the foundation, and several sections of green shingles were missing from the roof. It looked abandoned, but it had potential. *Maybe one day*, he thought.

A half hour later, Kim parked the Tahoe in the same spot

as before. "I have a feeling this isn't going to go well," she said, getting out.

Jack didn't reply, but he had a sneaking suspicion she could be right. From what he had heard, Corbin wouldn't welcome visitors. But there were too many questions Jack needed him to answer. He followed the deputy as she climbed toward Corbin's cabin. The air was crisp, and the sky, which had been a brilliant shade of turquoise, now threatened rain.

A hundred yards shy of their destination, Jack saw Butch Corbin open the door to his cabin and step outside with a shotgun laid in the crook of his arm. Jack glanced down at the firearm strapped to Kim's hip and was painfully aware he had come unarmed. He cursed himself under his breath. It was a rookie mistake.

As they got closer, Corbin stood his ground. He was a large man, with unruly hair and a grizzled beard that reached the center of his chest. He was cloaked in a worn buffalo-hide robe. Eli Wren had been right—Corbin did, in fact, resemble DiCaprio's portrayal of Hugh Glass in *The Revenant*, only older. Jack knew from Otto that he was in his late sixties, but he looked a decade older.

Corbin's face was weathered, creased deep like folded leather. "You folks lost?" There was no friendliness in his voice.

"Hi, Butch." Kim stopped several feet from the porch. She didn't appear even the least bit intimidated, which impressed Jack. "I want you to meet somebody," she said.

Corbin left her remark unanswered. His good eye narrowed, and Jack realized the other was glass. The guy was straight out of Hollywood casting.

"This is Jack Martin," the deputy continued. "He wants to ask you a few questions. And Tony said he'd take it as a personal favor if you'd talk to him."

Corbin grunted his displeasure.

Jack stepped forward and reached out a hand, but when

the large man didn't budge, he lowered it back to his side. This was going to be more difficult than he'd thought.

The conversation that ensued was one-sided and tense. Jack spent several minutes asking questions Corbin answered in one-syllable words and grunts. As hard as Jack tried, he couldn't get any more out of the man than what was already in the sheriff's report.

Dark storm clouds rolled over the peaks as they talked, yet Corbin didn't budge. And when it started to drizzle, he didn't invite them inside. Instead, the three stood in the rain.

"I warned you it wouldn't go well," Kim said as they got back into the Tahoe, shivering.

Jack was cold and wet, and his boots were soaked through. But what upset him more than anything was that the mountain man had gotten the best of him. Aside from meeting the infamous Crazy Corbin in the flesh, the trip to Shudder Basin had been a bust.

Corbin had proved an impossible nut to crack. And he stank like a rotten animal hide.

Rude and offensive, he hadn't even treated Kim with common courtesy.

Jack knew that emotion was often the death of a good investigation, but he was furious.

CHAPTER 22

JACK WAS STILL upset when they pulled into Telluride an hour and a half later. It had been years since he'd encountered anyone as irascible as Butch Corbin.

Interrogations were like a game. There were strategies and tactics, offense and defense. And although Jack wasn't one to brag, he knew it was something he was better at than most. During his time with the FBI field office in Houston, his superiors had pulled him in on numerous interrogations when other agents had failed to extract information.

Corbin might think he had won, but what the crazy mountain man didn't know was that Jack wasn't finished with him yet.

"What's going on up there?" Kim had slowed the Tahoe to a crawl.

A small crowd had gathered on both sides of the street, and everyone's eyes turned to the vehicles blocking both lanes. At the center of the mess were two delivery trucks stopped at odd angles. On either side of them were two trucks from the marshal's office with their lights flashing.

"I think it's an accident," Jack said, straining to get a better look.

"An accident that's escalated into something more." Kim pointed to a deputy who held a man by the shoulders. His hands were behind his back, indicating he was cuffed. Another deputy was questioning the second driver.

"This could take a while," Jack said. "You gonna help?"

"Not my jurisdiction. Marshal's office handles things inside the city limits."

Although she was right, jurisdictional lines had never kept Jack from butting in when it wasn't his business. "I'll get out here and walk," he said, opening the passenger door.

"Yeah, this doesn't look like it's going to clear up anytime soon."

As Jack passed through the crowd, he heard bits of conversation: *Cold-cocked him in the mouth…was making an illegal U-turn.* It looked like the deputies had things under control.

At the far end of town, the street was quiet, but Jack suddenly sensed a presence behind him.

"You're that famous detective, aren't you?"

It was a young girl. She was barefoot and smiling, one side of her mouth raised slightly higher than the other. Her face was covered with freckles, and she had a mess of auburn hair pulled back into something resembling a ponytail. Her large eyes were a peculiar shade of gray—almost purple. She fell into step beside him, mindlessly pulling at the bottom of her right sleeve.

"I'm a detective," Jack replied. "But I don't know about the famous part."

"Yeah, you're famous. Around here you are, anyway." Her dirty feet made slapping sounds on the concrete sidewalk. "Everyone knows who you are."

Jack had zero experience with kids and didn't want any. He didn't reply, hoping she'd go away.

No such luck.

"You're looking into that murder, aren't you?"

"I don't know what you're talking about."

"Yes, you do. You're just trying to keep it a secret." She twirled the ends of her hair as she struggled to keep up. "That mine is haunted, you know."

"What mine?"

"That one where that man died. It's called the Judas Mine."

Jack stopped. He looked down at her and frowned, surprised by how much she knew.

"*It is*," she insisted, pulling at her sleeve again.

"Is what?"

"Is haunted." Her voice had risen an octave. "Tommyknockers probably got him."

"Tommy what?"

"Tommyknockers. Gremlins in the mines. Haven't you ever heard of them?"

"No, I haven't." Jack made a mental note to ask Otto about Tommyknockers.

He started for the campground again. As he passed Pandora Cafe, he was tempted to stop, but continued on, the girl still following closely behind.

"He wasn't nice, you know?" she said.

"Who?"

"The man who died. He was mean."

Jack stopped again, and she nearly bumped into him. He wondered what she could possibly know about Dylan Montgomery.

"Why do you say he was mean?"

"Because he was," she said, suddenly shy and looking down at the sidewalk, pulling at her sleeve.

She had probably overheard town gossip. But it reminded Jack he needed to learn more about the victim. He glanced back at Pandora Cafe. Judith would be able to tell him more about Dylan.

"Listen," he said to the girl. "It's been nice talking to you, but I've really got to get going."

"You're probably busy, aren't you?" She dropped her gaze again and nodded. "Adults are always busy."

Jack stuck his hands on his hips and swiveled, looking for help. Surely the girl had a mother frantically looking for her.

"I don't know why anyone cares he's dead, though."

Jack stepped to the curb, looking for anyone searching for a child. Maybe her mother was in the crowd down the street, gawking at the accident.

The girl was still talking, but her voice had grown faint. "He burnt down his own house, you know?"

Burnt down his own house? When it registered what she had said, Jack wheeled around, half a dozen questions suddenly on the tip of his tongue.

But the girl was gone.

CHAPTER 23

JACK STEPPED INSIDE Pandora Cafe and found it nearly empty.

"Where is everybody?" Judith asked as he sat down at the table by the fireplace.

"Accident down the street."

She nodded, then set a small plate in front of him. "Try this," she said. "It's an apricot fried pie. It's a little late in the season, but I'm testing a new recipe."

Jack hadn't realized how hungry he was. He grabbed the warm pie and took a bite.

"How is it?"

"Like heaven in a crust."

Judith handed him a napkin, and Jack wiped his mouth.

"You don't happen to have some of your chicken and dumplings to go along with the pie, do you?" he asked.

"Special of the day." She shot him a mischievous grin. "But you already knew that. Let me get it for you."

A few minutes later, she emerged from the kitchen, set his order on the table, and then pulled out the chair next to him and sat. "You look like a man troubled by something. Unload it on me if it'll help."

She was fishing for information on the investigation. Jack trusted Judith—she was as good as gold—but he had to be careful. In Telluride, like most small towns, gossip traveled at lightning speed.

"Can I ask you something?" Jack poked at the dumplings with his spoon, letting them cool.

"You can ask me anything. Everyone knows I'm an open book."

"Tell me about Dylan Montgomery."

A shadow crossed her face, and she settled back in the chair. "What do you want to know? Dylan wasn't a regular customer, but I knew him. We all did. He lived here for the last twenty years or so."

"What was he like? It doesn't seem he had a lot of friends."

She frowned, considering the question. "I think people liked him for the most part. He was a loner, though. Kept to himself mainly."

"What about his family?"

"No family in Telluride. I think he's from Denver."

"Anything else you can tell me about him?"

She was quiet, then shrugged. For the congenial town gossip, Judith was being unusually tight-lipped.

"What about Cindy?" Jack asked. "His wife?"

Judith drew in a breath but hesitated. Something about the question made her nervous. When the front door opened, she immediately turned to look.

"Eli!" she said, getting up. "Excuse me for a second, Jack." The arrival of a customer was an excuse to evade the question. For some reason, she was avoiding talking about Cindy Montgomery.

Eli Wren looked exhausted. His hair was disheveled, and his designer outdoor clothes were covered with dust. Judith pointed him to a table near the front of the cafe, but when Wren spotted Jack, he made a beeline to the back.

Judith watched him nervously, then disappeared into the kitchen, and Jack wondered if she had purposefully tried seating Wren as far from him as she could. Something was up.

"Howdy-doo." Wren dropped a backpack onto the floor

at the adjacent table. "Fancy meeting you here again. Did you find that map at the museum yesterday?"

"I did."

"Well, I offered once, and I'll offer again. If you need any help, you just let me know."

Jack thanked him and watched as he pulled a flurry of papers and maps from his backpack and spread them across the table in front of him. He placed a red spiral notebook on the top of it all, opened it, and began making notes.

Jack noticed a large rock hammer in the backpack, a particularly nasty-looking geological tool with a flat head on one end and a pick on the other, used for splitting rock.

"I met Butch Corbin today."

Wren looked up from his work. "And you lived to tell the tale?" He shook his head, then began writing again in the notebook. "Orneriest SOB I've ever met," he added.

Jack finished the chicken and dumplings, then laid his napkin on the table. He glanced toward the kitchen, where, curiously, Judith had remained out of sight. The altercation between the two delivery drivers must have been resolved because the cafe slowly began to fill with customers. Sooner or later, she would have to come back out.

Wren had tracing paper over a topographical map and drew concentric circles using a protractor.

Jack watched him. "Trying to locate something?"

"Always," Wren said without looking up. He finished the last circle and set the protractor and pencil aside. "You interested?"

"In what?"

"Treasure hunting? Adventure?" He smiled, revealing a good portion of his large white teeth. "A life spent crossing the globe in search of unknown adventures and riches?"

Eli Wren was a character, but for some reason, Jack liked him.

Jack smiled. "Maybe."

The response had Wren beaming. "There's nothing like it to get the blood pumping. Nothing like it in the world. And don't listen to anyone who says it's all about the hunt. That's bunk. They say that because they never find anything." He laughed. "The satisfaction is in the spoils, my boy. To hell with the hunt."

Wren was on a roll. "I got the bug as a kid. Grew up in Denver. Spent a couple of summers pulling gold out of an old mine near Black Hawk. I guess you could say that's when I got hooked. Oh, sure, I went off to college—Wharton— got a finance degree. Made a bit of money on Wall Street before I couldn't stand it anymore and quit. Do you know how damned demoralizing it is being locked in a skyscraper all day wearing a suit and tie?" He shook his head. "Sucks the soul right out of a man."

Jack had researched Wren on the internet and knew he was downplaying his time on Wall Street. *Forbes* magazine estimated his net worth at just over two hundred million.

Jack decided to call Archie Rochambeau, an old FBI colleague and financial genius, to learn more about the flamboyant treasure hunter.

"So you quit Wall Street to travel the world."

"I did."

"You mentioned yesterday that you spent time in the Caribbean."

"The hunt for the *Santa León*. Now, that's the kind of experience that will change a man. We searched for almost three years but never gave up—the prize was too big. And boy, was she something." He leaned the chair back on two legs, remembering. "First launched in 1756, she was one of the largest Manila galleons ever built. Spanned nearly…"

Wren spent several minutes describing the ship, using terms Jack had never heard. The man was obsessed but brilliant.

"And now you're in Telluride looking for gold?" he asked when Wren's monologue slowed.

"Not just for gold," he said, pointing a finger. "For the legendary spur of the old Smuggler Vein."

Jack had never heard of it and was afraid to ask but did, setting Wren to talking again.

"It's what caused the San Juan rush in 1875," he explained. "John Fallon found it. He was high up in the mountains and literally saw a streak of gold a mile long shining in the sun. Couldn't keep his mouth shut, and soon, the valley was flooded with prospectors. The vein played out decades ago." Wren brought his chair forward and grinned. "At least, that's what they thought."

"You think there's gold left?"

"I know there is." He riffled through the papers and pulled a map from the stack in front of him, then set it back down on the table. "See here…"

Wren spent the next ten minutes pointing to places and reading sections of geological and seismic reports, none of which Jack understood. But he listened patiently, waiting for an opening.

When Wren mentioned Shudder Basin, he got it. "That's why you're interested in Corbin's mine."

Wren's demeanor changed, and he folded the map. "That one, among others."

Jack remembered the proximity of Corbin's Crystal Lake Mine to where Dylan Montgomery was found dead.

"What about the Judas?" he asked and saw Wren's animated face go slack. He suddenly looked gravely serious.

"The Judas holds the mother lode."

CHAPTER 24

Sunday, September 22

Jack woke the following day disturbed, remembering the auburn-haired girl who had stopped him on the street and wondering who she was.

How would a girl of eleven or twelve know about Dylan Montgomery? Surely, gossip as morbid as murder wouldn't have made its way to a child. But it obviously had. Then again, it had been kids who'd found him.

Something the girl had said still bothered him. *He burnt down his own house, you know?*

Kim mentioned that Montgomery had been inconsolable following his wife's death. Could he have intentionally set the fire, not knowing she was home? Had he accidentally burned her alive? It would explain the extreme grief.

It could also explain why residents of Telluride didn't want to talk about Cindy Montgomery. Had there been a tearful confession by her husband? Did people know—or suspect—that Dylan had deliberately set the fire?

Jack bypassed Kim and called her boss. "Tony, it's Jack. Sorry to bother you on a Sunday, but I've got a question."

Sheriff Burns filled Jack in on the details of the fire, information almost identical to what he'd already learned from the deputy. There had been an investigation but no proof of arson. It had been ruled a tragic accident.

But Jack wasn't satisfied. After wrangling enough details

out of the sheriff to be able to locate the old Montgomery homestead, he left Crockett with Otto and headed for Placerville. According to Tony, the property was thirty acres of mainly forested land, with several hundred feet of frontage along a tributary of the San Miguel River. The property was sold after the fire, but as far as Tony knew, it was still vacant. Just off the highway, Jack picked the lock on the gate to the property, hoping he was right.

The charred foundation sat on a clearing a hundred yards from the river. Jack walked across the blackened concrete, stuck his hands on his hips, and turned, facing the rising sun to think.

Even if Dylan *had* set his own house on fire, why would he do it? Greed and desperation were the most common motives for arson. Had Dylan been strapped for cash?

Jack fished his phone from his pocket and scrolled through his contacts.

"Jack! What's hanging, old buddy?" Archie Rochambeau spoke with a thick Cajun accent that was sometimes hard to understand. But after years of working with him for the FBI, Jack could decipher just about anything Rochambeau said.

"Sorry to bother you on a Sunday, Arch. I hope I'm not catching you at an inconvenient time."

"Got my toes in the water, ass in the sand. Know the song? Anyway, little vacay with the missus. What's up?"

"You're on vacation?"

"Got the kids back in school, and we're taking a sortie in Sarasota."

"You're in Florida?"

"That I am," he replied. "And it reminds me—what do you call a lobster that won't share?"

"I have no idea."

"Shell-fish." Archie laughed. "Get it? Shell-fish?"

Jack smiled. "Yeah, I get it."

"Here's another one—"

"Arch—"

"No, this is a good one. A pirate hobbles into a bar with a peg leg, a parrot on his shoulder, and a steering wheel in his pants. Bartender says, 'Hey, buddy, you've got a steering wheel in your pants.' Pirate says, 'Aarrgghh, I know, and it's driving me nuts.'"

Jack chuckled despite himself. He missed his old friend.

"I told you it was a good one," Archie said, laughing again. "Now, what's up, old buddy? I don't get these calls out of the blue to shoot the shi—"

"I need a favor."

"Jack Martin needs a favor. Now I've got a reason to live."

"The victim's name is Dylan Montgomery."

"Hold on. No paper on the playa. I'm gonna put you on speaker so I can type it into my phone, so I don't forget it. Laptop's in the room. Another hour in the sun, and I'll get on it. You said Dylan Montgomery?"

"That's right."

"Okay, what're you looking for?"

"He was murdered three weeks ago in Telluride. I want to know if he was in any kind of financial straits."

"Got it," Archie said. "Loans, mortgages, gambling debts?"

"All of the above."

"Alimony?"

"No wife. He was a widower."

"So an old dude."

"Not hardly," Jack said. He looked down at the charred foundation and thought of something. "Check his bank accounts. See if he had any large deposits twelve years ago, give or take a couple of years."

"Sure thing. Now, to satisfy my natural curiosity, how'd your vic check out?"

"Gunshot."

"Damn."

"Yeah," Jack said. "To the back."

Archie whistled, then started in on one of his notorious monologues. "You don't turn your back on an enemy. Then again, sometimes we don't realize who's an enemy until it's too late, do we? Could have been someone he trusted. Or maybe not." He cleared his throat. "But that's why you're the investigator, and I'm the financial gumshoe, your run-of-the-mill computer-hacking whiz. Any idea who capped him?"

Questions and theories swirled in Jack's head. He thought of Butch Corbin's arsenal of weapons. Dylan would never have trusted his cantankerous neighbor in the basin. But he also had an ex-girlfriend. Scorned lovers were one of the oldest motives in the book.

Dylan was murdered in the mine. Corbin and Graham would have known where to find it. Then again, so would Eli Wren. Although Jack couldn't imagine the outgoing treasure hunter being a killer, he knew that looks could be deceiving.

"Run a quick check on the finances of Eli Wren while you're at it," he added.

"The adventure guy?"

"Yeah. But don't spend a lot of time on him. I just want to know if he's really financially sound."

Archie blew air through his teeth. "I'm pretty sure the dude's loaded, but I'll get some numbers. Now, *that'll* be an interesting dig—no pun intended."

"Get the scoop on Montgomery first."

"Will do."

Jack remembered another suspect—the mystery man in the black Jeep. The one who'd had breakfast and a tense conversation with Dylan the morning he died. Had it been a coincidence?

"Poor guy," Archie said, breaking the silence. "Knowing your killer would be a particularly nasty way to check out. At least being shot in the back meant he probably didn't see it coming."

Jack watched the river flow languid and dark in the shadows of the forest. "Dylan Montgomery knew his killer," he said. "I'm sure of it."

CHAPTER 25

Jack's next stop was Earl's Tavern. He found Sean Sullivan sitting on a wooden bench outside the bar, facing a small grassy area at the side of the building. His motorcycle was just around the corner.

"Morning, Jack. I'll open the bar in a bit." Sullivan was holding a small paper bag, tossing peanuts on the ground at his feet. "If you stay really still, they'll come right up to you and get it."

Jack stood still as a squirrel snatched a peanut, then retreated to the base of a cottonwood tree, where it sat upright and chewed hungrily.

"They're smaller and darker here than in Texas," Sullivan said. "I don't know why, but I've always taken a liking to them."

Jack remembered the squirrels that had driven his grandmother crazy, raiding her arsenal of bird feeders. Reminders of his grandparents were creeping up more often, but he pushed the memory aside.

"If you've got time," he said. "I've got a few more questions."

"Sure. Have a seat."

Jack took the opposite end of the bench and watched him toss another peanut.

"You said that you met Dylan five years ago."

"That's right. It'll be five this December."

"Did he ever mention a house fire? It would have been six or seven years before that."

Sullivan was quiet, watching the squirrel grab the peanut and retreat before he answered. "He did. Not long after we met. The memory must have still been raw because I don't think he ever brought it up again."

"What did he tell you about it?"

"Not much. Just that it was a total loss. I'm sure it was something he didn't like to talk about."

Sullivan emptied the remaining peanuts onto the ground and brushed his hands on his jeans. "Let's move the conversation inside," he said, getting up from the bench. "I need to get ready to open."

Jack followed him into the bar, where he turned on a series of lights, brightening the dark room. He pulled two beers from a refrigerator, opened them, and slid one across the bar to Jack.

It was still early. For a moment Jack considered refusing but then thought better of it. *Put them at ease*, he reminded himself. Plus, it was a Shiner—his favorite.

"So, how's the crime-detecting business going?" Sullivan wiped foam from his mouth and set the bottle on the bar.

"Slow."

"Must be a tough case. The sheriff doesn't seem to have gotten very far with it either."

"What can you tell me about Dylan?"

Sullivan frowned. "Dylan was a complex guy. He'd get rowdy if he had too much to drink, but nothing too bad. At least nothing that I saw. He never hurt anyone that I know of."

"Did people like him?"

"I've heard of some who didn't."

"But you did?"

"I did." He took a sip of beer and set the bottle down. "Dylan had a high-strung personality. He was obsessed with his mine and was up there practically every day. Some weekends, he'd even spend the night there. I think some people didn't understand him. But he didn't deserve what happened to him. Nobody does."

"Any ideas who would want to kill him?"

Sullivan took in a slow breath, thinking. "I've asked myself that several times." He shook his head. "I know there were people who didn't like him, but for the life of me, I can't think of anyone who'd want him dead."

Jack let a few seconds pass. "What do you know about Eli Wren?"

"Eli?" Sullivan chuckled. "I know he's some famous fortune hunter. He comes into the bar regularly and seems like a nice enough guy, but you never know. I put up with all his talking because he's a great tipper."

"He's eccentric," Jack said. "But he doesn't seem to be what I would call crazy."

"Everyone's got a different definition of crazy."

"What do you mean?"

Sullivan pulled an assortment of bowls from behind the bar and began filling them with peanuts. "Eli's got gold fever. He was always bugging Dylan, wanting to get inside the mine and have a look around."

"Did Dylan ever let him?"

"He did once—which was probably a mistake. After that Eli wouldn't leave him alone." Sullivan shook his head, still dividing peanuts among the bowls. "I've heard he's been all over these mountains searching mines when the owners let him…breaking into others when they won't." He shook his head. "Gold fever can make a man crazy."

"Crazy enough to kill?"

Sullivan stopped pouring and looked up. "Maybe. But not crazy enough to buy my share outright." He stowed the bags under the bar.

"What do you mean?"

"Eli's obsessed with finding gold, but when I offered him my share of the mine after Dylan died, he said he wasn't interested. I figured selling it to him would do us both a favor. I'd unload the damn thing, score a little cash, and Eli finally gets what he wants—complete access to it anytime he wants. But he declined the offer. It doesn't make sense, if you ask me. Unless he wants to get in and look for free."

That had Jack thinking. "Did he know you were a minority partner before you offered to sell it to him?"

"No." Sullivan pulled a cutting board from a cabinet. "Not until I told him. I think he thought Dylan owned it outright."

Jack watched as Sullivan grabbed limes from the refrigerator and quartered them. Could Wren have thought that, with Dylan out of the way, he could search the mine for free? Then, when it turned out there was a second owner, his plans had been thwarted? Maybe Wren wasn't as wealthy as everyone thought he was.

With Dylan dead, Jack wondered if Sullivan was now in danger. But he decided to change the subject. "Do you know a woman by the name of Vanessa Graham?"

"Sure, I know Vanessa."

"I hear she's Dylan's ex."

"She is."

"Did they get along okay after the breakup?"

Sullivan shrugged, still cutting the limes. "As far as I know. But then again, Vanessa gets along with everybody."

Jack asked Sullivan for her telephone number. Vanessa Graham was the next person on his interview list.

Sullivan laid the knife on the bar. "Sure, I can get it for you. Hold on a minute." He disappeared into the back for several minutes. When he came out, he held out a sticky note to Jack. "You going to ask her about Dylan?"

Jack looked down at the number and recognized the backward slanted handwriting of a lefty, reminding him of his grandfather's. Another memory he immediately pushed aside.

"The more you learn about the victim," he said, "the more likely you'll be able to solve the case."

Sullivan nodded. "Makes sense."

Jack stuck the paper into his back pocket. "Did Dylan ever mention a man from Utah? Tall, dark hair, beard. Drives a black Jeep."

"No. Why?"

"A man fitting that description was seen with Dylan the day he was murdered."

Sullivan was putting limes in a plastic container but stopped. "You think he could have killed him?"

Jack left the question unanswered.

CHAPTER 26

Harriet Hughes had loved Sunday mornings for as long as she could remember, never tiring of the order and sanctity of her favorite day of the week.

The ritual had been the same nearly every Sunday of her seventy-three years. A warm bath, putting on her best dress, and a powerful sermon to help cleanse the week's sins from her soul.

After church, there was always Sunday lunch with family while she was growing up and brunch with friends at the New Sheridan with Opal and Ivy Waggoner as she got older. For the past thirty years, following services at Telluride's Wildwood Chapel, she dined with Opal and Ivy. The women were together—every—single—Sunday.

Harriet enjoyed Ivy's company. The younger and kinder sister wasn't the problem. Ivy might be a few bricks short of a load, but she was generous and kind.

The problem was Opal. Harriet had tired of her decades earlier. She was cranky and short-tempered and never met a person she couldn't find fault with—except for herself. And there was her annoying habit of striking the ground with her cane when she thought no one was listening or she wanted to make a point. There were times when Harriet wanted to take that cane and—

"Will you two slow down?" Opal hobbled between them,

her cane tapping rhythmically on the sidewalk with each short step. "These orthopedic shoes are killing my feet."

Oh, Lord, Harriet thought. *Here we go again with the shoes.* She knew exactly what Ivy would say next. It was the same conversation between the two sisters every Sunday.

"They're not supposed to hurt your feet, Opal. They're supposed to help."

"Well, they don't."

"You should wear your sneakers, like I do."

Opal harrumphed. "Ivy Waggoner, since when is it appropriate to wear sneakers to church? If I didn't know better, I'd think you were raised in a barn."

"Well, I'm sure the Good Lord won't sentence me to eternal damnation for wearing Keds."

It was the same conversation every—single—week.

Harriet sometimes fantasized about kicking the cane out from under Opal, sending her and the godforsaken shoes sprawling. But as she always did, she bit her lip.

Opal and Ivy were a package. If you took one sister, you got the other. And Harriet wasn't in a position to be picky. Telluride was a small town. And at their age, they didn't have many friends left, most having passed away or moved to live near grown children.

"Well, lookee there." Ivy stopped and stared across the street.

"Oh, Lord. He's back," Opal replied. "Keep moving, Ivy, or he'll see us."

"Who will?" Harriet asked.

Ivy pointed across the street.

"Good grief, quit pointing," Opal huffed.

"Who is he?" Harriet was still confused.

"That's Jack Martin," Ivy replied. "That famous detective. Isn't he handsome?"

Harriet glanced at the man walking in the opposite direction across the street. He was tall and lean, with brown hair that reached his collar and a beard that needed trimming. She had seen his photograph in the media and thought he was attractive. But straining to see from across the street, she couldn't tell if he was as good-looking in person or not.

Opal was having none of it. "The two of you should see yourselves ogling him like a couple of teenage girls. That man is a nuisance and a busybody. Sticks his nose into other people's business."

"Well, I believe that's what detectives are supposed to do, Opal." Ivy smiled, still watching him. "And I think he's nice."

"Ivy Waggoner, wipe that ridiculous grin off your face. You're too old for a crush."

"Am not."

"You need to check your hormones."

"You need to check your—"

"The detective?" Harriet was putting the pieces together and suddenly felt sick.

The women continued walking but stopped at the entrance to Waggoner Mercantile. Ivy waited patiently for her sister to unlock the front door, but Harriet stared at the man down the street. She wished she'd gotten a better look at his face.

She remembered how, only days earlier, Abby had come home, her large gray eyes wide with excitement and her ponytail swinging as she gestured wildly, telling Harriet about seeing the great detective. Now there he was, in the flesh, and Harriet wished she had gotten a better look. When the three women stepped inside the store, she went straight to the window and continued watching him. He was walking fast, then started to run, and Harriet wondered why. Opal suddenly rapped her cane on the wood floor, making her jump.

"Do you know what I think?" Opal asked.

"I can only imagine," Ivy muttered under her breath.

"I think that detective is back in town to investigate that murder."

Harriet felt a lump form in her throat. She turned and faced Opal. "Dylan's murder?"

"Yep. Who else's?"

Robbie Cruz, Harriet's handyman, entered the store but pulled up when he saw the ladies huddled at the window.

"I—I can come back," he said. He made eye contact with Ivy and held a paper bag aloft.

"Take it to my desk, dear," Ivy said softly. "I'll be back there in a minute."

Robbie scanned the faces of the three women, then nodded, knowing something was up.

"Well, go on, Robbie," Harriet instructed. "Do whatever it is Ivy needs you to do."

He nodded. "I'll go wait in the back, Ms. Ivy."

Harriet hadn't meant to be short. She took in a deep breath, trying to steady her nerves. But she was afraid that her worst nightmare was coming true.

"Do you think he could be a problem?" she whispered.

"The detective or Robbie?" Ivy whispered back.

The older sister rolled her eyes. "Well, of course she means the detective."

Harriet looked to Opal expectantly. But when she received only a silent stare in return, she felt something inside her clench. She turned back to Ivy, who immediately dropped her gaze to the floor, echoing her sister's sentiments.

It was then Harriet knew.

They were in trouble.

CHAPTER 27

It was Sunday. Although weekends were busy in Telluride, even in the off-season, town was unusually quiet.

Leaving Earl's Tavern, Jack had intended to go straight to Pandora Cafe. But what he saw up the street changed his mind. A black Jeep was parked up the hill in front of Telluride Bank & Trust. Ever since his visit with the waiter in Ouray, Jack had taken a second look at each one he encountered.

He started in the direction of the bank, intent on having a look. And when he realized the Jeep had an orange and blue license plate, he quickened his pace. He was still a block away when a man in a cowboy hat stepped out of the bank. But it was a Sunday. The bank should have been closed.

The man had a black beard, like the one the waiter had described. And when he opened the driver's-side door of the Jeep, Jack began to run.

"Stop!" Jack hollered, but the man either hadn't heard or had ignored him.

The Jeep swung from the curb and headed out of town. But not before Jack got a good look at the license plate.

He pulled his phone from his pocket and typed the numbers into a text to Kim O'Connor. Then he opened the door of Telluride Bank & Trust and stepped inside.

Ted Hawthorne looked surprised to see him. "We're closed."

"It doesn't look that way to me. I just saw someone walk out of here."

Hawthorne stumbled over an answer. "Well, he...That was...Actually, it's none of your business."

"Pretend it's my business. There's been a murder."

Hawthorne frowned. "What does that have to do with...?" His voice trailed off.

"Maybe nothing," Jack replied. "But I need the name of the guy who was just in here."

"Why?"

"Like I said, it's an investigation."

Hawthorne stuck out his chest, posturing. "Am I being questioned?"

"Some people would call it that." Jack was in no mood for his Napoleon complex. "All I need is a name."

Hawthorne glanced over his shoulder, then outside through the window, as if looking for help. Jack took a step closer, and the banker stepped back, bumping into a desk.

"Do I need a lawyer?"

"Only if you have something to hide."

Hawthorne stumbled around the side of the desk, groping for the receiver of the phone set on it. "I'm calling the marshal's office."

"Go right ahead. They know I'm working for the sheriff."

Jack watched him debate what to do next and hoped like hell the banker wouldn't call his bluff. His interrogation tactics wouldn't pass muster, and he wasn't sure if Tony had informed the marshal he was working on the case or not. But the last thing he wanted was for law enforcement more involved than they already were.

"Look, Ted," Jack said, holding up a hand. "All I need is a name."

Hawthorne eyed him skeptically, then laid the receiver back on its cradle. "I'm bound by a fiduciary duty not to disclose the name of the bank's clients."

"So the man is a client?"

Hawthorne stared back without answering. "I've told you enough already. Now, if you please. The bank is closed."

Jack stuck his hand in his pocket, then realized he'd left the safe deposit key in the trailer that morning, never thinking he'd be at the bank on a Sunday. He wished he had it, hoping something in the box would shed light on Dylan's murder.

"I'll be back," he said, turning to leave. But when he reached the door, he stopped. "You know, it's almost as if you don't want this murder solved."

The tendons in Hawthorne's skinny neck flexed.

"Why is that, Ted?"

The banker stood defiant.

But Jack saw the fear in his eyes.

CHAPTER 28

Jack called Kim the second he left the bank.

"I got your text," she said, answering the phone.

"Can you run the plate?"

"We're already on it." She was quick and efficient—another sign of a good cop.

"It might be nothing," he said. "But let's check. Just in case." He was downplaying the significance of the driver's identity, not wanting her too interested.

"Where'd you see the Jeep?"

"Parked outside Telluride Bank & Trust."

"Did you get a look at him?"

"Not good enough for a decent description," he lied.

Kim fell silent a moment. "Want me to talk to Ted Hawthorne?"

"Don't bother," Jack answered. "I just did."

"And?"

"Claimed it was his fiduciary duty to keep the man's identity confidential."

She was quiet, thinking again. "I'll let you know when I've got something on the plates."

"I need something else," he said. "Vanessa Graham's address."

"Hold on a minute."

Jack heard her typing on a computer keyboard. "Are you at the office?"

"Working from home." There were a few more clicks. "Here it is. She lives in Norwood."

Jack sighed. It was a forty-minute drive. He pulled his phone from his ear long enough to check the time. "Can you text it to me?"

"Will do. But I should go with you."

"No. Enjoy the rest of your day off." He thanked her and ended the call before she could protest.

Jack had been to Norwood several times before, but it always surprised him how fast the landscape changed once out of the valley. The terrain went from mountainous to flat. Gone was the proliferation of aspen and pine trees, replaced by scrub brush and farmland. Although still in Colorado, it reminded him of New Mexico.

He followed the GPS on his phone to a small house in a run-down neighborhood on the edge of town. There were two cars parked in front—a Chevrolet sedan and a Subaru hatchback. Both old and in need of paint jobs.

The house could have used a coat of paint as well. It had blue clapboard siding with white trim and was surrounded by a yard infested with weeds.

Jack got out of his truck and took a cracked sidewalk to the front door.

"Well, hello, handsome." The woman looked to be in her early fifties but could have been a decade younger. She leaned against the doorjamb, smoking a cigarette, and Jack instantly recognized the signs of meth. She was gaunt and pale. Her eyes sunken and ringed with dark circles. She wore a limp T-shirt with no bra and running shorts several sizes too small. There were sores on her arms and legs.

"I'm looking for Vanessa Graham."

"Ah, shucks," the woman said. "And here I was hoping you were looking for me."

Jack gave her a polite smile in reply.

The woman tossed the cigarette onto the porch and

ground the ash with her flip-flop. "Vanessa! You got company!" she hollered over her shoulder. She gave Jack another appraising glance, then disappeared inside, leaving him standing at the open door.

After several seconds, he heard footsteps inside.

Vanessa Graham was more attractive than her roommate. Thin, but not frail. Pale, but not a sickly shade of gray. Yet there were signs of past abuse—small scars from sores on her hands and the side of her face. He glanced at her arms, looking for track marks, but didn't see any. Although she had probably used drugs in the past, she appeared clean—at least for the time being.

"Can I help you?" She looked nervous, but her tone was curious and polite.

Jack introduced himself.

"I've heard of you," she said. "You're that detective, aren't you? You figured out who killed that congressman last spring."

Jack nodded.

"And now you're trying to find out who murdered Dylan."

"You haven't returned my calls." When she didn't reply, he added, "What can you tell me about him?"

"Dylan? I was raised not to speak ill of the dead." She sighed, then glanced over her shoulder. "I'd invite you in, but..." She stepped onto the porch, closing the door behind her. "Sorry, but Lynette is all ears. How about if we take a walk?"

They took the sidewalk to the street and fell into step with each other.

"So what can you tell me about him?"

"Dylan wasn't a nice guy." She hesitated before continuing. "Oh, he was at first—dinner, flowers, the whole bit. Said all the right things. He was handsome, too, in a scruffy sort of way. I should have known he was too good to be true. The good ones never stick around. Anyway, pretty soon he started drinking again. Friends warned me he was a mean drunk, but I didn't listen to them. Man, I should have."

"Did he ever hit you?" The look on her face answered his question. "Did you press charges?"

Vanessa shook her head. Jack was always disappointed when victims of domestic violence wouldn't press charges, but he understood it. Most wouldn't do it out of fear. But it meant criminals were left on the street to abuse again, which infuriated him.

"What about his friends? I understand Dylan had lived here a long time."

"He had a couple of drinking buddies, but I wouldn't call them friends."

After a few steps, Jack asked, "What about Sean?"

"Sean Sullivan?"

Jack nodded.

She was quiet a moment. "Sean was…" Her voice trailed off and her steps slowed. "Sean was more of an acquaintance, I guess you'd say."

"What do you know about him?"

"Sean?" When Jack nodded, she continued. "I know that before he came to Telluride, he worked road crews. Mainly in Texas, but he was working on one in New Mexico when he met Dylan."

"Did they get along?"

"They did." She was quiet for a few steps before she continued. "They were friendly but not friends, if that makes sense."

Jack told her it did. "Sean helped the sheriff find the mine after Dylan was murdered."

She seemed surprised. "Did he? Well, I guess it was because he knew where it was. He'd been up there with Dylan a couple of times, although never voluntarily."

"What do you mean?"

"He didn't like it. And Dylan was always trying to get him

to work in it with him. But it wasn't Sean's thing. I think he's claustrophobic or something."

"But he owns part of it."

Vanessa chuckled. "Again, not voluntarily." Jack waited for her to explain, and she continued. "Did he tell you how he got his share of it?"

"He said it was collateral for a gambling loan."

She nodded. "Yes. But did he mention he never wanted it? He always figured Dylan would pay him back with interest, like he said he would. Or at least, he'd be able to sell his share to someone else. Maybe make a little extra."

"But he hasn't yet."

Vanessa shook her head. "Dylan kept filling him full of lies, telling him he was on the verge of finding some long-lost vein of gold. But Dylan was good at lying." She sounded bitter.

The mention of lost gold made Jack think of Eli Wren. Wren was convinced he was on the verge of discovering a forgotten part of the old Smuggler Vein. Could Dylan have been looking for the same thing?

Vanessa was still talking. "Sean always thought Dylan would eventually buy his shares back. But now that Dylan's dead, I guess he's stuck with it."

A truck approached them and slowed as it passed, the elderly driver sticking his arm out the open window to wave. Vanessa waved back, but for some reason, she looked sad.

"A friend of yours?"

"He lives around the corner. His wife just died."

"I'm sorry to hear it."

"Yeah, cancer's a bitch."

They walked past the next several houses in silence.

When they got to the corner, Vanessa stopped. "I usually turn here," she said. "But my route takes me a mile and a half. I suppose we should go back."

Jack was enjoying the fresh air and being in the company

of an attractive woman but reminded himself that he was there on business.

"I have to ask," he said after they turned around. "Where were you the day Dylan was murdered?"

She pulled up short, surprised or offended by the question, Jack couldn't tell, and answered, "I was with Sean."

CHAPTER 29

"So much for taking a day off," Ted Hawthorne mumbled to himself as he unlocked the bank's front door and stepped inside. It was his second trip to the bank that day. He'd already had two visitors that morning. Eli Wren now made the third. Although Ted had been excited to snag Eli as a customer, the treasure hunter was quickly becoming a pain in his backside.

But the bank's second visitor that morning had been even worse. Jack Martin was more than a nuisance—he could cause trouble. The only visitor the banker had wanted to see that morning was his first.

"Top of the mornin' to ya, Ted," Eli boomed, stepping inside.

"Eli," Ted replied without enthusiasm.

"Oh, come now. Most bankers would be excited to receive a deposit."

Eli's humor fell flat. "Is the deposit cash this time?"

"Sorry, my good man. It's more samples for the box, but the cash is coming!"

Eli followed him to the vault, where Ted punched in the code to unlock it, careful to ensure Eli wasn't looking over his shoulder.

He swung open the heavy door. "I've told you before, Eli, I don't like opening the vault on the weekend. It violates the terms of the bank's insurance policy."

The vault was lined with dozens of steel drawers on three

sides. Ted took a key from his pocket and unlocked one of them.

"A great way to get robbed," Eli said, cuffing Ted on the shoulder as he stepped around him. "But, I assure you, my good man, the inconvenience will be more than worth it. I'm hot on the trail of that forgotten vein. And when I find it, I'll deposit cash with you faster than you can count it."

Yeah, yeah, Ted thought. He'd heard the same story for months. Although he appreciated the box rental, regularly meeting Eli at odd hours to let him into the dang thing had gotten old. He stood at the vault's threshold as Wren slid his key into the drawer's second lock and unloaded rocks from a canvas bag.

Ted had asked about the samples before, wondering why they needed to be stored at the bank. Eli had sworn Ted to secrecy and explained the significance of keeping them safe until he could get them tested.

Ted suspected Eli was prone to unnecessary drama. Who would want to steal a bunch of rocks? But as long as the bank got fifty dollars a month for the box rental, Ted would put up with him for a while longer.

"How long will you be in town?" he asked the treasure hunter.

"As long as it takes." Eli locked the box and stepped out of the vault.

Ted swung the door shut and locked it. "What if you don't find the vein?"

"I'll find it," Eli assured him. "I'm pretty sure I already know where it is, and I've got something in the works."

Ted eyed the man warily. If Eli was onto something, he hoped it wasn't anywhere near Shudder Basin. It could ruin his plans.

"Where've you been looking?"

Eli scoffed. "Where *haven't* I been looking is more like it." He rubbed the back of his neck. "If I weren't having so much fun, I'd say I was getting too old for this." He dropped his hand and grinned. "But it's still too much fun."

Ted felt a jolt of envy. He'd never had a job he felt passionate about. The bank had been in his family for generations. After inheriting it from his father, he had brought it back from the brink of insolvency out of desperation. Telluride Bank & Trust was the only thing his father left that was worth a damn. Gerald Hawthorne had been a gambler and had squandered everything else, including the family home. The memory caused bile to rise in Ted's throat, and he pushed it down.

"Thanks for your hospitality, Mr. Drysdale," Eli teased, referring to the banker on the sitcom *The Beverly Hillbillies*. "Jed Clampett is leaving the building!"

Eli strolled to the door but pulled up short, looking at something outside. "That guy is everywhere."

Ted came up beside him and saw Jack Martin on the sidewalk across the street. The men stood watching him through the window.

"What do you think he's up to?" Eli asked.

"He's investigating that murder."

Eli looked at him. "Dylan Montgomery's?"

"That's right."

They continued watching him. Ted hoped Martin wouldn't cross the street. He'd already seen enough of the detective that morning.

"He won't be a problem," Eli muttered under his breath.

"What was that?"

Eli shook his head. "Nothing. Just talking to myself."

When the detective glanced in their direction, both men stepped back from the window.

"Do you think he saw us?" Eli asked.

Ted's heart caught in his throat. "I hope not."

CHAPTER 30

THE TWO MEN inside the bank stepped back from the window into the shadows. Their behavior was suspicious, but Jack kept walking, resisting the urge to turn and let them know he noticed.

It made sense that Ted Hawthorne had avoided eye contact, afraid Jack would cross the street and hassle him again about the mystery customer in the black Jeep. What the banker didn't know was that as soon as Kim O'Connor had the man's name, another confrontation was inevitable.

What Jack didn't understand was why Eli Wren was avoiding him—unless he was hiding something. Although Wren seemed harmless, Jack decided to find out more about the flamboyant treasure hunter. For a Sunday, the bank was unusually busy, and that intrigued him.

He walked another block, then crossed the street and went into Pandora Cafe. The crowd was light, but he was disappointed the table next to the fireplace was occupied.

Judith pointed to an empty table closer to the kitchen. "Food tastes just as good at this one," she said, smiling. "What can I get you?"

"What's the special?"

"Fish and chips with a side of mac and cheese and a biscuit."

Not a hint of anything green.

"Perfect," he said. "I'll take it."

She returned several minutes later with his order and set it in front of him, then pulled out an adjacent chair and sat.

"How's the investigation going?"

Jack poked at the mac and cheese, letting it cool. "It's going slow, but maybe you can help."

She watched him without answering.

"Yesterday you were reluctant to talk about Cindy Montgomery."

Judith pursed her lips, then relaxed back into the chair. "It's a sore subject," she said. "What happened to Cindy was a horrible accident."

"But why do people avoid talking about her?"

She shrugged. "Probably because everyone was devastated by what happened. It's still hard to talk about. Everyone loved her."

It was a convenient answer. And Jack reminded himself that she'd had twenty-four hours to come up with it.

He let the subject drop. "What can you tell me about Vanessa Graham?"

Judith frowned. "Who?"

"Dylan's ex-girlfriend."

He could see it took a second for the name to register with her. "Ah, yes," she said. "Now I remember. But I don't know much about her other than her relationship with Dylan was brief."

"Were they seeing each other before the fire?"

She shook her head. "Not that I know of. I always understood they didn't meet until almost a year later. But it didn't last long."

"Was it an amicable breakup?"

"That I can't tell you. I know who Vanessa is, but she doesn't come in here. I don't think I've ever met her."

Jack wasn't sure why, but he was glad Vanessa Graham wasn't seeing Dylan before the fire. Although she had been helpful and appeared to have been telling the truth, at some point in her past, she'd been an addict. He was glad she had gone straight, and for some strange reason, found it a relief that she had an alibi for the day of Dylan's murder.

He shook thoughts of Vanessa from his mind and turned to scan the faces in the cafe. "Has Eli been in today?"

"Not yet."

Jack didn't mention that he had seen him at the bank. He took a bite of fish and nodded his appreciation. "Tell me about him," he said, cutting another piece.

"About Eli?" Judith thought a moment. "Well, aside from him being my best customer while you were gone, I guess I don't know much more than anyone else. But I hope you'll reclaim the title now that you're back." Her smile was warm.

"I'll make it my mission."

"You do that."

"How long is he planning on staying in Telluride?"

"I'm not sure. But he doesn't seem to be in much of a hurry to leave."

Jack had gotten the same impression. Then again, he could do a lot worse than Telluride for killing time between adventures.

Jack needed to ask Judith more questions, but he had to be careful. As the friendly town gossip, if she figured out Wren was a possible suspect, she could jeopardize the investigation. Jack would need to keep the conversation casual.

"Just curious," he said, "but did Eli ever mention Dylan or the Judas Mine? He's up in the mountains so much, I thought there was a good chance they'd met."

Suspicion immediately blazed in her eyes. "Why do you ask?"

Shit, Jack thought. "Just wondering."

"Uh-huh." She wasn't buying it. Judith was sly. Trying to get information out of her without her suspecting anything wasn't going to work.

Jack chewed a bite of fish, then wiped his mouth with a

napkin and set it back in his lap. "Alright," he said, dropping his voice. "I could use your help, but this conversation has got to stay between us."

"It won't leave this room," she said. "I promise."

"Judith, half the town dines in this room on a regular basis."

She waved off his concern. "I get it, Jack. But just because I'm known for running my mouth doesn't mean I can't keep a secret."

"That's not what I—"

"It's alright." She held up a hand. "I know what you meant. But you can trust me."

Jack held her gaze a moment and decided he believed her.

They spent the next several minutes discussing Wren. And from what Jack gathered, Judith liked him and couldn't fathom for a second he was capable of murder. Wren hadn't shown any more interest in the Judas Mine than he had in any of the others. And as far as she knew, she'd never heard him mention Dylan's name.

She described Wren as an amiable customer, never complaining and always polite to her and the staff. And he was an excellent tipper. He would have breakfast at the cafe most mornings and dinner several nights a week after a day spent in the mountains.

"If he's one of your suspects," she said. "I think you're barking up the wrong tree."

"I'm not saying he is or he isn't. But this conversation has to stay between us."

She lifted a hand from the table. "I already promised you that."

Jack nodded. "Thank you, Judith."

She studied him for a moment. "Most people wouldn't care what happened to someone like Dylan. But I'm sure you've found that out by now."

Jack didn't answer.

"I don't understand it."

"Understand what?"

Judith looked at him, concerned. "You've got some strange need to right the world's wrongs," she said. "Even when it's not your responsibility."

Not sure what to say, Jack stayed quiet.

"You see the world as it should be instead of accepting the way it is." There was a grave look on her face. "I just hope that someday it doesn't get you hurt."

CHAPTER 31

Jack hung around Pandora Cafe longer than he needed to, hoping Wren would stop in. But he hadn't.

He stepped outside the cafe and was hit by a brisk wind off the mountains that blew through his cotton shirt. The sun had dropped toward the horizon. The days were growing shorter and colder, but he wasn't ready for winter.

He felt his phone vibrate in his pocket, pulled it out, and saw it was Archie Rochambeau. He would have information on Dylan or Wren.

"Hey, Arch. That was fast."

"Faster than grass through a goose. Here's what I got. First of all, the treasure hunter. The guy's worth millions—hundreds of millions, in fact. No financial problems."

"Alright," Jack said. "What about my vic?"

"Here's what I found for one Dylan Montgomery, resident of Telluride, Colorado. Deceased August twenty-sixth of this year at the ripe old age of forty. Existing mortgage on one house, on Timberline Court. Want the address?"

"I've got it." Jack started for the campground.

"Could have had gambling debts. There were two sizeable wires to an Indian casino, both over ten years ago."

"Which casino?"

"The Ute Mountain."

The same casino where Dylan had lost a share of the mine to Sean Sullivan. Dylan could have been a regular. He made a note to ask Sullivan if his partner had stopped gambling, hoping he had. Jack was eager to cross casino debt collectors—who sometimes used nefarious means of settling debts—off his suspect list.

"Anything else?"

"One car loan that was paid off four years ago. Two credit cards. A handful of missed payments but no current delinquencies. Aside from the mortgage on his house, the only other significant debt he had was a secured personal loan for just under half a mil."

Five hundred thousand dollars? The loan could have been for gambling debts. That would mean expanding his investigation to the casino.

Jack sighed. "Can you find out what he put up as collateral?"

"Hold your horses, Kemosabe. I'm one step ahead of you. I have to tell you, though, it's a weird one—something I've never heard of being used as collateral."

"What do you mean?"

"And the loan has been in default for months. Your dead man made payments for several years but had recently stopped. In fact, the bank started foreclosure proceedings a couple of months ago."

"What was the collateral?"

"It's the strangest thing."

"Arch, what was it?"

"The loan was secured by a gold mine."

Jack stopped walking and looked toward Shudder Basin, hidden high in the mountains above town. The temperature was dropping, the frigid wind slapping his face as he thought about what the information meant.

Dylan Montgomery had taken out a large personal loan. But for what? A personal loan could be used for anything. Jack thought about the casino. Gambling was a rough business. If

Dylan had owed the wrong person half a million dollars, it could have easily cost him his life.

Then he remembered what Archie had said about the bank starting foreclosure proceedings—not a casino or an individual, but a bank.

"You still there, partner?" Archie asked, bringing Jack around.

"Yeah. Sorry."

Jack took another moment to gather his thoughts. In all his years investigating homicides, a bank had never been behind one. It probably meant nothing, but he was curious.

He turned and looked down Main Street. "Arch, what's the name of the bank?"

"Well, you see, that's another funny thing," he said. "It's the Telluride Bank & Trust."

CHAPTER 32

Monday, September 23

Vanessa Graham woke Monday morning to someone knocking on the front door. Although Lynette occupied the only bedroom on the first floor, Vanessa knew it was unlikely the noise would wake her. After one of her benders, Lynette could sleep like a bear in winter. And the one the night before had been particularly brutal.

Life would be easier with a roommate less prone to drama, but Vanessa couldn't bring herself to kick her old friend out.

She rolled over, took her phone from the nightstand, and saw that it was just before seven. Her alarm would go off in only a few minutes.

She closed her eyes and pulled her grandmother's quilt up to her chin, feeling its softness after decades of use. She remembered the Christmas her grandmother had given it to her. Life had been simpler then.

After another knock at the door, Vanessa threw off the quilt and swung her feet to the floor, then grabbed the tattered robe from the foot of the bed and padded downstairs. Although she hoped they'd go away, the visitor was persistent.

"Sean?" she said, opening the door. "What are you doing here?"

Sean Sullivan stood just beyond her threshold. He wore jeans and boots and had parked his motorcycle at the curb.

"I wanted to let you know that the detective came by the bar again yesterday. He asked me for your number."

Vanessa yawned. "You could have called me."

"We were busy. Those antique car people are in town for a festival, and I left my phone at the bar. I stayed at the hostel in Placerville. I would have stopped by last night to tell you, but it was too late."

"And you don't consider seven in the morning too early?"

"Sorry. But it's my day off, and I'm on my way to Montrose."

"Mondays." Vanessa nodded. "Yeah, I know. I got to get to work."

"I'll get out of your hair. I just wanted to ask you for a favor."

Vanessa rubbed her eyes, wishing she were back in bed.

"I've been evicted again," he said, and she looked up.

"No, Sean. You can't stay here—"

"Just for a week or so. Only until I can find another place. You know how expensive rent is in Telluride."

"Then live somewhere else." She blew out a breath and shook her head.

"Please, Vanessa. I'll pay rent this time."

"I really need to get ready for work."

"Just think about it," he said. "I'll come by this afternoon when I'm back. I just wanted to let you know about that detective in case he calls you."

"He already came by," Vanessa said, annoyed. "I really wish you'd warned me first."

"Crap, Vanessa. I'm sorry." Sean ran his hand through his hair. "I didn't think he'd look you up so soon."

"Well, he did."

"What did he want?"

"He had a bunch of questions."

"About what?"

"Mainly about my relationship with Dylan."

"What did you tell him?"

"I told him the truth. That it started out fine, and then it wasn't."

Sean stepped back and put a hand on his hip, thinking.

Vanessa hesitated, then added, "He also asked me about you."

"Me? What did he want to know?"

"He asked if you and Dylan were friends."

"What did you tell him?"

"I told him the truth again. I told him how Dylan duped you into lending him money for a share of that stupid mine."

He stared at her a moment, then shook his head. "Yeah, I was an idiot."

"So, I guess it's yours now," Vanessa said, studying him closely. "Now that Dylan's dead."

"Looks that way."

"So, what are you going to do with it?"

"Get rid of it somehow."

"What about working it?"

"What?" He seemed appalled by the question.

"Well, it's yours. Why not see if there's something to what Dylan said about there still being gold in it?" When he didn't answer, she added, "Maybe you could afford your own place if you found some."

An elderly woman walked her dog by the house, and Vanessa pulled her robe closed tighter, shielding herself from the prying neighbor. She needed to get dressed for work. But something was gnawing at her conscience.

Looking at Sean, she narrowed her eyes. "You didn't say anything to that detective about me, did you?" When he hesitated, she grew angry. "What did you tell him, Sean?"

"Nothing."

She didn't believe him.

"Honest, Vanessa. I've kept my end of the bargain. Why? Did he ask you where you were that day?"

Vanessa stiffened, fighting to control her anger…and her fear. "He did."

"What did you tell him?"

"I told him I was with you."

CHAPTER 33

SEAN SLAMMED HIS hand down on the handlebar of his motorcycle—damn woman. Vanessa was in a position to ruin everything. He should have never trusted a former drug addict to do the right thing. She had a history of making bad choices and would likely make plenty more in the future.

Life was finally going right. Sean was on the verge of getting what he wanted. Years of traveling like a vagabond, taking odd jobs here and there to make ends meet. Working long hours on road crews, he was never able to settle down anywhere. But he finally had a job he liked. And although he thought some of the locals were crazy, most were friendly enough. But more important, they left him alone.

Living in the mountains was easier than anywhere he'd lived before. No one seemed in a hurry. Oh, there were plenty of nut cases—he could name a few off the top of his head. But for the most part, as far as he could tell, people in Telluride kept to themselves.

He enjoyed living there and wanted to stay. Although he could never afford a house in town, maybe one day he could find a place down valley. Or in Ridgway. Ridgway was even smaller than Telluride, and the locals there seemed friendly, too. Maybe he could even open his own bar one day.

For several minutes, he let his thoughts race with the wind, letting the dashed yellow lines in the center of the highway slide past. It was good to dream again. It had been a long time.

Holding the bike steady, he used his left hand to carefully pull his phone from the pocket of his jacket and looked for a missed call. But there hadn't been any. Disappointed, he wriggled the phone back into the pocket again.

Although Sean had called the guy several times, it had been days since he'd heard from him. The guy was ghosting him. And no news was probably bad news. But Sean wouldn't let go of the sliver of hope that the guy was just busy and would return the calls later.

He took his eyes off the road long enough to admire the view of Mount Sneffels, its peak rising over fourteen thousand feet. The range sat majestically behind the Double RL, Ralph Lauren's ranch just outside Ridgway. Sean thought the snow-capped mountains, looming just beyond the sprawling pastures and evergreen forest, were breathtaking. A far cry from the views from the highway construction jobs he'd worked in Texas and New Mexico.

He turned his attention back to the road.

If it hadn't been for Dylan, Sean never would have moved to the mountains. He glanced at the sky. "Thank you for that," he said aloud to the man who would never hear him.

He had known Dylan for only five years before he died. And although the guy had his share of faults, he had seemed decent enough. Crazy, but decent. Who knows? Sean thought. If Dylan hadn't died, they might have even become friends.

But Sean had heard plenty of stories of Dylan's past and knew that, in his worst moments, he could be an odd kind of crazy—bar fights, beating up on women, and suffering from gold fever. The fever and that damned mine had cost him his life.

Sean thought of Eli Wren, another man obsessed with finding gold. If Eli had agreed to buy the mine, Sean would already be rid of the damn thing and not have to beg a former addict for a place to stay. Eli had another thing coming if he thought Sean would let him poke around in the mine for free. Although Sean hated the damn thing, he thought there might still be a way to get his money back—as long as Vanessa Graham didn't screw it up.

He pulled the phone from his pocket again and saw there was still no missed call. He shifted the transmission into a higher gear and pulled back on the throttle, sending the bike's engine whining. The cold wind blowing through his hair felt good and helped clear his mind.

He wouldn't waste any more time worrying about Vanessa. His luck was changing. He could feel it.

A black bear appeared on the road, and he slowed, letting it cross in front of him, then watched as it vaulted up the rocky hillside along the highway and marveled at its strength and agility. Seeing a bear in the Rockies was a thrill that never got old.

He smiled, turning his attention back to the road and feeling an affinity for the great furry beast. Another animal that preferred to live life alone.

CHAPTER 34

Jack stood on the sidewalk outside of Telluride Bank & Trust and watched the jumpy banker scurry around inside like a frightened rat. This time Jack wouldn't let Ted Hawthorne give him the brush-off. He'd come ready.

He slipped his hand into his pocket and closed his fingers over the key. He would get inside Dylan Montgomery's safe deposit box one way or another. He pulled open the door and stepped inside.

When Hawthorne saw him, he froze. A deer stunned by the headlights of an oncoming car couldn't have looked more afraid.

"We're not open yet," the banker said between breaths.

"Come on now, Ted. We both know you don't keep normal banking hours."

"We open at nine."

"What about Sundays?" Jack asked, taking several steps closer.

"We're closed on Sundays."

"You weren't yesterday."

Hawthorne stepped back, and the tendons behind his bow tie went taut. "Yesterday was a special circumstance."

"The mystery visitor you had yesterday morning—you still don't have a name?"

"I told you. I'm bound by a fiduciary du—"

"Your fiduciary duty." Jack stuck his hands on his hips

and looked down at the floor. "Yes, you've used your *duty* as an excuse already. But let me tell you about another duty you have, Ted."

Jack brought his gaze up from the floor and leveled it on Hawthorne, trying hard to channel his inner Clint Eastwood as he did so, and found he was enjoying himself. "You also have a *moral* duty as a citizen of Telluride to tell the truth—to do what you can to help solve the murder of a fellow citizen. A citizen who just happened to be one of your customers."

Hawthorne stood still.

"Here's how this is going to go, Ted." Jack took another step closer, pulled the key from his pocket, and held it to the banker's face. "You're going to let me have a look in Dylan's safe deposit box."

When Hawthorne began to protest, Jack held up a hand. "I'm not going to remove anything from it, but you're going to let me have a look. Something in there might lead me to the person who killed him. And after I look in the box, we're going to sit down and talk about a couple of your other customers—two men I saw in here at different times yesterday."

He paused before he continued. "I want to know about the mystery man who was in here early," he said. "And about Eli Wren."

The banker frowned. "Eli?"

"I saw you and Eli in the window. And I want to know what our friendly treasure hunter is up to."

Ted swallowed. "And if I refuse?"

"If you refuse, I'll let Tony Burns know you're obstructing the investigation. That means you're obstructing justice." Jack let it sink in. "This isn't up for negotiating, Ted. Now, I need to get in that box."

Hawthorne's thin lips tensed, turning them white. But his face burned fiery red. In his wire-rimmed glasses and tweed suit, he looked more like a cartoon character than a banker. Jack imagined steam blowing from the little man's ears and almost grinned. But he stood still, maintaining the Eastwood vibe as Hawthorne stared back at him.

The banker was the first to blink. His posture sagged as he said, "Alright, I'll let you have a look, but you can't touch a thing. Do you hear me?"

Jack followed him to the massive steel door to the vault.

Careful to hide the keypad, Hawthorne punched in a code and swung the heavy door open.

Jack followed him inside and was immediately struck by the stale dead air. The space was cramped and windowless. Tan steel drawers lined three sides, stretching from the floor to the ceiling. A small table sat along the back wall. Jack had never considered himself claustrophobic but decided to make his business quick.

He watched as Hawthorne removed a key from his pocket and slid it into the lock of one of the drawers. Then, with a smug look on his face, he pointed to a second lock. "If your key doesn't fit, you're out of luck."

Jack came forward and held his breath as he slid the key from behind the map into the second lock, then exhaled when it opened. He pulled the drawer from the wall, and Hawthorne immediately stepped in front of him and lifted the lid, stealing a glance inside. His eyebrows shot up before he took a step back.

"Okay," Hawthorne said. "Have your look. But don't touch anything."

Jack glared at him until he backed away, then returned his attention to the box and saw immediately what had surprised the nervous banker. It was an antique revolver, a Colt .45, the infamous Peacemaker—the gun that had settled the West. Jack recognized the famous model instantly.

Except for the pistol and a folded set of papers, the box was empty. Jack lifted the gun and pulled out the papers.

"I said not to touch anything."

"Back off, Ted." Jack flipped through the pages and realized it was a deed. But a deed to what?

He laid the document on the table, scanned the first page, and realized the deed was to the Budnick Mine.

"Budnick?" Jack said to himself, thinking. It was the legal name of the Judas Mine. But the name on the deed wasn't Dylan Montgomery's.

But the document was old. The pages were brittle, aged to a golden yellow. Jack flipped through them, looking for a date, and saw that it had been signed in 1912. He then remembered the woman at the museum had said the Judas belonged to Cindy Montgomery, not her husband.

Jack thought of the fire, remembering the charred foundation, and thought if the land had also belonged to Cindy and not Dylan, the pieces could start to fall into place.

He lifted the deed from the table and turned to the banker. "You gave Dylan a personal loan he secured with the mine."

Hawthorne froze.

"No more games, Ted." Jack shook the document at him. "I know you put the loan into foreclosure before he was murdered. What were you going to do with it once the bank had control?"

The vault was quiet.

"Ted?"

"I don't see how that's any of your business."

"Well, let me tell you the way I see it. There's a dead man, and you benefit from his killing."

"Now, hold on a minute."

"Or what?"

The vault fell silent again.

"Damn it, Ted. What are you planning to do with the mine?" Jack thought of Eli Wren. "Are you selling it to Eli?"

Hawthorne shook his head. "Eli doesn't want it. He says he doesn't buy real estate."

"Right." Jack ran a hand through his hair, thinking. "It's Sean Sullivan, isn't it?" he asked, looking up.

Hawthorne scoffed. "Sean Sullivan doesn't have a dollar to his name. Plus, he's scared to death of that place."

It was true. Jack wasn't sure how much the mine was worth, but an itinerant bartender would never be able to pay off half a million dollars.

He laid the deed on the table and pulled his phone from his pocket. And as he photographed each page, he thought of what it all might mean. Dylan had gone into debt trying to bring gold out of the Judas. But he was on the verge of losing the mine when he died. Who besides the banker stood to benefit? Jack couldn't imagine that Ted Hawthorne, the tweed-wearing banker afraid of his own shadow, had murdered Dylan Montgomery. But if not Ted, then who?

"He always said he had a large payday coming."

Jack looked up, his train of thought broken. "Who had a payday coming?"

"Dylan. He was a dreamer." Hawthorne continued. "He kept insisting that he was going to sell the mine—kept talking about a guy who was going to buy it. But he dragged his feet, and the deal never happened. By then I'd extended the loan for him several times." He shook his head. "That was a mistake. It only delayed the inevitable."

"So what are you going to do with it?"

It took a moment for him to answer. "I don't know."

He blinked twice, and Jack knew.

The banker was lying.

It was then Jack remembered the mystery man in the black Jeep.

CHAPTER 35

Jack left the bank in a huff, cursing Ted Hawthorne. The infuriating banker had again refused to give up the name of the mystery man who'd been in the bank Sunday morning.

But Kim was running the Jeep's license plate. Jack would give her an hour and then call to ask for an update. He was growing impatient.

His next stop was Earl's Tavern to see if Sean Sullivan could shed light on Dylan's finances. But the bar was empty.

"Hello?" Jack called out. "Sean?"

"I'll be right there." The voice came from somewhere in the back. But it was female.

A few seconds later, a petite woman in her thirties appeared carrying a box of liquor bottles. She set it down on the bar. She had cropped dark hair and wore no makeup but several earrings in each ear and a tiny diamond stud on one side of her nose. Tattoos crawled up both arms.

"We don't open for another hour." The look on her face said she was friendly but busy.

"Is Sean here?"

"Monday's his day off." She moved the box to the floor and pulled out a bottle of tequila. "Is there something I can help you with?"

"I haven't seen you in here before." As soon as Jack said it, he thought it sounded like a pickup line.

She smiled. "I'm Taz." She set the tequila on a shelf

behind the bar. "I work Mondays—Sean's day off—and whenever the boss needs me to fill in."

"Taz?"

"As in Tasmanian Devil." She grabbed another bottle from the box and grinned. "My nickname as a kid."

She was all business, but outgoing and pretty. Jack liked her. He pulled out a stool at the bar and sat.

"Try this," she said, opening a bottle and pouring him a shot. She then poured one for herself. "I make it a point of trying the new stuff before I serve it to customers." She winked, then threw back the liquor like a pro and smiled.

Jack studied the clear liquid in his glass. It was early, not yet noon. But he didn't know how to get out of it. Taz was watching him.

"Oh, what the hell," he said, lifting the glass. He took the shot, then immediately regretted it as the liquor scorched the back of his throat.

When he stifled a cough, she laughed. "Want another?"

Jack held up a hand. "No. One's plenty."

She set the bottle on the shelf with the others and turned back around. "Something tells me you didn't come in for a drink."

"Is it that obvious?"

She tapped her temple and laid her forearms on the bar. "It comes with the job."

"Mind reading?"

"Mind reading, psychoanalyzing. Whatever you want to call it."

"Can I ask you a question?"

"It's part of the job."

"What can you tell me about Dylan Montgomery?"

Her smile dropped, and she pulled back from the bar. "The dead guy?"

Jack watched her closely. "Yeah, the dead guy."

"Not much. He'd come in every now and then, but he wasn't what you'd call a regular."

"You didn't know him well?"

"No."

"What did your regulars think of him?"

She took a glass from a shelf, held it to the light, and polished it. "I've only been here for a year, but as far as I can tell, people mostly kept their distance. He had a reputation for being…difficult. But it's terrible what happened to him."

Jack watched her polish another glass. "Thanks for the drink," he said, getting up.

She smiled. "Stop in anytime."

Outside, Jack started for the campground but changed his mind. Waggoner Mercantile was across the street, and he hadn't seen Opal or Ivy Waggoner since he'd been back from the mountains. The octogenarian sisters were local legends, having lived in Telluride their entire lives and having run their father's store for decades. The sisters could be a handful, but Jack liked them.

He went to the corner and crossed the street.

"Well, lookee here," Ivy said as Jack stepped inside the store. She was short and round, with a wispy nest of blue-gray hair, and her voice was soft and sweet.

"Hello, Ivy." Jack hugged her.

"We heard you were in the mountains with Otto, didn't we, Opal?"

Opal had lumbered into the room, her cane tapping the wood plank floor with every other step. "Well, look what the cat drug in."

Not feeling compelled to hug the older sister, Jack smiled and nodded. "Opal. It's good to see you."

Opal was the crankier of the Waggoners. She was gaunt, with closely cropped gray hair. Despite her cantankerous disposition, Jack liked her, even finding her amusing at times. But he knew to keep his distance.

"When did you get back to town?" Ivy asked him.

"Last week."

"Well, it's good to see you again." She patted him on the arm. "I hope your summer excursion was fruitful."

"Playing Yosemite Sam with that crazy old coot." Opal shook her head. She had opened a glass case and was stooped over it, rearranging a display of turquoise jewelry. "Won't be much of a life if you keep digging in that old mine of his."

Jack remembered the stack of cash Otto gave him as his share of the summer's take. He wasn't sure yet what to make of his summer in the mountains, but it reminded him why he had crossed the street.

"I want to ask y'all something."

"I guess that means you're not here to buy anything," Opal said, still arranging jewelry. "I'm shocked."

"Oh, don't listen to her," Ivy replied, waving a hand at her sister. "You go ahead and ask us anything you like. Is it about that murder?"

"Ivy Waggoner!" Opal stood up straight and whacked her cane against the floor. "Now, why would you go and say a thing like that?"

"Well, because it's probably true." She turned to Jack. "It's true, isn't it? You're investigating that murder." There was a mischievous twinkle in her eyes.

Jack had figured that the news he was working on the case was all over town by now. "It's true," he said. "I was hoping you could help me with something."

"Us?" Ivy's eyes grew wide with excitement. She clasped her hands to her chest. "How could we possibly help you?"

Opal slammed the jewelry case door shut with a bang. "We can't help you, and we won't." She rapped her cane on the floor. "Even if we could, it's ridiculous to think the two of us would know anything about a murder."

Something about the convoluted way she said it made Jack wonder. "I want to ask you about Dylan Montgomery."

The sisters stood immobile, resembling the wooden totem pole propped in the store's back corner.

"We didn't know him," Opal finally said.

"Well, yes, we did," Ivy replied. She looked at Jack. "We knew him way back, even before his wife died."

"Then you remember the fire."

A shadow crossed Ivy's face. "It was horrible. Poor Cindy." She paused a moment. "Everyone liked Cindy."

"Including Dylan?"

"Ivy, you've said enough." Opal's bony knuckles had gone white, pushing down on her cane. Something had her upset.

"Don't you shush me, Opal." Ivy glared at her sister. "Why, I haven't hardly said a thing. And we should be doing everything we can to help Jack find out who killed that boy."

Opal scowled at her. "Well, I could care less if he solves that murder."

"Couldn't," Ivy corrected her.

"Couldn't what?"

"Couldn't care less."

"That's what I said."

"No, you said I *could* care less."

Opal hit the cane on the floor. "That's right."

"But it's not could. It's couldn't."

"Ivy Waggoner, why, I oughta—"

"Who is that?" Jack asked, interrupting their argument. He had noticed a girl on the sidewalk across the street and stepped to the window.

The sisters came and stood on either side of him.

"Who?" Opal asked.

Jack pointed. "That girl."

"Why, that's Abby," Ivy said.

It was the girl who had stopped Jack on the street Saturday night. The one who'd told him Dylan had burned down his own house, accidentally killing his wife. She was wearing shorts and the same long-sleeved shirt. Her messy auburn hair was pulled back in a ponytail again.

Opal clucked, watching her walk toward the edge of town. "Not wearing shoes again, I see."

"Oh, what difference does it make?" Ivy replied. "We didn't always wear them at her age."

"Who is she?" Jack asked.

"Just a local girl," Opal shot back. "One with a talent for five-fingered discounts."

"Opal!" Ivy huffed. "Abby's nice. And it's a sin to gossip."

"Then you don't have a prayer of seeing the pearly gates."

"You're one to talk."

Jack was still watching the girl. "What's her name?"

"Abby," Ivy answered. "Abby Mer—"

"Ivy Waggoner." Opal rapped her cane on the wood floor again, causing Ivy to fall silent.

For some reason, the sisters were acting suspiciously. And that only fueled Jack's curiosity about the girl who knew about a house fire that had taken place more than a decade earlier—probably before she was born.

Then he remembered.

Abby. The schoolgirl who had been in Shudder Basin when he'd first gone up there with Kim O'Connor.

Jack turned to Ivy. "Where does she live?"

"She lives with Harriet."

"Ivy!" Opal was inexplicably upset again.

Jack looked from Opal back to Ivy, where the younger sister stood wide-eyed with her hand over her mouth.

They were hiding something.

CHAPTER 36

Jack left Waggoner Mercantile and crossed the street to Pandora Cafe, where he took a seat at his usual table, facing the entrance.

"The town's gone mad," he said, running a hand through his hair.

Judith set a plate of cookies in front of him. "I'll leave you alone to cool off. I'll be back in a minute."

Jack watched her walk away. In the months he'd been in Telluride, she had become one of his closest friends. But even she'd been acting suspiciously since he'd returned to town a week earlier.

The Montgomery case was puzzling. Despite questioning numerous residents about Cindy, he still knew relatively little about her. It was as if the entire town was hiding something, protecting her, or keeping some secret even though the woman was dead.

Judith returned with a large glass of iced tea. "Drink this," she said. "It might help." She then pulled out a chair and sat.

Jack welcomed the tea, not mentioning the tequila shot. He took a large gulp and set the glass on the table.

"You look like the Wreck of the Hesperus," she said, watching him.

There was a tug at his heart. His grandmother had often used the same expression when he came inside the house after playing. Although it wasn't a compliment, it made him smile. "I've heard that before."

"Jack, are you alright?"

She looked concerned, but he left the question unanswered. "Do you know Harriet?"

"Harriet Hughes?"

"I take it you do know her then."

Judith settled back into the chair. "Yes. I know her."

Hughes. Jack now had a last name. It was more than he had gotten from the Waggoner sisters.

"What can you tell me about her?" he asked.

"What do you want to know?"

"What's her relationship with the girl?"

"The girl?" Judith's eyes widened a bit, but she shook her head, stalling. Jack had seen the same response to questions countless times before: a stall tactic meant to kill time while the person searched for an answer.

"Yes, the girl," he said. "If you're friends with Harriet, you must know the girl who lives with her." Jack was expecting a half-truth or a lie.

"Abby is a distant relative," Judith finally answered. "I don't know the whole story, but she had been living somewhere in the Midwest, and her family sent her here to live with Harriet."

"Why?"

"I heard it was because she was a handful."

"So they sent her to live with an old woman?" It didn't make sense.

"Watch it, Jack. Harriet's only a few years older than I am."

Jack had said it out of frustration and felt a pang of remorse. He laid his palms on the table. "I'm sorry. This hasn't been an easy case."

"Are they ever?"

He thought about it for a moment, then shook his head. "I guess not."

Judith reached across the table and laid her hands on top of his. "Whatever is going on, it doesn't have anything to do with an *old woman*, as you put it. Or her temporary ward."

The kindness in her eyes relaxed him. And although he was sure there was something she was holding back, he let the subject drop. His mind was going in a dozen different directions.

Had Dylan Montgomery been an arsonist? What was the story behind his ex-girlfriend? And who is the mystery man in the black Jeep? It didn't help that everyone Jack knew was acting suspiciously—Ted Hawthorne, Eli Wren, Opal and Ivy, the girl with the auburn ponytail, the crazy mountain man in Shudder Basin, and even Judith. Thank God for Otto.

Jack's head was spinning. There were clues pulling him in every direction, yet none seemed related. He missed the familiar feeling at this point in a case when things started to come together.

He was beginning to worry it wasn't the town that had gone mad, but him. What was he missing?

Damn tequila.

"Good morning, good people!" a man's voice boomed as he entered the cafe.

It was Eli Wren. Jack wasn't sure if he was happy to see him or not.

"It's almost noon, Eli," Judith said, standing to greet him. "I didn't think you were coming today."

Wren pulled out a chair at an adjacent table and dropped his backpack on the floor. "Took the day off. Had some work to do on my computer."

Judith pulled an order pad from her apron. "What can I get you?" She took Wren's order and disappeared into the kitchen.

Jack shook off his mounting depression. He had a job to do. "How's the hunt for gold going, Eli? Find any yet?"

Wren flashed a white smile. "Not yet, my boy, but I've got a strong feeling I'm on the verge of a great discovery. These things take time, though—years sometimes. You have to be patient."

Jack wished he could borrow some of Wren's enthusiasm. "You think you're getting close?"

"I *know* I am. The gold's out there. It just takes hard work, patience, and a little luck to find it." He hesitated before continuing, then dropped his voice. "It's going to be somewhere in or around Shudder Basin," he said, watching Jack closely. "Probably just south of Crystal Lake Mine."

"So, near the Judas?"

Wren hesitated again. "The Judas could be sitting smack-dab in the middle of it. But I need to get inside both of the mines up there and have a look." He sat back in the chair and sighed. "And I had the owner ready to help me."

"Butch Corbin?"

"Not Corbin," Wren said. "Best steer clear of that one. No, it was your dead fellow, Dylan Montgomery."

"Have you approached his partner?"

"Sean Sullivan? Only every other day." Wren laughed and shook his head. "Sean's only interested in selling. He's scared of the liability of letting someone in—not that I blame him. People are trapped or killed in abandoned mines every year. But buying's not my thing. I hunt, I find, I leave."

It was what Ted Hawthorne had said.

"But you're sure it's there?" Jack couldn't imagine going to all the trouble for odds worse than a crapshoot.

"Gold?" Wren beamed, settling back in the chair. "I'm positive."

"Then why hasn't someone found it?"

"Could be a number of reasons. One, few people are interested in looking for it. Most kids today lack a sense of adventure. But even if they were interested, these old mines are labyrinths of shafts and tunnels. Some have been walled off. Some have suffered cave-ins. Most are dangerously unstable. The safe ones are hard to find. But there are still plenty out there to explore. My guess is that the old guys mining years ago stopped short of finding it."

"Or they didn't know it was there."

"Exactly. There were always rumors, but they didn't have the geological and seismic data that we have available today." Wren pointed at him. "I'm telling you, my boy, there is still plenty of gold in these mountains above us. It's there for the taking. And my offer to you still stands. If you want a job helping me find it, just ask."

Wren's enthusiasm was infectious. For a second Jack considered accepting the offer. Then he remembered that Wren had talked about the hidden vein to anyone in town who'd listen. And despite the average local's love for adventure, none had yet volunteered to help.

There was something not right with the Judas Mine. Jack got the feeling most people in Telluride thought it was cursed. And what surprised him was that he was beginning to believe it, too.

CHAPTER 37

Jack spent the rest of the day searching the internet for anything he could find on Dylan or Cindy Montgomery. When nothing significant turned up, he researched Eli Wren. After hours of staring at the computer, he had grown weary. And if it weren't for the steaks Otto grilled for dinner, he would have turned in before sundown.

The two men spent several hours sitting on the riverbank, watching the dogs romp in the dwindling autumn flow. The change of pace was nice. The night was quiet and still, but after the sun dropped, a frigid wind began to blow, prompting the end of an enjoyable evening.

Back in the Airstream, Jack took his laptop and reclined on the bed, grateful for the warmth of the small trailer. Although he was still tired, the evening with Otto and the dogs had revived him. And there was still plenty of work to do.

Leaving the laptop on the bed, he opened the photos app on his phone and spent the next few minutes zooming in and out, reading the deed to the Judas Mine.

Aside from dated language, the document was straightforward. The only clause that caught Jack's attention was the right of survivorship. The title to the mine was a tenancy in common, which he knew meant that if one owner passed away, that partner's interest passed to their heirs. But in this deed, if there wasn't a living spouse or any direct descendants, the deceased's interest was immediately transferred to any surviving partners.

Jack wasn't an attorney, but if he was reading it correctly, it meant Dylan's share of the mine transferred to Sullivan upon his death. But Kim had said that Dylan's will was stuck in probate, so it could take weeks, or even months, to know for sure.

Jack set the phone down and thought about it for a moment. Then, because there wasn't an attorney he trusted, he called Archie to have him explain the significance.

"Not a problem, old buddy. Justice delayed is justice denied."

Jack read the clause in the deed and asked what it meant.

"That would keep *distant* relatives from poking their noses into things," Archie told him. "Muddy the waters, so to speak. Think about it this way. You got a business partner. He kicks the bucket. Now, do you want to be stuck dealing with the guy's parents? Or worse, a passel of greedy siblings or cousins?"

Jack could see how the arrangement would be desirable. "But it was an old deed."

"Deeds transfer to heirs upon death. No need to pay some fancy-pants ambulance chaser to create and file another one. If your dead guy died with no kids, his share goes to any surviving partners. Easy peasy."

Easy peasy. Except Jack knew that it wasn't.

The mine had passed down through Cindy's family, not Dylan's.

Jack thanked him and ended the call. He then spent several minutes searching the internet for mentions of Sean Sullivan. The guy didn't have a single social media account, which wasn't surprising, since Jack didn't have any either. But there was also no sign of a criminal record.

To be sure, Jack took his phone and called Kim. "What can you tell me about Sean Sullivan?"

"Evening, Jack." She took a moment. "Aside from what I've already told you, not much. No priors, no criminal record. He helped us find the mine after Dylan was murdered since none of us had ever been up to Shudder Basin."

"Well, I've been doing some research, and I think that Sullivan just inherited one hundred percent of it."

She chuckled. "If he has, he doesn't want it."

Jack had gotten the same impression but wanted to hear what the deputy had to say. "What do you mean?"

"He took us up there but wouldn't go inside. He couldn't get out of the basin quick enough. It could have been the sight of Dylan dead that had him spooked, but I got the impression he was hyperclaustrophobic. He didn't handle the drive up there well, either. About lost his breakfast when I made a couple of the switchbacks." She chuckled, remembering.

"He said he's trying to sell it."

"He's told me the same thing. Poor guy is probably stuck with it now. Nobody but Eli Wren or Butch Corbin would want it."

Crazy Corbin.

Jack would ask Sullivan if he had approached him to buy the mine.

"I was going to call you in the morning," Kim said.

"The license plate?"

"Yeah, I've got it right here. Hold on."

Jack could hear paper rustling on the other end.

"Here it is. Your black Jeep is registered in Utah to a guy named William Ammon Lockwood."

Jack thanked the deputy and ended the call, then typed the name into the search bar of his computer. He watched as hits flooded the screen, then opened the first one and began to read.

CHAPTER 38

Tuesday, September 24

Abby woke disoriented, thinking the dream had been real. But when the cobwebs in her sleepy brain cleared, she was disappointed to realize it wasn't.

She wrapped her arms around herself and hugged, trying to hold the dream close, imagining again the feel and smell of the woman who had been her mother.

Her few memories of the woman were fading. Secretly, deep down, she wondered if they had ever been real, suspecting it had only been her imagination. But that hurt her heart, and she pushed the horrible thought from her mind.

She lay in bed, listening to the wind and the creaks of the old house settling above her, still trying to conjure the image of the woman in the dream. After several minutes, she rolled over, pulled the old photo from the drawer of the bedside table, and ran her fingers along the edges, which had curled from the passage of time.

She thought of the family she had left in Chicago. It was her mother's family, but she had overheard them call her a "bad seed"—whatever that meant. They also called her a burden. She had even heard the uncle who was supposed to be her new daddy say he had never wanted her. But that was okay, Abby told herself. She didn't want them, either.

It was just over a year since they'd sent her to live with Harriet, which wasn't so bad. At first she'd thought she would hate living with an old woman in a small town with nothing to do. But Harriet had turned out to be nicer than the family in Illinois.

And living in the mountains was awesome. Abby loved them immediately and now spent as much time in the forests and high mountain tundra as she spent in school. A few weeks earlier, she'd even overheard Harriet tell Mr. Eli that she was like a mountain goat, which secretly made Abby happy, thinking the comparison was a compliment.

Although the mountains were her favorite thing about Telluride, she liked the town, too. Except for the boys in her grade—who she hated—and the mean old hag Opal Waggoner, the people were mostly nice.

But Abby couldn't help wondering what it would have been like if the woman in the photograph had lived. She rubbed the face in the picture with her thumb, the face that often came to her at night when she was asleep.

She squeezed her eyes shut hard, trying to bring back the dream, but it was no use. After a few seconds, she opened them again. It made her sad that she would never see her mother again, but she hoped, more than anything, that the woman was somehow watching and that Abby made her proud.

Still holding the photo, she pushed her fingers tight against her ears and listened to the whooshing sound it made in her head. For as long as she could remember, the dull hum was comforting.

She had plugged her ears in Chicago to shut out the yelling and cursing and so she wouldn't hear them call her names. But sometimes she did it when she didn't want to think about anything at all. Because when thoughts hurt, it was better to think about nothing.

Sometimes she plugged her ears while squeezing her eyes shut when she was scared. But since she'd moved away from her family in Chicago, she mostly closed her eyes and ears when she wanted to pretend she was somewhere else, like on a beach. She had never been to a beach and wanted to see one someday.

As she lay in bed staring at the ceiling, she couldn't help but hear the mean man's words again: "You have a real smart mouth, just like your mother." A heaviness pushed against Abby's chest. Tears prickled her eyes, but she squeezed them away, trying to crush the memory.

There was movement in the hallway, and she shoved the photograph under the covers. She strained to hear it again, knowing Harriet was probably coming to get her up for school.

But the hallway was quiet, and instead, she listened to a bird chatter somewhere beyond the window. She knew instantly that it was a magpie; she loved magpies—the patches of black and white feathers, the flash of blue on their chest. She rolled over to look for it. But the window was high on the basement wall, and she couldn't see anything except shrubs and the aspen tree above them, its leaves bright shades of yellow and red.

There was a rap on the door.

"Abby? Yoo-hoo." It was Harriet.

Abby rolled her eyes and sat up as the door opened.

"You need to get up this minute, young lady, and get yourself ready for school. Nothing good comes from lying around daydreaming. And don't go playing hooky again, do you hear me? Your truancy has cost me enough sleepless nights already. And I'm running out of excuses for you."

Abby swung her feet over the side of the bed and scratched her right arm. She always scratched it when she was tired or nervous.

Harriet took a hairbrush from a bureau against the opposite wall and sat down on the bed beside her. "You're a beautiful girl, dear," she said, running the brush gently through Abby's hair. "Do you know that?"

"No." Abby never thought of such things.

"Well, you are." She had gathered Abby's hair in her hand and twisted it. "And you remind me so much of your sweet mother. You're too young, but you'll appreciate that one day."

Harriet pulled a hair band from her pocket, finished the ponytail, then leaned over and set the brush down on the bedside table.

"There," she said, smiling and holding Abby's face in her cool, soft hands.

Abby pawed at her hair, enjoying the smoothness of it, and smiled back. "Thank you."

"Now, you go to school and stay out of trouble today. Deal?" Harriet kissed the top of her head.

Then Abby looked into the eyes of the woman she knew would give her the world if she had it. She felt a stab of guilt for what she had already done…and for what she was about to do next.

CHAPTER 39

JACK WAS ON the road to Utah early Tuesday morning after spending several hours researching William Lockwood the night before. After two calls to Lockwood's cell number went unanswered, he had decided to pay Lockwood a visit in person.

It was a two-hour drive, and the landscape changed quickly outside Telluride. The Rocky Mountains gave way to the grease flats of western Colorado and then to the desert terrain of eastern Utah. Driving through the parched red landscape, Jack noticed that the peaks that dotted the northern horizon were surprisingly already capped with snow. It was a rugged but beautiful landscape, and he enjoyed the trip.

His destination was La Sal, a small town in Utah's southeast corner. But more specifically, he was headed to Coyote 1, a nuclear power plant along West Coyote Creek. Through his online search, Jack had discovered that Lockwood was an executive with the plant's operating company. His bio on their website revealed his title was senior project facilitator, which Jack worried could mean anything. There were no mentions of specific duties or past employment, no excerpts from media interviews. The only qualifications listed for Lockwood were a degree in physical education from BYU and a spot on the school's football team.

The bio hadn't included even a photograph. But unless another William Ammon Lockwood drove a late-model black

Jeep Rubicon in Utah, Jack was confident this was his mystery man.

The plant came into view when he was still miles away. Two hyperboloid cooling towers, rising hundreds of feet into the sky, belched clouds of steam. A large concrete building with a dome roof sat nearby. The property included dozens of acres enclosed by a tall fence topped with razor wire. The plant wasn't huge—Jack had seen larger—but it was impressive.

He turned off the highway at the plant's entrance, the adjacent fence littered with warnings and No Trespassing signs. A large plaque mounted on a rolling gate identified the plant as the Coyote 1. Beyond the gate, in the distance to the south, rows and rows of large cylindrical drums sat baking in the morning sun—probably nuclear waste.

Jack pulled up to the guard shack, and a bull of a man emerged, carrying a clipboard. He had a firearm strapped to his hip and looked ready to chew nails. Two other men stood inside, watching. And Jack suspected that somewhere else, probably at a separate location, someone was monitoring all of them through the security cameras mounted on both sides of the gate.

Jack rolled down the driver's-side window as the man with the clipboard approached, the short sleeves of his uniform stretched taught over biceps the size of bowling balls.

"What's your business?" he asked without a hint of congeniality.

"I'd like to speak with William Lockwood."

"Who?"

"William Lockwood. The senior project facilitator."

"You mean Bill." He flipped through the pages on the clipboard, then eyed Jack skeptically. "You have an appointment?"

"I don't."

The guard stared at Jack for what felt like an eternity. "Name?"

"Jack Martin."

He made a note of it on his clipboard and looked up again. "The nature of your business?"

"It's personal."

The muscles in the man's jaws flexed. Without replying, he pivoted and left. Jack saw him say something to one of the other men, then pick up a telephone.

A minute later, he was back. "Bill is unavailable. You'll have to exit the premises."

The man's attitude was grating, and Jack wasn't ready to admit defeat. He glanced at the name tag on the guard's uniform.

"Listen, Emmett, I've driven two hours this morning to talk with Bill Lockwood. I'm sure there's something we can work out so that I haven't wasted my time." When the guard wasn't impressed, Jack added, "It's about the murder of a man in Telluride."

The statement had the desired effect. The muscles in Emmett's jaws twitched.

But he quickly recovered, and the scowl was back on his face. "Hold on a minute." He returned to the guard shack and picked up the telephone again. His second call took longer than the first.

"Bill is still unavailable," he said, back at Jack's window. "You'll need to exit the premises." He tore a sheet of paper from the clipboard. "But he told me to give you this. It's his cell number."

"I already have it."

Emmett held out the number. "You don't have *this* one." He lifted the paper, urging Jack to take it, then returned to the guard shack without saying another word.

It had been an odd exchange. And as Jack drove east toward the state line, he thought of what little he'd learned.

Security at Coyote 1 was impressive. And Bill Lockwood had a second cell phone number—one that was unpublished—something that didn't seem to be a surprise to the security guard.

The encounter had Jack wondering. What would a senior facilitator at a nuclear power plant in Utah want with Dylan Montgomery? And was it a coincidence he had met Dylan in Ouray on the morning he died?

Jack spent several minutes trying to decipher what it all meant and decided there was only one way to find out. He took his eyes off the road long enough to punch Lockwood's unlisted number into his cell phone and hit Send.

CHAPTER 40

TED STOOD AT the bank window, scanning the faces of pedestrians on the sidewalk and watching cars pass. Jack Martin had driven through town earlier that morning. And having the nosy detective back in Telluride had Ted jumpier than usual. Was it too much to ask to get the deal done before Martin could cause more trouble?

Ted turned from the window, determined to do *something* before that nuisance stuck his nose into the bank's business again and ruined everything.

It was still early, but Wanda would show up any minute to help open the bank. Ted had to work fast.

He plopped down on the chair behind his desk, snatched the phone's handset from its cradle, and punched in the numbers he knew by heart.

"Got anything for me yet?" he asked the woman who answered.

"Ted, I told you not to call me at work." She was whispering and chewing gum. "I said I would let you know when I found out something."

Ted blew out a breath. "I needed the information yesterday."

"I'm working on it," she insisted. "But you have to hold your horses. These things take time."

"I don't *have* time."

Her gum smacking had him wanting to reach through the

phone and throttle her. The blasted woman didn't have a clue what a sense of urgency meant.

"I don't understand what's taking so long," he said.

"It hasn't even been a week."

She was exasperated, but Ted didn't care. "And that's a week longer than I've got."

He drew a deep breath through his nose, then let it out slowly through pursed lips. *Zen in, Zen out.* He did it several more times—just like his therapist had taught him—and felt his heart rate slow.

A bubble burst on the other end of the line, bringing him immediately back to the present.

Blasted woman.

"Just get me that name, dammit," he spat into the phone, then slammed it down on the desk.

CHAPTER 41

Bill Lockwood had been short and to the point, and when asked about Dylan Montgomery, he'd been evasive.

"I won't talk over the phone," Lockwood said. "But I'll be at the New Sheridan for brunch on Thursday. You can meet me there if you feel it's necessary." He ended the call without giving Jack a time.

Getting ahold of Lockwood had only raised more questions. And Jack was more determined than ever to get answers. He would be at the restaurant when it opened Thursday morning.

Back in Telluride, Jack slowed as he passed the Bank & Trust. He saw several customers inside but no sign of Ted Hawthorne.

He stopped at an intersection to let a man cross the street headed in the direction of Waggoner Mercantile. Jack thought of the sisters. They were acting strange, and he was sure they were hiding something. So was Judith.

He found a spot along the curb in front of Pandora Cafe and parked but decided that, although he was hungry, food could wait. He pulled open the door to Earl's Tavern instead and stepped inside, then took a moment to let his eyes adjust.

He heard Eli Wren before he saw the man.

"Well, if it isn't Telluride's very own James Bond. Have a seat, 007. I'll buy you a drink."

Wren was sitting on a stool at the bar, dressed in cargo

shorts and a monogrammed long-sleeve cotton shirt. He had one designer hiking boot resting on the bottom rung of the stool and was swinging the other back and forth and grinning. Something about him reminded Jack of a kid at an ice cream counter.

Jack took the stool beside him. "Good day in the mountains, Eli?"

"A great day," Wren said, then slapped Jack on the shoulder. "Let's have a round or two. It's on me."

Sean Sullivan was stacking napkins behind the bar. Except for a table of tourists—Jack had become adept at spotting them—the tavern was empty. But the night was early.

"What's your poison?" Wren asked Jack.

Jack turned to Sullivan, "Can I get a Shiner Boch?" A cold beer sounded good.

"Shiner?" Wren laughed. "Boy, you must be from Texas. Sean, get us two Shiner Bochs."

Jack saw a flash of white teeth in the dim light of the bar. The treasure hunter's levity was infectious, and Jack felt himself relax.

Sullivan grabbed two bottles from a refrigerator, popped off the caps, and slid them across the bar. "How's the detective business going, Jack?"

"Slow." Jack took a sip of beer, letting the cold liquid slide down his throat, reviving him. He hadn't realized the extent of his exhaustion. It had been a long day.

"I've been thinking," Wren began. He gestured with his hands as he talked. "Hunting a killer's got to be a lot like hunting for treasure. Sure, there's the thrill of the hunt, but that's not what it's about, is it? We've already discussed that. The hunt is merely the means to an end. The pot of gold at the proverbial end of the rainbow! Or, in your case, the apprehension of the sorry son of a gun who committed the dastardly deed."

Wren drank and talked nonstop. "Have I mentioned the

time I was searching for a lost hoard of emeralds along the Ganges and got swept into the current? Spent a night huddled on the riverbank before I was rescued. I tell you, that was one of the most…"

Wren's stories got more elaborate as he drank.

Jack spent the next twenty minutes downing two bottles of beer and listening to him talk, then switched to water. At one point, he looked at Sullivan, who smiled and rolled his eyes as he wiped down the bar.

The two men continued listening as Wren reminisced about past adventures, telling stories of the places he'd been and the people he'd met. Some of which, Jack suspected, had been embellished.

Jack asked him about the eccentric characters he'd met through the years and slipped in a question about Butch Corbin.

"Watch your back with that one," Wren said, pointing a finger and slurring his words.

"I think I might go up and see him tomorrow," Jack said.

The treasure hunter's brows shot skyward. "Well, don't say I didn't warn you."

Jack thought about it a moment. "What is it about the mines in Shudder Basin?" he asked. When Wren didn't answer, Jack looked at Sullivan, who shrugged and shook his head.

An hour later, Wren had finally finished talking. He emptied his fifth Shiner and set the bottle down on the bar, then slapped his hands on his knees and stood up. "Well, my boys, it's back into the mountains tomorrow to search for gold. So that's probably enough for me."

Sullivan leaned across the bar. "Can I get someone to help you home, Eli?"

"You underestimate me, son." Wren laid a hundred-dollar bill down and started for the door. "Next time I come in, remind me to tell you about the time I held my own with

Ernest Hemingway at Sloppy Joe's in Key West." He threw a hand up as he exited the tavern.

Jack was quite sure Hemingway was dead by the time Eli Wren was of drinking age. Although he doubted much of what Wren had told them, the guy was entertaining.

"He's quite a character," Sullivan said, tossing empty beer bottles into the trash.

Jack agreed. "He's convinced there's still gold up there. He admitted he's interested in the Judas."

"Wants to get in and have a look for free," Sullivan replied. "He'd been working on Dylan for some time."

"And Dylan let him in."

Sullivan nodded. "He did."

"But Dylan was looking for gold, too, wasn't he?" Jack asked. "Seems he'd want to let the world-famous treasure hunter have a look."

"A look, but not unlimited access."

"Why not?"

Sullivan chuckled. "You don't know many miners, do you?" He jerked a chin toward the ceiling. "The guys still mining the mountains around here are half-crazy—some *completely* crazy. And they can be very territorial."

"So I've heard."

Jack remembered how Otto had sworn him to secrecy, promising never to divulge details regarding the location of the mine or that it was rhodochrosite he looked for, instead of gold. Next, Jack thought of Butch Corbin and had to agree—miners were a peculiar bunch.

"The mine's yours now. Why not let Eli have a look?"

"If he'd buy it, that would be one thing," Sean said, wiping down the bar. "But why give a guy the milk for free when he can afford to buy your cow?"

"What if he paid you to have a look?"

Sullivan shrugged. "He's never offered rent."

Jack thought about the Judas, hidden high above town

in Shudder Basin. He couldn't imagine someone wanting it. Then he remembered Butch Corbin.

"What about Corbin? Have you ever approached him about buying it?"

"No, but I might have to." Sullivan refilled Jack's water glass. "Trouble is, the guy's never in town. He's always at his cabin."

Jack remembered the conversation with Kim. "And you don't like going up there?"

"Not if I can help it. I like the view of the mountains just fine from down here in town."

Jack thought a moment. "What are your other options?"

"I'll admit, I'm running out of them." He sighed. "I'll probably have to go talk to Corbin one of these days."

"You could have Eli talk to him for you."

Sullivan laughed. "You know Eli well enough now. How do you think that would go over? Sending him up there to negotiate a sale with Crazy Butch Corbin?"

Jack had to agree. Having the gregarious treasure hunter approach Corbin for *anything* would likely infuriate the reclusive mountain man. It would be oil negotiating with water.

"Then why not let Eli have a look? What could it hurt? If there's gold there, finding someone to buy it would be easier."

"Eli's a loose cannon." Sullivan shook his head. "And you've been up there. That place is a death trap. A couple of months before he died, Dylan almost buried himself alive."

"What happened?"

"Cave in. He could have killed himself." Jack saw the irony of what he had said register on his face, and Sullivan sighed. "Anyway. There are all sorts of things that could go wrong. Accidents happen all the time in those old mines. There's no way I want some millionaire treasure hunter with a lawyer-rich family getting killed and suing me."

Sullivan shook his head. "I can't afford that kind of liability. Plus, I offered to sell it to him outright, but he refused.

He was all hot-to-trot to get into the mine before Dylan died. But now, for some reason, he no longer seems interested." He shrugged. "I think he *knows* there's no gold in it."

"So what are you going to do with it?"

"Nothing right now. I'll probably end up sealing the entrance with concrete, make it so that no one can get inside. They do that with a lot of the old mines around here. If a buyer comes along later—great. I'll sell it to them, and they can open it back up. But Eli's not one to put down roots, so why let him kill himself without buying the thing first?"

Jack finished his water and stood up.

"Plus, he might seem nice enough," Sullivan added, "but I'm not sure I trust him."

Outside, Jack stood on the sidewalk thinking. He wondered if Sean Sullivan was right. Eli Wren was friendly, and his enthusiasm for life was infectious, but he had a manic energy about him that made Jack nervous. And he was beginning to think the flamboyant treasure hunter might not be as harmless as he seemed.

CHAPTER 42

Harriet was washing her hands at the sink when Eli stumbled into the kitchen. He reeked of beer, which irritated her. Any discussion of their plans would have to wait. For that, she needed him sober.

"Good evening, Eli," she said, drying her hands on a dish towel and forcing a smile. "I just put a meat loaf in the oven. Dinner won't be ready for an hour."

"Sounds delicious." Eli tossed a spiral notebook on the table and dropped into a chair.

"Busy day?"

"Always," he said without looking up.

Harriet watched as he flipped through pages and scribbled notes with a ballpoint pen. He was strangely quiet. She cleaned the kitchen, pretending not to notice but stealing sideways glances, wondering what was wrong with the usually gregarious boarder.

When she had put away the last of the pots, she looked into the living room but saw that it was empty and became exasperated. *Where is that child?*

Although Harriet loved the girl, she didn't have the faintest clue how to keep her out of trouble. She had instructed her to come straight home after school, but school had been let out hours earlier. Harriet hadn't seen her since morning.

Then again, the child was like a cat, slinking around spying and eavesdropping. She could have snuck in without being seen. Harriet decided to check and descended the stairs to the basement but found the girl's room empty.

Back in the kitchen, she took two glasses from a cabinet and filled both with water, then set one down in front of Eli and had a seat at the table.

"Thank you," he said without looking up from his work.

Harriet watched him for a minute, glad to have the company, even if they both sat in silence. Eli was a better guest than her previous boarders. Almost all had been single men in town for work and representing an eclectic mix of professions. She had rented the spare room to day laborers and engineers, construction workers and businessmen. Most had been young and not prone to conversation.

From the beginning, Eli had been different, regaling her with stories of world travel and adventure. Harriet had spent her entire life in Telluride and enjoyed the last few months of living vicariously through Eli's stories.

And what luck. A famous treasure hunter landing on her doorstep just before Dylan Montgomery was murdered? She wouldn't wish Dylan's fate on anyone—even her worst enemy—but she wasn't heartbroken that the evil scoundrel had finally gotten his comeuppance.

She pressed her palms against the polyester slacks over her thighs, pushing the memories aside.

Eli still reeked of beer, but Harriet decided he was lucid enough.

She cleared her throat. "Eli."

"Hmm?" He flipped a page in the notebook and ran a hand down a row of dates.

"Eli," she repeated more firmly. "We need to talk."

He looked up, his eyes taking a moment to focus. He closed the notebook and laid the pen on the table.

"What is it, Harriet?"

"You seem…upset about something." She didn't know how else to put it.

"I do?" Eli shifted in his chair, stifling a belch. "Well, I guess maybe I am a bit distracted."

"You're not having second thoughts, are you?"

He frowned. "About what?"

"About our deal."

"Oh, that." He relaxed back into the chair. "Good heavens, no."

Harriet sighed with relief. Getting her ducks in a row was taking longer than she had expected. "I should have an answer for you next week."

"That's fine," Eli replied. "I'm glad to hear things are moving along. I'll be ready when you are."

Harriet studied his closed notebook. She wasn't sure what he did every day in the mountains but was relieved he wasn't growing impatient. It had seemed too good to be true the way everything had fallen so neatly into her lap. But she only had one shot to get the deal done.

Eli took a sip of water and set the glass on the table. "I spoke with Sean Sullivan today."

"Who?"

"Sean Sullivan. He owns the minority interest in the mine."

Harriet nodded, trying to dislodge the mothballs from her brain. "He won't be a problem, will he?"

"Not at all." Eli hesitated. There was a faraway look in his eyes. "But he's a nice young fellow. Polite. Great company for an old geezer who likes to reminisce at the end of a long day." He twisted the glass on the table. "It's been weighing on me, and I've decided to make sure we take care of him."

Harriet nodded again. She wasn't sure what Eli meant, but as long as he kept his end of the bargain, she didn't care about the details of his plan.

Eli picked up the pen and tapped it on the notebook's cover, looking more sober. "I saw that detective again today."

Harriet was lifting her water glass but stopped.

"Would you believe he went up and talked to Butch Corbin? Even after I warned him not to. And I think he's going *back* to see him tomorrow." He shook his head.

Butch Corbin. Harriet knew him by reputation only, but he seemed like a vile man. But Corbin wasn't her concern. It was that pesky detective she worried about. The best she could hope for was that Jack Martin would lose interest in the murder and go away.

She glanced over her shoulder, ensuring there were no young ears listening. She couldn't afford to be careless around Abby, having made that mistake too many times before.

She dropped her voice to a whisper. "You need to watch out for yourself."

Eli frowned. "What do you mean?"

"That detective," she said. "Does he know about…?" Her voice died as she looked over her shoulder again.

Eli shook his head, fidgeting with the pen. "He's asking everyone about that dead fellow, but I don't see how he could possibly know."

Harriet swallowed, worrying about what could happen next. As much as she had impressed it upon him, Eli would never understand the significance of her secret.

CHAPTER 43

Wednesday, September 25

Everyone warning Jack to stay away from Crazy Butch Corbin had only inflamed his curiosity.

Dylan Montgomery's neighbor in Shudder Basin had motive and means to kill him. There was also a history of threats, and Corbin had an arsenal of weapons. The reclusive mountain man checked all the boxes, yet that was Jack's problem. It was too easy.

Jack had met him only once, but Corbin hadn't seemed stupid. Would he have bumped off his neighbor, knowing he didn't have an alibi and would be a prime suspect?

Jack wanted to see for himself if the rumors about Corbin were true. And he had a hunch the man wasn't as crazy as the locals made him out to be.

Before reaching Ouray, Jack swung the truck off the highway at the For Sale sign and noticed a placard attached to it indicating the property was sale pending. He wondered how a change of ownership of the land that straddled both sides of the gravel road might affect access to Shudder Basin.

He leaned over to pet Crockett, glad for the company. The dog sat on the passenger seat, staring through the windshield with his tongue lolling. After nearly a week of being left at the campground with Otto and Red, he was enjoying the morning outing.

Jack returned his hand to the steering wheel as the road

narrowed and started to climb. He then said a quick prayer he wouldn't meet a vehicle coming in the opposite direction. He tightened his grip as he made the first switchback. And for the next half hour, he steadied his nerves by running through all the possible suspects in his head.

First there was Corbin. Jack hoped his visit would answer questions about his relationship with Dylan Montgomery.

There was also Sean Sullivan, Dylan's reluctant partner. Although Sullivan didn't want anything to do with the mine, had there been a dispute between the partners? Maybe when Dylan hadn't paid him back? But it was hard to get money out of a dead man.

Vanessa Graham, the disgruntled ex-girlfriend and former drug user, could have been hell-bent on revenge. A woman scorned was an old cliché, but one that was often deadly. He would need to make another trip to Norwood and see if she could shed light on Dylan's precarious finances.

Next Jack considered Ted Hawthorne, the unethical banker foreclosing Dylan's loan secured by the mine. Did Hawthorne want the mine for himself? Or was there a plan to dispose of it once he had control?

It made Jack think of Bill Lockwood, the mystery man who'd dined with Dylan on the morning of his murder. Jack had a slew of questions for Lockwood when they met the following day face-to-face.

But now at the top of Jack's list was the flamboyant treasure hunter, Eli Wren. The fast-talking, fabulously wealthy adventure seeker was likable but used to getting his way. And Jack was beginning to suspect there could be something sinister behind the congenial demeanor.

Soon after the last switchback, Jack reached the clearing where the road ended. He parked in the same spot Kim had twice before. He and Crockett would have to go the rest of the way on foot.

"Let's go," he said to the dog, opening the door.

The sun was shining, but dark clouds boiled over the peaks to the north and threatened rain. The air was cold and damp. Jack started for a trail of smoke that rose in the distance, where Corbin had a fire lit in his cabin.

The temperature quickly dropped as they climbed higher, and Jack felt the cold seep into his boots, numbing his feet. He wiggled his toes as he walked, trying to warm them.

After several minutes, he noticed a trickle of water like a white ribbon snaking its way down from the snowy peaks, finally emptying into a small lake in the distance he hadn't noticed on his previous trip. The water was a fluorescent shade of turquoise that nearly took his breath away—Crystal Lake—the namesake of Corbin's mine.

After a while, realizing Crockett was no longer at his side, Jack turned and looked back down the trail. The dog was stopped behind him, wagging his tail and staring at something down the mountain. Jack squinted at the trees below them but didn't see anything.

"Come on, boy."

With Crockett back at his side, Jack ran through the list of suspects again as they continued toward Corbin's cabin. But as he went through the names for the umpteenth time, he couldn't shake the nagging feeling there was someone he was missing.

CHAPTER 44

ABBY CROUCHED BEHIND a tree when she saw the man and his dog on the trail above her. At first the dog didn't see her, but it stopped and stuck its nose in the air. She stayed frozen as it turned in her direction and, after a few seconds, began wagging its tail. She was sure it could see her hidden behind the thick pine branches.

The dog seemed friendly, and Abby wanted to pet its shiny brown coat more than anything. But she stayed frozen, holding her breath and feeling her heart thump in her chest. When she looked closer at the man, she recognized him. It was that detective.

The man saw that the dog wasn't following him and called to it. Then the two started hiking away again. Abby waited until they were gone, then stepped out from behind the tree and started for the mine.

She had set out before Harriet woke that morning, sneaking into the kitchen to quietly make herself a sandwich, then stuffing it into a knapsack with a leftover biscuit and a bag of chips. On her way out of town, a peach, filched from an unsuspecting vendor setting up produce, had been added to her stash.

Then, under cover of morning darkness, as she had done so many times before, Abby had slipped past the last few houses on Telluride's east side and disappeared into the mountains.

As she climbed, the sky had dawned pink and gold, prettier than anything she'd ever seen in Chicago. She had lived in the mountains for a year and never tired of watching the sky change colors in the early morning and at night. And after spending the first ten years of her life seeing nothing but buildings and concrete and people and cars, the mountains were like heaven. Which meant that somewhere in the trees and snow and rivers high above town was her mother.

Before moving to Telluride, she had only seen mountains in books. She didn't miss Chicago. There weren't even hills there. And the air had stunk, too. The smog and pollution sometimes stung her throat and burned her eyes. The worst was trash day, when everyone dragged all their gross stuff outside to bake in the sun before the giant blue trucks covered in grime roared down the streets to pick it up. Thinking about it made her gag. She always heard there were nicer parts of town, but her family never went there.

She remembered red-faced old-man Louis—Pee-yooey Louis—who owned Schmidt's Deli and always smelled of liver and onions and cursed at her when she'd sneak a pack of gum from below the register. He had no right to complain, stinking up the neighborhood like he did. The least he could do was offer up a lousy stick of gum now and then to pay for his smell.

The mountains were different. The mountains smelled clean, like pine and wildflowers. Harriet complained about how much time Abby spent in them and that she was rarely home before dark. But Harriet didn't understand—grownups never did.

Abby picked her way around a large boulder, careful not to twist an ankle, and drew a deep breath, smelling the cold wet air. Just before it rained, the mountains smelled even better.

The wind began to blow harder as she started up the mountain again, adjusting the knapsack on her back and pulling her jacket tight around her. Fall would soon turn to winter, and although she liked the snow, it would cut back on the time she could spend in the mountains.

The year before, her first winter in Colorado, the snow had come heavy in November, and she hadn't been able to explore the mountains again until late spring. She strained her mind, trying to remember the month, and decided it was probably April when she had been able to come back up again. She used the fingers on her right hand to count the months. Six. She had been stuck in town for six whole months.

But town wasn't so bad. Telluride was small, and there wasn't much to do when you couldn't be in the mountains, but she had freedom here that she'd never had before. She would wander around town watching the tourists, and she liked spying on girls her age or older. She would listen to them talk about clothes and music—and boys. Although she wasn't interested in any of those things, listening to them talk was like listening to aliens.

Some days she would take the gondola up to Mountain Village and watch people ice-skate. It looked like fun. Sometimes she wanted to try.

School was better here, too. Abby stopped and looked down the mountain. She couldn't see town but pictured the redbrick school building at the far end. She would be in trouble for skipping again, but the teachers here were nicer than the uptight ones at the school she went to before.

Although being stuck in town wasn't so bad, being alone in the mountains was her favorite—even before she found out about the mine. She was glad she had overheard Harriet and Mr. Eli talking that night several months earlier—even though Harriet had caught her and sent her to her room.

Abby remembered how she had come in through the front door and heard them talking in the kitchen. And since she was bored and had nothing to do, she had decided to listen for a while but had ended up listening to their whole conversation. That was when she learned about the Judas Mine and about a secret Harriet was keeping.

The next day, Abby had pretended to go to school, but instead, she'd hid outside the house and followed Mr. Eli into the mountains. She knew where he was going from the conversation the night before. So she followed him that morning, climbing higher than she ever had before and memorizing the way.

When they finally reached the mine, she saw a man come out and talk to Mr. Eli. She couldn't hear what they said, but after a while, they disappeared inside. She waited, but they didn't come back out, and she left.

Ever since the night she overheard Harriet and Mr. Eli's conversation, she had been drawn there. She had been back many times, even sneaking inside when she thought no one was there. It was like a magical tunnel to another world, and she liked exploring it.

But one day the man who worked there caught her inside. He was mean and said terrible things. But he was dead now.

Abby had reached her destination and stood staring into the magical tunnel that led deep into the mountain, feeling tears sting her eyes as she remembered the mean man. She squeezed the tears away, trying to squeeze the ugly memory from her mind. But it was no use.

After a few minutes, she opened her eyes and looked up at the dark clouds now swirling in the sky above her, letting frozen mist prickle her face. It felt good, but she had been in the mountains enough to know that bad weather was dangerous.

She wiped the moisture from her face and stared into the magical tunnel again, wondering what to do next.

CHAPTER 45

BY THE TIME Jack and Crockett reached Butch Corbin's cabin, it was beginning to sleet. Still a dozen yards out, Jack heard violin music playing inside.

The cabin was small but larger than Jack remembered. And since Corbin was nowhere around, he took a moment to admire it. Built from stacked logs, with a porch that stretched several feet to either side of the wooden door. A metal flue spewed smoke over a split-shake roof that sagged slightly to one side. Although the old cabin was weathered by wind and snow and unrelenting sun, it looked sturdy.

Jack's gaze drifted past the cabin to the alpine meadow and the mountains behind it. There were no signs of modern innovation anywhere—no electrical pole or cell tower marring the landscape, not even a road. It was as if time stood still in Shudder Basin.

As Jack got closer to the cabin, the music grew louder. A slow, sad tune that abruptly stopped as Crockett approached the steps to the porch. Seconds later, Corbin stepped outside with the Winchester resting in the crook of his elbow.

He turned his head, narrowing his good eye. "You lost?" His voice was deep and gruff, a semi-intelligible growl.

Jack stood just off the porch. He wouldn't go any closer unless invited. "I have a few more questions I'd like to ask you."

Corbin grunted in response, and the two men stared

at each other for several moments, the frigid wind wailing through the trees, flinging sleet like frozen grit against Jack's face. He felt it melt and trickle down his neck. Although he was cold and wet, he didn't budge.

Crockett broke the standoff when he bolted onto the porch and landed at Corbin's feet, wagging his tail. He then shook furiously, slinging the moisture in every direction.

Jack started to call him back, but Corbin spoke first.

"He's a fine-lookin' dog."

Crockett rolled onto his back, twisting it against the porch's rough-hewn boards. Jack tensed, then saw a hint of a smile beneath Corbin's grizzled beard and relaxed.

"Weather's turnin'," Corbin said. He stared at Jack a moment longer, then slowly lowered the shotgun. "Why don't y'all come inside."

Without waiting for an answer, the wild-looking mountain man disappeared into the cabin. And to Jack's horror, Crockett jumped up and followed him inside, leaving a trail of wet footprints in his wake.

Jack hesitated, still standing just off the porch. He felt for the comfortable bulge of the Glock tucked into his waistband, debating what to do next. But when the rain came down harder, he took the steps to the porch and followed Corbin and the dog inside.

Jack closed the wood door behind him, surprised at how warm it was in the cabin. The room was small but neat. It smelled of wood and smoke. The only furnishings were a table and chair, a potbelly stove, and a cot with a small table beside it. Various tools hung from steel pegs driven into the log walls. Two square windows provided natural light, but they were small, and the room was dark. To help make up for it, a single candle flickered on the center of the table.

Crockett had already made himself at home, lying on a large oval rug woven in bright colors in the center of the room, his head resting on his feet.

Corbin sat on the bed and gestured for Jack to take the chair, and for several seconds the men sat in awkward silence. Jack figured it was as much hospitality as the mountain man had ever mustered.

He noticed a violin propped against a wall where Corbin had set the shotgun and pointed to it. "Do you play?"

Corbin took his time to answer. "On occasion."

"I heard the music," Jack said. "You're good."

Jack saw him steal a quick glance at a small framed photo of a woman on the table beside the bed. He hadn't noticed it when he'd come in. Had the woman been Corbin's wife, or maybe his mother? Jack was curious, but he didn't ask. He wondered if she was the reason for the music. Did Corbin play to remember…or to forget?

Jack took a sheet of paper from the pocket of his jacket, unfolded it, and held it out. "Have you ever seen this man in Shudder Basin?"

Corbin leaned forward and studied the photo of Bill Lockwood, then rested back and nodded. "Once."

Jack held his breath. "When?"

"I don't remember exactly."

"Can you give me an estimate? Last year? Last month?"

Corbin scratched at his beard. "A month ago. Maybe more."

"Where did you see him?"

"At the flats."

"The flats?"

"Where the road ends."

Jack thought a moment. "You mean where people park when they come up to the basin?"

"That's right."

A burning log in the stove popped and shifted. Crockett raised his head, then, satisfied everything was fine, laid it back again.

"Did the man go to the Judas Mine?" Jack asked.

"Don't know."

"You didn't ask where he was going?"

"Not my business."

Fair enough, Jack thought. But it raised more questions. "Was he with anyone?"

"Montgomery was there." Corbin hesitated. "And someone else."

"There was a third man with them?" Jack struggled to keep his surprise in check.

Corbin nodded.

"Can you give me a description of the third man?"

Corbin pulled at his beard, thinking again, then shook his head. "There was nothing noteworthy about the third man." He pointed at the photo of Bill Lockwood. "I remember that one because of his cowboy hat and beard."

So, Bill Lockwood had been in the vicinity of the Judas Mine sometime before Dylan was murdered. It was a significant clue, and Jack was getting excited. He pulled his phone from his pocket, intending to find a photo of Eli Wren on the internet, but there was no cell service.

"Those things aren't much good up here," Corbin said.

Crockett got up to move and settled on the floor at Corbin's feet. And Jack was surprised when the mountain man reached down and petted him.

Jack stuck the phone into his pocket. "Do you know Eli Wren?"

Corbin grunted an acknowledgment.

"Have you ever seen him in Shudder Basin?"

Corbin grunted again, then picked at something stuck in his teeth.

"Was he the third guy at the flats? When you saw Dylan with the man in the photo?"

Corbin rubbed at his beard and said, "No."

Jack let out a breath, disappointed. "But you've met him?"

"Who?"

"Eli Wren. He told me he's met you before."

Corbin nodded. "He wanted to look inside my mine."

The conversation was excruciating, but Jack hid his impatience. "And what did you tell him?"

Corbin bent to pet Crockett again but stopped. "I told him no."

"Has anyone else come up here to ask you about your mine?"

"On occasion."

"Anyone recently?"

Corbin shook his head. "Only Wren."

Jack sat back, wondering what it was about Shudder Basin that was so appealing. He looked over the cabin again. As far as he could tell, no one up here was getting rich.

CHAPTER 46

Jack decided to take another look at the Judas Mine before he left the basin. For the life of him, he didn't understand the obsession and wanted to see again the dark recesses of the mountains that held men's imaginations.

When he and Crockett reached the flats, instead of stopping at the truck, they continued in the direction of the Judas.

With the storm over, the sun cast rays haphazardly through the clouds, pocking the ground with patches of sunlight. There was a fresh layer of snow on the cliffs above them. It never ceased to amaze Jack how fast the weather changed in the Rockies.

The moisture from the storm had dampened the rocky soil, making it an easier climb. They made good time, reaching the Judas in under twenty minutes.

Jack stood just outside the entrance, where there were tools and an old gas can scattered about, everything as he had seen it before. Next, he studied the huge iron door already open, as if beckoning him inside. But he stood still, for some reason, something inside him resisting.

Crockett darted away, chasing a marmot into the trees. Knowing the dog wouldn't go far, Jack turned back to the mine and drew in a deep breath, then stepped from the sunshine into the darkness of the mountain.

He stopped several feet from the entrance, letting his eyes

adjust, then pulled his phone from his pocket and switched on the tiny beam of light.

The mine was humid, and the air smelled like cold, damp earth. There was something unnatural about mines—man-made tunnels blasted through the earth's crust. Although Otto's hadn't bothered him, for some reason, this one did.

He noticed a flashlight on the ground just inside the entrance that he didn't remember seeing before. But it didn't surprise him. Otto had several scattered throughout his mine in case of an emergency or the batteries in another one died. Jack picked it up, switched it on, and was surprised it worked but was grateful for the stronger light. He stuck his phone back into his pocket.

He used the flashlight to sweep the walls around him. Everything was as it had looked before. The main tunnel sloped toward the entrance, letting a small stream of water drain to the outside. Jack had learned over the summer that water was the enemy of miners, seeping down walls and rotting supports. And the most common way of fighting it was gravity.

A set of iron rails ran down the center of the tunnel, laid a century earlier to whisk ore out in carts. Between the rails, not far from where Jack was standing, was where Dylan Montgomery had been found dead.

Crockett barked somewhere outside the entrance, still chasing the marmot, and Jack went farther inside. He spent the next several minutes venturing deeper into the mountain, the air growing colder and the sound of the barking growing faint. He passed a connecting tunnel with its own set of rails and eventually reached an area he recognized as a stope, used to store ore before it was carted from the mine.

He continued down the main tunnel but stopped when he reached an offshoot set at an odd angle. Remembering the map at the museum, he knew there would be dozens more shafts and tunnels crisscrossing one another at different depths and angles before the mine eventually played out nearly half a mile in.

He pointed the beam of light inside and saw that the ground sloped up sharply and there were no rails. The floor of the smaller tunnel was dry, not muddy. It was an adit, a narrow passageway that provided access to other parts of the mine. There had been several in Otto's.

He turned and looked back toward the entrance and was surprised to see that he hadn't come far despite having been in the mine for several minutes. The mud made moving through it slow. It would be a nightmare to work in.

Jack stood still a moment, listening to the silence, broken only by the sound of water dripping somewhere deeper inside. It was an eerie feeling being there completely alone. The Judas was nothing like Otto's mine, and he was ready to get out.

Before leaving, he shined the flashlight into the adit one last time, and something near the farthest reaches of the light caught his eye. He squinted at it. It looked like a tarp with something protruding from underneath. He held the flashlight farther out and stepped closer. Was it a boot?

He swept the light over the crossbeams overhead, studying the supports at the adit's entrance. Satisfied it looked secure, he took another step.

As he did, his ankle caught on something—a string or a wire.

The explosion hurled him farther inside the adit, slamming him against the rock. The blast was tremendous, splintering wood and bringing boulders and debris crashing down around him. The sound reverberated for several seconds as rocks and gravel continued to rain.

When it was over, Jack lay on his side, gasping for air but breathing in dust and grit that sliced the back of his throat like a thousand needles. He rolled over coughing, trying to catch his breath, and struggled to his knees, then groped for the flashlight with bloody hands.

When he swung the light back toward the adit's entrance, what he saw through the dust-filled air caused his heart to catch in his throat. He was trapped in the bowels of the Judas Mine.

CHAPTER 47

As dust swirled around him, Jack crawled deeper into the tunnel until he reached the tarp. The beam of light had grown weak, but it was still strong enough that he saw the tarp was actually a coat, and under the coat was a pair of boots. He lifted the coat gently and was grateful there wasn't a body.

But he was alone.

He pulled his phone from his pocket, but as expected, there was no service.

Each of his senses was on high alert. He sat still, letting the dust settle around him and trying to blink grit from his eyes, which only made it worse by scratching them.

He switched off the flashlight to save the battery and was immediately engulfed by a sea of darkness. For several minutes, he closed his eyes, letting them recover. When he thought most of the dust had settled, he opened them but saw nothing, not even the hands he held out in front of his face.

He sat a while longer, catching his breath and assessing his injuries. Even in the dark, he could tell that his palms were bloody. He ran his bloody hands carefully over his arms and legs, finding spots that were bruised and sore, but nothing broken. The dust had finally settled, and the air was now as still as a tomb.

Jack continued to sit in the dark, thinking, and decided there were only two possibilities for what had happened.

Either Dylan Montgomery had booby-trapped the adit before he died, or someone else had set the explosives later. But investigators from the sheriff's office had combed through the mine following Dylan's murder. They would have stumbled upon the trip wire, just as Jack had. It meant someone had set the trap after their investigation. But why?

With the flashlight still off, Jack looked toward the main tunnel, but there was only darkness. Not even a sliver of light escaped the pile of rock blocking his exit. Realizing the explosion had sealed the way out, he felt a sudden wave of claustrophobia wash over him when it registered that he had been buried alive.

He braced himself against the cold rock wall and struggled to stand, sending his right knee and shin screaming. He switched the flashlight back on and swept the adit with the dying light, assessing the debris that blocked his escape. But what he saw made his heart sink.

From the distance the rubble had advanced toward the discarded coat and boots, he estimated that nearly twenty feet of rock and timber lay between him and the adit's entrance. There was no way to tell, but it was possible the slide had also sealed the main tunnel. Digging his way out would be impossible.

He walked slowly in the opposite direction, following the adit deeper into the mine. The map had shown a web of passageways, and although he hadn't seen one, maybe there was another way out. But in the back of his mind, Jack knew that, if he reached another dead end, he was a dead man.

Running one hand gently along the cold rock wall and holding the dying flashlight in the other, he carefully made his way deeper into the mine, passing several shallow crosscuts that led nowhere. Several times, he felt the slight movement of air, but he worried it was only his imagination.

His sore legs grew weak, but he kept going, losing track of time.

Jack's mind began to wander. He thought of Crockett and desperately hoped he was still chasing the marmot far from the mine's entrance but worried the dog had followed him into the mine and was buried in the rubble. His heart ached thinking about what could have happened.

The Judas Mine—the *cursed* Judas Mine. Sean Sullivan's words came back with a vengeance. If only Jack had heeded his warning or listened to the premonitions he'd felt in his gut. But it was too late now.

For hours, he searched a labyrinth of tunnels that seemed to go on forever, tentacles stretching deeper and deeper into the mountain.

Sometime later, when the flashlight battery finally gave out, he was plunged into total darkness. He pulled his phone from his pocket, switched on the tiny beam, and turned back. If he was lucky, the light would last long enough to get him back to the adit's entrance. But what then?

After what seemed like an eternity, he stood staring at the debris pile that was preventing his escape and decided there was only one thing left to do. Dig.

But he had to be careful. An unexpected slide could bury him. It would take search and rescue days to find his remains if they found them at all.

He carefully climbed to the top of the rubble and removed several large stones, letting them roll down to the mine floor, then stuck his phone between the rock and peered as far as he could into the debris. What he saw was devastating.

Pushing thoughts of death aside, he kept going, tossing rocks and handfuls of gravel down the slide until he could no longer feel his hands.

After a while, he checked the time on his phone and saw that he had dug for over an hour. But the amount of rock and timber he removed had barely made a dent.

Giving up, he slid down to the ground and shined the

light from the phone in the opposite direction. There *had* to be another way.

He retraced his steps, rechecking the same crosscuts as before. And as he ventured deeper, he hoped his mind was playing tricks on him, that it was only his imagination that he was running out of air.

Feeling his throat tighten, Jack pulled at the collar of his shirt, his head swimming as images and memories flashed randomly through his mind.

He leaned against the wall and slid down, scratching his back until he reached the ground. As he did, his thoughts turned to Otto, and he wondered if his old friend had ever been in a similar predicament.

Jack wasn't sure how long he sat there, but when his thoughts turned again to Crockett, he pushed himself off the ground with shaky legs. No one knew he was there. There would be no one coming. The beam of light on his phone had grown weak. He had to find a way out.

But he grew disoriented. He had turned back toward the entrance, but had he doubled back again? Or maybe a third time? He couldn't remember. He stared into the darkness, not knowing which way he was facing, and dropped to the floor.

He rested his head against the wall, falling in and out of consciousness. Or was it sleep? He didn't know.

A flurry of tiny colored lights swirling in the dark roused him. He blinked, afraid it was his dying brain playing tricks on him. But being entombed in the unforgiving basin wasn't how he wanted to go, and he forced thoughts of death aside again.

He struggled to his knees and began to crawl. But his bloody palm landed on the sharp edge of a rock and he cried out in pain, then crumpled to the side, dropping his phone. He lay staring where the waning light illuminated the ceiling above him. There was a strange void—a darkness overhead, like the rock had melted away.

He was going crazy.

He blinked several times, clawing back a sliver of lucidity, and thought there was a mine shaft above him. But was he dreaming?

Even if the shaft was real, he had no rope and no energy. And even climbing up, there would only be more tunnels. No matter what he did, he would be lost in the mine forever.

His phone battery died, taking with it the last bit of light.

Time passed as he continued to fall in and out of consciousness. Hours. Maybe days.

He was hungry and shivered uncontrollably, still lying on his back.

Staring into the blackness—mustering his last ounce of strength—he cupped a hand to his mouth and, in desperation, hollered out for help.

As his shout echoed away in the dark, he finally closed his eyes in surrender.

CHAPTER 48

ABBY PUSHED HER hair from her eyes and dropped her head into the wind, pulling her jacket tight around her. As she did, she caught a glimpse of the toes of her shoes and noticed the rubber soles were separating from the tops of her hiking boots.

She hated the boots, hated the feel of them, like her feet were stuck in buckets of sand, sometimes making her feet sweat, which was gross. And the clomping sounds they made on the sidewalk as she hurried toward Harriet's was annoying.

As long as it wasn't too cold, most days it was easier to go barefoot. But not on the days she went into the mountains, where there were too many pine needles and rocks. Not long after moving to Telluride, she had learned that lesson the hard way when, after stepping on a nasty pine cone, Harriet had taken her to the medical center, where they wrapped her foot like a salami. The kids at school had teased her for two solid days. It was the only time in her life Abby would have done anything to wear a second shoe.

As she walked home, she studied the horizon. She didn't know what time it was but could tell from the position of the sun that school had let out hours earlier. She quickened her pace.

If she was lucky, she could slip into the house and get to her room without Harriet noticing, and pretend she had been home all along. And if she got *really* lucky, she would see Robbie first.

Although Robbie was old—maybe even over thirty—he was her friend. And on the days she skipped school, he would let her hide her sneakers in the greenhouse behind Harriet's garage, where he worked. "Learned heaps more in the mountains than I ever did in any classroom," he had said many times. Robbie was the only grown-up who understood.

If Abby asked nicely enough, she knew Robbie would cover for her if Harriet suspected she had been in the mountains. He would say she had run errands for him or been helping him with something in the greenhouse. And Harriet would believe him. Harriet liked Robbie, too.

But there was no avoiding being in trouble when Harriet found out she had skipped school for the second time that week—and it was only Wednesday. It would mean another trip to the principal's office. But Abby didn't care. She knew there was nothing the school could do except stick her in detention for a couple of days again—Robbie had told her so, saying something about a state law.

Harriet sending her to live with another relative would be the worst thing that could happen. But Harriet wouldn't do it. Abby had overheard her tell Mr. Eli that she would never "toss the child out like trash" like her other family had. Instead, Harriet wanted Abby to go to some fancy school in Dallas. Which sounded almost as horrible, but not quite.

Thinking about leaving Telluride made her stomach hurt. If someone else had said they wanted to send her to a school far away, she would have put rocks in their shoes or swished their toothbrush around in the toilet. But Harriet was nice, so Abby would never do those things to Harriet.

When Harriet would say the boardinghouse was now her home, Abby would merely smile, not wanting to hurt the old woman's feelings by telling her she felt more at home in the mountains with the elk and the deer than living in some crummy old house with a revolving door of strangers.

Abby took the corner at the end of the block and started the climb to Harriet's. As she did, she studied the rocky cliffs hanging above town and wondered if there were mountains in Dallas.

CHAPTER 49

Before he sat down, Ted Hawthorne used his handkerchief to wipe the rain from the park bench in front of the courthouse. The storm had cleared, and Main Street was quiet.

He was grateful only a handful of people milled about. The locals could be nosy. And the last thing he wanted was to be forced to come up with a reason for why he was sitting on a park bench in the middle of the day if someone asked.

He pulled up his sleeve and glanced at his watch. *Where is the blasted woman?*

As he waited, he bounced one of his legs furiously, a nervous habit his teachers had unsuccessfully tried curing him of when he was a schoolboy. He rechecked the time on his watch and huffed.

The call from the woman earlier that morning, saying her friend in the Department of Health and Environment had found the name, had Ted excited but nervous. He had never held bureaucrats in high regard, but finally, one had proven their worth.

The sun was drying the puddles along the curb, and the afternoon was warming. He glanced at the courthouse, looking for her. He hoped their business wouldn't take more than a couple of minutes. But the blasted woman was already late.

Several minutes later, the courthouse door swung open, and the woman he'd been waiting for finally descended the steps.

"You got my lunch?" She plopped down hard on the bench beside him.

Ted handed her the paper sack and watched as she stuck her hand inside and shuffled through its contents. He had picked up her order at the deli down the street twenty minutes earlier—a BLT with pesto aioli on homemade toast, a bag of chips, and a slice of key lime pie, precisely what she'd requested. Then, on his way to the park bench, he had discreetly slipped the envelope containing three one-hundred-dollar bills into the bag with her lunch.

The woman drew out the envelope and counted the bills.

"Keep it out of sight, will you?" he said, looking over his shoulder.

She threw him a perturbed glance, then stuffed the envelope into the pocket of her oversized blazer and pulled the sandwich from the bag.

Ted watched her unwrap it. "The meal wasn't part of our original bargain," he said, anxious to get back to the bank. "Now, what's the name?"

She swallowed a bite of BLT, dipped her hand into a pocket, and handed him a crumpled scrap of paper.

"There you go." She took another bite of the sandwich.

Ted's heart thumped in his chest as he smoothed the paper. The information could either bail him out or sink Telluride Bank & Trust into oblivion.

As he read the name scrawled in pencil, a grin slowly spread across his face, and under his breath, he mumbled, "This is going to be easier than I thought."

CHAPTER 50

Thursday, September 26

In the deep recesses of his mind, Jack heard a dog bark. It stirred him to a consciousness that confused him. Where was he?

He opened his eyes but couldn't see. The world was black, and his body felt like lead. He tried to move but couldn't. For a second he thought he was dead.

Then he remembered being trapped in a narrow underground tunnel where no one would find him. He heard the dog again and fumbled in the dark, searching the ground for his phone. Then, remembering the battery was dead, he sat still and listened.

There was a scuffling sound somewhere above or beside him—he couldn't tell which. It was as if the darkness had yanked away his spatial awareness.

He heard the sound again and realized it was rock shifting. Somewhere, something was moving.

"Hello!" he hollered into the dark. Once again, his words echoed painfully away as they reverberated through the mountain.

But this time there was an answer.

"Jack?" It was a man's voice. He sounded in distress.

"I'm here." As soon as he said it, Jack realized it was a ridiculous response. He had no idea himself where *here* was.

A second later there was a dance of light on the rocks above him. But as quickly as it appeared, it was gone.

"Hello?" Jack called out again.

"I'm coming." The response echoed against the rock.

It was a voice Jack recognized. "Corbin?"

The dog barked again, and Jack knew instantly it was Crockett. Tears of relief welled in his eyes.

The light appeared again, brighter this time, blinding him, and Jack used a bloody hand to shield his face.

Corbin was now directly over him. "Hold on a minute," he said. "I'm going to throw down a rope. Do you think you can climb up it?"

Despite bloody and bruised palms and weak legs, Jack thought he could sprout wings and fly if it would help him escape the suffocating tomb.

But the climb was more difficult than he had imagined. The wounds on his hands reopened and began to bleed, his swollen knee throbbing and refusing to bend.

When Jack finally reached the top, Corbin grabbed him and hauled him away from the drop to keep him from falling back into the adit.

Exhausted, Jack coughed, his breath sputtering dust, which Crockett instantly turned to mud as he licked his face.

"Hey there, boy," Jack said, resting his arm across the dog's back. He tried to stand but staggered when pain shot through his right knee.

Corbin grabbed his arm and kept him from falling. "Watch out behind you," he warned, carefully maneuvering Jack to the side. He handed him a canteen and told him to drink, then set the flashlight on the ground. "Hells bells, I thought I was lookin' for a dead man."

Jack gulped water and coughed again, then wiped drips from his chin. He rested his back against the cool rock wall, letting it soothe his scratches. His mind was reeling.

He was free. But he was confused. "Where are we?"

"You're now in the Crystal Lake Mine," Corbin said, winding the rope over an elbow as he pulled it from below. "Praise the Lord you had the good sense to pass out under the ventilation shaft. Ten feet in either direction, and you wouldn't have made it."

"Ventilation shaft?"

Corbin pointed the flashlight at the floor, and Jack squinted into the gaping hole where he'd been.

"Back in the day, that spur in the Judas killed a passel of men before they figured out the air was bad. Bored the ventilation shaft straight through to the outside, clipping the adit we're in now before they reached fresh air." Corbin shined the light upward into another black hole. "We're a long way down from the top, and the shaft angles with the mountain. That's why there's no sunlight."

He clipped the coiled rope to a carabiner and attached it to his waist. "This way."

Crockett ran ahead, occasionally stopping to look back, making sure the men were following him. Jack limped slowly behind Corbin, each step sending stabs of pain through his knee and up his thigh to his hip.

Water dripped from a spring hidden somewhere in the rock. The air was cold and wet, and Jack started to shiver but continued on in silence, following the man and the dog through the maze of tunnels in the Crystal Lake Mine.

After minutes or hours, there was finally a pinpoint of light in the distance, an escape from the hard rock tomb where Jack thought he would take his last breath.

From the dim gray light, Jack knew that it was early morning or evening. He didn't know which and didn't care. He kept moving forward, placing one foot in front of the other despite the pain, and recognized the signs of hypothermia. But he was almost there—almost free.

Crockett stopped at the mine's entrance, waiting and wagging his tail. He was muddy and wet and panted with his tongue lolling, making it look as if he were smiling. Jack had never loved him more than he did at that moment. When he reached the entrance, the dog spun in a circle and whined.

Jack drew in a long breath, letting the fresh air fill his lungs. "It's alright, boy," he said, bending to pet Crockett. "It's alright now."

"I knew that was a good dog," Corbin said, standing beside them. "Now you owe him your life."

Jack frowned, looking at Corbin. "What do you mean?"

"He's the only reason I found you."

Jack had been so distracted by the relief of being rescued that he hadn't stopped to wonder how it happened. But he had more pressing questions.

"What day is it?" he asked Corbin.

"Thursday morning."

With a muddled brain, Jack struggled with the math and realized he'd been stuck in the mine for just under twenty-four hours. But now he was free.

Despite the pain and the urge he felt to collapse, exhausted, he turned his face to the stars still littering the morning sky and thought it was the most beautiful sight he'd ever seen. He drew in another deep breath, welcoming the sting of the frozen crystals suspended in the frigid air.

As they took the trail away from the mine, the normally reticent mountain man took his time to explain how Crockett had led him to the rockslide.

"He showed back up at my place, whining. And since you weren't with him, I knew something was wrong." He spent the next several minutes describing in detail how the tunnels of the Judas and Crystal Lake Mines intersected and how he had eventually found Jack.

"I've seen a map," Jack said as his truck came into view, still parked at the flats. "They looked close, but I couldn't tell they overlapped."

Corbin shook his head, stopping at the fork in the trail

that led to his cabin. "Maps aren't accurate. These old mines crisscross each other all the time. It caused many a dispute back in the day." He paused a moment and frowned. "You okay to drive? You're welcome to stay a night if you need to."

The supposed crazy man surprised Jack again. He remembered the violin music and the black-and-white photo of the woman. Butch Corbin was an enigma who had saved his life.

Jack thanked him but declined the invitation.

"Suit yourself," Corbin replied, and nodded. "But I'd watch my back if I were you."

Jack didn't know how to respond.

Corbin started to go but turned back. "That trip wire you described wasn't an accident, you know?" Jack frowned, and Corbin added, "Seems to me there's a person who wanted someone dead."

CHAPTER 51

Two hours later, Jack was at the Telluride Medical Center, reclined on an exam table dressed in a ridiculous-looking gown and feeling like a fool. Despite the protests of medical staff, Crockett lay on the floor at his feet.

"I'm fine," he insisted, still angry at having a perfectly good pair of jeans cut off to examine his knee.

"You're fine when *I* say you're fine," the doctor said.

She was a massive woman with a bedside manner that would frighten Frankenstein. Although Jack remembered her from a previous visit to the medical center months earlier, he made a point of not mentioning it.

She had his leg in the air, bending and poking at his knee, which had swelled to the size of a cantaloupe. "You drove with it like this?" When Jack didn't reply, she frowned and added, "You're lucky there's no ligament damage."

She poked at it some more. Jack clenched to keep from crying out in frustration and pain.

"Yep. Just a strain." She dropped his leg to the table and pulled off her latex gloves. "I'll get a nurse to bandage it. You'll be free to go as soon as I get them your discharge order."

Jack breathed a sigh of relief.

The doctor jerked open the door but turned back. "It just dawned on me why you look familiar," she said, pointing at him. "Cracked ribs a few months ago. Got yourself shot." Without saying anything else, she shook her head and left.

Despite being bloodied and bruised, coming to the medical center hadn't been Jack's choice. But on his way back to Telluride, he had called the sheriff to tell him what'd happened, and Tony insisted.

The exam room door swung open, and Kim O'Connor rushed in. "I heard what happened. Are you alright?"

"I'm fine," Jack said, tired of saying it and frustrated at being caught wearing a gown.

She came closer and frowned, studying his swollen knee. "Well, you don't look fine."

Jack held up his right hand and wiggled his fingers, mercifully left free from the thick gauze binding that wrapped his palm. "Just a few bumps and bruises."

"That's more than a bruise," she said, shaking her head. She bent to pet the dog. "Hey, Crockett."

"You didn't have to come. But thank you."

"Tony's got a couple of guys up at the mine now. They've already found the trip wire and evidence of dynamite. It wasn't there when we searched the mine after Dylan's murder." She stared at him a moment. "It was really Crazy Corbin who saved you?"

When Jack confirmed it was, she took a moment to think about it, then frowned. "Jack, who knew you were going up there?"

When it registered what she was implying, theories swirled in his head. Had someone set the explosives, hoping he'd be the next person in the mine? Jack remembered the boots and felt a surge of adrenaline, realizing someone had staged the scene.

Whoever was responsible could have waited a couple of days, then returned to the basin and driven his truck off a cliff, hiding evidence that Jack had been there. It could have been years before anyone found the truck or his body—maybe never.

He remembered Corbin's warning to watch his back. It might be true that Jack was the target, but he wasn't convinced.

"It could have been set for anyone," he said. "Someone from the sheriff's office was just as likely to have been in there next. I just happened to draw the short straw."

Kim shook her head. "We've been out of the mine for weeks. We weren't going back in."

"That doesn't mean—"

"Jack, you need to look at this objectively. Maybe we didn't broadcast the fact that you're helping with the investigation, but people found out." She let it sink in. "Now, the question isn't Who knows you're investigating the case? We have to assume that everyone knows. The question is Who knew you would be in Shudder Basin?"

Deep down Jack knew she was right. By now half the town probably knew he was working the Montgomery case. And it was an easy guess that he would eventually revisit the crime scene.

He squeezed his eyes shut and rubbed his throbbing temples.

"Jack, are you alright?"

He had almost forgotten the deputy was in the room. "I'm fine," he said, dropping his hands back to the exam table, rustling the paper. "Just a little sore."

"And understandably so." She laid a hand on his arm. "Now, think for a minute. Who knew you were going up to Shudder Basin?"

Jack shook his head. "It could have been anybody. And the dynamite could have been set days ago."

Kim released his arm and dropped into a chair against the wall. "You're probably right. Nobody from the sheriff's office has been up there since you and I were there last Thursday. I wish we had gone back in when we went up to see Corbin."

Lost in his thoughts, Jack had stopped listening. "Let me ask you something," he said. "Whoever rigged the trip wire knew their way around explosives. That narrows the list of suspects."

Kim nodded, following his logic.

Jack lowered his voice. "What can you tell me about Eli Wren?"

"Eli?" She came forward in the chair. "He would definitely know about explosives."

Jack nodded. "And he was in the mountains the day Dylan was murdered."

"But he wasn't in Shudder Basin."

"How do you know that?" Jack had already heard Wren's alibi. But now, after the explosion, he wanted to hear the details to ensure something hadn't fallen through the cracks.

Kim sank back into the chair, thinking. "First of all, Eli admitted during questioning that he was in the mountains that day. In fact, he volunteered the information before we asked. But second, a couple of tourists from Texas hiking Ajax confirmed it. They saw him that morning. It would have been nearly impossible for him to get from Ajax to the Judas, kill Dylan, and get back to town. And the boys who found Dylan said they never saw him."

Ajax was the iconic mountain at the far end of the box canyon. With spectacular views of town, it was a popular day hike for locals and athletically inclined tourists. Jack had hiked it once and knew it wasn't anywhere near Shudder Basin.

"What time did the couple from Texas report seeing him?"

"They didn't remember exactly but said it was sometime before lunch." She shook her head. "And Eli was back in town by late afternoon. Judith confirmed he had an early dinner at the cafe."

Jack knew from the autopsy report that the coroner wasn't able to pinpoint an exact time of death. Despite a wound to the back of Dylan's head that actively bled before he died, the cold temperature in the high-altitude basin made it impossible to determine. Instead, the coroner had estimated a range that spanned several hours.

But Wren was fit, and Jack wondered whether he could get from Ajax to Shudder Basin within the coroner's time range. It would have been difficult, but there was a chance he could have hiked to the Judas, killed Dylan within the coroner's time frame, and been back in town before dark. Although the theory was unlikely, it was possible.

Jack wanted to talk to Wren again. "He's in the mountains most days, isn't he?"

"He was up there almost *every* day this summer," she said. "But he's spent more time in town the last few weeks."

More time in town since Dylan died? Jack wondered if that was a coincidence. "Where's he staying?"

"He's renting a room at a boardinghouse on Galena."

"Do you have the address?"

She leaned over and pulled a phone from her pocket. "Harriet Hughes owns it. Let me find it for you."

"Harriet?"

Kim nodded, scrolling through the contacts on her phone.

Jack had heard the name. It took him a moment to remember where. "Does Harriet have a girl named Abby staying with her? Red hair, maybe eleven or twelve years old?"

Kim looked up from her phone and frowned. "Yeah, why?"

Wren was staying in the same boardinghouse as the peculiar girl who knew too much about Dylan. Jack's head was pounding again, wondering what the connection meant, if anything. But that was a puzzle to solve another time.

He checked the time on his phone and looked up at the deputy. "I need you to do me a favor."

CHAPTER 52

AFTER BEING DISCHARGED from the medical center, Jack rushed to the New Sheridan, but the closest parking spot was a block from the hotel. He hobbled the rest of the way, favoring his bandaged right knee and grateful the deputy had taken Crockett to the campground and brought back a pair of jeans.

He cursed the bandage, which made him unable to bend his stiff leg, and vowed to remove it when he returned to the trailer.

But it was nearly noon, and his priority wasn't the knee; it was getting to the restaurant before Bill Lockwood left. Although Lockwood had mentioned *where* he would be that morning, he hadn't divulged the time he would be there. Jack hoped he wasn't too late.

He stumbled on the step as he entered the hotel. Looking up, he saw an attractive young hostess smiling at him. He cursed the bandage under his breath but smiled back at her.

"I'm here to see Bill Lockwood."

The girl tucked a lock of hair behind her ear. "Mr. Lockwood is at his usual table in the back corner of the parlor." She swept a hand toward the hallway that led to the restaurant.

Jack started for the dining room, taking in breaths redolent of omelets and bacon, causing his stomach to growl. He hadn't eaten in over a day, but food would have to wait.

The restaurant's painted wood paneling and furniture upholstered in red velvet reminded Jack of a hotel in the Old West. And although he had been in the restaurant several times, he had never dined there. It was too expensive. Diners sat at tables with gleaming silver set on crisp white tablecloths. Only a few were occupied.

Jack turned toward the small parlor in the back. It was a diminutive space with only a handful of small tables, which provided more privacy than the main dining room. But it was the off-season, the months between summer and ski season, when the number of tourists dwindled to a trickle. Jack wondered why Lockwood would want to dine in a remote corner of the parlor when the restaurant was nearly empty.

Lockwood was reclined in a chair at a corner table with a half-eaten plate of food in front of him. He was talking on a cell phone. Jack sized him up as he limped closer.

Behind Lockwood's carefully trimmed beard was a face with sharp edges and cruel dark eyes. He wore a starched plaid shirt and black lizard boots that stuck out from under the table. There was a hard look about the man. He talked on the phone with an air of superiority that was apparent even from a distance.

Jack knew the conversation wouldn't be easy.

When Lockwood noticed Jack, he abruptly ended the call, then laid the phone on the table, leaving his right hand covering it.

"I didn't think you'd come," he said as Jack approached the table.

There was no need for introductions. Like Jack, Lockwood had done his research.

"Why wouldn't I?" Jack took the chair across from him and sat, leaving his swollen leg extended to the side.

Lockwood glanced from Jack's bandaged hands to where his jeans stretched tight across his knee. "What happened?"

Jack wondered if the question was a ruse and searched

the man's eyes for a sign he already knew what had happened in the mine. But his poker face was impeccable.

Jack left the question unanswered. "What business did you have with Dylan Montgomery on the day he was murdered?"

"Right to the point," Lockwood said. His mouth tensed. "I'm a busy man. And although I appreciate the direct approach, I don't think that's any of your business."

"I'm asking on behalf of the San Miguel County Sheriff's Office," Jack replied, getting comfortable in the chair. "The way I see it, that *makes* it my business."

Lockwood's stare was long and hard. It might have shrunk another man, but after decades working in law enforcement, Jack had encountered worse. He waited for the other man to respond.

After a few tense seconds, Lockwood took his napkin from his lap and laid it on the table. "I would offer you something," he said, sweeping a hand over his plate. "But as you can see, I'm already done eating."

"I didn't come for food," Jack said. "I need answers."

The ensuing conversation was like a chess match. The two men spent the next several minutes exchanging questions and cryptic answers, each trying to outmaneuver the other.

Lockwood was good, but Jack was better. After threats to involve the sheriff, Lockwood finally broke.

"Alright," he said, settling back into the chair. "If you must know, I was negotiating with Dylan when he died."

"Negotiating what?"

"The purchase of the mine."

"Why would you want the mine?"

The men fell silent as a busboy cleared dishes from the table.

When they were alone again, Lockwood continued. "My reasons for purchasing the mine are, again, none of your business. But if you must know, I wanted it for personal reasons."

"Personal reasons?"

Lockwood glanced around the room as if searching for an answer. He lifted his hands from the table and let them fall back, covering the phone with his right hand again. He drummed the table with the fingers of his left. His fingernails were filed and buffed, and he wore a gold signet ring on his left pinkie.

"I wanted the mine for personal reasons," Lockwood repeated. "It's a hobby of mine."

"What is?"

"Prospecting."

Glancing at his soft, smooth hands, Jack didn't believe it for a minute. "Dylan was going to sell you the Judas?"

"He was," Lockwood replied. "At least until that treasure hunter muddied the waters. But I still think we could have gotten a deal done."

"You mean Eli Wren?"

"That's him. But Wren wasn't willing to buy the mine outright. And I was. Once Wren got involved, the deal was going to take us longer to get done, but I'm confident we would have."

"What makes you so sure?"

"Wren wasn't offering Dylan cash. But I *was*."

Lockwood's confidence didn't square with the fact Dylan had recently purchased mining equipment.

But Jack wanted to keep the arrogant man talking. "Now that he's dead," he said, "why not negotiate a deal with Dylan's partner?"

Lockwood looked annoyed by the question and checked the time on his phone. "I think I've answered enough questions. I really don't have time for—"

"I would argue you have plenty of time to convince me you're not guilty of murder."

The other man stared hard at Jack. "Do I need to call my attorney?"

"Only if you're guilty of something," Jack replied.

Lockwood pressed his palms against the table, causing his fingernails to go white. He resembled a mountain lion ready to pounce.

"Listen," Jack said, coming forward in his chair. "This doesn't need to be contentious. I just want to know why you're no longer interested in the mine."

Lockwood stared for a couple more seconds, then relaxed. "Alright. Not that this matters to your investigation, but I *was* trying to work a deal with Sean Sullivan."

"Past tense?"

"Yes," Lockwood replied. "Past tense. I quit negotiating when things with the title got messy."

"What do you mean?"

"I was informed that someone's inheriting Dylan's interest in it when his estate is probated. Why work a deal with a minority partner? At that point, I was wasting my time."

"What?" Jack was surprised by the revelation that someone besides Sullivan had a controlling interest in the mine.

Lockwood smiled. "You didn't know."

The information changed everything. "I didn't," Jack admitted. "Who's going to inherit it?"

"That's a good question," Lockwood said. "I don't know yet."

Jack sat back, wondering why Sean Sullivan hadn't mentioned negotiating with Lockwood. But more importantly, he wanted to know who now controlled the Judas Mine.

He looked at the man across the table. "And your intention for the Judas is to mine it?"

"Why else?"

But Jack still wasn't buying it. "When was the last time you were up there?"

"At the Judas?" He drummed his fingers a moment, thinking. "Probably a week or two before Dylan died. So… maybe a month ago."

"You haven't been up there in the last week?"

Lockwood frowned. "No. Why would I?" He picked up his phone and checked the time.

Jack noticed his hands again. "You don't seem the type to dig for gold on the weekends."

Lockwood pushed his chair back from the table and stood up, indicating the conversation was over. "People can surprise you."

"They can," Jack replied, "but they rarely do."

He watched as Lockwood walked out, snatching a cowboy hat from a hook beside the bar. Like his lizard boots, the hat looked new.

Lockwood was slick—one of several things Jack didn't like about him.

He watched through the windows as Lockwood strolled past the restaurant. Jack suspected that much of what he had said was a lie, having decided long ago never to trust a man with a manicure.

CHAPTER 53

"I missed you yesterday," Eli said as he stepped into Earl's Tavern.

"Good afternoon, Eli." Sean set aside the beer glass he was polishing. "What can I get you?"

"Rum on the rocks."

"This early?"

"It's never too early when you're taking a day off."

"Any preference on the rum?"

"Not that expensive swill you hawk to tourists. Give me that good cheap stuff."

"Flor de Caña?"

Eli snapped and pointed his finger at him. "You're a good man, Sullivan. And put it in a highball," he added. "Not one of those double old-fashioned glasses Taz serves it in. I had to order twice as many yesterday to drink half as much."

Sean smiled. "I'll have a talk with her about that."

Eli pulled out a stool from under the bar and sat, then rubbed his palms over its cool surface, waiting for the drink. "You hear what happened to Jack Martin yesterday?"

"I did." Sean set the rum in front of him. "It's a miracle he wasn't killed. It's why I want to be rid of that damn place—it's a death trap."

Eli took a sip of his drink and nodded. "I don't think you have to worry about Martin. He doesn't seem the type to sue."

"Maybe not. But what about the next guy?" Sean asked. "Or the next *kid?*"

"Well, the good news is you probably won't have to worry about the mine much longer."

"What do you mean?"

"Word's out somebody's inheriting Dylan's share. You might be bought out once the estate settles."

Sean frowned. "Dylan had an heir?"

"Ted Hawthorne mentioned it this morning at the bank. Wouldn't say who the person was, but I'm pretty sure he knows. Guess that means you could have a buyer for your share any day now. Or at least someone with deeper pockets for somebody to sue." He threw back another swallow.

Sean raised his brows. "So I might," he said. "You don't have any idea who it could be?"

Eli ran a finger around the rim of the glass. "Not a clue. But you'll have to beat me to them when we find out. I plan to offer them a cut of a deal they can't refuse."

"You want to buy it now?" Sean looked hopeful.

"Not buy it," Eli replied. "I'm going to convince them to let me have a look. Pay for a lease if I have to. I don't care what people say—the lost Smuggler Vein runs somewhere right through the Judas, and I intend to find it. They'll get a percentage of the take on the back end."

"I'll never understand the lure of gold." Sean shook his head. "As far as I can tell, no one's getting rich looking for it anymore."

"Just wait." Eli drained the last of the highball and dropped the glass to the bar with a thud. "One more, then I've got to call it a day."

"Big plans tomorrow?" Sean asked, taking the glass from him.

"Heading up to talk to Butch Corbin."

"You, too? Are you sure that's a good idea? Look what happened to Jack Martin after he went to see him."

"Corbin didn't have anything to do with that explosion. Didn't you hear? Corbin's the one that saved him."

Sean shook his head. "Maybe he did, but I still think it's a mistake."

CHAPTER 54

AFTER HIS MEETING with Bill Lockwood, Jack had more questions than answers, so he called the one person he knew could help—Archie Rochambeau.

"See what you can dig up on a nuclear power plant in Utah called the Coyote 1."

"Nuclear power plant? Holy atom-splitting, Batman. Who are you taking on next? Global crime syndicates?"

Jack was in no mood for humor. "There's a man named William Lockwood who works there. He goes by Bill. See what you can find out about him while you're at it."

"Gotcha, boss."

Jack listened as Archie typed something into his computer. The meeting with Lockwood had him discouraged. Lockwood had lied—at least about prospecting as a hobby. No man with lizard boots, a perfectly coiffed beard, and manicured nails mined for gold in the Colorado Rockies for fun. But if Lockwood didn't want the Judas for its gold, what *did* he want it for?

Archie had stopped typing. "Anything else, my caped crusader friend?"

"That's it," Jack said, hearing the weariness in his voice.

Archie fell silent for a moment. "Hey, Jack, are you alright?"

Jack dropped his face into his free hand, intentionally not mentioning the explosion in the mine. "I'm just a little tired."

"No worries, mate. I'll hit you back faster than you can say 'holy nuclear meltdown.'"

After the call, Jack crossed Main Street and went into Waggoner Mercantile.

"Jack! For goodness' sake. We heard what happened." Ivy Waggoner made a beeline for him, her arms stretched wide. She enveloped him in a voluminous hug, the scent of her gray-blue hair reminding him of the rose perfume his grandmother had worn.

"Let me look at you," she said, pushing back to study him head to toe. Her eyes lingered on his bandaged hands, then where his jeans were pulled tight over his swollen knee. "Are you alright?"

"A little banged up. But I'm fine."

"Well, you don't look fine." Opal Waggoner had emerged from the back of the store, carrying a canvas bag in one hand and holding the knob of her cane in a death grip with the other. "You look like you've been drug through hell and back."

Ivy took Jack's arm and dropped her voice. "Don't listen to her. She's constipated. I think you look just fine." She patted his arm and let go. "Now, what can we do for you?"

"I'd like to ask you a few questions."

Opal harrumphed. "And here I thought you'd finally come to buy something."

Ivy shook her head, then turned to Jack. "What did you want to ask us, honey?"

Questioning the Waggoner sisters was an unorthodox way of gathering information, but Jack knew that clues often came from sources not connected to the crime. And right now the sisters were low-hanging fruit.

"What can you tell me about Eli Wren?"

"Eli?" Ivy was confused by the question.

Opal spoke next. "He's a Hollywood pirate. Putting up flyers all over Telluride advertising for help, littering our good town and polluting young minds with ridiculous dreams of gold."

"He's not a pirate, Opal." Ivy rolled her eyes. "He's a treasure hunter."

"A swashbuckling idiot, if you ask me."

"Well, we didn't ask you. Did we, Jack?"

Jack stammered, not knowing what to say.

"And I think he's handsome," Ivy added.

"Thinking with your hormones again," Opal huffed. "Shouldn't those have dried up decades ago?"

"Along with your hemorrhoids, I suppose?"

Jack cleared his throat, interrupting their argument. "I understand Eli lives with a friend of yours."

The sisters suddenly fell silent.

"I believe her name is Harriet. You mentioned her the last time I was here."

"Um..." Ivy struggled for words.

"We do have a friend named Harriet," Opal said. "She runs a boardinghouse. But we aren't privy to the identity of her guests. They come and they go."

"They do." Ivy's chin bobbed. "They come and they go."

"I've been told Eli is renting a room from her."

Opal rapped her cane on the floor. "Maybe he does, maybe he doesn't. It's none of our business."

"But it is mine," Jack said, impatience seeping into his exhaustion. "I'm going to talk to Harriet, but I was hoping you ladies might answer a few questions for me first."

They remained silent.

"What is her relationship to Eli?"

"There's no relationship," Opal said. "He's merely a boarder."

"So he *is* staying with her?"

Opal's mouth went hard when she realized she'd slipped.

"Oh, for goodness' sake, Opal," Ivy said. "Jack said he

already heard Eli was staying at Harriet's. What difference does it make if we confirm it for him?"

Harriet Hughes's name had come up too many times, and Jack wanted to know how she fit into the equation. Eli Wren was the primary suspect in the murder of Dylan Montgomery, and he lived with Harriet.

And Abby, the girl who knew more than she should about the victim, also lived with her. Had the girl overheard Eli and Harriet talking about the murder? But that could mean the two were closer than what the Waggoner sisters were letting on.

Jack turned to Ivy. "Did Harriet know Dylan Montgomery?"

"Why would you ask that?" Opal interrupted. "Harriet didn't have anything to do with what happened to Dylan. That boy got what he deserved."

"Opal, don't say such a thing," Ivy reprimanded. She turned to Jack. "We all knew Dylan. Telluride's a small town."

"So what does Harriet say about Eli Wren?" Jack asked, steering the conversation back to where he wanted it.

"Just that he's been driving her crazy about that mine," Ivy said.

"What mine?" Jack asked. "The Judas?"

Opal whacked her cane against the hardwood floor. "You're speaking out of turn, Ivy. It's not our business to say."

"What about the mine, Ivy?" Jack asked. "It's the Judas, isn't it?" Ivy's eyes widened with fear, and he had his answer.

She turned to Opal, not knowing what to say.

"We won't speak another word about Harriet," Opal said. "Will we, Ivy? She's our friend, and we refuse to gossip."

Ivy looked at Jack and shook her head apologetically.

Not willing to give up, Jack asked several more questions but got only vague answers. For some reason, whatever was going on between Harriet Hughes and Eli Wren regarding the Judas Mine was a well-guarded secret.

CHAPTER 55

Harriet's purse was tucked safely under her arm, where she squeezed it tightly against her chest. Although she had known Ted Hawthorne since he was swaddled in diapers, she would never let her guard down around a banker.

Banks were for suckers who didn't mind paying fees for everything but the air they breathed. And Harriet was sure that if Ted could figure out a way, he'd gladly charge a fee for even that while she was inside his bank.

Harriet had always been happy to tuck her savings safely between the box spring and mattress of her bed—a cliché so worn-out that she was sure no one would ever suspect it.

But here she was, standing in the lobby of Telluride Bank & Trust, its president staring up at her. His phone call the day before had surprised her. Their conversation had been pleasant but brief, and she had reluctantly agreed to meet him the following morning as much out of curiosity as from fear.

Ted adjusted the glasses on the bridge of his nose. "Step into my office."

Harriet eyed him skeptically but relented. She took a chair and waited as the banker rounded his desk and sat facing her.

He laid his hands flat on the desk that separated them and cleared his throat. "Have you thought any more about what I'm offering?"

Harriet fidgeted with the clasp of her purse, now resting

in her lap. "I told you yesterday I've already got a deal with Eli."

"Is it in writing?"

"No."

"Then it's not a deal." When she didn't reply, he added, "Listen, Harriet. I'm offering a sure thing, not some ludicrous pipe dream of some treasure hunter."

"But—"

"And it's what's best for the girl." He raised his hands from the desk, then let them fall back.

She was frustrated he knew which buttons to push. She looked into the beady eyes behind the glasses, searching for something sinister, an ulterior motive he was trying to hide.

"You promise not to disclose her identity?"

"I promised you I wouldn't," he replied. "And I'm a man of my word."

What troubled Harriet was that she would be going back on *her* word. She didn't know what to say. What Ted proposed seemed like a better deal than what she had arranged with Eli.

But she liked Eli. And he had readily agreed to keep the truth secret. Eli had treated her fairly, but if she accepted the deal with Ted, he would be furious.

Harriet reminded herself that Ted's offer was better for the girl. But still, her conscience was torn, and she shook her head.

"I know this is hard," Ted told her. "But it makes more sense." When she didn't reply, he added. "Eli won't be a problem."

"He'll be furious."

"He'll get over it." Ted laced his fingers together and twiddled his thumbs. "Now…do we have a deal?"

The banker's gaze made Harriet nervous, and she squirmed in her chair. She took a minute to think, then nodded.

"Great!" Ted jerked open a drawer under the desk. "I'll

get the paperwork drawn up immediately." He laid a manila folder down in front of him.

Harriet wondered why—if it was the right thing to do—her stomach was tied up in knots. She fiddled with the clasp of her purse. "I don't know what I'll tell him."

Ted was scribbling something on a sheet of paper but stopped to look up. He grinned. "You'll think of something."

CHAPTER 56

JACK KNEW THAT Bill Lockwood could have set the explosion that nearly killed him. But it could have just as easily been Eli Wren.

He would have to wait for Archie to get back to him to find out just who the hell Lockwood was. In the meantime, confronting Wren was the next item on Jack's to-do list.

After leaving Waggoner Mercantile, he opened the Notes app on his phone to where he'd stored Harriet Hughes's address. Several minutes later, he was standing on the sidewalk in front of her house.

It was a cookie-cutter Victorian like countless others in old mining towns scattered throughout the Rockies. Built of clapboard siding with a steep gable roof, it had a porch that stretched from one front corner to the other. What made Harrie's home different was that it was buried in landscaping—trees, shrubs, and flower beds, some stubbornly hanging on to their late-summer blooms. Flower boxes filled with fall perennials were attached to the porch railing, and ivy draped from hanging pots overhead. On the front door, a wreath of giant sunflowers welcomed visitors. It could have looked a mess, but it didn't. There was order to the chaos. Everything was meticulously planted and trimmed and almost looked fake.

Jack took the steps to the porch, favoring his sore knee. He knocked on the door and waited. A few seconds later, a tall, lanky man appeared from around the side of the house, holding garden shears. He was in his early thirties and wore jeans, a flannel shirt, and work boots caked in mud, and walked with a loose gate like his limbs were only attached by tendon.

When he saw Jack, his eyes widened, and he immediately turned back.

"Excuse me," Jack called out as the man disappeared around the side of the house.

He reemerged a few seconds later. "You need something?"

"I'm looking for Eli Wren. I was told he's staying here."

The man hesitated. "He's in the kitchen—it's around back. The TV is on inside. It's probably why he didn't hear you."

"What about Harriet?" Jack asked. "Is she here?"

"No." The man shook his head. "She's running errands."

Jack came off the porch. "My name's Jack Martin." He extended a hand.

The man swallowed, then fumbled the gardening shears from his right hand to his left.

"Robbie," he replied. His handshake was clammy.

"No last name?"

"Cruz," the man replied. "Robbie Cruz."

"Nice to meet you, Robbie Cruz. Mind if I try the back door?"

Robbie hesitated, then led the way around the side of the house. Jack saw his grip tighten on the garden shears, turning his knuckles white. Something had him nervous.

The backyard was small but stuffed with plants and flowers. There was a dirt bike leaning against the garage. Harriet clearly kept Robbie busy.

"Back door." Robbie pointed with the clippers. "That's the kitchen."

"Thank you." Jack stepped onto the small covered porch

and heard the drone of a television somewhere inside. He knocked.

A few seconds later, Eli Wren opened the door and gawked. "Jack! Holy hell, I heard what happened. Come in." He pulled the door open farther. "Give me a minute while I shut off the idiot box in the living room. Have a seat."

Jack pulled out a chair at the breakfast table and took a seat, then looked over the small kitchen. It was a step back in time, with ancient-looking appliances and a linoleum tile floor. But it was immaculate—not a thing out of place. Sunlight streamed through a spot-free window over the sink, reflecting off the black laminate countertop polished to a high sheen. Except for a couple of canisters labeled for flour and sugar, and a set of knives attached to a magnet strip on the wall to the left of the sink, everything must have been stowed in the few cabinets and drawers.

A backpack leaned against a table leg, the same one Wren had with him at Pandora Cafe a few days earlier.

Something ticked behind him, and Jack twisted in his seat. A plastic clock in the shape of a cat hung on the wall, its tail swinging in rhythm with its bulging eyes, counting the seconds. Something about it gave Jack the creeps.

"Can I offer you a drink?" Wren asked, coming back into the kitchen. "Although there isn't much. Harriet disapproves of imbibing in things she deems sinful," he added, smiling.

Jack shook his head. "No, I'm fine. Thank you."

Wren took an empty chair. "Well, I don't believe that for a minute," he said, shaking his head. "I can see from the limp that you're *not* fine. Been in my fair share of scrapes. You need to take it easy. It'll take a day or two to get over the shock. Now, what the hell happened?"

Jack watched Wren closely as he recounted the explosion and his time stuck in the mine. When he finished talking, Wren scratched the back of his head, taking a moment to consider it all.

"Could have been leftover dynamite set decades ago but not detonated," he said. "But Dylan would have already tripped it. And there have been so many people in there since he died. It doesn't make sense. It's probably more likely that someone rigged it recently. But why would anyone do that?"

Jack agreed, seriously considering Kim O'Connor's theory that he was the intended target and wondering if she was right.

"You make someone mad?" Wren said, trying to lighten the mood. But the joke fell flat.

"Let me ask you something," Jack said, wanting to see Wren's reaction. "Where were you yesterday?"

"Yesterday?" He thought about it a moment. When he realized what Jack was implying, he leaned forward in the chair and shook his head. "Oh, come on, now, Jack. You don't seriously think I had anything to do with it."

"When was the last time you were up in Shudder Basin?"

Wren sat back. "I don't remember exactly, but I can tell you I wasn't there yesterday."

"When was the last time?"

"Hold on a minute, and I'll tell you." Wren pulled a red spiral notebook from his backpack and dropped it on the table, then flipped through the pages and pointed to an entry. "Right here. The last time I was in Shudder Basin was over two weeks ago." He spun the notebook around and pushed it across the table to Jack.

Wren's handwriting was difficult to read, but it was apparent the notebook was a log of his time in the mountains. Entries were listed chronologically by date and included the location where he had been each day.

Jack looked to where Wren was pointing and saw that—according to the diary—he was telling the truth. He had been in Marshall, Savage, and Gold King Basins during the past several days, but hadn't been anywhere near Shudder Basin in over two weeks.

Jack started to scan earlier dates, but Wren pulled the notebook back and shut it.

They spent the next few moments in heavy silence.

Jack was the first to speak. "I keep hearing your name in the same sentence as the Judas Mine. Why is that?"

"Because I'm looking for gold." Wren's friendly demeanor had disappeared. "And everything I've learned and seen indicates the Judas could be sitting right on top of it."

"Why not buy it from Sean?"

"Because I'm not in the real estate business."

"What if he let you in and you found something?"

"I'd pay him a fair share."

"But you'd need help. You couldn't mine it yourself. It would take a lifetime."

"Ah," Wren said, nodding. "You're talking about my crew. But that's not how it works." He settled back in the chair, getting comfortable. He ticked the points off on his fingers as he spoke. "My expeditions are always the same—even the undersea ones. First, I need proof that I'm onto something. Then comes funding—I need evidence to attract investors. Only *then* do I bring in my people—and a few others that I'll hire locally."

"I thought you funded your expeditions yourself."

Wren laughed. "That's how you go broke. I'm in the business of *making* money, not losing it. Oh, I'll put in plenty of my own, but with enough proof of the vein's existence, I'll have backers lined up to invest."

"Spread the risk, spread the wealth," Jack said.

Wren pointed at him and winked. "You're learning."

Jack thought a moment, studying the red cover of Wren's daily log and wondering if there was more to the story than what he was saying.

"I'm sure you have experience with dynamite."

Wren sat back again. "Of course I do. But I didn't have a damn thing to do with that explosion in the Judas."

From across the table, Jack saw the veins in his neck tense and decided to change the subject. "Tell me about your relationship with Harriet."

"Relationship?" Wren frowned. "I rent a room from her."

"It seems there's more to it than that."

The treasure hunter dropped his voice. "I might appear ancient to you, Jack, but Harriet is old enough to be my mother."

"That's not what I mean."

"Then what *do* you mean?"

Wren spent the next several minutes fidgeting and blinking while he answered Jack's questions—signs he was probably telling half-truths and lies. He also embellished the conversation with unrelated stories of adventure as a distraction.

Jack left the boardinghouse frustrated. Despite Wren having been evasive and still the prime suspect in Dylan Montgomery's murder, damned if Jack didn't still like him.

CHAPTER 57

JACK FOUND EARL'S Tavern nearly empty. Two men sat in a booth near the door, and Sean Sullivan was arranging liquor bottles on a shelf behind the bar.

It smelled of old wood and beer, and the light was dim, augmented by neon signs scattered around the room. Country music played from speakers somewhere overhead. Jack decided he could get used to the place if he wasn't careful.

When Sullivan caught Jack's reflection in the mirror, he whirled around. "Jack..." Anything else he had intended to say got caught in his throat. He set the bottle of tequila he was holding down on the counter.

Jack realized he should have expected the reaction. Sullivan had probably heard about the explosion in the mine—*his* mine.

Jack limped forward, holding up his bandaged hands. "Don't worry. I'm scratched up, but I'm fine." When the bartender didn't reply, he added, "And I don't believe in suing people for something they're not responsible for."

Even in the low light, Jack could tell Sullivan's face had drained of color, but he saw it relax.

Jack pulled out a stool. "Can I get a beer?"

"I heard what happened," Sullivan said without moving. "Everyone in town has."

"Yeah, it's been a wild twenty-four hours." When Sullivan didn't budge, Jack added, "A beer would help."

Sullivan shook his head. "Sorry, man. Tap or bottle?"

"Bottle will be fine."

He opened a refrigerator behind the bar. "Shiner Boch, right?"

"A bartender's memory never ceases to amaze me," Jack said, trying to lighten the mood.

"This one's on the house." Sullivan popped the bottle cap off, then hesitated. "I warned you about it. That mine is a death trap. I thought you were going up to see Corbin."

"I *did* see him." Jack took the bottle from his outstretched hand, careful not to drop it because of the bandages. He took a drink, then held the amber-colored bottle aloft, admiring the outline of the liquid inside. He couldn't remember a beer ever tasting as good. He sat back and, for the first time since the explosion, relaxed.

The front door swung open, flooding the room with light as Robbie Cruz stepped into the bar, holding a small paper bag. He pulled up when he saw Jack.

Robbie's gaze slid to Sullivan. "I can come back."

"No, it's alright," Sullivan said. "Just put it in the office."

Jack fell silent, sipping on the beer as he watched Robbie cross the room and disappear through a door in the back.

A few minutes later, he reemerged. Avoiding eye contact with Jack, he threw a hand up. "See ya, Sean."

"Interesting guy," Jack said when he was gone.

"Who? Robbie?" Sullivan chuckled as he pulled a couple of glasses down from a shelf. "Interesting is putting it mildly, don't you think?"

"I just saw him across town."

"It doesn't surprise me." Sullivan filled the glasses with beer on tap and set them on a tray. "Robbie does odd jobs all over town—cleaning, deliveries, stuff like that. He might even house-sit, but I wouldn't trust him."

"Dishonest?"

Sullivan shook his head. "No, just a knucklehead." He

slid the tray off the bar and carried it to the booth near the front. Jack watched him exchange words with the two men, who laughed at whatever he said.

When Sullivan was back behind the bar, Jack said, "I met a man named Bill Lockwood."

Sullivan was surprised and looked up. "Where was he?"

"At the New Sheridan."

"Is he staying there?"

"I don't know. He was there having breakfast. Why?"

Sullivan shook his head, dumping a bowl of uneaten peanuts into a small paper bag. "The guy ghosted me."

"He mentioned he was talking to you about buying the mine."

"*Had* been talking to me," Sullivan said, folding the top of the bag and setting it aside. "Like I said, he ghosted me."

Jack didn't mention Dylan's heir, feeling it wasn't his place to tell Sullivan if he didn't know. "Any idea why he's avoiding you?"

"No clue. Did he happen to mention anything to you about it?" When Jack didn't answer, he added, "Probably no chance of selling it to him now after what happened to you."

Another customer came in, and Sullivan helped him.

When he was back behind the bar, Jack asked, "Do you know Harriet Hughes?"

"The lady who owns the boardinghouse?"

Jack nodded.

"I've heard of her, but she's not a customer. Why?"

"Robbie was at her house earlier. It looked like he was gardening or something."

Sullivan nodded but didn't reply. He wiped liquid from the tray, tossed the rag under the bar, and gestured at the empty Shiner bottle. "Another round?"

Jack hadn't realized he had finished it. "No. One's good. I've still got work to do."

Sullivan tossed the bottle into the trash. "Shouldn't you be taking it easy after what happened?"

"Maybe I should. But I won't," Jack replied. "Not yet."

CHAPTER 58

Harriet opened the back door, saw Eli at the kitchen table, and felt a pang of guilt. She was going to renege on their deal. And although Ted said it wasn't a deal if it wasn't in writing, Harriet felt like a heel.

"Jack Martin came by," Eli said, looking up from whatever he was reading.

Harriet's heart clenched as she set the market bags on the counter. She kept her back to Eli, hiding her face. "The detective came to see me?"

"No. Came to see *me*. Nice enough fellow, but a bit intense. Then again, after what happened yesterday—"

"What did he want?"

"Now that I think about it, I'm not really sure. But I think it was to check if I had an alibi."

"An alibi?" Harriet pretended to busy herself unloading groceries. "For what?"

"He asked me where I was yesterday."

Harriet turned around, holding a cucumber. "He thinks *you* were responsible for the explosion in the mine?"

"You heard about it, too, then."

"Of course I have. Everyone in town has."

Eli thought about it a moment. "Well, he seems to think I could have had something to do with it."

"But that's ridiculous."

"Is it?"

"Of course it is," Harriet replied, wagging the cucumber at him. "Everyone knows someone like you couldn't have had anything to do with that."

Eli pretended to look stunned. "Now, Harriet, I find talk like that downright insulting. Who's to say I'm not capable of something as nefarious as trying to kill a man? You must think I'm a complete bore. And here I thought I was the mysterious type."

She frowned, confused. Eli let a smile curl the edges of his mouth, and she turned for the refrigerator.

"Your parents obviously needed to tan your backside more often than they did," she said, shaking her head. "Maybe you wouldn't be so insolent."

Eli laughed. "Seriously, though," he said, picking up the papers he'd been reading. "You can't tell what's in a man's heart by looking at his face."

He was right. Harriet had met plenty of people who weren't what they seemed.

There was a knock at the back door just before it opened. "Miss Harriet?"

"Come in, Robbie. I'm just putting away the groceries."

Robbie saw Eli and hesitated at the door. "Uh. Do you mind if we talk outside? It's—it's about them lupin bushes you want me to move."

"Bless your heart, Robbie," Eli said, looking up from his reading. "Harriet, you're going to work that poor boy to death. Moving flowers?"

"I'll be right out."

"Yes, ma'am." Robbie shut the door behind him.

Harriet sniffed, emptying the last bag. "I wouldn't have to move them if that old Jezebel down the street wouldn't lop off my blooms every summer. I oughta have Robbie burn that woman's house down instead."

Eli laughed.

Harriet folded the market bags and placed them in a

drawer. "I'll be right back. Dinner might be a few minutes later than usual." She started for the door but paused. "I don't suppose Abby's home?"

"Haven't seen her."

Harriet sighed. "If she doesn't get into that boarding school, I don't know what will become of the child." She left the kitchen and closed the door behind her.

Robbie was waiting, but Harriet was the first to speak. "I was thinking it might be better if we wait until spring to move the lupin," she said.

Robbie shook his head and shifted his weight nervously from one foot to the other. "That's not really what I needed to talk about."

"Well, spit it out then. What is this all about?"

"It's that detective."

Harriet stood still, waiting for him to continue.

"He was here, Ms. Harriet. He asked about you—and about Mr. Eli. He was watchin' me funny—lookin' at me all suspicious-like. And when I went over to the tavern, he was *there*. I think he suspects something."

"Now, Robbie, do you really think the famous Jack Martin is interested in what you're doing?"

"I *do*, Miss. Harriet," he insisted. "He's been turning up everywhere I go. Why, just the other day, I was walkin' by the bank, and out he comes. Acted like he didn't see me, but I know he did."

Harriet felt a knot in her stomach. "He was at the bank?"

"He was. He came walkin' out right as I—"

"Which bank?"

"The Bank & Trust. Then he was here at the house today and at the tavern."

Robbie continued to talk, but Harriet quit listening.

What business did Jack Martin have at the bank? Everyone knew he was staying in a trailer at the campground. Surely someone who lived like that didn't have enough money to bother going into a bank. But if he had been poking around asking questions, why hadn't Ted mentioned it when she was there earlier?

Harriet turned and stared into the mountains, thinking. She needed more time to get the deal done, but Jack Martin made her nervous.

Robbie was still talking, and Harriet laid her hand on his arm. "Now, Robbie, calm down. There's nothing for you to be worried about."

"But—"

"No buts. Have I ever told you wrong?"

He shook his head. "No, ma'am."

"No, I haven't," she said, releasing his arm. "And I'm not wrong now. I promise I won't let that detective ruin anything."

CHAPTER 59

ON HIS WAY to the campground, Jack thought of Eli Wren. Although Wren was wealthy enough to purchase the mine outright, he had insisted he didn't want to buy it. He wanted Sean Sullivan to let him have a look inside for free.

Jack wondered if Wren was a freeloading millionaire. He had encountered a handful during his career—people with a high net worth and an aversion to spending their own money, preferring to filch off others.

Sullivan had excused Wren's eccentric behavior by calling it "gold fever." But had the illness driven him mad enough to murder?

As Jack drove toward the campground, one thought led to another. Even if Wren *had* killed Dylan, his being responsible for the explosion in the Judas didn't make sense. Why would Wren bury a man alive in a mine he wanted to search? Then again, Corbin said the air in the adit was toxic. So, would it matter if that section had been sealed forever?

But something about the theory that Wren was a killer didn't sit right, and Jack hoped it wasn't because he liked the man.

Jack swung the truck into campsite twenty and shut off the engine. His knee was throbbing, and he regretted refusing a prescription for painkillers.

The sun had dropped behind the mountains, leaving the sky a dull gray haze.

He sat in the truck, thinking about everything that had happened since he'd left the trailer the day before. The shock he'd felt following the explosion was slowly morphing into anger. Jack knew that pretty soon he'd be mad as hell that someone had tried to kill him.

But for now he was mostly exhausted.

He got out of the truck and crossed through the patch of trees that separated campsites twenty and twenty-one and was surprised at what he saw.

Otto sat in a folding chair beside the river, a kerosene lamp flickering on the picnic table beside him. Sitting next to him on the tarp was the girl with auburn hair. She wore tattered shorts, a long-sleeve T-shirt, and hiking boots. She threw a stick across the shallow river that landed on the opposite bank and then laughed as Crockett and Red raced through the water to fetch it. Otto chuckled along with her.

"You've got a good arm," Jack said, coming closer.

The girl turned with a crooked smile, then blushed and scratched at her right arm.

"Well, look who finally decided to grace our presence," Otto grumbled, twisting in his chair.

Abby got up from the tarp and crossed the river, expertly hopping from stone to stone, keeping her boots dry.

Jack watched her play with the dogs on the far side. "Do you know her?" he asked his old friend.

"Who? Abby?" Otto pulled at his beard and nodded. "For over a year now."

Jack didn't remember seeing her there. "She's been to the campground?"

"Several times. She comes around now and then."

Jack had never noticed her there. Then again, he wasn't in the habit of paying attention to kids. He watched as she threw the stick downriver, then ran with the dogs to get it—a flurry of fur and pigtails, dancing and laughing in the waning daylight. Something about his previous encounter with her still haunted him. She was an odd child.

"How's the leg?"

Otto's gravelly voice brought Jack around. He looked to where the jeans pulled tight over his knee. "Hurts a little," he said. "But I'll be fine."

Otto looked him over and grunted. "I saw men carried out of the jungle in Nam that looked better."

"I didn't know you were in Vietnam."

"You didn't ask." He looked across the river at the girl and the dogs, his thoughts momentarily half a world away. He fished a pack of Camels from his shirt pocket and shook one out. "That pretty redheaded deputy told me what happened when she brought me Crockett."

"I hope it was alright that I had her bring him to you. I had some business to take care of in town and didn't know what else to do with him."

"It's always alright." Using a cheap Bic lighter, Otto lit the cigarette dangling from his lips. He then drew in a breath, causing the ash to burn fiery red.

Jack followed his gaze across the river to the girl. "Do you know a woman in town by the name of Harriet Hughes?"

"Went to school with her."

He turned to Otto. "Here in Telluride?"

"We didn't go nowhere else."

Jack took a moment to process the information. Telluride was a small town, but the web of connections among its residents continued to surprise him.

"I heard Abby lives with her," he said.

"She does."

"What do you know about her?"

Otto pulled the cigarette from his mouth and blew a ribbon of smoke toward the evening stars, taking his time to answer. The moon had risen, casting his face in a ghostly shadow.

"Abby's got a wild spirit," he finally answered. "I'd think she was part Ute if I didn't know better."

"What do you mean?"

He took another draw of the cigarette. "Spends most of her days in the mountains."

"Have you ever seen her up there?"

"Plenty of times."

Jack remembered seeing her in Shudder Basin. "Shouldn't she be in school?"

"From what I understand, she doesn't like it much." Otto studied the end of the cigarette, then hauled himself out of the chair, still holding it aloft. "I got four chapters left in the book I'm readin'," he said, starting for the tent. "I'll leave the flap unzipped for Red."

Jack sat in the vacated chair. A few minutes later, the girl was back across the river with the dogs, all three breathing heavily, fogging the air, the dogs wagging their tails.

Abby plopped down on the tarp at Jack's feet, then draped an arm across Crockett's back.

After a while, she looked up and pushed hair from her eyes. "You ever shoot somebody?"

The question took Jack by surprise. He didn't know how to answer it from someone so young. "I…uh…yeah, I have."

"Was it somebody bad?" she asked, staring up at him. "The guy you shot?" She had stopped petting the dog and was listening intently.

"Very bad," Jack answered, hoping she'd drop the subject. She thought about it, making him uncomfortable.

After a few seconds, she nodded and scratched her arm. "Then it was alright that you did it."

But it wasn't. Jack never thought it was "alright" when he shot someone. The times he'd done it, he'd had no other choice, but he was never comfortable with the decision.

He felt the need to say something. "It's never alright. But if the person poses an immediate danger or is threatening to harm someone, then sometimes it's necessary." The conversation was unsettling.

"So you only shoot people when you have to," she said, nodding. "Makes sense."

The conversation still didn't feel right, so he added, "But it's always more important to know when *not* to shoot," he insisted.

Abby frowned, thinking about what he'd said. After a few minutes, she asked, "Have you ever been shot?"

He wouldn't tell her that he'd been shot outside of Telluride a few months earlier—the memory was still too raw, and it could scare her. So he lied. "Luckily, I've never been shot."

She seemed relieved by the answer. Several seconds passed, and she had another question. "Has anyone ever shot at you and missed?"

Jack worried the questions might never end. "Several times," he admitted.

The girl's eyes grew wide. "Really?"

Jack nodded.

"Were you scared?"

"Of course I was scared."

"What happened?" she asked, excited.

Jack thought a moment, then told her about his encounter with Luther Byrd outside of Denver the year before. Abby asked question after question, but he gave a simplified version of being held at gunpoint. She sat riveted while he talked, listening to what had happened.

"You got so lucky," the girl exclaimed.

Amused by her curiosity and careful not to further aggravate his knee, Jack demonstrated the drop and roll technique he used to evade Byrd's shotgun blast.

"When you're in danger, it's important to keep a cool head," he told her. "You have to think clearly if you want to figure a way out."

She nodded dutifully and had more questions.

Although Jack typically guarded his past, avoiding discussions of old cases, he found himself revealing more to the girl than he would have to an adult. It could have been because of her innocent enthusiasm. But it was more likely because it felt safer to let his guard down around a child.

When she asked about his investigation into the murder of Dylan Montgomery, Jack turned the tables. "Did you know him?" he asked.

Abby shook her head. "No." She paused a moment. "I saw him around town, but I didn't know him." She scratched at her arm.

Jack stayed quiet, hoping she would fill the awkward silence. She knew more than she was saying.

But she dropped her eyes to the dogs and rubbed them fiercely.

Several minutes passed.

The daytime noises of the campground had grown quiet, and the sky burned with the light of a thousand stars.

Jack checked the time on his phone and saw that it was almost nine o'clock. "Shouldn't you be getting home?"

The girl got to her feet. "It's not really my home."

Even in the dark, Jack saw pain in her eyes and understood. He had learned that she'd been passed around among relatives for years and somehow ended up living with an old woman in Telluride. It couldn't have been easy.

"Do I need to walk you?" he asked.

"No, I can do it myself," she said. "I do it all the time."

He watched her give Crockett and Red a few last pets, then turn to go. At the campsite's edge, she turned back and waved.

"Goodbye, Jack," she hollered.

Jack nodded and whispered, "Good night, Abby." But she had already disappeared into the shadows.

Jack recognized the pain of a tortured childhood and had

questions about the girl's past and her family. But he knew to leave it alone. It wasn't his place.

Sensing the night was over, Red stood and yawned. Jack watched as he meandered to the tent, stuck his muzzle through the zipper, and then disappeared inside. Otto had a light on in the tent, casting the dog's shadow in silhouette against the canvas wall.

"Come on, Crockett," Jack said, starting for the trailer.

As he made his way to campsite twenty, he couldn't get the mysterious girl out of his mind. He suspected there was an old soul in the young body and that she was more intelligent than most children her age.

He thought of their first encounter on Main Street. Now she had shown up at the campground. It was as though she was intentionally seeking him out. But why?

Jack unlocked the trailer door and opened it, letting Crockett inside. As he closed it behind him, he wondered if Abby had been in the mountains the day Dylan died. She knew the way to Shudder Basin—Jack had seen her there.

The girl was a puzzle.

And there were still too many pieces missing.

CHAPTER 60

Friday, September 27

It was another glorious day in the mountains. Eli Wren shielded his eyes from the sun to study the turquoise sky, a stiff morning breeze chilling the exposed skin on his hands and face. He drew a deep breath, filling his lungs with the morning cold that felt like winter. As much as he loved exploring exotic oceans, only the Rockies made him feel so alive.

Although he didn't need to be in the mountains that morning, he wanted to be. He had found it was the best way to kill time. The alternative was to wait in town until finally given the green light to explore the Judas Mine.

The rock hammer in his backpack shifted, causing the pack to pull to one side. He stopped and repositioned it, distributing the weight evenly on both shoulders. An unfortunate accident while moving diving gear in the Caribbean a decade earlier had resulted in a dislocated collarbone. The recurring pain that flared up now and again reminded him that he was getting old. But facing his eventual mortality only fueled his drive to accomplish more. The thought of running out of time scared him.

It also made waiting on Harriet to get her ducks in a row even harder, and he hoped it wouldn't take much longer. Harriet had reassured him that it was only a matter of days, but her demeanor had changed recently. She had become evasive, even hesitant to talk about the mine, making Eli nervous.

Once he got the go-ahead, he would have to assemble a crew of men. There would be supplies to purchase and have shipped to the basin. But winter was approaching. And if he was to start work before the first major snow, he was running out of time.

But there were other hurdles.

Eli stopped at the edge of a steep embankment and swept his gaze over the forested canyon below, admiring the aspens mixed with pine that blanketed the slopes with a quilt of yellow and gold. As he scanned the far horizon, he thought of the other obstacles that could get in the way—the young girl, Robbie Cruz, and Jack Martin.

Eli suspected Robbie knew everything that had happened. Robbie was too close to the family, working nearly every day in Harriet's yard and the greenhouse. He hoped Robbie was smart enough to keep his mouth shut.

There was also the girl. Eli wondered how much the mischievous child knew. He had caught Abby eavesdropping on more than one conversation and suspected she had rifled through the things in his room. It would be harder to keep a child quiet.

Next, he thought of Jack Martin. Of the three, the detective posed the greatest threat to his plans. Although Martin was a nice enough fellow, he was getting dangerously close to discovering Harriet's secret. If he did, it could be catastrophic. It was that damned investigation. If only the sheriff hadn't asked for his help in solving Dylan Montgomery's murder.

The wind carried the sound of tumbling rock, and Eli turned and saw a figure in the distance. He was used to running into occasional hikers—or even Abby playing hooky now and then—but this was different. He had never seen this person in the mountains before.

He squinted into the wind, watching the figure come closer, and something inside him stirred and his heart beat faster. Remembering the rock hammer in his backpack, he wanted to reach for it but didn't.

Eli smiled nervously as the person approached. "Well, hello there," he said. But something about their demeanor was off, and he asked, "What are you doing all the way up here?"

When the person came closer without replying, Eli took a step back.

CHAPTER 61

JACK WAS AT his usual table at Pandora Cafe, massaging his swollen knee, glad that the cuts on his palms had scabbed over and were beginning to heal. They still hurt, but not as much as the day before—a small concession for feeling like he'd been hit by a semi.

"I thought I was going to have to come look for you," Judith said, sounding irritated. "What's the idea of getting yourself trapped in that old mine and not letting me know you're okay? I had to hear about it from a customer."

"I'm sorry."

She stood watching him, her eyes reflecting the gas flames from the fireplace beside the table. "Late start this morning?" She took a pad and pencil from her apron. "Can't say that I blame you with what you've been through the last forty-eight hours."

It was after ten thirty. Jack didn't mention he'd been up most of the night, tossing and turning, trying to find a position that didn't hurt. Finally falling asleep as the sun came up, he had slept soundly until Crockett woke him with wet kisses a few hours later.

"Seriously though," Judith said, her eyes filled with concern. "Are you alright?"

Jack smiled. "I've been better, but I'm fine."

She glanced over her shoulder with a worried expression,

then dropped her voice. "There's lots of tongues wagging about this not being an accident. Is there any truth to that?"

She searched his face, looking for reassurance he couldn't give her.

"I was clumsy," Jack finally said.

Judith stared at him. When it became apparent he wasn't going to say anything more, she frowned. "Well, alright," she said. "If you say so. But if you ever have to go back up there, you be more careful."

He nodded, glad she was letting the subject drop.

She had her pencil poised over the order pad. "Now, what can I get you?"

Before he could answer, the front door opened, and Kim O'Connor rushed inside. With her hand resting nervously on her sidearm, she scanned the crowd until her eyes locked on Jack. She made a beeline for his table, and the grave look on her face had him worried.

Judith saw her coming and stepped aside. The restaurant fell silent.

"Jack, you've got to come with me."

"What is it?"

"Tony asked me to find you," she said, out of breath. "A couple of hikers just found a body west of Royer's Gulch."

When Jack didn't reply, she stepped closer and added discreetly, "It's Eli Wren."

CHAPTER 62

KIM WAS ALREADY behind the wheel when Jack climbed into the Tahoe beside her.

"What happened?" he asked.

Her red ponytail swung as she shook her head. "We're not sure yet. But it looks like he fell."

Fell? Jack thought of the considerable time Eli had spent in the mountains since coming to Telluride. He was an experienced climber, having spent months in the Andes and the Himalayas, as well as the Rockies. How was it possible? Had Eli really fallen to his death less than a mile above town?

Jack didn't believe it. He glanced at the deputy as she drove and could tell by the muscles in her face and the way her hands worked the steering wheel that she didn't believe it either. Plus, why would Tony have sent her to find him if Eli's death was an accident?

"What do you know about the hikers who found him?" he asked.

"Husband and wife in their early fifties. Second homeowners from Florida. Got into town two days ago. They're clean." She swung the Tahoe onto Tomboy Road and headed higher into the mountains.

"Where were they?"

"On the trail below the road, just west of the gulch. They said they saw a backpack on the ground just off the footpath. It's a steep section on this side of the gulch. When they didn't see anyone around, they looked over the side and spotted him about twenty yards below."

"Was he conscious?"

She shook her head, sending the ponytail swinging again. "D-O-A. We're lucky they had cell service. They called the office as soon as they found him. Tony came up with some guys immediately."

"Did they see anyone else?"

"No one after they left town this morning. Which they said was around eight."

If the Florida couple hadn't seen anyone in the area near the time Eli fell, Jack worried they wouldn't be much help. Witnesses were sometimes prone to speculation, or worse—making things up—when offered the chance to participate in an investigation.

"Where's the couple now?"

"Still there."

"I'd like to talk to them."

Kim steered the Tahoe around a nasty switchback that had them bouncing in their seats. She was an expert driver, but a fast one. Jack rode with one hand on the door and the other on the dash to prevent him from losing his teeth.

The ride was jarring and steep, but they got there within minutes. Five vehicles were already at the scene—two from the sheriff's office, an unmarked truck, and a white van with Coroner painted on the side. The rear doors of the van were open, exposing a gurney and an empty body bag inside.

There was a flurry of activity—sheriff's personnel and civilians milling about. Two men in street clothes, probably with search and rescue, were lowering a basket over the side of the mountain.

"The trail's below us," Kim said when she saw Jack watching. "But the easiest way to get Eli out is from up here."

Jack walked toward the van, wondering what it meant. Eli

had been at the top of his suspect list for Dylan murder. But now Eli was dead.

His gaze raked the rugged landscape, knowing that every year a handful of people died from falls in the Rockies and that most happened because the deceased had ventured into terrain more challenging than their abilities.

The trail below them was difficult, but Jack had hiked it several times with Crockett and knew it wasn't particularly dangerous—especially for a climber as experienced as Eli.

Sheriff Tony Burns came up behind him. "Thank you for coming, Jack."

"Kim said he fell."

The sheriff shifted his weight from one foot to the other. "That's the working theory," he said, apparently not comfortable with it.

"Sheriff?" It was a man's voice from somewhere below.

Burns walked to the slope's edge where the rescue basket had disappeared. Jack followed him and looked down at the commotion. Investigators from the sheriff's office were taking photos and measurements. Others talked on their phone or were taking notes. Kim was already descending the rope and had almost reached them.

"What is it, Anders?" Burns called down the slope.

Jack remembered the tall, Nordic-looking member of search and rescue from a previous investigation.

"Greenwald wants to talk to you." The county coroner.

"Ah, hell," Burns said under his breath, turning for his truck. "I was hoping I wouldn't have to climb down." He took two harnesses from the bed. "You've climbed before?"

Jack glanced over the side of the mountain. It was steep but not treacherous. "I've done a little."

Burns tossed him one of the harnesses. "Well, strap in."

The sheriff went first, clipping on to the rope and slowly lowering his bulk to the trail below. Jack followed, grateful for the rubber lug soles of his Red Wings, and said a quick prayer of thanks when he reached the bottom. By the time he unclipped from the rope, Burns was clipped into the second set, preparing to descend farther.

"You're next," Anders said, grinning at Jack without humor.

Jack remembered why he didn't like the man and glanced over the side. The second descent was short, but it was steeper than the first. Where it flattened, providing a natural shelf, several people had gathered around the crumpled body of Eli Wren.

Burns had reached the shelf and motioned for Jack to follow.

Up close, Jack was surprised by the condition of Eli's body. There were gashes to his face and arms, and his legs had come to rest in an unnatural position. The fall should have been instantly fatal, but there was too much blood. Eli had been alive for some time before he died.

Despite having viewed countless bodies in his career, Jack had never gotten comfortable with the sight of death and looked away.

Mike Greenwald, the coroner, was talking. "You can see from the lacerations to the head and extremities that the deceased suffered severe injuries from the fall."

Jack hoped it had been an accident, that Eli had died of natural causes following the fall. It could mean a murderer was now off the streets, that karma had intervened, and justice was done.

"So the fall killed him?" Burns asked the coroner.

The look on Greenwald's face, and his hesitation, had Jack worried.

"It could have," the coroner said, then shook his head. "But I don't think it did."

Burns frowned. "What do you mean?"

Greenwald pointed to a spot on Eli's bloody scalp with his ballpoint pen. "This wound isn't indicative of one typically seen in a fall." He then turned and pointed to something away from the group, and everyone turned. "And then there's that."

Nearly twenty feet away, nowhere near the gruesome body—too far to have resulted from the fall—lay a large stone bathed in blood.

CHAPTER 63

Jack and Kim spent the drive back to town in silence, processing what they had learned.

As Eli lay helpless after falling, sustaining injuries that would have eventually been fatal, someone had taken a large rock and bashed him over the head, finishing him off. Jack shuddered, thinking it was a horrible way to die.

Something stirred inside him as he remembered the gregarious explorer's infectious laugh. Although Eli had always been at the top of his suspect list, Jack liked him. He had enjoyed their conversations, the endless stories of Eli's adventures across the globe. Although Jack was going to miss him, he knew there was no place in a murder investigation for emotion and pushed the feelings aside.

He ran through everything he knew as the deputy maneuvered the bumps and turns on the way back to town.

Eli's death made it unlikely he was responsible for Dylan's murder. What were the odds two killers had been walking the streets of Telluride at the same time? But if not Eli, then who? And why would Dylan's killer now want Eli dead?

Although the list of suspects had grown shorter with the murder of the famous treasure hunter, it raised more questions than it answered.

Next, Jack considered the explosion that had trapped him inside the Judas. He was now convinced someone had intended to bury him alive.

His cell phone buzzed. He pulled it from his pocket and saw that it was Archie Rochambeau. "Mind if I take this?" he asked the deputy.

"Not at all."

The Tahoe dropped into a rut washed out by the recent rain.

Jack held the phone to his ear with his left hand and held on to the grip above the door with his right. "Yeah, Arch. What do you have for me?"

"Man, where are you? Your voice is as jerky as a bag of Jack Link's. You alright, old buddy?"

Jack waited for the Tahoe to clear the rut before he answered. "I'm fine. Just on a rough road. What do you have for me?"

"Your nuclear power plant—the Coyote 1—is limping on its last electron."

"What do you mean?"

"Lawsuits, government fines. They filed for bankruptcy protection a few months ago to keep it going, but I don't know how they're still in business."

"Who's suing them?" he asked.

"Don't know, but I can find out—"

"Don't worry about it just yet. I'll let you know if I need it."

"Suit yourself."

So, Bill Lockwood's company was deep in debt, probably threatening his job. Why would someone facing unemployment be interested in an old mine? Was it another case of gold fever? Maybe Lockwood was, in fact, interested in mining it.

"Thanks, Arch."

"There's one more thing," Archie said before Jack could end the call. "I ran Lockwood's social. No priors, but he's got a property under contract not far from Telluride. It's outside a town called Ooo-something."

"Ouray," Jack said, pronouncing it *your-ray* like he'd heard it said dozens of times.

"Ouray," Archie repeated. "So, that's how you say it. I'll never understand why some towns are named in ways people won't know how to pronounce. You know there's a town in West Texas called Knippa? You'd think the 'K' was silent, that folks from there would call in 'Nippa.' But they articulate the 'K.' I drove through there once on the way to—"

"Arch," Jack interrupted, afraid of getting caught up in one of Rochambeau's notorious diatribes.

"Sorry, old buddy. You gotta be busy. Now, what was I saying?"

"Ouray."

"Oh, yeah. That town—Ouray. A title company there just ran a credit check on the Lockwood fellow. Seems he's buying a house on some acreage on the north side of town, just off the highway."

Jack thought of the little white house with the green roof and remembered the sale-pending sign just off the road.

"I know the place. Thanks, Arch." He ended the call.

A mine, now a house on several acres? It was a lot of spending for someone about to lose his job. It didn't make sense. Jack spent the next few minutes thinking about it and decided that maybe it did.

If Lockwood owned the property where he could control access to the Judas Mine—or at least monitor traffic—he could keep people out of the basin.

Jack remembered the rows of metal drums baking in the desert sun, and another piece of the puzzle fell into place. "Son of a bitch," he said under his breath.

"What was that?" Kim asked, making the last turn toward town.

"Nothing. Just talking to myself."

But it finally made sense. Lockwood wasn't interested in

gold. He was planning on using the Judas to store nuclear waste.

CHAPTER 64

The theory that Bill Lockwood was buying the property outside of Ouray to restrict access to Shudder Basin was the only one that made sense.

Jack thought of the shiny boots, the new hat, and the manicure—Lockwood had no intention of mining the Judas for gold. He intended to use it to illegally store nuclear waste.

The basin was far too remote for him to be concerned about the occasional hiker. A few well-placed No Trespassing signs threatening fines would take care of that. It was vehicle access from Ouray that Lockwood would want to control, or at least mitigate. Purchasing the property that flanked both sides of the only road that provided access would ensure that he did.

Jack wondered if there had been a connection between Lockwood and Eli.

"I'd like to talk to Harriet Hughes," he said when they reached town. If there was evidence among Eli's things in his room at the boardinghouse, Jack wanted to find it.

Kim glanced at him. "Now?"

"If you have time." He would rather go alone and not have her looking over his shoulder, but he knew it was unlikely Harriet would let him search Eli's room without the presence of law enforcement.

Kim made the turn onto Galena. "You know, Eli's not your case, Jack."

"Not yet."

She looked at him. "You think the murders are related?"

"Do you?" Kim was a good cop—green, but good—and Jack wasn't going to let her whitewash the dirty truth.

She took a moment to answer. "I *do* think they're related," she admitted reluctantly. "I just don't know how."

She was squeezing the steering wheel, working out her frustration. Jack had done it himself countless times. But being frustrated was an inherent part of the job of an investigator that she would have to get used to.

"I need a copy of today's incident report as soon as you get it," he said. "And the autopsy report. We'll go through both of them together. These murders are connected. We just need to figure out how."

She took her eyes off the road long enough to look at him and nod.

Harriet opened the front door and greeted Kim with a smile. But when she noticed Jack standing behind her, her face dropped.

"Can we come inside?" Kim asked.

Harriet hesitated, shifting her gaze from the deputy to Jack, then back again. "What's this about?"

"I think it would be better if we discussed it inside."

Harriet searched Kim's face for a few seconds, then pulled the door open wider. "Of course," she said. "Y'all come in."

She ushered them into the living room, where Harriet took an upholstered chair and waved them to the sofa, where they each took an end. For the next several minutes, Jack stayed quiet, letting Kim tell her what had happened to Eli, carefully leaving out their suspicion it was murder.

As she spoke, Harriet's eyes grew wide until she closed them and dropped her face into her hands. "This is horrible," she said, her voice trembling. "Poor Eli."

They gave her a moment.

"Harriet," Kim said. When she had her attention, she continued. "I'd like you to let Jack search Eli's room."

Harriet looked at Jack and frowned. "Why him?"

"Jack is helping with the investigation."

"I thought he was helping find out what happened to Dylan."

"He is."

"But why does he need to search Eli's room?" The horror of the truth hit her, and she brought her hand to her mouth. "Was Eli murdered? Was it because of the Judas?"

Jack was startled by her response. "Why would you think it had something to do with the mine?"

Harriet dropped her hands to her lap and massaged them nervously. "I—I don't know why I said that. It's just that Eli was always talking about the mine." She then turned to the deputy, her face contorted in disbelief. "Was he really murdered?"

Kim didn't answer her, probably not knowing what to say. She looked at Jack, and he jumped in.

"Harriet, the sheriff is determined to do everything he can to find out what happened to Eli. And I'm going to help him do it."

"But murder?" The sound of her voice had risen several octaves. She clutched the reading glasses that rested against her chest.

"We're going to investigate *every* possibility," Jack replied.

They gave her another minute, letting it sink in.

"Harriet," Kim said gently. "It would really help if Jack took a look at Eli's room."

Harriet shook her head, her eyes filling with tears. She kept one hand on her chest but swept the other in the direction of the stairs.

Kim looked at Jack and nodded. They had agreed in the car that she would keep Harriet occupied while he searched the room. He got up from the sofa.

The stairs went down to a basement and up to a second floor. Guessing that Eli Wren probably hadn't rented a room in the basement, Jack grabbed ahold of the banister and started up.

At the top of the stairs was a short hallway with three doors. The first was open, and Jack peered into the room and figured it belonged to Harriet. It smelled of roses and baby powder, reminding him of his grandmother. Pink floral paper covered the walls, and a four-poster bed with a peach quilt and matching pillows sat between two windows. The room was cluttered with knickknacks, porcelain figurines of flowers and birds carefully organized on crocheted doilies.

The remaining two doors on the floor were closed. Jack opened one and found it was a cedar closet. It smelled stale and woody. Long coats and old furs shared space with an assortment of shoes and snow boots set on the floor against the red walls.

He went to the third door, at the end of the hallway. When he opened it, he knew he'd hit pay dirt.

The room was simple but furnished tastefully with a bed, a single bedside table, a large wardrobe, and a desk. The doors to the wardrobe were open, exposing an array of canvas pants and expensive shirts Jack recognized as Eli's. They were arranged by color, each spaced equally from the other. Jack searched through the clothes but found nothing of interest.

Next, he looked through an assortment of papers and maps littering the small desk, hunting for anything to connect Eli with Bill Lockwood. There were charts and pages of numbers, geographic coordinates, and diagrams but nothing to suggest Lockwood knew the treasure hunter.

Jack pulled open the desk drawer and found office supplies. He sifted through it all, then went to the bedside table where Eli had set a Clive Cussler novel. The book was three inches thick and, from the illustration on the cover, appeared to be an adventure story set somewhere in the Caribbean. As

Jack flipped through the pages, a small scrap of paper slipped to the floor. He picked it up and noticed a phone number scribbled in pencil. He turned it over in his hand, but there was no name. He stuck the paper into his pocket and placed the book back on the bedside table.

Next, he went into the tiny connecting bathroom, and it was like stepping back in time. It was straight out of the '50s. Mint-green tiles covered the floor and the lower half of the walls. The fixtures included a white tub and toilet and a simple pedestal sink. A small window covered by sheer white curtains offered a view of the backyard.

Jack opened the small medicine cabinet above the sink and found a toothbrush, toothpaste, and a couple of prescription medicine bottles lined up with their labels facing out.

For an eccentric millionaire, Eli Wren had lived a life of relative simplicity, probably a necessity for a man who was always traveling the world. Except for the papers and maps strewn across the desk, the only remarkable thing about his living quarters was how clean and tidy they were.

Disappointed, Jack returned to the living room. When he walked in, Kim looked up, her eyes searching his, hopeful he'd found something. When he shook his head, her expression fell.

Jack spent several minutes questioning Harriet on Eli's comings and goings and if he had ever received visitors. Nothing Harriet told him shed light on why someone would want him dead. Eli had been a model guest who kept regular hours, leaving the boardinghouse early every morning and never returning too late at night. There were no women or rowdy visitors. No loud music or complaints about the room or the food.

The longer Harriet talked, the harder it became for her. Her eyes filled with tears again, and her voice caught in her throat.

When it was evident she couldn't add anything of significance to the investigation, Jack stood up from the couch and thanked her. There was no sense in putting her through the misery of more questions. She had obviously been fond of her most recent tenant and was now grieving his death.

"Thank you, Harriet," Kim said at the door, hugging her. "Someone will be in touch on what's going to happen with Eli's things. I expect you will want to relet the room as soon as you can."

Harriet dabbed at her eyes with a tissue. "There's no rush," she said, opening the front door.

"Well, if you need anything, you call me anytime."

Harriet smiled sadly. "I've got your number."

When they were back in the Tahoe, Kim turned to Jack and asked, "Did you find anything in Eli's room?"

He remembered the scrap of paper in his pocket. The telephone number was probably insignificant. Then again, it could be the clue to solving both murders. "I didn't find anything," he lied.

When they reached Main Street, Jack asked her to drop him off at the corner.

"Are you sure? I can take you to the campground."

"Thanks, but I've got a few things to do before I go back to the trailer."

"Suit yourself," she said as she pulled to the curb.

Jack unlocked the door and got out but turned back. "Get me copies of the crime scene and autopsy reports when you have them," he said. "We're going to figure this out."

Kim looked unsure but nodded.

"After the evidence is processed, I'd like to see the things in Eli's backpack." Jack wanted a look at Eli's red notebook, where the treasure hunter kept a detailed account of his daily activities. There was a good chance that if Eli had met with Bill Lockwood, it would be recorded in the diary.

Jack shut the door, tapped the Tahoe's hood, and waved

goodbye. He then waited for it to clear the rise, not wanting the deputy to see where he was headed next.

CHAPTER 65

When the Tahoe disappeared, Jack turned away from Main Street and started uphill. It was slow going as he favored his sore knee, trying to push the pain from his mind. He crossed over Harriet's street and kept climbing. His destination—the museum.

Upstairs, he went straight to the map of the mines above town and studied the spiderweb of tunnels and shafts crisscrossing each other. It took a minute to find what he was looking for—the location of Eli's murder.

He traced the distance from the crime scene to Shudder Basin and the Judas Mine, then studied the network of tunnels until he located the adit that had entombed him for almost twenty-four hours. Using his finger, he then followed the trail from the Judas back down the mountains to where Eli was found, wondering if he had been heading for the basin.

Had the killer accompanied him into the mountains that morning? Or had Eli encountered them on the trail?

Jack stepped back from the map, letting a visitor pass by, then glanced over the other exhibits in the room, thinking. Eli's murder was somehow connected to the Judas, and Jack scoured his brain, trying to figure out how. What was the motive for murder? Had Eli discovered something incriminating or gotten in the killer's way?

Dylan Montgomery had owned the mine. But why kill Eli? The famous treasure hunter only wanted access to search for a fabled lost vein of gold. He had no intention of buying it.

Then it dawned on Jack that, as a partner in the mine, Sean Sullivan's life could also be in danger. He decided to stop by Earl's Tavern on his way back to the campground and warn him.

Jack looked again at the map, and in particular at Shudder Basin. He spent several minutes checking whether there were any other mines besides the Crystal Lake that might overlap the Judas. When he decided there weren't any, Jack knew he would have to question Corbin again. Although the reclusive mountain man had rescued him from certain death, Corbin was still a suspect.

But Bill Lockwood now occupied the top of the list.

It was time for Jack to sit down with Tony Burns and reveal everything he had learned about Lockwood and the nuclear power plant. The sheriff would have to take the next steps. There would be surveillance, scouring through phone records, and interrogations. Since Jack wasn't with law enforcement, that was out of his hands. But he would damn sure insist on being informed. As far as Jack was concerned, it was still his investigation. And he wanted to ensure they nailed Dylan and Eli's murderer to the wall.

He took the stairs down to the museum's ground floor. Near the bottom, he spotted a black-and-white photograph hanging on the wall that stopped him short. It was of a man, probably mid-sixties, wearing overalls, work boots, and a determined expression on his face. He was standing at the entrance of what looked like the Judas.

Jack leaned in to read the plaque mounted below the photo and learned his name was Clarence Mercer.

"Mercer?" Jack said aloud. He had heard the name before.

The museum attendant chimed in. "That's old Clarence Mercer," she said. "Lived in these parts all his life. Interesting old guy. He—"

"Is that the Judas Mine?" he interrupted.

"It is. He owned it until—"

Owned it. Jack remembered what Otto had said about mines being passed down through families.

"Do any Mercers still live in the area?"

The woman seemed perturbed by the second interruption.

"I'm sorry," Jack said. "But it's important. Do you know if any of Clarence Mercer's descendants still live in Telluride?"

The woman's scowl softened. "As far as I know, there aren't any Mercers around these parts anymore."

But Jack had heard the name somewhere. He turned back to the photograph, searching his memory.

Behind him, the woman said, "No Mercers that I know of, but old Clarence does have one descendant still living in Telluride."

Jack whirled around, his pulse quickening.

"Who?" he asked.

"Her name is Harriet Hughes."

CHAPTER 66

Jack left the museum and immediately started for Harriet's. Remembering the scrap of paper he'd found beside Eli's bed, he pulled it from his pocket and glanced at the number. From the area code, he knew it was probably local. It could be nothing, he thought. Then again, it could solve it all.

As Jack limped from the museum, he punched the number into his phone.

"Hello?"

Jack was surprised when he recognized the voice. "Ted Hawthorne?"

"Speaking."

He took several more steps, not knowing what to say, not having expected the number to belong to the banker.

"Hello?" Hawthorne said again.

"Yeah, Ted. This is Jack Martin."

There was silence on the other end of the line.

"I want to know what business Eli had with the bank." He heard the other man scoff at the request.

"You may be some hotshot detective," he said, "but I've told you before—ongoing concerns of the bank will *never* be any of your business."

His smug tone irritated the hell out of Jack. "Eli's no longer an ongoing concern of yours. He's dead."

The line went quiet again.

"That's not true," Hawthorne finally managed to say, clearly surprised by the news. "I talked to him just yesterday."

"Well, he was murdered this morning." Jack reached Galena and took a left.

"What?" It had come out as a squeak.

"Eli was murdered this morning. Probably because of something to do with the mine. Now, listen to me, Ted. He had your phone number stuck in a book beside his bed. Nobody else's. Just yours. I know he did business with the bank, and I need to know what that was."

"No, no, no," Hawthorne repeated into the phone. "It can't be true."

Jack almost felt sorry for the man. "Ted, it's important."

"Give me a minute."

Jack took several steps before he continued. "Did Eli's business have something to do with the Judas?"

"Yes."

"What? I need to know. That mine's been a curse to everyone associated with it. There's been three murders because of it," Jack said, including Cindy Montgomery's. "And I have a feeling this isn't over. Help me out here, Ted."

Jack walked nearly a block before Hawthorne finally replied.

"Jack, listen to me." His voice had dropped to a whisper. "If people are being murdered because of that damn mine, then there's someone else in danger."

Jack stopped dead on the sidewalk. "Who?"

"You know more than you realize."

"What? What do I know?"

"I've said enough already." The banker clicked off the call.

"Damn it!" Jack exclaimed, then shoved his phone back into his pocket. What in the hell did he mean? Who was in danger? Was it Sean Sullivan? Or Harriet?

CHAPTER 67

Jack rang the front doorbell and waited, then looked through the window. He saw movement inside through the sheer curtains, but no one came to the door.

He had left Harriet's house less than an hour earlier. He was positive she was home, but for some reason, she wouldn't answer the door.

Jack went around the side of the house, determined to confront her about the mine. He wanted to know why she hadn't disclosed her connection to it and why she had kept her relationship to Clarence Mercer, the mine's previous owner, a secret.

When Jack reached the back of the house, he heard something rustling behind the garage, then heard a door shut.

He walked across the yard to investigate. But just as he reached the garage, Robbie Cruz appeared from around the corner, carrying a plastic jug used for spraying chemicals. When he saw Jack, he jumped.

"Sorry, Robbie. I didn't mean to scare you."

Robbie froze, unable to speak for a moment. "N-no problem, man." He shifted the container to conceal it behind his legs. "Can I help you with something?"

Jack was curious what he was hiding and wanted to ask, but decided to let it go. There wasn't time. "I'm looking for Harriet."

Robbie nodded at the house. "She's inside."

Jack held his stare a moment, making the younger man nervous, then turned for the back door.

It took several knocks, but Harriet finally answered. "Jack?" Her voice was strained, and her eyes were red from crying.

"I need to talk to you."

Her thin lips quivered. "I've told you everything I know about Eli—may he rest in peace."

"This isn't about Eli. It's about the Judas."

She took hold of the reading glasses that hung around her neck and worked them nervously. "I don't know what on earth I could possibly tell you about it."

Jack was tired of the secrets. "I know, Harriet," he said.

"You know what?"

"I know your grandfather owned it."

She shook her head.

"Clarence Mercer," Jack said. "I know he was your grandfather. And that he owned the Judas. Cindy must have been, what…your niece?"

Harriet's body went limp. "First cousin, once removed." She sighed, then pulled the door open wider. "Come inside."

They went into the kitchen.

She gestured for Jack to have a seat at the table. "Can I get you a glass of water?"

Jack pulled out a chair. "I need the truth, Harriet." A part of him felt bad for being brusque with the elderly woman. But there had been three murders and countless secrets. It was time for answers.

Harriet took the chair beside him. "What do you want to know?"

Jack laid both palms on the table. "Do you own the mine?"

"No."

"Harriet?"

"As God as my witness, Jack, I don't own a single share of that mine."

She looked him in the eye, never blinking, and Jack believed her.

"Then tell me how Dylan got ahold of it."

She sighed. "He was married to Cindy."

"I know that. But *you're* Clarence Mercer's heir, not Dylan."

"And I thank the Good Lord every day that he wasn't." There was acid in her reply.

"You didn't like him."

"Dylan?" She shifted in her seat, agitated. "No, I didn't like him. And I told Cindy that."

"But she was married to him."

Harriet's eyes flashed. "She wouldn't have been much longer. She was going to divorce him. I told her from the beginning that he was no good. If only she had listened to me, she would still be here."

Jack could tell that she instantly regretted having said it. She worked the glasses around her neck with her hands again.

"Harriet, I need to know the truth. Other people could be in danger." The revelation stirred something inside her. Jack wasn't sure what, but he pressed. "I heard a rumor that Dylan could have intentionally started the fire that killed Cindy. Is that what you meant by saying she would still be here?"

Harriet let the glass fall to her chest as her face went hard. "He *did* start that fire. Nobody will ever convince me he didn't."

"But why would he do it?"

"For the mine. Dylan knew that Cindy was going to divorce him, so he killed her before she could do it. He was always obsessed with that mine. But it wasn't his—it was *hers*."

"So why did he get it when Cindy died? Shouldn't you have inherited it? *You* were Clarence Mercer's heir."

"Dylan took control of it after the fire."

"And that made you angry."

"Dylan was a monster." Her eyes narrowed. "And as far as I'm concerned, his death wasn't an accident. It was justice."

Jack watched her, wondering if she was capable of murder. But Dylan had been killed inside the mine. There was no way Harriet could have gotten up to Shudder Basin.

Then he remembered Robbie. He made a mental note to ask Kim about Harriet's gardener.

"So you don't own *any* portion of the Judas?" Jack asked again.

"I told you I didn't."

"Does that mean it now belongs to Sean Sullivan?"

Harriet shrugged. "I don't know, but it's none of my business." Her lips twitched when she said it.

And Jack knew she was lying.

CHAPTER 68

It was early evening. Jack stopped at Pandora Cafe on the way back to the trailer—to rest his knee as much as for a bite to eat.

Judith approached the table and called over her shoulder, "Casey, bring Jack a bowl of chili and a glass of iced tea." She turned to him. "You look tired. The chili will give you energy—and put meat back on your bones. I think you lost ten pounds in that mine."

Jack hadn't thought about it but knew she was right. He was thin…and exhausted.

She thought of something else and turned back to the girl. "And bring him a large slice of that cherry pie."

Jack smiled. "And the pie is for?"

"Your limp. Cherries are good for inflammation." She stared at him a second, then winked.

The evening crowd was light, and she pulled out a chair and sat, then leaned in and whispered, "What happened to Eli?"

Jack shook his head. "Sheriff's looking into it."

Judith pinched her lips together. "But you went up there with Kim. Jack, Eli wasn't only one of my best customers; he was a friend."

Jack debated how much to tell her. "We don't exactly know what happened yet."

"I don't need *exactly*. Just tell me it was an accident."

When Jack didn't answer, she knew what it meant and sat back in the chair.

Jack leaned in. "We're going find out who did this."

She nodded silently, then took a napkin from the table and turned to the fireplace, putting her back to the room and staring into the flickering gas flames.

"There's something you can do to help."

"Anything," she said, dabbing her eyes.

"Explain Harriet's connection to the mine."

"Harriet?" She twisted in the chair to look at him. "What does she have to do with any of this?"

"Maybe nothing. But I need to find out."

Judith shook her head. "I can tell you for a fact that Harriet Hughes didn't have anything to do with Eli's murder. Or Dylan's."

"Then help me understand, Judith."

"How can I?"

"Have you ever heard Eli or Harriet mention a man by the name of Bill Lockwood?"

Judith frowned, thinking. "I don't think so," she said, shaking her head.

Jack took one of her hands. He risked angering her, but he had to press the issue. "Judith, I know Harriet owns the mine."

"You're wrong," she said, frowning, pulling back her hand. "Harriet isn't the one who inherited it."

"Then who did?"

She stared at him, and Jack saw the wheels in her head turning, trying to find a way out of the conversation.

"Judith, whoever owns the Judas Mine could be in danger. Three people have already been murdered—Dylan, Eli, and Cindy." He let it sink in. "I don't know what's going on yet, but I'm getting close."

She stared at him, and he continued. "I need to know who owns the mine."

Judith watched him a moment longer, then slowly shook her head, and Jack knew the conversation was going nowhere. She gave him some made-up excuse about being needed in the kitchen and got up from the table.

Jack spent the next several minutes staring into the dancing flames beside him, wondering what it was about the Judas Mine that had good people keeping so many secrets.

CHAPTER 69

JACK LIMPED DOWN Main Street toward the campground. Judith hadn't helped, but the chili and the cherry pie had. He felt a surge of energy and was even more determined than before to find out what in the hell was going on in Telluride.

Three people were dead—all somehow connected to the Judas Mine. One victim had owned it, the second wished he had, and the third had been dead set on finding its lost vein of gold. But what was the connection?

Jack thought about Dylan Montgomery, a man not liked, who some had even hated. Jack remembered the fury in Harriet's eyes as she talked of the fire.

But Harriet wasn't the only one who had a problem with Dylan. Even Opal and Ivy Waggoner had confessed to not liking him. Sean Sullivan had tolerated his former partner but readily admitted his shortcomings. And there was Vanessa Graham, the spurned ex-girlfriend who had been abused. But Vanessa and Sean had an alibi.

Jack knew that when he figured out who killed Dylan, he would know who murdered Eli.

At the top of the suspect list now was Bill Lockwood. Jack wondered if Dylan had rebuffed Lockwood's attempts to buy the mine. Had Dylan found out that Lockwood planned to use the Judas to store nuclear waste? Could it be what got him killed?

Nearing the campground, Jack crossed Main Street,

frustrated. None of his theories explained Lockwood's motive for killing Eli. Unlike Dylan, the famous explorer had been liked by everyone. Had Eli somehow gotten in Lockwood's way? Although Lockwood was his prime suspect, Jack wasn't ready to pull the trigger and say he was the only one. There were still others.

But it was time to call Tony Burns. Coyote 1was across state lines; the sheriff would have to pull in the FBI.

When Jack reached the campsite, he was surprised to find Abby playing with Crockett and Red, holding a stick aloft as the dogs danced around her.

"Where's Otto?" he asked as he got closer.

Crockett started for Jack, wagging his tail, until Abby threw the stick, sending both dogs racing. Jack was secretly hurt, but seeing the trio having so much fun warmed his heart and he quickly got over it.

"Otto went to the liquor store for cigarettes," Abby told him. "He asked if I would watch the dogs for him." She took the stick from Red's mouth and threw it again and giggled wildly as the dogs tangled and fell over each other to chase it.

The sun was flirting with the horizon, streaking the sky with soft shades of orange and pink. A gentle breeze had the pines whistling. Jack needed to call Tony but decided to wait. There was nothing the sheriff could do until morning.

After the last couple of days, an evening spent beside the gurgling water, watching the dogs play, was appealing. Jack took a folding chair from a compartment on the outside of the Airstream and set it beside the river. He started back to the trailer to grab a beer but stopped.

"Abby, you want a glass of water?"

"You got a soda?" The girl grinned her crooked smile and wiggled a pair of crossed fingers.

Jack smiled back and nodded. "Coming right up."

A few seconds later, he emerged from the trailer, a Shiner

in one hand and a Coke in the other. The girl took the soda and thanked him.

There was still no sign of Otto, and Jack was disappointed. He wanted to know more about Shudder Basin and the mine, hoping to discover why it elicited so many secrets.

He sank into the chair, and Abby sat on the ground at his feet. The dogs settled on the grass beside her, tired and panting.

Jack watched as she drank the soda. She was a peculiar child. But she lived with Harriet and Eli, which had Jack thinking. She could have seen or heard something that would help with the investigation. But Jack had to be careful—she might not know that Eli was dead.

"Look!" Abby shot an arm at an eagle circling overhead.

They watched the bird swoop and dip for several minutes as it danced in the wind. Then Red barked, scaring it away.

Abby laughed. "No, Red!" With one arm over the dog, she took another drink of the soda, spilling some. When she used her arm to mop it from her chin, the long sleeve of her shirt shifted, exposing several inches of skin above her wrist.

Jack recognized the silky scars of a burn, and the truth hit him like a sledgehammer. He felt the color drain from his face, and he set the beer on the grass.

He stared at her. "Abby?"

"Yeah?" The girl looked up and smiled the crooked grin, a Coca-Cola mustache across her upper lip.

"I need to ask you something." Jack waited until he had her attention. "Abby, is your last name Montgomery?"

She shook her head violently. "No way. Harriet changed it back after I came to Telluride."

"Back to what?"

"To my mama's last name," she said proudly.

"And what is that?" Jack asked, then held his breath.

The girl grinned again. "My last name's Mercer."

Abby Mercer?

It was the name Kim O'Connor had mentioned the week before.

One thought immediately led to another, sending them racing through Jack's mind.

Abby's mother's maiden name had been Mercer. And the girl lived with Harriet. It wasn't a coincidence—Jack didn't believe in them.

He shuffled the puzzle pieces and tried putting them together.

"Abby, what was your mother's name?"

She looked up, still petting the dog. "It was Cindy."

Cindy Mercer. Cindy Montgomery. Mercer had been her maiden name.

Jack felt his heart beat faster. If Abby was Cindy Montgomery's daughter, she would inherit the mine. Not Harriet.

Jack remembered the house fire and felt a lump catch in his throat. He looked down at the girl's arm, now covered again by her sleeve. She would have been just a baby but somehow had escaped the fire.

Abby finished the Coke, crushed the can with her hand and then held it aloft. "See, I'm stronger than I look." She was beaming.

"Abby, I need to ask you another question."

"Okey dokey."

Jack hated to do it; she was having so much fun, but he needed to know. "Abby, what's your father's name?"

A look of anger immediately replaced the smile on her face. She bent over Crockett to pet him.

When she didn't answer, Jack asked again, "Abby, what's your father's name?"

She shrugged, petting the dog harder. "I know what it used to be."

"*Used* to be?" She had used the past tense.

She was quiet, her back still to him. Then Jack saw her

drop her head and run a hand across her face. Was she crying? He didn't want to push too hard, but he didn't know what else to do. He needed the truth. And the girl could be in danger.

"Abby?"

"He's dead."

She stroked Crockett furiously. Suddenly, the dog darted to chase a squirrel, and Red followed, leaving Abby alone. Jack watched as her bony shoulders sagged and her small body began to quake.

He asked gently, "Abby, who's dead?"

The girl looked up, tears blazing in her large gray eyes. "The man they say was my father. But he wasn't my father. He was just some man. I heard Harriet tell Eli who he was, but I wish I never knew!"

Jack didn't understand her emotions and didn't know how to respond. "I'm sorry," he said. "I'm sure he wasn't that bad."

"But he *was* that bad, don't you see? He burned down his own house on purpose. He deserved to die. I didn't mean it, but he deserved to die." She bent forward and laid her head on the ground, crying.

Jack reached for her. "Abby—"

In a muffled voice between sobs, she said, "Bad people should die. Not good ones."

Jack was startled by her raw emotion; then it hit him without warning. She had said she didn't mean it. *Didn't mean what?*

When the horror of what she was saying hit him, Jack's breath caught in his throat. It took him a moment to recover.

"Abby," he said, struggling with the hideous truth. "Abby, did you shoot Dylan Montgomery? Did you shoot your father?"

She looked up. Her ponytail had come loose, and strands of auburn hair hung wildly around her face. "He wasn't my father!"

"But did you shoot him?"

She dropped her face to the ground again. "No." But after a while, she slowly nodded. In a shaking voice, her forehead resting on the ground, she quietly added, "Maybe."

Jack got out of the chair and sat beside her on the grass. "Abby, it's alright. Tell me what happened."

She faced him, drawing a forearm across her dripping nose. "He was talking to himself like he was crazy. I tried to be nice. But he didn't know who I was."

"You went to the mine?"

She nodded, pressing her hands against her eyes. "I went there a lot after I heard Harriet tell Eli that it was my mine. I followed Mr. Eli there one day. But he didn't know."

So it was true. Jack couldn't believe it. Abby Mercer was the heir to the Judas Mine.

"What happened when you saw Dylan?" Jack was almost afraid to ask, but he had to know.

"He was really mean to me," she said. "When I told him who I was, he said, 'I thought I got rid of you.' When I got mad, he said he could kill me and hide my body in the mine, and nobody would find me."

They were monstrous things to say to a child. Jack remembered that Dylan had been intoxicated when he died, but why would he threaten to kill the girl? When Jack caught another glimpse of the silky scar on her arm, it started to make sense.

"The fire," he said under his breath.

Abby was no longer crying, but her face was flushed with a child's fury. "He burnt our house down on purpose—with me and Mama in it. And Mama died." She fought back tears welling again in her eyes and dropped her voice to a whisper. "But I lived."

Jack heard the guilt beneath her grief and anger, and her pain suddenly became his own. He understood. Mothers gone too soon. Being unwanted and shuffled among relatives.

"He was so mean." She was crying again. "He said mean

things about Mama. He said she had to die and that he wished I did, too. And I saw a gun."

"Who's gun? Dylan's?"

She shrugged and shook her head. "I just saw it. And when he kept saying mean things, I picked it up and said I would shoot him if he didn't stop."

"And what did he do?"

"He started laughing at me." She had raised her voice again, pleading for him to understand. "He came closer like he was going to hurt me."

"It's alright, Abby," Jack said, trying to calm her. "Stop and take a deep breath."

But she didn't. "I only did it because he was going to hurt me," she said, wiping her nose. "I didn't mean to kill him—honest. But I shot him, and he fell back."

"It's okay, Abby."

She dropped her chin to her chest and quaked with silent sobs.

Every atom in Jack's body screamed for him to stop, but he continued. "What did you do after you shot him?"

"I ran."

"Where?"

"Home. I didn't want to be by myself. I wanted to be home with Harriet."

"I would have done the same thing," Jack said, reassuring her. But then he thought of the gun and realized she could be a danger to herself—or someone else—if she still had it. "Abby, what did you do with the gun?"

"It hurt my hand, so I dropped it. I never shot a gun before. And I never want to again." She got to her feet, wiping her eyes, and turned for town. "I want to go home now."

"Abby—"

But she disappeared into the trees.

Jack wasn't sure how long he sat there, processing what

had happened. He heard Otto return to his tent and whistle for Red.

Jack didn't move but continued staring into the blackness of the night, having gone numb from cold and disbelief, his heart frozen by a chain of events he wished he could somehow go back in time and undo.

How was it possible?

The girl. The freckles, the messy ponytail, and the crooked smile.

A mother, killed at the hands of her husband. Burned to death. And the child who had survived.

Jack's stomach lurched with nausea.

Dylan Montgomery had been a murderer. But he wasn't the only one.

The girl was a murderer, too.

Abby Mercer.

It meant someone else killed Eli.

But he couldn't get the girl out of his mind.

A murderer? It couldn't be true, but it was.

And now, Jack wondered, *just what in the hell do I do about it?*

CHAPTER 70

Saturday, September 28

ABBY WOKE BEFORE dawn and could feel that her eyes were swollen—from not sleeping or from hours of crying into her pillow. She didn't know which and didn't care.

She crawled out of bed, scratching her arm, then silently snuck up the stairs, careful not to wake Harriet.

She made a sandwich in the kitchen and stuffed it with a few other things into her backpack. Then, as quietly as her tiny hands could, she unlocked the back door, opened it, and slipped out into the dark.

Robbie was usually at the house when she left in the mornings, letting her hide her shoes in the greenhouse so Harriet wouldn't see that she had changed into hiking boots and gone into the mountains. But not that morning. It was still too early. Robbie wasn't there.

The detective was nice, but Abby knew that she had told him too much and worried about what would happen. He would probably tell Harriet. He might even go to the police. They could send her to jail. Or worse—they might send her back to Chicago.

Abby told herself she wanted to get away to think. But maybe she just wanted to hide. The only thing she knew for sure was that she needed to be back in the mountains.

She didn't know how long she would be gone but knew

exactly where she was going—the only place she could be alone. The only place in the world that was her own.

The Judas Mine.

CHAPTER 71

JACK'S DREAMS WERE haunted by images of a young girl holding a gun on her father, her small, pale hands gripping the weapon tightly but shaking. The man reached out to stop her. And although his lips moved, there were no words. A black void opened behind him, threatening to suck him inside as the cave's rock walls spun around them. Jack could feel the girl's anger and saw the fear on the man's face. And when a gunshot exploded—the only sound in the dream—it startled him awake.

Despite the chill in the trailer, Jack woke in a pool of sweat. He was drowsy, his head still swimming with a kaleidoscope of images from the dream. The beer he had downed the night before pounded in his ears.

As he woke slowly, his thoughts turned to Dylan Montgomery and the girl with the crooked smile. His memories of the conversation the night before came to him in warped confusion, and Jack prayed they had been part of the dream.

But lucidity finally brought him fully awake, and he remembered—the girl was a killer.

Crockett was lying on top of the covers, and Jack gently nudged him with his foot. "Let's go, boy. Time to get up."

He opened the door and let the dog out, then sat on the trailer's steps, letting the cold morning air wash over him. The night was still a blur, but he remembered that hearing Abby's confession was a burden too great for him to bear, and he had tried drinking away the shock.

As details of their conversation came flooding back, he remembered her tiny body quaking with emotion. She would live the rest of her life with the scars on her arm as a permanent reminder of a fire and a father who had tried to kill her.

Jack ran his hands through his hair, wondering how she would live with the memories. His heart broke for her, but he had to push his feelings aside.

But now, in the clarity of the morning, some things she had said didn't make sense. He couldn't put a finger on what they were and sat racking his brain. He massaged his throbbing temples, trying to recall her exact words. When they came to him, he froze.

Abby said that firing the gun had hurt her hand, and she dropped it. But law enforcement didn't find the weapon.

Jack's eyes shot open. But there was something else stuck in his subconscious he needed to work loose.

She said that she had fired a single shot, but investigators found *two* spent casing inside the mine.

Jack's pulse quickened. He stood and called for Crockett, then dashed back into the trailer. He pulled the investigation file from the cabinet over the sink, laid it on the table, and shuffled through its contents until he found what he was looking for.

As he studied the autopsy report, his mouth went dry. The bullet that killed Dylan Montgomery had entered through the left side of his back.

"His back," Jack said aloud.

But Abby had pulled the trigger as he had been coming toward her.

"She missed."

Jack threw the photo onto the table and turned for the bed. Feeling a surge of relief and adrenaline, he snatched the clothes he'd worn the day before from the floor and got dressed.

On his way out of the trailer, he grabbed the Glock from inside the bench under the table and stuck it into the waistband of his jeans.

It was still early, but he walked Crockett through the trees to Otto's tent and spoke through the flap. "Otto, are you awake?"

There was rustling inside. "Been up for nearly an hour."

"I know it's early, and I'm sorry, but can I leave Crockett with you?"

The old man unzipped the tent and stuck his head out. Jack could see Red dancing and wagging his tail inside.

"We would appreciate the company, wouldn't we, Red?" Otto's breath fogged the morning air. He unzipped the flap farther, releasing the excited hound, and stepped outside carrying a coffeepot. Within seconds, the dogs were hunting along the bank of the river.

"Thanks, Otto. I owe you one."

Jack got into his truck and saw that it was almost seven o'clock. Tony Burns would be at the office soon.

As Jack made his way through town, he remembered something else Abby had said; Dylan was talking to himself like he was crazy. Jack had thought it was because he was drunk but knew now that wasn't the reason why. There had been someone else in the mine.

The murderer shot Dylan nearly point-blank from behind. Not the girl, but a coward. And the same person killed Eli.

Jack squeezed the steering wheel and slowed the truck, letting a man cross the street. The man nodded and threw up a hand of thanks. His *right* hand.

Jack let the truck idle at the corner a moment, thinking.

The wound. The bullet had entered the left side of Dylan's back but exited near his navel. The shot was pointblank, meaning the killer was probably left-handed.

Jack accelerated and pounded the steering wheel with his fist. They had all missed it.

He glanced at the bank as he passed, wondering how Ted Hawthorne knew Abby was in danger. The mine had fallen into foreclosure before Dylan died. He must have known she'd inherited it and was working a deal with Eli. But Eli was dead.

Jack turned his attention back to the road and shook his head. "Not Eli?" he said aloud. "Bill Lockwood."

His thoughts then returned to the girl. *Abby.*

She was in danger. She owned the mine and was now the one in the killer's way. But Tony would be able to protect her.

So many pieces to the puzzle had fallen into place. But something significant still eluded him. Who had murdered Dylan Montgomery and Eli Wren?

Then he remembered the handwriting that had reminded him of his grandfather's.

And he knew.

CHAPTER 72

FOR A SECOND, Jack considered turning the truck around for Earl's Tavern, but it was early, and the bar would be closed. So he pressed the accelerator to the floorboard and sped past the turn for the sheriff's office. He was going to Norwood.

Vanessa Graham opened her front door wearing a robe.

"Where's Sean?" Jack asked her.

"I—I don't know. Why?"

"I know from his previous landlord that he's lived here before. And since he's been evicted, it's an easy guess that he's living here now."

Shame washed over her face. "Jack, I—"

"I'm not your father or your preacher. I don't give a damn who you live with. Now, where is he?"

Anger flashed in her eyes. "He left early this morning."

"Where did he go?"

"I don't know."

"Well, he's not here, and the bar isn't open yet. Did he go to Ridgway? Montrose?"

"I don't know. I don't keep tabs on him."

"But you lie for him."

She frowned. "What are you talking about?"

Her roommate stuck her head around the corner, eavesdropping. Vanessa stepped outside and closed the door.

"You lied to me," Jack repeated, bluffing. "You told me that you were with Sean the day Dylan was murdered."

"I *was* with him."

"The whole day?" From her silence, Jack had his answer. "How did he do it?"

"Do what?"

"Coerce you into giving him a false alibi."

"Alibi? What are you talking about?" She took in a quick breath.

"I need to know exactly what time you were with Sean that day. Be specific."

She shook her head. "I don't remember. It was a few hours, at most. Why? Is Sean in trouble?"

Jack didn't answer, and her eyes grew wide. "You think he killed Dylan?"

Jack stepped off the porch, debating how much to tell her. The killer was probably left-handed, and Sullivan was a lefty. Jack had noticed it when he'd written Vanessa's telephone number in stilted handwriting that reminded him of his grandfather's. It was a seemingly insignificant clue until viewed in the light of all the others.

But the evidence against Sullivan was mounting. He was the minority owner of the mine. Get rid of Dylan, and the Judas would be his to sell. Except, he didn't know about Abby.

Jack realized he should have considered Sullivan sooner. But Sullivan had claimed he was with Vanessa on the morning Dylan died, and she had corroborated his alibi.

"Jack," she said, getting his attention. "You don't honestly think Sean could have killed Dylan, do you?"

"That's what I'm trying to figure out."

She shook her head. "He told me that he was scared they'd think he did it—because he was Dylan's partner. They would think he killed him for the mine. But Sean didn't want anything to do with the mine."

"He was negotiating with a man who wanted to buy it from him," Jack said. "He would have made a lot of money."

She shook her head. "There's no way he killed Dylan.

He didn't like him—nobody did—but there's no way Sean killed..." Her voice trailed off as she considered the possibility. Suddenly, there was fear and uncertainty in her eyes.

"You need to think carefully about this, Vanessa. If Sean is guilty and you provided him with an alibi, that makes you an accessory."

She started to protest, but Jack cut her off.

"Unless you want to get into a lot of trouble for protecting him, you need to tell me exactly what you know about his whereabouts." He gave it a moment to sink in. "Now, what time were you *really* with him that day?"

Vanessa dropped into a rusted patio chair and held her head in her hands. "This can't be happening. He couldn't have."

"You need to listen to me," Jack said. "There could be someone else in danger. I need you to tell me exactly what time you were with Sean on the day Dylan was murdered."

With her head still buried in her hands, she said, "I wasn't."

CHAPTER 73

By the time Jack regained cell service, he was only a quarter mile from the sheriff's office.

"Come on, Tony—pick up, pick up."

It was the second time Jack had called but, again, the sheriff didn't answer. He called Kim O'Connor next.

"Sorry, Jack, it's not a good time. The media's gotten wind of Eli's death. We're up to our eyeballs in—"

"Kim, listen to me. Abby Mercer could be in danger."

"What? What are you talking about?"

"Meet me at the school. We need to find her."

"Jack, it's Saturday."

"Shit." Jack pounded a fist on the steering wheel. The girl could be anywhere. He quickly ran through several options in his mind. "Alright," he said. "Meet me at Harriet's."

"Jack, what's going on?"

"One more thing," he said. "Put out an APB on Sean Sullivan."

"Why?"

"Kim, just do it. Now!"

"Jack, you've gotta give me *something*. We don't issue APBs willy-nilly. We can't go around picking up citizens without a reason."

Jack knew she was right.

He took a deep breath, steadying his nerves. "There's a good chance Sean is responsible for the murders. And Abby could now be in danger. Just get to Harriet's. I'll explain it all when you get there."

She must have heard the urgency in his voice. After a few seconds, she replied, "I'm on my way."

Jack tossed the cell phone onto the passenger seat and pressed the accelerator as a multitude of worst-case scenarios raced through his mind. He had to find the girl.

Sean Sullivan was the killer. Jack was sure of it.

When he reached Harriet's, he rang the doorbell, and when no one answered, he sprinted around the side of the house and ran into Robbie Cruz. He had stepped out from behind the garage, carrying a box full of mason jars, but pulled up short when he saw Jack.

His eyes were bloodshot and wide with fear. "I—I only sell to friends," he said, taking a step back. "Honest, man. Just friends."

Jack glanced at the jars and saw they were filled with dried marijuana. It explained his behavior—and the greenhouse behind Harriet's garage.

"I got an idea," Robbie said nervously. "Maybe we can work a deal." He took a jar from the box and held it out.

Jack frowned. "I don't care about your weed, Robbie. Where's Abby?"

Robbie was confused by the question. He shrugged. "I haven't seen her."

"Is she home?"

"It's Saturday. She always goes into the mountains on the weekend. But you can ask Harriet."

Jack stepped onto the porch and opened the back door without knocking. "Harriet," he called into the house.

She entered the kitchen, clutching the glasses at her chest. "Jack? What on earth has gotten into you?"

"Where's Abby?"

There was a blank look on her face. "I don't know. She's probably in her room."

"Check and see."

"What's this all about?"

"Harriet, just make sure she's in her room. Kim's on her way here. We'll explain everything."

She frowned, considering his request, then turned and disappeared down the hall. Jack could hear her call down the stairs.

A few minutes later, she returned to the kitchen with an expression of concern. "She's not here. But I forgot it's Saturday. I can't keep that child out of the mountains—especially on the weekends."

"We need to find her."

Harriet became frightened. She pointed a bony finger at him. "Jack Martin, you tell me what's going on this instant, or you can wait outside until Kim gets here."

Jack steered her to the table and had her sit, then took the chair beside her. He needed to calm his own nerves, as well as hers. But he checked the time on his phone, growing more impatient. *Where is Kim?*

"I know Abby is Cindy's daughter," he said. Harriet's mouth fell open. "And I know that Dylan was her father."

"Who told you?"

"She did."

"Abby?"

"And that's not all. She said that she overheard you and Eli discussing the mine and figured out that it was hers. That's why she's been spending so much time up there."

Harriet groped for the glasses at her chest and shook her head. "I couldn't keep the child away from it. I insisted she never go back up there after…after what happened."

"After Dylan's murder," Jack finished for her.

She dropped the glasses and stared down at her hands, working them nervously in her lap. "I told her it wasn't safe."

Something was off. Jack watched her for a minute and knew she was still hiding something.

"You thought she killed him, didn't you?"

She looked up. "I don't know what you're talking about."

Jack came forward in the chair. "Yes, you do, Harriet. You know *exactly* what I'm talking about. You knew that Abby was in the mountains the day Dylan was murdered, didn't you? That's what you've been hiding. You've been afraid she killed him."

She started to say something but stopped and began to shake.

Worried she would topple out of the chair, Jack laid his hand on her arm. "Harriet, Abby didn't do it."

Her eyes filled with tears.

"She didn't kill Dylan," Jack said.

Harriet began to cry. "What have I done? Oh, that poor child."

"Tell me about Eli."

It took her a moment to compose herself. "Eli and I were working a deal."

"What kind of a deal?"

"It was for Abby," she said. "Eli was going to pay money to explore the mine. Abby was going to get a cut of the gold he found. She could have made millions."

"And what if he didn't find anything?"

"Then what harm would it have done? Abby doesn't have any money of her own. I'm leaving her what little I have, but that's not much. I was doing it for her—for that sweet child. But then Eli…" Her voice trailed off.

"Then Eli died."

She took Jack's hand in hers. "You have to believe me. This was always about Abby—about making it right for her after everything that's happened. I've had a long life, Jack. I've loved and lost. And now, with that dear child here, I'm blessed to be able to love again."

Jack looked into Harriet's eyes and saw her heart. He believed her.

She continued. "That mine doesn't deserve the reputation it has. It needs new karma. And I had hoped that Eli would change it." She fell silent a moment. "But then Ted Hawthorne told me he knows a man who wants to buy it outright. I forget his name…"

Jack felt things coming full circle. "Bill Lockwood," he said.

"That's it," she said. "Ted says he would pay cash. The amount of money is significant, and the deal would be a sure thing. He said that even though Abby wouldn't own the mine any longer, the man wanted to search for gold and could finally return the mine to its previous glory like my grandfather intended. He said people might call it the Budnick again, not the Judas. It's what my grandfather wanted to do but was never able to."

"Ted's lying."

She frowned. "What do you mean?"

"I don't have time to explain." Jack checked his phone again and got to his feet. "I can't wait any longer."

"Where are you going?"

"I have to find Abby."

"She'll be back tonight." Then her face slowly contorted with fear. "Jack, what's going on?"

"Do you have *any* idea where she could be?"

Harriet stood up and grabbed his arm, fighting back tears again. "Is she in danger? Tell me, Jack—is Abby in danger?"

"She could be."

"Oh no," Harriet said, bringing her trembling hand to her mouth. "God have mercy on that poor child. She's been through too much already." She pushed Jack toward the door. "Go, Jack. Please find her. You *have* to find her."

CHAPTER 74

As Jack closed the back door, Harriet's pleas to find Abby echoed in his ears. He stood in the yard, staring at the rocky cliffs above town, not knowing what to do next. Abby could be anywhere but was probably somewhere in the mountains.

He pulled his cell phone from his pocket.

"I'm almost there," Kim said, answering his call.

"We've got to find her before Sean Sullivan does."

"Jack, I don't think Sean's our man."

"What about the APB?"

"We got a hit in Ridgway. He filled up his motorcycle at the Shell station about an hour ago. Probably on his way to Montrose. He's not our guy."

But Jack knew that he was. He turned and looked back at the house, thinking. If Sullivan wasn't in Telluride, it would give them time to find the girl. Then it hit him.

"He's going to the mine."

"What?"

"Sean," Jack said. "He's not going to Montrose. He's going to the mine."

It was Saturday, and everyone knew that Abby went into the mountains on the weekends. If she went to the Judas, she would be easy pickings. Sullivan could make it look like an accident—push her off a cliff—or hide her body where no one would find her.

"We've got to get someone up there," Jack said.

"There's no time. If that's where he's headed, he's got over an hour head start on us."

"Damn it." Jack turned in the direction of the basin, thinking. "What about a helicopter?"

"There's no way we can get one that fast," Kim said. "I can call Ouray. We'll get someone from the sheriff's office over there to go up and check."

Jack shook his head. Even if they agreed to do it, there might not be enough time.

He noticed Robbie's dirt bike leaning against the garage. "I've got an idea."

"What?"

"Call Ouray. But I'm going up there."

"Jack—"

He ended the call and stuck the phone in his pocket. "Robbie!" he hollered, whirling around. "Robbie, where are you?"

Robbie came running from behind the garage. "What is it? You change your mind about the weed?"

"I need to borrow your bike." Jack was already on the motorcycle. He squeezed the clutch and kicked down on the starter lever. It was an older-model bike, but the engine roared to life. "When the deputy gets here, tell her that I'm on my way to Shudder Basin."

Jack twisted the throttle and raced out of the yard.

"Hey! Wait!" Robbie hollered behind him.

Jack took Tomboy Road above Telluride and headed up into the mountains. The bike jumped and lurched, in and out of ruts in the gravel road, speeding away from town. As Jack went higher, the air thinned and turned bitterly cold. His fingers, wrapped tight around the handlebars, were soon frozen stiff.

He wasn't sure how to get to the Judas from Telluride, so he stayed on the road as long as he could. He turned off at Marshall Basin and climbed higher.

The bike's engine screamed in protest as he bounced over rocks and around trees. He stopped several times to search for landmarks and finally spotted the familiar row of rock fingers, the vertical granite formations, in the gray cliffs above him. It was the entrance to Shudder Basin.

Ignoring the pain in his knee, Jack left the bike behind when it became impossible to ride it any higher. He would have to go the rest of the way on foot.

After twenty minutes of navigating crevasses and dangerous scree fields of broken rock, the gaping black hole of the Judas Mine finally came into view.

Jack raked the surroundings with his eyes, checking for movement, then started forward. A few seconds later, when he heard a girl scream, he began to run.

She was there. Abby was inside the Judas.

Already out of breath, he felt his heart race faster. He took cover just outside the mine's entrance, then stopped to listen and heard voices inside. He pulled the pistol from beneath his shirt and released the magazine, then pushed out the cartridges, counting them into his scabbed palm.

With the magazine back in the pistol, he leaned over and hollered into the mine, "Abby?"

"I'm here!" she screamed.

"Shut up."

Jack recognized the voice. "Sean, I'm coming in," he called out, then stepped from behind the entrance and into the mine, not knowing what he was walking into.

"Jack!"

Abby's scream caused Jack's blood to run cold, and he heard a scuffle. The light inside the mine was dim, and it took a second for his eyes to adjust.

"Don't do anything stupid, Sean," he said and heard the other man laugh.

When his eyes adjusted, Jack quickly assessed the situation. What he saw terrified him, and he stood frozen.

Sullivan had grabbed Abby from behind and was holding a knife to her throat. The child had gone stiff from fear, her large eyes even more enormous. A lantern glowed on the ground at their feet. A bag of chips and a half-eaten sandwich lay beside it. Sullivan had surprised her while she ate.

Jack held the gun out in front of him. "Put the knife down."

Sullivan laughed again. "Or what? You'll shoot me?" His voice was strange, almost detached from the man Jack thought he knew. "Throw the gun down, or I slit her throat."

He jerked the girl closer, and she whimpered.

Jack slowly lifted his hands, still holding the gun. "Why, Sean? What's in it for you?" Outwardly, Jack was calm, but his heart was hammering in his chest.

"I would have gotten a cut of the deal if Dylan had sold it."

"To Bill Lockwood."

Sullivan smiled without humor. "You've done your research. But Eli got to Dylan, and he balked on the sale. Damn fool had Dylan convinced he could find gold. Dylan was an idiot."

"So you killed him."

Sullivan took a moment to answer. "All he had to do was sell out to Lockwood—we would have made a killing. But along comes Eli, filling his head with dreams about being rich and famous." He shook his head. "Lockwood would have been a guaranteed payday. Dylan was going to do it until Eli got in the way."

"But the mine's in foreclosure now. You're going to lose your share."

"Not if I sell it to Lockwood first and pay off the loan."

"Except now the girl's in the way." When Sullivan didn't reply, Jack asked, "How did you know?"

"Eli. He was running his mouth. Mentioned that banker

told him Dylan had an heir. So I paid the man a visit." He grinned, but Jack wasn't amused.

"Why kill Eli?"

"He was in the way. Going all over town, bragging to anyone who'd listen that he knew where the gold was. It wasn't much of a stretch to figure out he was talking about the Judas. Eli needed to be shut up. Permanently. Lockwood was gonna get spooked if people suddenly started paying attention. It was going to kill the deal."

"What if someone had found out what Lockwood was planning to do with the mine?"

Sullivan grinned again, then took the knife from Abby's throat long enough to point it at Jack. "I'm impressed. You really *have* done your research, Martin."

He laid the knife against the girl's throat again, and Jack took a step closer.

Sullivan shook his head. "Stay where you are. I don't want to have to kill a kid," he said. "Give me the gun."

Jack looked into Abby's eyes, and she shook her head, telling him not to do it. She was a smart kid. She thought that by turning over the gun, Jack would seal their fate. But Jack knew better. He had a plan.

Jack turned the gun around, holding it by the muzzle, and stepped forward.

Sullivan took it from his outstretched hand. "I was thinking I should have kept Dylan's," he said. "But yours will do just fine." He folded the knife and tucked it into the back pocket of his jeans.

"What did you do with it?" Jack asked, wanting to keep him talking.

"Well, you, of all people, should know that I had to get rid of it," he said. "It's a rookie mistake to get caught with the weapon."

"Where is it?"

"In the San Miguel River outside of town."

"So that's how you did it," Jack said, putting more pieces to the puzzle together. "You killed Dylan, then got back to Telluride in time to be there when the boys who found him got to town."

"Nice alibi, huh?" Sullivan smirked. "Helping the sheriff find the mine was a nice touch, too, don't you think?"

"That, and getting Vanessa to lie for you." Sullivan's smirk was gone. Jack now had his full attention. "How'd you get her to do it?"

"Threatening a drug addict is easier than you would think. Tell them you'll turn them in for breaking conditions of parole. Besides, I had photos I could have used against her." He smiled, proud of how he had covered all his bases.

Jack was disgusted. "Nothing says coward like blackmailing a woman."

Sullivan's eyes narrowed, and Jack saw the monster inside.

"The blast should have sealed you in that worthless tunnel." When Jack didn't reply, he added, "Yeah, that was my handiwork, too. Working road construction all those years finally paid off. But it should have killed you."

"How did you know I would be here?"

Sullivan scoffed. "You practically told me the night before. When you said you were coming up to see Corbin, I figured you couldn't resist another look inside the crime scene."

Sullivan had read him like a book, which made Jack angry.

He locked eyes with Abby. "It's going to be okay," he said, trying to reassure her. "Do you remember the story I told you about my friend Luther Byrd?"

The girl frowned, confused. After a few seconds, recognition registered in her eyes, and she blinked twice.

"Sorry, folks," Sullivan interrupted. "There's no time for trips down memory lane. Now, we're going to all take a walk a little farther back into the mine."

There was no way Jack was going to let that happen. "Abby? Do you remember?"

She blinked twice again. She was smart.

"Now!" Jack yelled.

The girl elbowed Sullivan in the gut, loosening his grip enough to drop to the ground and roll to the side.

Sullivan hesitated, surprised by the move. He raised the pistol at Jack and pulled the trigger. But the gun was empty.

Jack lunged, falling on top of the other man before he could reach the knife in his pocket. The two men kicked and clawed, rolling over and over, stirring up mud and toppling the lantern.

Jack's injured knee crashed into the cold steel of the mine's rail track, shooting a bolt of pain up his leg and into his hip. He cried out in agony and heard the girl scream.

Sullivan's fists seemed to come from every direction, and Jack felt the wounds on his hands reopen and bleed.

Jack threw a punch that missed.

Sullivan had rolled to his side. When he started to get up, Jack swept him with his good leg, and Sullivan fell back to the ground.

Jack jumped on him. Then, with the last ounce of strength he could muster, he lifted Sullivan's head and slammed it down onto one of the metal rails.

CHAPTER 75

Tuesday, October 1

It had been three days since the fight with Sean Sullivan in the Judas Mine. Jack was happy to finally have nothing to do but sit alongside the river with Otto, watching the dogs romp in the water.

After Jack had explained to Tony Burns that Bill Lockwood probably intended to illegally store nuclear waste in the mine, the sheriff had alerted the FBI, which, in turn, alerted both the Nuclear Regulatory Commission and the Environmental Protection Agency. It meant hour after hour of sitting in a windowless interrogation room, being questioned by various law enforcement agents and bureaucrats.

And there was the press conference. Eli Wren's murder had attracted the attention of media outlets worldwide, many of which had quickly descended on Telluride looking for a salacious story. The San Miguel County Sheriff's Office and the FBI had held a joint press conference. Both agencies had insisted on Jack's participation.

Although Jack had spent his career doing everything he could to avoid the media, he had attended out of respect for Tony. However, when it was time to stand before the crowd of reporters and cameras, he had strategically chosen a spot in the back—close enough to the talking heads to be photographed, proving he was there, yet strategically positioned to sneak away once reporters started asking questions.

Kim later told Jack that several questions had been for him. The media wanted a firsthand account of how the famous detective had apprehended Sean Sullivan—the man responsible for murdering the celebrity treasure hunter.

Jack wasn't surprised when Kim told him there was very little interest in the death of Dylan Montgomery. But Eli's murder was big news that captured the attention of both mainstream media and paparazzi. And Jack knew from experience that he hadn't heard the last from them yet.

But for now he was content to sit beside the river.

He had turned off his cell phone after the fight and had no intention of turning it back on anytime soon.

Otto sat beside him, pulling at his beard. "You mean to tell me you walked right in there unarmed?"

"I had my pistol," Jack said. "So, technically, I wasn't unarmed."

"But it didn't have any bullets in it."

"I had put them in my pocket. But Sullivan didn't know that. I couldn't risk an accident with Abby in there with him."

"Where was Burns?"

"On his way," Jack replied. "Tony called the sheriff in Ouray before he left Telluride. They immediately dispatched a couple of their deputies to the basin and found Sullivan's motorcycle just below the mine. It threw everything into high gear. By that time, Tony and a couple of his guys weren't far behind."

Otto sat quietly for a while, pulling at his beard as he processed the information. He'd heard some of what had happened on the police scanner he kept in his tent. But there were gaps in the story he needed Jack to fill.

After a few minutes, Otto shook his head. "So, the son of a bitch was going to kill the girl." He leaned over and spat on the ground. "There's a special place in hell for a man who'd hurt a child."

Jack nodded, massaging his knee. Following the fight, it

was bandaged again. Although the fresh swelling had subsided some, he knew it would be a few more days before he would walk without a limp.

Otto chuckled, still contemplating the story. "And Opal and Ivy were in on Harriet's secret all along?"

"Harriet wanted to protect Abby," Jack replied. "None of them would talk about Cindy or the fire either. Harriet was convinced Abby had something to do with Dylan's murder, so she swore them all to secrecy. Deputy O'Connor admitted that she didn't know for sure but had suspected it, too."

"And that banker?"

Jack thought about his conversation with Ted Hawthorne after Sullivan was arrested. "Ted was between a rock and a hard place. He was about to take back the Judas as collateral for a loan, but didn't want it. Especially with the reputation that it was cursed. It was going to be nearly impossible to sell. He was afraid he'd be stuck with it forever, putting a financial burden on the bank."

"So he thought he'd make a mint selling it to store nuclear waste instead." Otto shook his head. "Bankers," he muttered under his breath.

Jack continued. "Once he started foreclosure, he found out Dylan had an heir and panicked. But when he found out it was Abby, he convinced Harriet to let him help sell the mine to Lockwood, thinking he'd collect a large finder's fee. The deal would probably have been unethical, if not illegal, but he didn't care. It would have been a win for everyone. Who was going to complain? Harriet didn't know about the nuclear waste."

Crockett brought Jack a stick, and he hurled it across the river, then picked at a new scab on his palm. Several of the wounds on his hands had reopened during the fight, but they were beginning to heal. His body was on the mend, but his mind needed a few more days to process what had happened.

Otto pushed on the arms of the chair and struggled to

stand. "I forgot I had something for you," he said. "Hold on a minute. I'll be right back."

Jack watched him hobble toward the tent using his cane. When he heard footsteps on the campground's gravel road, he turned and saw Abby walking toward him.

She wore shorts and a T-shirt that covered her arms. And she wasn't wearing shoes. She had a long face but smiled when the dogs came bounding out of the river to greet her. Although they were soaking wet, she draped a skinny arm over each of their backs, giving them hugs and not seeming to notice.

Thinking of everything that had happened in the girl's short life, Jack's heart went out to her. He hadn't seen her since the incident in the mine and thought she looked even younger and more vulnerable than before.

"I came to tell you goodbye," she said, rubbing the dogs.

"Where are you going?"

"Harriet's sending me to that boarding school in Dallas." She sighed. "They heard about what happened and gave me a skawler-something."

Jack thought for a minute. "A scholarship?"

She shrugged, then laid her head on Crockett. "Something like that," she said. "It means I can go there without paying."

"I've heard of scholarships," Jack said. "As a matter of fact, I got one a long time ago, too."

Her eyes lit up, "You did? They felt sorry for you, too?"

Jack laughed. "No, I had to play football for mine."

"Football?" She scrunched up her nose.

The dogs took off in pursuit of a squirrel, and Abby stood up and shrugged. "Harriet's taking me to Montrose tomorrow," she said, watching the dogs with a wistful look. "We're going on an airplane to Dallas."

Her sadness was palpable. Jack didn't know what to say, so he remained quiet.

After a while, she turned back to him. "Do you think there are mountains in Dallas?"

Jack suppressed a smile. "No, I'm afraid not," he said, thinking of the city's acres of concrete and steel. When he saw her face fall, he quickly added, "But I used to live in Texas. The people are nice there. I think you're going to like it."

Abby looked at him skeptically, then smiled. "You're just saying that to make me feel better. You're a fibber."

Jack chuckled. "I'm *not* a fibber."

"Are, too." She laughed.

For a moment she looked like the happy, carefree kid she should have always been. It reminded Jack of his own childhood, growing up in Baton Rouge, and the memories that both haunted him and made him smile.

Her expression turned serious again. "I remembered what you said you did when that man tried to shoot you."

Jack was confused, then realized she was talking about Luther Byrd and the drop and roll technique he had used to evade gunfire.

"You did remember."

"Now I did it too."

Jack smiled. "You're very smart," he said. "And very, very brave."

She blushed at the compliment. "I saved us." A few beats later, she added softly, "I think my mama would be proud of me."

Jack's hurt nearly burst his chest. He pushed down the lump in his throat and blinked back the threat of tears.

"I *know* your mama would be proud," he said and saw her lips curl at the edges, giving him a hint of the quirky, crooked smile.

"Maybe I'll be a famous detective like you one day."

Jack smiled and nodded. "Maybe you will."

Abby kicked at the ground with her bare feet. "Well, I have to go now," she said. "Harriet thinks I'm packing."

Without waiting for a reply, she turned and waved to the dogs. "Bye, Crockett. Bye, Red."

Otto emerged from the tent in time to see her disappear into the trees. He came closer, holding his cane in one hand and a letter in the other. "Was that Abby?"

"She's leaving."

"Going to that boarding school in Dallas. But she'll be back."

Jack was surprised. "You knew?"

Otto handed him the letter.

"What's this?"

"Picked it up for you when I was at the post office yesterday. Looks important."

Jack read the return address on the envelope, then slid a finger under the flap and tore it open.

Otto was cleaning the undersides of his fingernails with a pocketknife, pretending not to notice. When he couldn't stand it any longer, he asked, "None of my business, but what is it?"

Jack was still studying the official-looking certificate, double-checking the spelling of his name.

"It's a detective license," he said, running his thumb over the embossed gold seal at the bottom. "From the State of Colorado."

Otto grunted. "I guess some piece of paper from the state makes you legitimate."

There was a twinkle in the old man's blue eyes, and Jack smiled.

"I guess it does."

ACKNOWLEDGMENT

Echoes in the Dark depicts several real locations in and around Telluride and Ouray, Colorado, but all events and characters are entirely fictional. Anything negatively portrayed is done so purely for literary effect.

Shudder Basin and the Judas Mine are fictional locations created for the story, but I can't tell you how much fun I had imagining them and bringing them to life. I've wanted to write a mystery set underground in the Rockies for several years, and a tour of the historic Bachelor Syracuse mine outside of Ouray a couple of summers ago provided the timely inspiration for *Echoes in the Dark*.

It's not a secret that I've had a long-running fascination with the subterranean world, even occasionally suggesting to my children in jest through the years that I must have been a prospector or spelunker in a previous life, eliciting responses ranging from laughter to groans of exasperation because, although my fascination with stories of extreme adventure is well known, so is the fact that, in the event of heightened danger, my mental and physical shortcomings would undoubtedly result in my quick demise!

But if I can't live one of the stories of adventure I love to read, the next best thing is to write one. And I've had a lot of help along the way.

First, to my husband, Chris, who has followed me underground into caves, caverns, and mines more times than he would want to admit. A heartfelt thanks for his continued unwavering support of my writing journey.

To my editor, Kristen Weber. I thank my lucky stars every

day that she continues to help me write a better story than I can write on my own.

Thank you to my brother-in-law, Sid Cauthorn, for once again answering a slew of questions about banking. And who, by the way, is a much nicer (and more ethical) banker than Ted Hawthorne!

A very special thanks to my daughter, Abby, who has hounded me relentlessly for years to name a major character after her in one of my books. Although I never model characters after real people, she provided much of the inspiration for Abby in *Echoes in the Dark*. My 'real' Abby might not share her fictional namesake's freckles or proclivity for going barefoot, but I hope she recognizes her curiosity and kindness as her own. I also hope she enjoys reading the fictional Abby's story as much as I loved writing it!

And finally, a huge shoutout to you, the reader. I can't thank you enough for your ongoing support and encouragement. I love continuing to hear from you more than I can say. Thank you for your messages, emails, letters, and reviews. You're the reason I keep writing, so please stay in touch!

Printed in Dunstable, United Kingdom

SUSAN SCARLETT
SUMMER PUDDING

SUSAN Scarlett is a pseudonym of the author Noel Streatfeild (1895-1986). She was born in Sussex, England, the second of five surviving children of William Champion Streatfeild, later the Bishop of Lewes, and Janet Venn. As a child she showed an interest in acting, and upon reaching adulthood sought a career in theatre, which she pursued for ten years, in addition to modelling. Her familiarity with the stage was the basis for many of her popular books.

Her first children's book was *Ballet Shoes* (1936), which launched a successful career writing for children. In addition to children's books and memoirs, she also wrote fiction for adults, including romantic novels under the name 'Susan Scarlett'. The twelve Susan Scarlett novels are now republished by Dean Street Press.

Noel Streatfeild was appointed an Officer of the Order of the British Empire (OBE) in 1983.

ADULT FICTION BY NOEL STREATFEILD

As Noel Streatfeild

The Whicharts (1931)

Parson's Nine (1932)

Tops and Bottoms (1933)

A Shepherdess of Sheep (1934)

It Pays to be Good (1936)

Caroline England (1937)

Luke (1939)

The Winter is Past (1940)

I Ordered a Table for Six (1942)

Myra Carroll (1944)

Saplings (1945)

Grass in Piccadilly (1947)

Mothering Sunday (1950)

Aunt Clara (1952)

Judith (1956)

The Silent Speaker (1961)

As Susan Scarlett
(All available from Dean Street Press)

Clothes-Pegs (1939)

Sally-Ann (1939)

Peter and Paul (1940)

Ten Way Street (1940)

The Man in the Dark (1940)

Babbacombe's (1941)

Under the Rainbow (1942)

Summer Pudding (1943)

Murder While You Work (1944)

Poppies for England (1948)

Pirouette (1948)

Love in a Mist (1951)

SUSAN SCARLETT

SUMMER PUDDING

With an introduction
by Elizabeth Crawford

DEAN STREET PRESS

A Furrowed Middlebrow Book
FM92

Published by Dean Street Press 2022

Copyright © 1943 The Estate of Noel Streatfeild

Introduction copyright © 2022 Elizabeth Crawford

All Rights Reserved

The right of Noel Streatfeild to be identified as the Author of the Work has been asserted by her estate in accordance with the Copyright, Designs and Patents Act 1988.

First published in 1943 by Hodder & Stoughton

Cover by DSP

ISBN 978 1 915393 22 7

www.deanstreetpress.co.uk

Introduction

When reviewing *Clothes-Pegs*, Susan Scarlett's first novel, the *Nottingham Journal* (4 April 1939) praised the 'clean, clear atmosphere carefully produced by a writer who shows a rich experience in her writing and a charm which should make this first effort in the realm of the novel the forerunner of other attractive works'. Other reviewers, however, appeared alert to the fact that *Clothes-Pegs* was not the work of a tyro novelist but one whom *The Hastings & St Leonards Observer* (4 February 1939) described as 'already well-known', while explaining that this 'bright, clear, generous work', was 'her first novel of this type'. It is possible that the reviewer for this paper had some knowledge of the true identity of the author for, under her real name, Noel Streatfeild had, as the daughter of the one-time vicar of St Peter's Church in St Leonards, featured in its pages on a number of occasions.

By the time she was reincarnated as 'Susan Scarlett', Noel Streatfeild (1897-1986) had published six novels for adults and three for children, one of which had recently won the prestigious Carnegie Medal. Under her own name she continued publishing for another 40 years, while Susan Scarlett had a briefer existence, never acknowledged by her only begetter. Having found the story easy to write, Noel Streatfeild had thought little of *Ballet Shoes*, her acclaimed first novel for children, and, similarly, may have felt Susan Scarlett too facile a writer with whom to be identified. For Susan Scarlett's stories were, as the *Daily Telegraph* (24 February 1939) wrote of *Clothes-Pegs*, 'definitely unreal, delightfully impossible'. They were fairy tales, with realistic backgrounds, categorised as perfect 'reading for Black-out nights' for the 'lady of the house' (*Aberdeen Press and Journal*, 16 October 1939). As Susan Scarlett, Noel Streatfeild was able to offer daydreams to her readers, exploiting her varied experiences and interests to create, as her publisher advertised, 'light, bright, brilliant present-day romances'.

Noel Streatfeild was the second of the four surviving children of parents who had inherited upper-middle class values and expectations without, on a clergy salary, the financial means of realising them. Rebellious and extrovert, in her childhood and youth she had found many aspects of vicarage life unappealing, resenting both the restrictions thought necessary to ensure that a vicar's daughter behaved in a manner appropriate to the family's status, and the genteel impecuniousness and unworldliness that deprived her of, in particular, the finer clothes she craved. Her lack of scholarly application had unfitted her for any suitable occupation, but, after the end of the First World War, during which she spent time as a volunteer nurse and as a munition worker, she did persuade her parents to let her realise her dream of becoming an actress. Her stage career, which lasted ten years, was not totally unsuccessful but, as she was to describe on *Desert Island Discs*, it was while passing the Great Barrier Reef on her return from an Australian theatrical tour that she decided she had little future as an actress and would, instead, become a writer. A necessary sense of discipline having been instilled in her by life both in the vicarage and on the stage, she set to work and in 1931 produced *The Whicharts*, a creditable first novel.

By 1937 Noel was turning her thoughts towards Hollywood, with the hope of gaining work as a scriptwriter, and sometime that year, before setting sail for what proved to be a short, unfruitful trip, she entered, as 'Susan Scarlett', into a contract with the publishing firm of Hodder and Stoughton. The advance of £50 she received, against a novel entitled *Peter and Paul*, may even have helped finance her visit. However, the Hodder costing ledger makes clear that this novel was not delivered when expected, so that in January 1939 it was with *Clothes-Pegs* that Susan Scarlett made her debut. For both this and *Peter and Paul* (January 1940) Noel drew on her experience of occasional employment as a model in a fashion house, work for which, as she later explained, tall, thin actresses were much in demand in the 1920s.

Both *Clothes-Pegs* and *Peter and Paul* have as their settings Mayfair modiste establishments (Hanover Square and Bruton Street respectively), while the second Susan Scarlett novel, *Sally-Ann* (October 1939) is set in a beauty salon in nearby Dover Street. Noel was clearly familiar with establishments such as this, having, under her stage name 'Noelle Sonning', been photographed to advertise in *The Sphere* (22 November 1924) the skills of M. Emile of Conduit Street who had 'strongly waved and fluffed her hair to give a "bobbed" effect'. *Sally-Ann* and *Clothes-Pegs* both feature a lovely, young, lower-class 'Cinderella', who, despite living with her family in, respectively, Chelsea (the rougher part) and suburban 'Coulsden' (by which may, or may not, be meant Coulsdon in the Croydon area, south of London), meets, through her Mayfair employment, an upper-class 'Prince Charming'. The theme is varied in *Peter and Paul* for, in this case, twins Pauline and Petronella are, in the words of the reviewer in the *Birmingham Gazette* (5 February 1940), 'launched into the world with jobs in a London fashion shop after a childhood hedged, as it were, by the vicarage privet'. As we have seen, the trajectory from staid vicarage to glamorous Mayfair, with, for one twin, a further move onwards to Hollywood, was to have been the subject of Susan Scarlett's debut, but perhaps it was felt that her initial readership might more readily identify with a heroine who began the journey to a fairy-tale destiny from an address such as '110 Mercia Lane, Coulsden'.

As the privations of war began to take effect, Susan Scarlett ensured that her readers were supplied with ample and loving descriptions of the worldly goods that were becoming all but unobtainable. The novels revel in all forms of dress, from underwear, 'sheer triple ninon step-ins, cut on the cross, so that they fitted like a glove' (*Clothes-Pegs*), through daywear, 'The frock was blue. The colour of harebells. Made of some silk and wool material. It had perfect cut.' (*Peter and Paul*), to costumes, such as 'a brocaded evening coat; it was almost military in cut, with squared shoulders and a little tailored collar, very tailored at the waist, where it went in to flare out to the floor' (*Sally-Ann*), suitable to wear while dining at the Berkeley or the Ivy, establishments to which her heroines – and her readers – were introduced. Such details and the satisfying plots, in which innocent loveliness triumphs against the machinations of Society beauties, did indeed prove popular. Initial print runs of 2000 or 2500 soon sold out and reprints and cheaper editions were ordered. For instance, by the time it went out of print at the end of 1943, *Clothes-Pegs* had sold a total of 13,500 copies, providing welcome royalties for Noel and a definite profit for Hodder.

Susan Scarlett novels appeared in quick succession, particularly in the early years of the war, promoted to readers as a brand; 'You enjoyed *Clothes-Pegs*. You will love Susan Scarlett's *Sally-Ann*', ran an advertisement in the *Observer* (5 November 1939). Both *Sally-Ann* and a fourth novel, *Ten Way Street* (1940), published barely five months after *Peter and Paul*, reached a hitherto untapped audience, each being serialised daily in the *Dundee Courier*. It is thought that others of the twelve Susan Scarlett novels appeared as serials in women's magazines, but it has proved possible to identify only one, her eleventh, *Pirouette*, which appeared, lusciously illustrated, in *Woman* in January and February 1948, some months before its book publication. In this novel, trailed as 'An enthralling story – set against the glittering fairyland background of the ballet', Susan Scarlett benefited from Noel Streatfeild's knowledge of the world of dance, while giving her post-war readers a young heroine who chose a husband over a promising career. For, common to most of the Susan Scarlett novels is the fact that the central figure is, before falling into the arms of her 'Prince Charming', a worker, whether, as we have seen, a Mayfair mannequin or beauty specialist, or a children's nanny, 'trained' in *Ten Way Street*, or, as in *Under the Rainbow* (1942), the untrained minder of vicarage orphans; in *The Man in the Dark* (1941) a paid companion to a blinded motor car racer; in *Babbacombe's* (1941) a department store assistant; in *Murder While You Work* (1944) a munition worker; in *Poppies for England* (1948) a member of a concert party; or, in *Pirouette*, a ballet dancer. There are only two exceptions, the first being the heroine of *Summer Pudding* (1943) who, bombed out of the London office in which she worked, has been forced to retreat to an archetypal southern English village. The other is *Love in a Mist* (1951), the final Susan Scarlett novel, in which, with the zeitgeist returning women to hearth and home, the central character is a housewife and mother, albeit one, an American, who, prompted by a too-earnest interest in child psychology, popular in the post-war years, attempts to cure what she perceives as her four-year-old son's neuroses with the rather radical treatment of film stardom.

Between 1938 and 1951, while writing as Susan Scarlett, Noel Streatfeild also published a dozen or so novels under her own name, some for children, some for adults. This was despite having no permanent home after 1941 when her flat was bombed, and while undertaking arduous volunteer work, both as an air raid warden close to home in Mayfair, and as a provider of tea and sympathy in an impoverished area of south-east London. Susan Scarlett certainly helped with Noel's expenses over this period, garnering, for instance, an advance of £300 for *Love in a Mist*. Although there were to be no new Susan Scarlett novels, in the 1950s Hodder reissued cheap editions of *Babbacombe's*, *Pirouette*, and *Under the Rainbow*, the 60,000 copies of the latter only finally exhausted in 1959.

During the 'Susan Scarlett' years, some of the darkest of the 20th century, the adjectives applied most commonly to her novels were 'light' and 'bright'. While immersed in a Susan Scarlett novel her readers, whether book buyers or library borrowers, were able momentarily to forget their everyday cares and suspend disbelief, for as the reviewer in the *Daily Telegraph* (8 February 1941) declared, 'Miss Scarlett has a way with her; she makes us accept the most unlikely things'.

Elizabeth Crawford

THE train ran out from London. Straggling narrow streets and cramped houses, little gardens flapping with washing and chickens and crowded with rabbit hutches and the family effort at digging for victory, dreary gaping bombed areas, all gave way to fields, hedges, and a blue distance.

Janet had managed to get not only a seat, but a corner seat. She sat relaxed, her grey eyes staring through the window. It was early summer, the fields were spangled with daisies and buttercups, the first dog roses were opening. She took a deep breath, and in doing so moved and her book slipped off her knee and in retrieving it her elbow dug into the person sitting next to her. "I'm so sorry," she apologized.

Her neighbour was a girl, slim, with red hair and brown eyes. She was, Janet noticed, expensively dressed. The sort of clothes that look good always, no matter how long they have been owned. The sort of clothes, in fact, that she had always wanted herself, and was sure it was an economy to buy, only she never had the money to do it.

"It's all right," the girl laughed. "We can't very well turn without knocking each other. Sort of 'when father turns we all turn'. Awful travelling these days, isn't it? Daddy told me to travel first, but I won't in wartime, and anyway it wouldn't be any better, everybody gets in everywhere, and it would just be a waste of money."

"I suppose it would," Janet agreed. "I never travel first so I didn't know it was as bad." She turned back to the window. "Isn't the country looking lovely?"

"Yes. You haven't been out of London much lately, have you?"

"No. How did you know? Only for one week since the war started, as a matter of fact."

"You sat down with a sort of pleased 'now we're off' look, and then as the last of the houses disappeared you were like a cat that's going to purr."

"It's not only going to the country. I've had an awful time packing up, and settling things, and getting off."

"You bombed out?"

"Not at home. The office where I worked was."

"How miserable!"

"Yes. My old boss was killed, and his partner's in the army and overseas, so I couldn't get at him."

"What are you going to do now?"

Janet did not find these questions impertinent, she liked her red-haired neighbour, and could feel every question came from friendliness.

"I've not quite made up my mind. I'm a secretary so I expect I'd better put in for the same sort of thing in one of the services; the W.R.N.S. is what I should like."

"Wouldn't you rather have a change?"

"I would, but I've been a secretary for years, so I'd be more use in that than anything."

"You can't have been very many years."

"Why not? How old do you think I am?"

The girl studied Janet. The small, slim figure. The pale, square, not pretty, but alive face, made noticeable by wide-set, beautiful grey eyes. She watched Janet's smile. It was a lovely thing. It not only lit her up as though a light were switched on inside her, but seemed to spread outwards to make other people smile too; she was smiling in answer herself.

"Twenty-two? Twenty-three?"

"Twenty-five!"

"Are you? I shouldn't have thought you were that much older than me. I'm twenty-one. I'd like to do something. I want to join the W.R.N.S. too, but I can't just yet because of Daddy." She lowered her voice, not that the five soldiers, two sailors, and three elderly women who filled the rest of the carriage were listening, but her dropped voice suggested that she was confiding something personal. "He was terribly ill last winter. The doctor thought he was going to die; he says he's much stronger now, but he mustn't have any worries. You know, no upset in his life. So of course just now I can't leave him to join the W.R.N.S. or . . ." she hesitated and finished lamely, "or anything."

Janet's sympathetic eyes caught a faint flush on the girl's cheek. She felt a wave of pity. The 'or anything' sounded suspiciously like marriage. Of course she was very young, but in these uncertain times it would be hard to put off getting married even for a month or two.

"I hope your father's soon better. I'm lucky I'm not tied. My mother's not very strong, but I've a younger sister who lives with her. She's rather delicate, not fit for war work, but she can manage the work of the cottage they're living in, so I'm not needed at home, thank goodness. I'm simply longing to join up, would have done it ages ago only I couldn't leave my boss."

The ticket collector came in from the corridor. He could not reach the end of the carriage so Janet gave her ticket to be passed to him. The girl took it casually then turned an amazed face.

"You're going to Worsingfold."

"Yes."

"But that's where I live."

"So do my mother and sister."

The girl's eyes widened, and Janet thought looked somehow not too pleased.

"You can't be Sheila Brain's sister."

"Yes, I am. How did you guess? Do you know her?"

"Of course I know her, everybody knows everybody in Worsingfold. Anyway, she and your mother live in one of Donald Sheldon's cottages, and he's a tremendous friend of Daddy's and mine. Your sister's going to teach his little girl, Iris."

"Sheila is! I'm sure she can't be. Besides, she's got enough to do with the cottage."

The girl gave her a rather odd glance.

"Your mother's an awfully energetic person, I should think."

"She shouldn't be." Janet's face took on a worried look. "As a matter of fact her heart's not very strong. She doesn't know it, nor does Sheila. I got her down to the country on a trick. I got the doctor to say Sheila ought to get away; she never would have gone except for that."

"I expect it's difficult for your sister." The girl's voice had lost its easy naturalness and sounded forced. "I know how difficult it is to keep Daddy in order. I say, I wish you'd come and see Daddy and me while you're in Worsingfold. Our name's Haines, Daddy's a retired colonel, and I'm Barbara. It's awful to have a retired colonel for a father; he knows just how the war ought to be run, and gets so angry when the Government doesn't do things his way. You can hardly see our walls for maps, and they're ruined with pin-holes where the flags have gone in."

Janet laughed.

"I'd simply love to come. I suppose Sheila knows where you live?"

Barbara stared at her feet.

"Oh, yes. Yes, of course she does." She looked up. "Anyway, you can't miss it. It's called Worsingfold House. That sounds awfully grand, but it isn't really. It's the only house in the village, everything else is cottages except for the vicarage, and the Old Oast House which belongs to the doctor, and, of course, the farm. Donald Sheldon has the biggest of those, but you know him, don't you?"

"Me! No, I don't know a soul in Worsingfold. My sister found the place and fixed the cottage and everything."

"Did she?" Barbara gave her shoulders a faint shrug. "I can't think why, but I thought it was through you. I mean I thought I'd heard it was through a sister of Sheila's that you knew Donald, but I expect I've got muddled."

"No, we knew nobody, the cottage was just to let and we took it." Janet was looking at her watch so she did not see the puzzled expression on Barbara's face. "We must be nearly there, aren't we?"

Barbara looked out of the window.

"Not far off." She stretched as much as the cramped conditions would let her. "I'll be glad to get back."

"Have you been away long?"

"No, only one night. The dentist."

Janet's grey eyes ran over her thoughtfully.

"I should have thought it would be fun for you to get away now and again."

Barbara put on her gloves. Her voice lacked colour.

"Oh, it can be fun, of course, but just now it happens that everybody I know is overseas."

Janet was moved by the naïveté of this. Barbara was very young in some ways; nobody could be deceived by her 'everybody'. It was obvious that what she meant was 'my special somebody'.

Barbara became conscious of how her words had sounded, for she turned pink and said hurriedly:

"You do promise to come and see us, don't you?"

"Of course, it's awfully nice of you. As a matter of fact I shan't be in Worsingfold long. I shan't take more than a week's holiday before signing on."

"Let's hope they don't call you up for a bit after you've joined, for I should think you need more than a week's holiday."

"A fortnight or three weeks would be nice, but I'd like to get down to real war work. It's nice to feel free now to do it. My boss was awfully old, and though not past his work, found it a bit heavy once his nephew, who was his partner, was called up." Janet had quick movements, she swept round now to Barbara. "I can't get over what you said about Sheila teaching. Apart from having heaps to do with the housework, and shopping, she's not the type to teach." She sighed. "I can see part of my holiday will be spent putting my family straight. Sheila must be talked out of that idea."

"But it's a promise," said Barbara bluntly. "You can't make her let Donald down like that. Iris is eight and ought to be doing some lessons. Donald was frightfully pleased when she promised. He's been very disappointed she hasn't been strong enough to start yet. You see, his wife died two years ago, and though he's got an awfully good housekeeper called Gladys Batten, she hasn't much time for Iris, though she says she adores her."

A smile flooded Janet's face.

"You don't like Gladys Batten."

"I can see she's a marvellous housekeeper, looks after the house awfully well and cooks and everything, but I don't really like her. I can't think why, for I'm sure she's a very good woman, but you can't like people just because they're good, can you?" She got up. "We're nearly there." She stretched up to the rack for her case. "I am glad I met you. I've a feeling we're going to be friends."

Worsingfold was a halt not a station. Sheila was sitting on its only bench. She was a beauty and never forgot it for a second. Now on an empty station she was nicely posed for the edification of everybody on the train. She was wearing a blue linen frock the exact colour of her eyes. She had moved to the end of the bench where the sun caught the gold in her fair curls. On the seat beside her was a straw hat with a ribbon round it that matched her frock. Her face and bare legs were becomingly tanned.

She knew she looked like the cover of the summer number of a magazine, and felt it was a treat for the people on the train to have a look at her. She did not get up too quickly to spoil the effect, but sauntered over to Janet enjoying the male eyes that gazed admiringly out of every window.

"Hullo, Janet." Then she saw Barbara and her voice changed. "Good afternoon, Miss Haines."

Barbara nodded, and said a cheerful "Hullo". It seemed normal enough, but Janet had one of those fleeting thoughts, that you can't pin down, that something was not quite right; then even before the thought had taken shape she had forgotten it in her pleasure at seeing Sheila, and after months of loneliness being in touch once more with home.

"I've managed to get the taxi," Sheila announced.

"I wish I'd known your sister was coming," said Barbara. "I put my car in the station garage and I could have driven you home."

Sheila did not look grateful.

"Thank you, but I was able to get the taxi all right, and even if people can scrounge plenty of petrol one doesn't like to use it."

Barbara flushed.

"I've no more petrol than anybody else, but it wouldn't have been out of my way to drop you." She turned to Janet. "Goodbye. I hope you enjoy your holiday, and don't forget your promise to come and see us."

Sheila stared after Barbara, scowling.

"I could have driven you home," she minced.

A very ancient taxi was standing outside, with a grey-haired, bent old driver at the wheel. When he saw Janet carrying her suitcase he began to move preparatory to getting out. She stopped him with a smile.

"Don't bother, I can lift it in."

The driver shook his head.

"'Tisn't right; my grandson what this taxi rightly belongs to, him that's serving in the Navy, he says to me before he goes: 'no need to tell you not to smash the taxi, grand-dad, 'cos at the speed what you can drive you couldn't, and no need to tell you not to fiddle with 'er, but to take her to the garridge if she's actin' queer. All you got to do is just to treat 'er gentle same as if she was a 'oss, and if there's any luggage lift it in. Folks don't like payin' for a taxi and liftin' their stuff theirselves.'"

Janet laughed.

"I don't mind lifting mine. Have you good news of your grandson?"

"Yes. 'Is wife 'eard only this week. He seems rarely pleased with the way the Navy's doin'."

Inside the taxi Sheila eyed Janet disapprovingly.

"You shouldn't encourage people like him."

"Why not? He's an old pet."

"He's too familiar. They all are in this village. It's just because we live in a cottage. They're quite different to the Haines. They talk about Barbara Haines as if she was royalty, and there's no difference between us except that she lives in a big house."

Janet glanced anxiously at Sheila. She looked well, but of course that might be the sunburn. She did hope she wasn't taking a dislike to Worsingfold. The cottage was so miraculously cheap, and it was so unlikely to be bombed, it would be a disaster if she wanted to move.

"She was awfully nice on the train." Janet spoke cautiously, not wanting to annoy Sheila the moment she got home. "How's Mum?"

"Oh, she's all right."

Janet felt that Sheila was on the offensive and could not imagine why.

"You look marvellously well."

"I'm not. I still get terribly tired and my nerves are ghastly; they keep me awake at night. Do you know, sometimes I lie just shaking like a jelly about nothing at all. I was telling Mr. Sheldon, and he says he supposes it's the awful time I went through, and I expect he's right."

Janet's eyes opened.

"What awful time?"

Sheila flushed.

"Oh, the bombing and all that."

"But you didn't have much of it. The doctor ordered Mum away almost as soon as it started. The worst part was after you'd gone, thank goodness."

"I'm very highly strung. Even a siren upsets me."

Janet had heard this too often to want to start it all over again. "What's Mr. Sheldon like? He's our landlord, isn't he?" Sheila lit up. She thought all men an engrossing topic of conversation.

"He's rather good-looking in a he-mannish brown way. He's a farmer, of course, so he's not polished like the sort of men we're used to, but . . ."

Janet was laughing.

"You are a scream. I didn't mean what does he look like, I mean what's he like as a person. And I like all that about the men we knew being polished. What polished men did we know?"

Sheila wriggled, a way she had when her bluff was being called. "The men in my office had lovely manners."

"You always said you hated everybody in it."

"That was after the men were called up; nobody could like being in an office with only women. Women are cats and not half as understanding as men. Anyway, I never ought to have been in an office, I ought to be in pictures, everybody says so."

Janet shot away from this age-long argument.

"Miss Haines told me you were going as governess to Mr. Sheldon's little girl."

Sheila flinched as if something had hurt her. Janet saw there were tears in her eyes.

"I'm in an awful muddle about that. I did sort of say I would. You see, he was quite kind helping us to move in and all that, and then he's a widower, and you feel you must be nice to them, don't you? So I said I would teach Iris, but I never meant to, really. I couldn't, my nerves wouldn't stand it."

"The housework wouldn't, anyway. That's a full-time job, isn't it?"

Sheila wriggled again.

"Well, yes, of course it is; but he's got so horrid about Iris, you'd think I'd promised, which, of course, I never did. It's not my fault if he hasn't the time or the petrol to take his kid into a town to school." She turned her eyes to Janet. She had a trick of opening them wide with a look of childish candour. She did this now. "I expect truly he wants me in the house. You know how men are."

Janet knew only too well how men were about Sheila. From the age of three she had captivated any of them that set eyes on her. Little boys in the kindergarten with her, later big boys and schoolmasters, then every errand boy and postman that came to the house and, of course, the office staff. Janet had always suspected that until the men were called up Sheila's office life had been to sit around being worshipped and given presents while somebody did her work; it had not surprised her at all when the men had gone, and the elder women took charge, that they had delighted in making Sheila work, and that she had described them as cats. However, she was not going to judge her unknown landlord on Sheila's word only; her mother would know if she really had offered to teach the child.

"We must settle that somehow," she said lightly. "I dare say he sounds rougher than he means; it's that lack of polish you say we're not used to."

"I wish you wouldn't be sarcastic."

Janet was looking out at the village, whose first cottages were coming into view.

"I don't mean to be, but putting on side is silly. We're very ordinary people, and we know very ordinary men." Sheila's voice rose.

"Oh, do we! Do you call Richard Trent ordinary?"

Janet gaped at her sister.

"Mr. Trent! But you've never seen him." Something in Sheila's face eluded her. "Or have you?"

Sheila stared at her toes.

"You know I haven't."

Janet turned back to the window. She saw a picture postcard village street. White cottages, each one covered in a patterned thatch. A square Norman church sitting in a grassy graveyard. A village shop, its small windows bulging with everything from boots to worm powders, an inn called 'The Lamb', its sign a pascal lamb with its pennon over its shoulder. She saw all this with her eyes, but her mind was back in London. She was looking at her bombed office, and her employer's shattered flat above it. Poor old Horace Pringle, he must have died instantly. She was glad he had been spared the misery of knowing that his clients' papers had been destroyed. A solicitor has such intimate papers belonging to other people, it would probably have worried him into his grave. If only she knew where Richard Trent was so that she could send him a cable. Of course, Horace Pringle had his address, but it was destroyed with everything else. If only she knew what regiment he was in. On leave he had always got into mufti to get comfortably down to the mass of work waiting for him. It had really been idiotic of her not to have had an address for him, but he hadn't offered it, and she had not thought to ask for it. They were more than employer and employee, they were almost friends, but friends solely over business; she had never been interested in his private life nor he in hers, and so the question of his address had never crossed either of their minds.

"It's quite a pretty village, isn't it?" said Sheila. "Look out of this window; that's the Haines' house."

Janet turned and saw a Georgian house behind high iron gates.

"It looks very grand. She asked me to go and see her, but I shouldn't like to go there."

Sheila swung her foot angrily. Janet was as tiresome as ever, she thought. Always saying things to make other people feel small. She did hope she wasn't going round saying that sort of thing in Worsingfold. People were quick enough to look down their noses at you without you going about saying you weren't used to big houses. It was sickening Janet had come at all; she was certain to grumble and make rows, she always did. It would be a help if she could think of something to put her into a good temper before she got to the cottage. Her methods for pleasing were the same for women as for men. Her face broke into a sweet, wistful smile.

"It's simply lovely you've come. I feel awfully young to be looking after Mum and everything by myself."

Janet refrained from pointing out that Sheila was nearly twenty, and that when she herself had been that age she had been daily breading, parting with every penny she earned to lift a little of the anxiety off her mother's shoulders, and chief provider of luxuries for which a spoilt little sister of fourteen whined. She had a fear that the dismay which she often felt at Sheila's ways and goings-on might not be inspired simply by her dislike of affectation and fecklessness, but have a root in jealousy. She never did feel jealous, but it seemed so peculiar that she didn't, with, as she often told herself, me so plain and Sheila so lovely, that she tried to sift each aggravated thought that Sheila inspired, to find where its roots lay. She changed the subject.

"How far is it to the cottage?"

"We turn off in a moment up the lane to the farm. Our cottage is on a sort of track across some fields. The taxi can't go up that bit."

The words were scarcely out of her mouth when, with a violent jerk, the taxi came to a stop. With the careful slowness of an old person, less sure of the behaviour of their limbs than they were, the driver climbed out. He came to the open window. He looked anxiously at Sheila.

"Would it be too much for your sister to walk from here like? That time when I drove you and your mother up to the farm, when you just come, I had a terrible time gettin' back. Reversin' isn't no different to goin' forward, that's what my grandson said, not when you understand it, but maybe I haven't understood it."

Sheila made an annoyed movement, but before she could speak Janet broke in.

"Of course we'll get out here. My suitcase isn't so terribly heavy. If it's too much I'll borrow a wheelbarrow." She opened the taxi door. "How much?"

The old man said two shillings and eyed Janet while she found half a crown.

"You ain't bred same as your sister. Put me in mind of my old setter. She had a litter of pups so different that you wouldn't know they was come by same way." He held out his hand. "Let me carry that case a bit of the way."

Janet shook her head.

"Of course not, and when you next see your grandson you tell him that the women have got proud in this war, and won't let you carry their luggage for them however often you ask them."

The old man turned away, then struck by a thought he came back.

"We keep pigs, my wife and me. We got a right to kill one next month what hasn't to go Lord Wooltonin', but is for ourselves like. You step along down there and I'll find you a nice pork chop. Reckon you can do with it after being bombed and that in Lunnon."

Janet was charmed.

"I do think that's kind of you, Mr. . . . ."

"Jus' Tom. Nobody don't call me nothin' different."

"Well, Tom, I can't tell you how nice I think you are, but I'm afraid I shan't be here next month. I'm going to join the W.R.N.S."

Tom gave a nod of acceptance, and climbed laboriously back into his taxi, but before he shut the door he leant out and gave Sheila a wicked grin.

"That offer of a chop was made to your sister, so it's no good you steppin' round, for it won't be there, see!"

Sheila turned to Janet, her eyes blazing.

"I told you not to be familiar. You see what happens, they're all just waiting to be rude."

Janet picked up her suitcase.

"I shouldn't mind him. I think he's what's known as a character. Do we go through this gate?"

In spite of her brave words to Tom, Janet found the suitcase appallingly heavy, but not so heavy that she could not manage to look around and love what she saw. A winding, white, dusty road lay through fields of what her town-bred eyes took to be very green grass. At its end she could see a farm lying behind another gate set in a stone wall. After some minutes walking they came to a track on the left of the road. Sheila led the way up it; she was still offended and said nothing, so Janet, not to re-open a sore subject, changed her suitcase from her right arm to her left without asking for the rest for which her muscles were crying out. At the end of the field they came to a gate in a fence. Janet put down the suitcase, not because of its weight, but from amazement.

"That's not our cottage!"

Her obvious surprise made Sheila wriggle. Her voice was truculent.

"Yes, it is. Why not?"

"All that for ten shillings a week!"

"It's only a workman's cottage, and awfully out of the way."

Janet's thoughts shot back to battered London.

"Awfully out of the way," she repeated softly. "I should have thought people would pay a lot for that."

The cottage lay across a field in which cattle were grazing. It was whitewashed, and as Janet drew nearer she could see it was beautifully thatched. The fence of the field and its gate were the entrance to a little garden, the garden of a Londoner's dream. A flagged path bordered with lavender hedges, flower-beds behind blue with delphiniums and silver with lilies, a honeysuckle over the porch and roses everywhere.

"Goodness!" gasped Janet. "Fancy us in a lovely place like that." Then she gave a cry, for a figure came out of the porch and waved. "Mum!"

Sheila looked at the suitcase standing forgotten in the field.

"I suppose she expects me to carry it, but I won't, and I only hope the cows kick it."

Janet, tearing through the gate and up the path, was too excited to see her mother clearly. It was only when her first hugs were over that she was conscious of how little there was of the frame in her arms. She drew away and looked up, and fright laid clammy fingers on her heart. This was not even the mother that she and the doctor had beguiled away from the bombing; that woman had been frail, but this one was sick.

Maggie Brain never thought of herself except as a mother. Long ago, when Sheila was a baby, she had thought of herself as a wife. She had been so happy then, so loved, and so understood, that when her husband died it had seemed as if something of her died with him. She pulled herself away from her grief for the sake of her babies, but she was never again the laughing, soft Maggie her husband had known; she never again thought of herself as a person to be cherished and loved, but gave herself body, mind and spirit to her children.

Maggie's eyes searched her daughter's face for signs of the strain she had been through, for tiredness, for thinness, for lack of sleep. She was puzzled by Janet's expression.

"What's the matter, child? You're staring at me as if I were a ghost."

It was on the tip of Janet's tongue to say that nothing could have been more descriptive, but words said by the doctor stopped her. He had looked after the Brains since they were small. "Look here, Janet," he had said. "I'm not very pleased with your mother's heart, but I'm not saying anything to her about it, it'll only worry her, and it won't stop her doing too much. The thing for us to do is to get her away from this bombing, and put her somewhere quiet, where she can't overwork." That was when this country scheme had come about. Pinning it on Sheila had been the doctor's idea. "I'm going to tell your mother that I want that little puss, Sheila, out of London; it's the only way we can get her to leave you. We'll tell Sheila to see she rests, and in a couple of months you won't know your mother for the same woman." Janet, staring now up in her mother's face, thought grimly how horribly true were his words, but in the opposite way to which he had intended them, and it was not two months but seven. Maggie had always been thin, but now she seemed transparent, the blue eyes had sunk back into her head, and the bone structure of her face stood out too prominently. Even her hair looked different. She had grey curls which had defied brushing and pins, and stood up gaily in waves and tendrils, but now it lay meek and lank. Janet gave her a little affectionate shake.

"You miserable old woman, you're all skin and bones, and I sent you to the country to get fat."

Maggie linked her arm in her daughter's and led her into the cottage.

"I never was the fat kind; besides, you know what a worrier I am, and worrying is thinning."

"What have you got to worry about?"

"You for one thing. Do you think I didn't mind your being in London through all those terrible raids?"

"What else?"

"Oh, lots of things." Maggie squeezed her daughter's arm. "We'll have a nice talk later on."

The cottage was as charming inside as out. There were beautiful oak beams in all the rooms, and they showed well against white distempered walls. There were two good sitting-rooms, a stone-flagged kitchen, a small scullery, four bedrooms, and halfway up the queer-shaped oak staircase, the pride of the cottage, a bathroom.

"Not that we can use it much," said Maggie. "We have our own well, but wells don't seem affected by rain, no matter how wet it is we have a drought."

"What do we do about washing then?"

"Have a kettleful each and wash in bits. I've got quite good at it now, but I found it very trying in the winter. Whichever half you wash first seems to freeze while you're washing the other half."

Janet looked at the wide porcelain bath and the fitted basin.

"It seems awfully odd that you can get a lovely cottage like this for ten shillings a week, doesn't it?"

"And you haven't seen the half of it yet. There's an orchard at the back, and I'm making a nice vegetable garden."

"You are! You're not digging!"

Maggie nodded proudly.

"Of course I am, for victory." She put her arm round Janet. "Come down, darling, you must be dying for a cup of tea." She led the way into the kitchen, and put a kettle on to boil, and started to lay a tray.

"Where's Sheila?"

Maggie went on quietly setting out the tea things.

"In the other room, I expect; most likely she's reading, she's still crazy on those film papers."

"But doesn't she get the tea?"

"Sheila!" Maggie laughed. "Surely you know her better than that. Can you see her doing housework? It's all I can get her to do to make her own bed."

Janet said nothing for a moment, but took the tea-pot off the shelf. Then she spoke in a voice she forced to sound casual.

"How do you find time to garden if you've all the housework to get through?"

Maggie, unaware she was being catechized, answered easily. "Just a little organizing does it. I manage cold dinners and then I'm free in the afternoons. Of course I can't do much on shopping days, but I keep that down to twice a week. Seems funny after London where one was always slipping out for something."

Janet spoke more casually than ever.

"How does Sheila amuse herself?"

"Not very well, I'm afraid. She has little tasks, fetching the milk from the farm, and she did help in garnishing camouflage nets for the W.V.S. twice a week, but she had to give that up because she said the stuff they're woven of made her cough. Now she sometimes helps at a soldiers' canteen." She lowered her voice. "I'm not very happy about her. I'll tell you later. I think her health's better, I've made her rest up, and feed up, but of course she's still a bundle of nerves."

Janet fiddled with the tea-pot lid. Her eyes glowed with rage. So this was what Sheila had been up to! The little devil. She had not been told about her mother's heart because she could never keep anything to herself, but she had been told her mother was not well and must be got away and must rest, and that she was going to be told that she, Sheila, had anaemia as a means to lure her into the country. And this was how she had played up! Lazy little beast, trading on what she knew to be an imaginary illness in order to slack about doing nothing.

"It's lovely having you here," said Maggie. "I've such a lot of little problems to talk over."

Janet looked out of the window. The sun was shining on a rambler rose; there was a grassy mound near it, just the place to lie and look at the sky, and rest on your first holiday in two years. Then she straightened her back and threw up her chin.

"I can see with half an eye I shall have tons to talk about, and tons to do."

SHEILA had gone to a cottage to fetch the eggs. Janet had taken three chairs on to the lawn, gently pushed her mother into one, and picked up her feet and put them on another. Maggie looked at her feet as if they didn't belong to her.

"Really, Jan! Making me look silly! Whatever will people think!"

"That you're an incurable Cockney. You live in the country now, you haven't got neighbours to think anything."

Maggie was knitting a khaki sock. She laid it down to laugh.

"It's you that's the Cockney. You'd be surprised how much Worsingfold knows. Why, there won't be a soul who didn't know you were coming today, or that old Tom had been engaged to drive you from the station. And they'll know about my feet too. I don't know how they see things, but they do. In a day or two's time someone will say to me: 'You'll be feeling stronger now your daughter's home.' That'll mean that a story's gone round that you came because I was ill, and it will have started because you put my feet up."

Janet lay back in her chair and stared at the sky. She felt round for the right way to start the conversation. Could her mother really not realize how ill she looked? Maggie always had held a theory that giving in was a mistake, that you felt worse once you lay down. Was this theory keeping her going now? "She's a funny person, your mother," the doctor had said. "She's got so much grit and nervous energy, she'll go on working when any oilier woman would be an invalid; but just for that reason we've got to go carefully with her. She's never been really ill in her life, and like so many healthy people, she's inclined to think that a lot of so-called illnesses are imagination. If I were to tell her now that she's got a bad heart, it would be a nasty shock. If I say it's bad, she'll believe me. Have you ever seen a kid learning to swim? As long as they think they can do it they get along fine, but lose confidence and they sink." Janet had never forgotten that talk; it had given her a cold feeling at the pit of the stomach then, and the memory of it gave it to her now. She swallowed her feelings and spoke cheerfully.

"Well, what about these worries?"

Maggie took her time. Her needles clicked quite a while before she said:

"It's Sheila. I've failed with her, Janet. As you know, I never meant to force her into a life she didn't like. I knew her heart was set on going on the films, and though I didn't like it, and your dad would have hated it, I'd have let her have her way if she got a chance, but it's such an insecure life, I felt I had to see that she was properly trained for something else. Once she was trained as a shorthand-typist I didn't mean to insist on her working in an office for more than six months. I couldn't know the war was coming. Like everybody else, I hoped we'd escape it."

"She knows that."

"She doesn't. She blames me for what she calls 'ruining her life'. Can't you see how discontented she's looking?"

"But it's nonsense!"

"I know, but she doesn't see it that way. She thinks if I'd let her try for film work as soon as she left school, she'd have got a contract before the war started, and that now she'd be making films for the Ministry of Information and all that. She cuts bits out of the paper about all these film girls who get parts, and she slams them down under my nose and says, 'Look, that might have been me!'"

"She seemed quite pleased to move to Worsingfold."

"I know. I suppose she was glad of any excuse to get out of the office. She was even keen on coming to this place; I always thought that funny, it seems a very quiet spot for her to like."

"I heard from that Miss Haines on the train that she was going to teach our landlord's child, but when I asked her she seemed in a state about the idea. She seems to think she's being forced into it on an imaginary promise. What's the truth of the story?"

Maggie's face was worried.

"I don't know, and that's a fact. I don't like running down one of you girls to the other, but Sheila doesn't always speak the truth. It's not that she means to lie, I think, but she was always a fanciful little thing; you remember how when she was three she believed she was royalty, and we had to curtsy, well, she's like that still; she imagines a lot and doesn't always know what she's imagined and what's true."

"You think she may have promised?"

Maggie's forehead screwed into worried lines.

"Mr. Sheldon seems to me a nice man. Of course you never can tell with any man, but he doesn't seem the sort to get a girl to the house because of her pretty face. He's a busy farmer, and full of sense, and I should have thought if he said he wanted a governess, a governess is what he means."

"All the same, you're not sure."

Maggie's face cleared and her eyes twinkled.

"This is like old times. You were always so sharp it was a wonder you didn't cut yourself. Never could keep anything from you, could I? Well, then, I'm not sure. I met him in the village the other day and he stopped and said in a nice way, but abruptly, 'When is that daughter of yours coming to teach my Iris?' I was quite flustered by his tone and said she wasn't very strong, or something like that. Then he looked at me as if he were going to pat my arm and say something kind, but what he did say, though in quite a different voice, was: 'I don't want you to be bothered, but a bargain's a bargain, you know.'"

"A bargain! In a dictionary that means 'an agreement on terms of give and take'."

"I dare say, dear, but country people use words in funny ways, and I think he just meant that she'd promised."

"Well, if she did, she's a little fool; she couldn't teach in a million years, and she knows it."

"Yes, dear." There was a pause. Then, as if making a plunge, Maggie leant forward. "There's no need, you know, for either of you girls to be with me, I can manage alone." Janet moved and

Maggie stopped her. "But if one of you means to keep me company it should be you, Jan, and not Sheila."

Janet felt as if someone had given her a punch in the ribs. She had been earning her living for so long that going out every day, and being independent, was part of her. She adored her mother, and loved living at home, but there had always been her other life, the office, Friday's pay envelope, her desk, the warm glow that came from knowing she was valued by Horace Pringle and Richard Trent. That life was over; it had finished the night the bomb demolished the office, but once she had got over the shock of Horace Pringle's death, she had grasped that the shutting of the one door meant the opening of another. She had been hankering to do war work, and she was the type to whom the services appealed, particularly the W.R.N.S. She saw the life as a glorified office, in which she would not only be of value, but have the fun of being part of a community with all it offered, a warming picture after months of living alone. Now here was her mother in that gentle, matter-of-fact way of hers which was so compelling, suggesting that she give up her freedom and her dreams to live in the country, being just the daughter at home. Her face flamed, and though she tried to steady her voice, it was frill of resentment.

"Why should it be me?"

Maggie may have felt a pang at the obvious insinuation that living with her was a martyrdom for someone, but she didn't show it.

"It hasn't got to be either of you. I'm a perfectly healthy woman, and I can look after myself, but I won't have Sheila here any longer, hanging about, doing nothing, it's bad for her. I've been making up my mind about this for some time. If she had taken on this teaching that would be different, but she never meant to. Your being at home, even if it's only for a short time, is my chance to get her away."

"How?"

"I've no idea, but as you ought to know by now, when Maggie Brain sets her mind to a thing it's as good as done."

Janet got up.

"I'll go and meet Sheila."

The eggs came from a distant cottage. There was no Sheila in sight. Janet sat down in the field, she had it to herself, the cows had been driven home. The grass was young and green, the buttercups shook pollen on to her frock, an ox-eye daisy and a head of clover were dividing the attention of a sleepy, already heavily laden bee. Janet saw these things, but with no pleasure. She was bitter, and it took the colour from the grass and flowers and sky. Sheila! Since the day Sheila was born she had been giving up something for her. "No, darling, Mum can't play with you, she's got to look after baby Sheila." "I know you don't care very much for pink, darling, but I do like to dress you two children alike, and Sheila looks such a duck in pink." Her headmistress had said: "We rely on you, Janet, to coach Sheila in the evenings; she's a lazy little creature, but there, I suppose one can't have everything." Can't have everything! Sheila had very nearly had it. Janet's precious spare evening hours, every shilling that could be screwed from her earnings, all the looks, all the admiration, and she had never grudged her any of it. Now this? "Surely," she thought, thumping an impotent foot on the ground, "I needn't give in to her over this! It isn't even as if she wants it. She wanted to come here, she chose the place. Doing the housework and being the village beauty ought to be exactly her cup of tea." But it was no good arguing with herself; Janet was incapable of not looking the truth in the face. Sheila wouldn't do the housework. If her mother were not looked after she would die. "If Mum hadn't said what she did I'd have come to the same conclusion myself in the end, I suppose. I'd have taken a bit of time over it, it's so awfully disappointing. I do so want . . ." Janet was shy of tears. She seldom cried, and she certainly was not going to cry in front of Sheila, who would be coming along any minute now. To the left of the house across a field of mustard she could see a copse. Round the side of the house she would be out of sight of anyone coming up the main footpath. She had no idea if her mother could see her from the garden, and did not care very much if she did. She had reached that point when her throat ached so that she couldn't swallow, and any cover would do so long as she was alone to sob undisturbed.

Maggie raised her head from her knitting. She saw Janet's bent, scuttling figure crossing the field. An understanding smile twisted her bps; there had been times in her life when she had run to a bit of cover to have a good cry. There were times now when she would be glad to break down a bit. She was never going to tell the girls how queer she sometimes felt, especially in the night, a feeling as if she were being smothered, and falling through the bed. Of course it was just fancifulness, but it scared her all the same. The girls would laugh if they knew how many nights she sat up with the light on, just too scared of the smothered feeling to lie down. Work was the thing, of course; with plenty to do she would teach herself not to be so foolish. Her eyes rested on Janet just entering the copse. What a relief it would be to tell her, to be hugged and told not to be a silly old woman; but she mustn't say anything, mustn't let Janet know how the mere thought of living alone, as she had said she would do, brought her out in a cold sweat. Fancy having one of her silly night attacks, knowing there was no one to cry out to. Of course in the day hours it was easy to call yourself a fanciful fool, imagining you were going to die, when all that was wrong was a touch of indigestion; but in the night hours it was not so simple. There was something about the night, it sapped your courage.

In the copse Janet pushed her way through the undergrowth. Young bracken was popping up amongst last winter's dead leaves, it was bent and curled like a baby's fingers. She lay down amongst it, pressing her face into it, and sobbed as she had scarcely done since childhood. Between her sobs she moaned out broken, disjointed sentences: "It isn't fair . . ." "I did so want to do war work." "I don't mind being the plain one, I don't mind being pitied for having so lovely a sister, but I do want to live my own life my own way." "I know I've got to give in, but I do feel miserable."

"I beg your pardon, but is anything the matter?"

Janet raised a patchy, blotched face. A bit of moss had stuck to her chin. Then she sat up. A man was standing beside her. He was tall and slight, but gave the impression of wiry, muscular strength. He had a thatch of untidy brown hair, and honest brown eyes. He was wearing an old tweed coat and leggings and breeches. He had a gun under his arm. No woman likes any man, even a husband, to see her at her worst, and this was a stranger. Janet was furious, and her fury killed her wish to cry. Her voice still wobbled a bit, but it was as much with anger as tears. "Nothing is the matter. Why should it be?"

The man's lips twitched.

"You've got a bit of moss on your chin."

Janet's hand flew to her face, then as she found the straggling piece of moss she saw how silly the whole scene was. His question if anything was wrong, when it so palpably was, her proud reply, and then her appearance as the bearded lady. She began to laugh, and he joined in, and for a moment they rocked helplessly.

"I must look an idiot," she said at last, "but there's nothing wrong really; I was indulging in a nice basinful of self-pity." The man took out his cigarette-case and offered it to her. "Try my cure."

"Have you got enough to spare one?"

He nodded, and lit hers and his own.

"How did you come here?"

She smiled.

"I'm not a parachutist, if that's what you mean. I just walked. Why wouldn't I come here? Is it private?"

"Yes."

"How did you, if it comes to that? Are you a poacher?"

"I've done a bit of that when I was younger. As a matter of fact this is my land."

"You're not Mr. Sheldon?"

"Yes."

"I'm Janet Brain. My mother's a tenant of yours."

"Are you? Now I remember my housekeeper said you were expected. Well then, we aren't strangers, almost old acquaintances by proxy."

"What on earth does he mean?" she thought. Out loud she said:

"I'm sorry I'm trespassing, but I was very careful crossing the field; I came by what seemed to be a bit where things weren't growing."

"I'm sure you did. I gave your family leave to go anywhere provided they were careful, and shut the gates and all that. Your sister's a bit uncertain about which is crops and which is grass, still luckily she's light as a feather, and she's learning. She's going to teach my child, you know."

Janet was not one to let a thing slide to save herself trouble.

"I'm afraid she isn't. She never could teach anybody." She watched a stubborn look settle on his face. "As a matter of fact that's what I was howling about. Mother thinks Sheila ought to go away and get a real job. And that means that I"—stating her new plans as a *fait accompli* gave her a stab, her voice faltered—"I've got to stay here." His face softened, his voice was sympathetic.

"Is that so hard?"

"Yes. I've earned my living since I left school. I've had an independent life outside my home. I've been stuck in an office so far, but it's been bombed, and now I'm free I'd promised myself I'd join the W.R.N.S."

"I can sympathize. Drives me mad to be stuck here, hard-worked, of course, but living pretty well. When I read of what the civilians, even the women, do in the towns, and we've never heard a bomb. Of course I'm Home Guard, but if I had my way I'd have joined the Navy."

"I suppose as a farmer your place is here."

"Of course." There was silence. In it Janet heard the twittering of innumerable birds chatting as they settled down for the night. Some rooks cawed overhead. The baa of a sheep came from a distant field. London had been so noisy, with its crashes at night, and blastings and hammerings at smashed buildings by day, that the quiet and peace fell on her spirit like a cold hand on a sprained ankle. "If you're stopping at the cottage instead of your sister, couldn't you take on teaching Iris?" She moved and he hurried on. "She's a nice kid, though I say it myself. Her mother died two years ago. I can't give her much time. I've a housekeeper, but she's got her hands full. I don't want to send Iris to the village school because she's delicate. If I can't get her taught here it means a boarding school. Besides . . ."

Janet's eyes were on his face. She saw the stubborn, dogged look come back.

"Besides," she broke in, "Sheila promised."

"Well, a bargain's a bargain."

"And nobody's ever got the better of you over one," she thought. To him she said:

"It's a new idea. I don't know how it will fit in with everything else. I don't want my mother doing so much, and the only way to stop her is to be there to do it for her."

"I don't care a bit about Iris being forced on, it's more companionship she needs. You could take her along to the cottage with you."

She did not want to answer until she had time to think. She looked at her watch.

"I must go or they'll imagine I'm lost. I'll let you know tomorrow if I may. Will I find you at the farm?"

"I'll be about, one of my men will tell you."

He watched her go, and as he turned away he began to whistle 'The Poacher's Song', a gay, carefree whistling.

His shepherd was passing up the lane on the far side of the copse. "That's master," he thought. "Haven't heard him so jovial since missus went."

Janet, hurrying across the field, felt in her pockets and took out her powder-puff. "Gosh!" she murmured, seeing her face. "He must think we run to extremes in our family. Must tidy up; don't want to come in looking like a wet Sunday." Then a thought came to her which startled her. She paused, her powder-puff halfway to her nose. "How queer! How very queer! I don't' mind the idea of stopping half as much as I did. I suppose I've cried it out of me!"

§

THE Brains sat round the supper-table. Janet had cleaned and powdered her face, and had managed to get most of the signs of tears away. Maggie beamed as she carried in three boiled eggs.

"I wouldn't do anything to them, dear," she told Janet, "except boil them. A nice fresh egg will be a treat to you."

Janet took a piece of bread.

"I met your farmer while I was out."

Sheila flushed and her eyes slid round to Janet.

"What did he say?"

Both Maggie and Janet were surprised by a note of truculence in her voice. Janet looked at her squarely.

"He said you'd definitely promised to teach his kid, Iris. Did you?"

"No, I told you I didn't. He was kind when we moved, and I was sorry for him, and . . ."

"I expect you more or less did," Janet said resignedly, "but you don't mean to, do you?"

"Well, I would if I could, but I don't like children and—"

"Come on, do you mean to, or don't you?"

Sheila jabbed at her egg with her spoon.

"I wish you wouldn't bully. What's it got to do with you, anyway!"

"Only that if you're not going to take on the job, I am."

Maggie's teacup clattered into its saucer. There was a ring of happiness in her voice which warmed Janet's heart.

"You're not, Jan!"

Janet nodded at her mother.

"Yes, I am. I told you that you were too thin, you bad old woman. I'm looking for some job near here where I can keep an eye on you. Well, Sheila, do you mean to take the job or don't you?"

Sheila wriggled.

"I'm not sure. I can't be rushed."

"Don't talk nonsense about being rushed," said Maggie. "You had the job offered you last autumn, and now it's June."

"Well, I haven't been strong enough."

Janet's voice was quietly determined.

"Now you are strong enough, do you want the job or don't you? You were offered it first. I'm not butting in if you're going to take it."

Sheila looked stubbornly in front of her, and then with a cry which had a real ring of suffering in it, she put her head in her hands and burst into tears.

"Goodness!" thought Janet. "We are a lot of cry babies in this house. We're like Jo and Beth in *Little Women*. Whatever's come over us!" Unwillingly she found herself pitying Sheila.

"Come on. Don't cry. What's the matter?"

"It isn't fair!" Sheila wailed. "I ought not to be shut up in a little village being expected to be a governess. The best years of my life are passing and no . . . nobody cares."

Maggie laughed.

"Don't be a little goose. You've got plenty of best years left at nineteen. It was you who chose Worsingfold, you know."

"But I didn't know how things would turn out. I thought it would all be so different."

Janet stared at Sheila's heaving shoulders.

"What on earth did you hope would happen here?"

"Never you mind. But I did. And here I am with nobody to see me except a lot of cows."

Maggie and Janet, though realizing Sheila's grief to be real, could not help laughing. Maggie patted Sheila's curls.

"Cheer up, child, and eat your supper. As a matter of fact you and I have been thinking exactly the same thing. It's time you got away and took a job, you . . ."

Sheila's head shot up.

"Now! Why should I? I've put up with this dead and alive hole for months; it would be idiotic to go now." Maggie placidly sipped her tea.

"Why, dear? Do you mean because it's summer time? But wars don't wait because it's summer. I think you ought to go into one of the services."

"Me!"

Janet lost her temper.

"Yes, you! Why not? You sound as if there was something special about you which kept you from working like an ordinary person."

Sheila turned on her.

"So there is. You'd know it fast enough if I'd gone on the pictures, and was as famous as Vivien Leigh."

Anger died in Janet, to be replaced, as it had so often been before, by a feeling of helplessness. You couldn't treat Sheila as an ordinary person, she was wrapped round in an armour-plated sheath of belief in herself, in her beauty and charm, and it cut her off from common everyday people as if she were actually of different clay. She finished her egg before she spoke, and then used a quiet, reasoning voice.

"You don't want to stay here doing nothing, do you?"

"Where, as you say, nobody but the cows see you," Maggie added.

Sheila looked from Janet to her mother with a hunted expression.

"Of course I don't. But it won't go on. I mean the war might finish, or—or anything."

"Even if it did, which at the moment doesn't seem very likely, I shouldn't think Worsingfold would be a riot of gaiety."

"The quickest way to finish the war is for everybody to get down to working," Maggie pointed out.

Sheila looked more hunted than ever.

"Of course, if you're going to drive me out."

Maggie laid aside her egg-cup, and helped herself to some jam.

"Don't talk nonsense, dear. You always understood that you had to work for your living."

"Only for six months, and then I was going into pictures."

"Yes, if there hadn't been a war," Maggie agreed.

"If you hadn't made that idiotic fuss and made me learn to type, I'd have been in pictures before the war started."

"Don't let's have all that again," Maggie pleaded. "The point is the war did come. I don't know what the position of actresses is, but I feel sure only the very high-ups are allowed to go on working; the rest, together with all you other girls, will sooner or later be called up like the men, and only fair too, if you ask me."

"Then Jan will have to go too. She won't be able to stop round in the country teaching one kid."

Janet, her eyes on Sheila's resentful face, struggled to get at what was at the back of Sheila's mind. "I'm sure she wants to stop here for some reason," she thought. "A reason with Sheila is a man. It can't be Mr. Sheldon or, of course, she'd have taken on teaching Iris. I wonder what other men there are round here. I must ask Mum."

"Janet won't mind," said Maggie. "If it's her duty."

Sheila gave Janet a malicious look.

"She pretended she was going to join up. She told Old Tom she was going in the W.R.N.S. Swankpot. You won't half look a fool in Worsingfold when they find that all you've done is to take on the job I didn't want."

"The W.R.N.S.!" Maggie looked at Janet. "It's the first I'd heard of that."

Janet bent her head to hide a flush.

"It was only an idea."

"We'll have a talk later on." Maggie turned back to Sheila. "I think you should give yourself a week to make up your mind, dear, then you must register at a Labour Exchange."

"Labour Exchange! Me!"

Janet sighed.

"Yes, even you."

Sheila was scratching a pattern on the cloth with her nail.

"I like the way Janet plans to live in the cottage and turn me out. Who got the cottage, anyway?"

"You did," Janet agreed. "And if you like to take on the job of teaching Iris you can stop in it. Or how about the Land Army? I expect you could get a job somewhere round here when you're trained."

Maggie chuckled.

"I'd get a real laugh at Sheila in the Land Army!"

Sheila had to smile.

"So'd I. That's one thing I'll never do."

Maggie took Janet's cup to refill it.

"I should go and have a talk with the Labour Exchange people. They'll have a lot to tell you about jobs, but I should think, being a shorthand-typist, you'll do something in that line."

Sheila held out her cup for more tea. Her eyes were lowered so her mother could not get an idea of her thoughts.

"I'll see. If you turn me out, it's my business what I do." Maggie and Janet washed up and cleared away. Sheila lit a cigarette and strolled off into the garden, and Janet said nothing. There had been enough argument for one night. For quite a time there was silence in the kitchen, both Maggie and Janet turning over in their heads the scene at the table. Maggie was trying not to feel wretched. Sheila was her baby, and what she would have liked to have done was to run out and give her a hug, and tell her that of course she was only to do just what she wanted, that Mother wasn't really hard and unkind. In fact she wanted to take back not only what she had just said, but what she had been working herself up for weeks to say. Instead she wiped the dishes, and made herself stay where she was. She knew she had done the right thing, and only the foolish side of her mother-love was saying she had been cruel. All very well if you were rich, and if there wasn't a war, to give in to a lovely, idle little creature, but this was not a world of fairy-tales but of exceedingly cold reality.

Janet, her arms in the basin, her hands busy, was still puzzling over Sheila. Why had she picked Worsingfold? What had she hoped for?

"Mum," she said suddenly, "is there a film studio near here?"

Maggie at once got on to where Janet's thoughts had landed. "No, dear. I'd thought of that. Nothing of the sort. Nor does anyone connected with the film industry have a house here."

"Then there must be a man."

"Well, who? You never saw a neighbourhood with less men. There's Mr. Sheldon, and Dr. Nelson, but he's married with grown-up daughters, and the vicar, but he's an old man, sixty-five at least. There's Colonel Haines, he's not young, of course, but he's nice looking; but it certainly isn't him, for although Miss Haines has been very kind Sheila doesn't seem to like her or her father, and never goes near them. Mr. Sheldon has a half-brother, known locally as Mr. Dick; he's young and attractive, I believe, but he's in the Army and has never been home since we've been here, and as a matter of fact local gossip says that he and little Barbara Haines are very sweet on each other. In fact I think the village expected a wedding before this."

"I can tell you about that if that's the man she's fond of. When we were in the train she told me she couldn't do anything to upset her father as he'd been ill. She said she couldn't go and do war work or anything, but I guessed she was talking about getting married."

"Poor little girl! What a shame! Still, the colonel has been terribly ill, I believe, and he's very dependent on his daughter. I dare say she's done right to put off marriage until he's stronger."

"I should have thought, if he's in the Army, she could have got married and then lived at home."

"It wouldn't be the same thing; there's no security in a married daughter, her husband has first right. Mind you, of course, I'm sure her father doesn't know she wants to get married; they say he's a very fine man, and I'm certain he would be horrified if he knew he was standing in her way. I expect he's as surprised as anyone that she hasn't announced her engagement."

"What's his name besides Mr. Dick?"

"I haven't any idea. I've heard little Iris speak of him, and, of course, she calls him Uncle Dick. Whenever he's spoken of in the village it's either as 'Mr. Dick, him that's half-brother to Mr. Sheldon', or else as 'Mr. Dick, him who's sweet on Miss Barbara'. They keep a special voice for him as they do for Mr. Sheldon; they've belonged here for generations and are accepted and looked up to; it's rather as though they were relations who'd done well in the world. We don't seem to have that sort of connection with people in London."

"Getting quite a country bumpkin, aren't you, darling! You've even caught the accent."

Maggie had put away the last of the dinner things. She hung her cloth on a line to dry, then came and leant against the sink, which Janet was scrubbing down.

"Did you want to go in the W.R.N.S.?"

"Yes, if I'd done anything. You see, I hadn't thought of stopping here."

Maggie took Janet's chin in her hand and turned her face towards her.

"Had you set your heart on going? You'd been crying, hadn't you?"

Janet grinned.

"Yes, Mrs. Sherlock Holmes."

"Was it about missing the W.R.N.S.?"

"Yes."

"Are you doing this for me?"

Janet moved her head.

"Can I have my chin back and finish cleaning your sink?"

"Not until you've answered my question."

Janet swung round and faced her mother.

"If you must know, yes. I think you're too thin, and I love you too much to want to come home and find that you've slipped down the pipe with the bath water."

"Your being here won't make me fat, darling."

"That's all you know." Janet turned back to the sink. "You'll be surprised what's going to happen to you. Probably bed; certainly a long chair in the garden, and not getting up until eleven. Tonics and milk and eggs and . . ."

Maggie's voice was sharp.

"I'm not seeing the doctor."

"Oh, yes, you are. Fair's fair. I love you better than the W.R.N.S., so for love of me you can give up your old-fashioned ideas that doctors are only required when one is dying. I don't suppose he'll find much the matter with you, but there'll be something wrong if I let you get any thinner."

"If I promised to take things a little easier, wouldn't that satisfy you?"

"It would not. I know you, you're a bad old woman, and this weak daughter could never keep you in order; you need a savage doctor for that."

Maggie let the point drop for the moment.

"You know, dear, I shouldn't like you to give up the W.R.N.S. if you've set your heart on joining. It may be that it's the right thing for you, and missing the experience is something you'll regret all your life."

Janet had finished the sink. She dried her hands and took off her apron. She spoke with conviction.

"Staying here is the right thing for me." She hooked her arm through her mother's. "Do you remember Mrs. Rose at the cake shop at home, how she used to say, 'It's meant, Mrs. Brain. It's meant.'"

§

JANET walked to the farm in a bad temper. It was all very well in an overnight glow of self-sacrifice to assure her mother that 'it was meant' she should stay in the country. In the morning she knew that 'meant' or not she was going to hate it. To begin with it was pouring with rain. A cottage which is two fields from the farm road is considered in bad weather inconvenient by the country woman. To Janet it seemed an idiotic position. No wonder her mother was ill if she had struggled across those tracks in midwinter. Her temper was not improved by finding her mother down before her. She gave her a kiss, and spoke in a teasing voice, but her tone was not convincing.

"You are a bad old lady. I told you not to come down until eleven."

"I've been awake since six, and I wanted a cup of tea."

"Well, take your tea and go and sit down in the sitting-room." Maggie opened her mouth, then seeing the glint in her daughter's eye, did as she was told.

The morning went on like that. Janet got Sheila out of bed, and brought her down to help, and had her, grumbling and tousled, laying the breakfast table. After breakfast she still insisted that Maggie rested, and put her on the couch in the sitting-room with her feet up. She dragged Sheila round with her making beds, washing up, dusting and cleaning. At eleven she made a pot of tea and brought it in to Maggie. She put the tray on a chair by the sofa and sat on the floor with her back against her mother's legs. Maggie looked at her with a loving twinkle.

"Feeling pleased with yourself?"

Janet was at that moment feeling smug. She had made Sheila work, she had made her mother rest, she had slaved uncomplainingly herself, but something in Maggie's voice made her go carefully.

"Why?"

Maggie poured out the tea.

"You've made Sheila do all the things she hates most—"

"It's good for her, lazy little beast."

"Where is she now?"

"Lying down. She said she felt too tired to swallow."

"I dare say it's true."

"Well, she must do her share of the work"

"You plunged her into it a bit suddenly, poor child. You never warned her you were going to treat me as an invalid. Just as you've plunged me into it rather suddenly. I'm bored and I'm cold. If I must rest I'd like to come to it gradually, and not start on a wet, cold day." Janet gave an exasperated movement. Maggie patted her shoulder. "I know, darling, just how you feel, but I know, too, just how Sheila and I are feeling. Now you put on the gumboots you'll find in the passage cupboard and run along up to the farm. I'm going to take a cup of tea up to Sheila, and then I'm going to cook the dinner."

The farm was a low-lying, white thatched building, with its innumerable barns, milking sheds and outhouses lying round it like a litter of puppies. The farm road curved through a white gate round the side of the house to the yard. Obviously that was the normal way of entry. There was a hedge dividing the road from the farm front garden. A little path ran in front of the hedge and the front door was reached through a latched gate. Janet stood a second considering. Should she ring the front-door bell and ask the housekeeper where Donald Sheldon was, or should she go on, and do as he had suggested, and ask one of his men where she could find him? The state of her boots decided her, she was much more fitted for a farmyard than a front door.

An aged man carrying a bucket was crossing the yard. He had a buff-coloured, wrinkled face, and buff-coloured, infinitely old clothes. He was like a leaf that had been lying where it fell since some long past autumn.

"Excuse me," said Janet, "but do you know where I can find Mr. Sheldon?"

The man raised unexpectedly bright eyes and fixed her with a childlike stare. It seemed as if her question had a long way to go before it contacted his brain.

"Master," he said at last, "he'm up to long acre."

"Where's that?"

There was another immense pause.

"A tidy step."

"How do I go?"

"You do'ant. You bides here."

Janet could not be impatient with anything so old, and, to her, rather pathetic. She spoke patiently.

"I must find him. Will you show me the way?"

An iron gate behind her clanged, and Donald came striding across the yard.

"There you are. Ben's given you my message, I see."

Janet smiled politely and waited until old Ben had plodded into a shed before she said:

"I didn't exactly get a message, but then he's very, very old, poor thing, isn't he?"

Donald laughed.

"Old, yes, but you've no need to pity him. There's a lot of life in him yet. He'd have given you the message in time. He was just keeping you hanging about so that he could look you over."

"Isn't he too old to work?"

He led her towards the house.

"He's slow, but then he always was. He worked for my grandfather, and then my uncle, and then my father, and now me. He's an old-age pensioner, but he wouldn't think of leaving the farm; if I told him to go he wouldn't, any more than he'd leave my cottage. I told him the other day I might need it for some Land Army girls and he said, 'They besoms can wait till I'm carried out.' He meant in his coffin. Of course I shan't turn him out, he knows that. I'll manage somehow. We go in at the side. We never use the front. My housekeeper, Miss Batten, is a grand woman, but house-proud. Iris and I are terrified of leaving a dirty mark in the front, but we're allowed to at the back."

The side door opened into a long stone passage. Donald stood in the doorway and shouted.

"Iris! Iris!" He lowered his voice and turned to Janet. "I'm not going to ask you if you'll take your sister's job until you've seen the kid."

A door opened and a woman came towards them. Janet's eyes goggled. Was this the housekeeper? She had imagined somebody inconspicuous and middle-aged. This woman looked about thirty.

She had sleek, blue-black hair smartly cut, a white, dissatisfied face, beautifully curved eyebrows, and an unusually large mouth. She had on a white overall, but it couldn't hide an exceptionally nice figure. She spoke in a low, husky voice.

"Don't be silly, Donald, Miss Brain can't see Iris out here, bring her in. It is Miss Brain, isn't it?"

Donald made the introduction.

"I'm dirty," Janet apologized.

"Perhaps you wouldn't mind the kitchen," Donald suggested. "I've got some work to do in the yard. Will you find me before you go?"

The kitchen was enormous, stone-flagged, with a long low window looking across fields to a distant hill. Early yellow roses were hanging over the panes.

"Please sit down." Gladys pulled out a chair. "I'll fetch Iris. I make a rule she doesn't run about the house in the mornings. I'm sorry to bring you in here, but you've no idea what this house is like to keep clean. I have the wife of one of Mr. Sheldon's men to work for me, but even then the place is never fit to be seen."

Janet looked round at the dresser with its rows of spotless china, at an almost unique collection of shimmering copper saucepans standing on a shelf, at the bright, clean cretonne curtains, at the well-washed flags and the scrubbed paint and woodwork, and she laughed.

"I'm a Londoner. Nothing in London ever looks like this, you know, however much you clean it. I've never seen a kitchen like this before. We only had a small slip of a house. I imagine if I had a kitchen like this I'd never leave it."

Gladys' eyes were taking Janet in.

"You're not a bit like your sister."

Janet untied the handkerchief she had fastened peasant fashion over her hair.

"I'm always an awful shock. People ought to be warned, really, or better still, see me first, then they wouldn't be disappointed;

but two beauties in one family would be a bit much to expect, wouldn't it?"

Gladys' voice was truculent.

"I like your sister."

Janet was surprised. Sheila was seldom liked by women, especially not good-looking ones.

"You'd have liked her to have been Iris' governess, then," she said sympathetically, "but it would never have worked."

"She never had any intention of coming as governess. I told Donald so dozens of times. I advised him to send the child away as a boarder. I still think it would be better."

Janet had been chatting vaguely. She was slow at making up her mind about people. She had registered Gladys' good looks and got no further. Now, in one sentence, said in that deep, husky voice of hers, Gladys had come out into the open. "Goodness," thought Janet, "she doesn't want me to come here, and she's telling me so. Why?" Out loud she said casually:

"She's rather small, isn't she? Can I see her?"

Gladys went to the door and opened it, then, as if a thought struck her, she turned.

"She'd be better at school; her mother was artistic. Iris inherits it. That sort of stuff is no good on a farm; besides, women are needed and it's ridiculous to waste woman-power on one child."

Janet made a funny little face as the door closed.

"Getting at me, are you?" Then she shrugged her shoulders. "Silly idiot, either she's afraid I'll interfere with the house, which I won't, or else she's in love with Mr. Sheldon, and, if it's that, she'd much better have me about than Sheila. She ought to be thankful to see my plain face."

Gladys came back leading Iris by the hand. The child was small for eight. A thin, angular little creature, with long brown pigtails with neat bows on their ends, a spotless check cotton frock, white socks carefully pulled up, and well-polished shoes, without the stub-toed look customary in a child's house shoes. Neat, tidy, colourless were the words she brought to mind.

"Say how do you do," Gladys said sharply.

The sharpness seemed unnecessary, for Iris had already released her right hand and was politely holding it out. Something about the depressing neatness of the child caught at Janet's heart. She held the hand and drew the child to her and kissed her.

"Good morning, not that it is a good morning, it's a perfect beast, isn't it? I hate rain, don't you?"

"Iris is a farmer's daughter and knows water is needed. We've had nearly a drought here."

Janet laughed.

"I may know I need medicine, but it doesn't make me like it."

Iris' face changed. It broke into a wide grin, her eyes were raised to Janet and she saw they were an unusually lovely blue. Laughing, the child looked a different person.

"I hate rain too," she agreed. "I've got gum boots, and a mackintosh and a sou'wester, and I'd like to go out and help Ben."

Gladys put a saucepan on the stove.

"You'll have a cup of coffee, Miss Brain." As Janet smiled assent she looked over her shoulder at Iris. "When you are old enough to clean your own boots and mackintosh, you can do what you like about going out, but while I've got to look after you as well as do all the housework, I can't put up with any extra mess; your father and the men stamping in and out are bad enough." Iris had a clear little voice.

"I could clean them myself, but you won't let me."

"It only makes more work if I do, slopping water everywhere." Gladys evidently felt she was sounding hard, for she turned to Janet with a note of apology in her voice. "I sound rather fierce, but if you knew what there was to do in this house. Sometimes when Iris comes in with a torn frock, or has fallen down and made herself in a mess, I could cry. I do all the washing myself. The laundry tears everything to bits. I have the woman, Mrs. Honeywell, to help me, but she's no good at fine work. All Iris' little things I iron and wash myself."

Janet thought how wretched for the child to hear what a burden she was; but at the same time she felt for Gladys. She was obviously overstrained and nervous. She was evidently one of those women who must have everything just so, and was driven distracted at anything untidy or torn. It seemed a pity she had chosen to live on a large, rambling farm; a little labour-saving flat or villa was what she needed.

"If I come and give Iris lessons, I can help look after her things."

Iris clutched at Janet's arm.

"Are you going to? Daddy said Sheila might be, but I heard her tell Gladys she was too ill to. Please do. Mummy used to teach me lessons, and I can read and write, but I write crooked unless there's ruled lines. Of course I was only little when Mummy taught me, and we read *Brer Rabbit*, and about Baba, but she read out loud to me too, *Alice in Wonderland* and the *Just So Stories*. I can read those to myself now, but we haven't got many books for me. Daddy doesn't know what to buy."

Gladys turned to Janet.

"I hardly ever get into town, and when I do I don't get time to go to bookshops; but you can't say you never get any new books, Iris, you had those two great annuals at Christmas, there ought to be enough in them to keep you quiet for a year."

Iris looked trustingly at Janet, expecting perfect understanding.

"It's all short. I like a book to be all one and go on and on."

"Well, off you run to your books now." Gladys' voice was brisk. "I want to talk to Miss Brain."

Iris moved unwillingly.

"You will learn me, won't you?"

Janet blew her a kiss.

"I expect so. Good-bye."

Gladys poured coffee and milk into two cups and put one down beside Janet.

"You don't take sugar, I expect," she said firmly. "We none of us do nowadays, do we?"

Janet hated coffee without sugar, but she accepted it with an agreeing smile. At the same time she was surprised; of course sugar was precious, but she had not yet reached the point where she had none to offer a visitor, and Gladys did not look the sort to be parsimonious. Her big mouth seemed more likely to show a tendency to give too much.

"Iris seems a pet."

Gladys stirred her coffee some while before answering.

"I do my duty by her, goodness knows, I couldn't have done more if she were my own. You should have seen me nursing her with measles. The doctor said I was wonderful, and so did Donald."

"All right," Janet thought. "I'm not arguing with you." Out loud she said:

"Sad for her having no mother."

"That's just it." Gladys' voice was eager. "She misses her. Try as I will I can't give the attention to her I should like. I'm sure if you come you will do your best, but what she needs is other children. I've worked for months to get her away to a boarding school. I know it's the best thing for her, and so the doctor thinks. I was thankful Sheila never meant to teach her. I do implore you don't upset all my hard work. If you refuse to teach her, then Donald will have to agree to her going away."

Janet felt awkward. Gladys was obviously sincere in her pleading. She had been looking after the child, and if she and the doctor believed she should be in a boarding school, it was tough a possible governess arriving out of the blue.

"She wouldn't be going to school until September," she suggested cautiously. "I might take her over until then and see how we got on."

Gladys' tone was rude.

"Well, of course, I can't stop you."

"Goodness!" thought Janet. "What is this?"

"After all, even if I don't teach her, I suppose Mr. Sheldon might decide to have a resident governess rather than send her to school."

"Oh, no, he won't! I put a stop to that. If a governess lives in, I said, I go out."

Janet, for a person of twenty-five, had led a sheltered life. There had been no other women in her office to chatter, and discuss things with her. At home their friends were the children of Maggie's friends. They had their faults like everybody else, but on the whole they were simple and straightforward. They liked a good time and a good laugh. They fell in love, some of them, and if so they got married. They were not a complex lot. Now, listening to Gladys, Janet felt as if she were on the edge of something new. Gladys' husky voice had deepened and smouldered as she spoke of Donald. "She loves him," she told herself, and, even as the thought reached her, she felt a revulsion. This was not love as she knew it; it was not love as she wanted to know it. It was fierce and possessive. The glimpse she had of Gladys' heart was as if, used to an English wood, she had peered into a tropical forest. She got up, awkward as a schoolgirl.

"Thank you for the coffee. I . . . I must go."

Gladys looked as if she were going to say more, but she changed her mind. She seemed to accept that Janet intended to take the job. Her manner altered. Janet was no longer a guest. She nodded towards the door into the passage.

"You'll find Donald in one of the barns. Ask Ben, the yardman."

Donald was deep in a discussion with his horse-keeper. He smiled at Janet and said he would not be a minute, then went on with what he was saying. A lot of the talk was incomprehensible to her, especially the horse-keeper's replies. The blacksmith was apparently ill, and a horse called Samson was in need of a shoe. Donald was arguing with the old man on the advisability of taking him somewhere called Molston to be shod. The discussion finished by Donald laughing, and giving the old man an affectionate push to send him off. He turned to Janet.

"Stubborn old fellow. I often wonder whose farm this is. Well, what did you think of her?"

They were in one of the stables. She leant against the manger.

"I've never had much to do with children, but she seemed to me interesting. She's very advanced for eight, isn't she?"

"Too advanced, I think. That's why I'm against a school. All schools push clever children on. I want her talked with and played with, but not worked; she's too much alone."

"At a good boarding school she'd have other children—" He moved; she stopped him with a gesture. "I'm not trying to get out of teaching her. As a matter of fact, I want the job, but I'm thinking of her."

"Gladys has been talking. She's full of this boarding school idea, she's even got the doctor on her side. But that's because she's over anxious. The kid had measles pretty badly, and Gladys has been scared ever since. She's as fond of Iris as if she were her own child, and it worries her she can't give all the time to her she'd like. She thinks a governess in the daytime isn't enough, she'd like her where there are matrons and all that. Before I came to the arrangement with Sheila I had thought of a resident governess, but, of course, that was impossible, it was stupid of me to think of it." He looked apologetically at Janet as if he were afraid she was thinking him a fool. "Difficult for a male to get the hang of how a woman feels; I saw directly I suggested it that Gladys could not possibly be asked to share the drawing-room and all that with a woman she didn't know."

Janet lowered her eyes to hide the expression in them, which was not sympathetic to Gladys.

"All right, then, I'll take Iris on."

His voice vibrated with pleasure.

"Good. When will you start?"

"Tomorrow."

"Better still." His eyes ran over her. "I can see we are going to get on fine." She walked to the door, and he kept pace with her. "Now, mind you, you've a free hand. Teach her what you like, but not too much sitting indoors. You can spend what you like within reason, you know, for books and all that. Just let me know what you want."

They stood in the stable door. The rain was beating down in a sheet before them, turning the yard into mud, but neither of them noticed the weather. There was a warm glow of understanding and fellowship between them, that was as good as the sun coming out.

"You won't hold it against your governess that you found her crying in a wood?"

He smiled.

"With a bit of moss on her chin."

She stepped out into the yard. Then a thought struck her.

"By the way, we haven't discussed money. I used to know a girl who lived out and came in to teach, and lend a hand, she got two guineas a week. Would that be all right?"

His face completely changed. He looked at her as if she were not the same woman he had been talking with a few seconds before.

"Two guineas! But . . ."

She tried to laugh away the discomfort between them.

"It sounds a lot, but, honestly, it's quite fair, and I'm afraid I must earn that, or look for some other job." His face was like iron. She laughed again, this time rather nervously. "Do I sound very mercenary?"

He hesitated as if he had something cutting to say. Then he changed his mind.

"Yes, you do. Under the circumstances you might have left it to me to do the fair thing. Your terms are not fair, but you're holding a pistol to my head. I want Iris taught. You can have your two guineas."

Janet stared at his back striding across the yard. She was horribly hurt. What did he mean? Under what circumstances'? Because Sheila had promised and let him down? That was no reason to get her sister cheap. She forgot to be hurt and, instead, was angry. She longed to run after him, to hold him by the arm and make him listen. He was spoilt by Gladys Batten. You can have your two guineas! What a way to talk! But she'd show him! She'd earn every penny of it. She'd make him ashamed.

Old Ben had been watching Janet and Donald from the shed where he had been mixing food for the turkeys. He watched Donald's departure, and then Janet's quick, angry march out of the yard. He shook his head.

"They do be wholly interested each in t'other." He chuckled to himself. "Gladys has a time coming, shouldn't wonder."

§

Janet kept her anger to herself. She told her mother quietly that she had agreed to take on the job of teaching Iris. Maggie was puzzled; she felt there was something not quite right, but Janet would not be drawn.

"Did you see Iris?"

"Yes."

"She's a dear little thing, isn't she?"

"Yes."

"What did you think of Miss Batten? I've only spoken to her once, and I found her not my type, but Sheila likes her."

"I didn't see her long enough to form an opinion."

"I'm sure you'll like Mr. Sheldon. Don't you think he seems nice?"

"I didn't think about him except as Iris' father."

Maggie sighed. Really, her daughters were difficult! Sheila, who could think of nothing but men, and Janet, who never thought about them at all. She had been just the same about Mr. Trent. It was not until the war started that she had even known that he was young. You could, as she had told herself, have knocked her down with a feather when Janet had said he had joined up. "Joined up!" she had gasped. "But surely they aren't taking old men."

"Old men!" Janet had looked amused. "I don't think he's thirty."

"Janet Brain," Maggie had said, "do you mean to tell me you've been working in that office all these years and you never told me Mr. Trent was young?"

"Why should I?" Janet had asked, puzzled. "I didn't know you'd be interested!" Really, an exasperating daughter, and here she was at it again. "I didn't think of him except as Iris' father!" Maggie could have shaken her. Of course she did not want her thinking of all men in a silly way, but it really was time she began to notice they existed.

Sheila also questioned Janet; she used her own oblique method. "Did you get muddy going up to the farm? Awful, isn't it, on a wet day?"

"I don't mind a little mud. How about you getting a little on you walking to the bus to go to the Labour Exchange?"

"There's not all that rush. I suppose I can wait for a fine day. It's the duty of everybody to keep well in wartime. I heard that on the wireless. It won't be any good my going to the Labour Exchange if I get a chill from it, and have to stop in bed for weeks."

"I shouldn't think it's much of a risk."

"I suppose, as you're in such a rush about me getting a job, you've decided to teach that awful Iris."

"I don't think she's awful, she seems a nice kid. As a matter of fact, I have."

Sheila wandered round the room fiddling with the ornaments.

"Well, I hope Mr. Sheldon's satisfied now." As Janet did not answer she shot her an anxious look over her shoulder. "Is he?"

"At having me instead of you? I think so. I gather, as a family, we were expected to produce a governess, and we have."

"Did he say that?" Sheila gave Janet another fleeting, anxious look. "What else did he say?"

Janet was in no mood to have her hurt probed.

"I don't remember. Why are you so interested? I've taken on the job and that's all that can concern you, isn't it?"

Sheila gave one of her wriggles.

"There's no need to be cross. I was just being friendly. It isn't a sin to be interested in what your sister earns and all that, is it?"

Janet saw the wriggle, and being used to Sheila, knew that she felt cornered. She also knew that they had come to the crux of the conversation on the word 'earn'. It was so true to Sheila's method to produce casually the object of a talk, as if it had been under discussion for quite a while. Often, when Sheila had tried to screw information out of her in this way in the past, she had teased her by holding it back. This time she did not feel like teasing. The word 'earn' was like a clumsy finger prodding her hurt. She could not conceive why Sheila should care what her money was to be, and she certainly was not going to tell her. To avoid an angry answer, she took a grip on herself, and said lightly, "I've fixed everything," and went out of the room.

Janet would have been startled if she could have seen Sheila's reaction to this remark. She looked after Janet, a flush spreading over her face. "She is mean," she muttered. "I believe he's told her, that's why she's cross, and she just isn't telling me because she wants me to go on worrying."

Janet gave a lot of care to her appearance the next morning. The rain had gone and it looked like being a fine day. She had some pretty, short-sleeved summer frocks, one of which she would have liked to have worn, but she rejected them and put on a long-sleeved, navy-blue dress, made of light woollen material that she had worn in the office. It had a neat white pique collar, and gave her a tidy, trim look. She wore her hair cut rather short, but long enough at the sides to curl back over her ears. This morning she put pins in these curls to hold them severely in place. When she was dressed she examined herself in the glass. There was no long mirror in her bedroom, so she tilted the dressing-table mirror backwards and forwards and saw herself in bits. "I'll do," she told herself. "Lisle stockings, flat-heeled country shoes, quiet dress, up to the throat and down to the wrists. Mouse-coloured hair, neat enough to be unbecoming; I shouldn't think anybody could look more like a governess than I do. He shan't say that he doesn't get something that looks right for his two guineas."

It had been agreed between Janet and Maggie the night before, that just for two or three days, until Janet had settled down in her new job, Maggie might do the cooking, and get the breakfast. In return she promised not to touch the garden, and to use Sheila for part of the housework, leaving the rest for Janet when she got back from Iris. Maggie had agreed the more readily because she was sure Janet would find Iris a whole-time job, and by degrees she would be able to slip back into doing everything, just as before. She had the breakfast on the table when Janet came down. Her lips twitched at the corners.

"A nice plain sailor hat, and some good gloves, would finish off the picture."

Janet grinned.

"I haven't overdone it, have I?" She helped herself to toast. "I don't want to look as if I were playing at the job."

"You don't. I had to laugh because you've tried so hard you look self-conscious. Are you coming back to dinner?" The thought of meals had not crossed Janet's mind. She stopped spreading her toast while she considered. What luck her mother had mentioned the subject! She imagined she was meant to feed with Iris at the farm, but how awful if she had taken it for granted. How still more awful if she was expected to go home; it would look as if she were trying to pick up perquisites on top of the two guineas.

"I think I'll take bread and cheese today. I forgot to ask about dinner."

"No need to take anything; either you're having it here or there. You can ask Miss Batten what's expected. I don't know if farms get more to eat than we do; if they don't I expect they'd rather you came back because of your rations, but if they want you to stay you could register with their butcher, and take up some cooking fat and sugar."

Janet interrupted Maggie's planning.

"No, I'd rather take bread and cheese, if you can spare it. Sheila could take my books to the Food Office and get my other books today, couldn't she?"

"Don't be silly, of course you can have the cheese. It's not your ration I'm worrying about, it's only it's so silly to eat scrappy bits out of a bag when you've a good dinner waiting for you a couple of fields away."

"Just for today I'd like to be independent. You do see how I feel, don't you?"

"No, I don't!" Maggie looked amusedly at her daughter. "I think you're behaving like a goose, which is not like you."

At a quarter to nine Janet, with her parcel of bread and cheese hung on one finger, started for the farm. She had not dared to put on a hat for fear of further teasing from Maggie. In spite of her uneasiness about the day ahead, she could not help her heart uplifting as she walked. It was such a lovely morning, the rain had brought out all the scents of the country. The good smell of wet earth, the mixed smells of clover, beans, hay, mustard, wheat, barley and wild flowers. Overhead a lark, rising higher and higher, sang as if he wished to burst with joy at being alive.

Her arrival at the farm, which Janet was dreading, was made easier by Iris. She was waiting for her at the gate, and as she came in sight gave a pleased whoop and ran towards her and flung herself on her.

"Good morning, Miss Brain. Gladys says I've got to call you that, but I call Sheila, Sheila, so couldn't I call you Janet? I call Barbara, Barbara, but that's different because Uncle Dick told me to. You see, he says she's almost a relation, at least he hopes she will be one day. I know that because Mrs. Honeywell, who helps Gladys, told me she was what she'd call 'Uncle Dick's steady', and I asked him if she was, and that's when he told me to call her Barbara."

Janet was turning over the child's request. What would Donald feel about Christian names? Gladys Batten seemed to be called by hers. It would be humiliating to give permission if Iris was then ordered by her father to revert to the formal 'miss'.

"We'll have to see," she said, making her voice warm and friendly so that Iris could not feel snubbed. "Your father may not like Christian names for a governess."

"I shouldn't think he'd mind. He's very silly about names. He never thinks of new ones. It's me that christens nearly all the animals. Sometimes the men change what I've called them. I called the new bull Blue-eyes, but George, he's the cowman, you know, he just calls him 'Bluey'. He says Blue-eyes is fancified. What lesson are we going to start with?"

"Grammar, I should think, if you are going to talk about fancified."

"I know it's wrong, but I was just telling you what he said, and it wouldn't be him if I said fanciful."

Janet looked down at the child with concern. Not a great many children had crossed her path, but she remembered them, and herself and Sheila distinctly, and none of them were at all like this child. She did hope she was going to be able to teach her; it would be awful if, after the money fuss, she was a failure.

"How far have you got with arithmetic?"

"Terrible. Do you know, I can only just add, and then not always right. You see, when Mummy taught me I was only six and couldn't do sums. Daddy has tried sometimes in the evenings, but he says I'm a hopeless ignoramus. Mummy and me did adding with bricks, but we didn't do it much, neither of us liked it much. We liked acting and reading. We acted all the people in the books, and lots in hist'ry. Can you act?"

"No, I'm afraid not."

"I expect you could be courtiers and people, couldn't you, who just curtsy and bow? Like this." Iris sank in an elaborate curtsy, and Janet, laughing, made her a deep bow.

They were just inside the farm gate, and at that moment Donald came round the side of the house. He stood watching them. Iris felt his eyes on them and looked up.

"Daddy, I was making Miss Brain a courtier because she says she can't act, but I thought she bowed beautifully, didn't you?"

Donald looked awkward.

"Fine. Good morning, Miss Brain."

Iris bounded to him and hung on his arm.

"Oh, Daddy, that does remind me! Gladys says I've got to call her Miss Brain, and I said to her need I? Could I call her Janet, and she said we must see, you mightn't like a governess to have a Christian name, but I said you wouldn't mind because you aren't interested, like when you weren't about the one for the new bull."

Janet gazed at her feet and struggled not to laugh. Donald made no effort, he laughed out loud. Iris, uncertain of the joke, laughed too, and after a second Janet joined them.

They were interrupted by Gladys. She was leaning out of a bedroom window looking down on them. The tone in her voice would have killed any laugh.

"Everybody seems to have a lot of time to waste this morning." Donald was apologetic.

"It was Iris. She was asking what she should call Miss Brain. She said I shouldn't care because I hadn't cared what she called the new bull."

Gladys' voice was full of expectation.

"Yes?"

"Well, that was all."

"Then I must add to my first statement, you've not only got time to waste, but breath, laughing at nothing."

Janet felt sure it would be wise to hold her tongue, but whatever Donald and Iris put up with, she was not going to be spoken to in that tone of voice.

"Miss Batten's quite right. Come on, Iris, show me your schoolroom." She turned to Donald. "And the question of the name is settled, since it's of no interest to you. Iris will call me Janet."

Iris seemed cowed by Gladys, but she gave a tiny skip and whispered "Goody."

"Bring Miss Brain in, Iris," Gladys emphasized the surname, "and I will show her your schoolroom." She smiled at Donald. "Quite a breath of town, isn't she, to we simple country folk? We're not used to Christian names to strangers."

Janet followed Iris with her chin high, but her heart was beating extra quickly. "What I'd like to do to her," she thought savagely, "is to give her a good slap across the face." There was just one small piece of balm to soothe her spirit. She had seen a look in Donald's eye as if he would have liked to have said, "Don't mind her." The look had died almost at once, and had been replaced with a hard 'I'm not going to like you, so don't try and make me' expression; but the first look had been there, and the thought of it was comforting.

The schoolroom was an attic. It had a sloping roof, and windows looking across the fields. It was a charming room, perfect for a child. In the windows were yellow curtains with nursery rhyme figures appliqued on in gay cottons with wool hair. The walls were distempered white and showed up the glorious oak beams. There were pictures blazing with colour. A flower group, a winding road through cornfields, some children playing on wet sand, all beautiful reproductions. The furniture and mantelpiece were the same gay yellow as the curtains. In the centre of the table was a bowl of buttercups. Janet's irritation disappeared; she turned, smiling, to Gladys.

"My word, this is nice!"

Gladys, too, forgot herself.

"It's Iris' mother's doing. She furnished this and Iris' bedroom. The rest of the house is full of what Donald has been left. What a difference!"

"Mummy made the curtains, and she did all the painting. She gave me the bowl and she said I was always to keep it pretty in winter and in summer, and I always have except when I've got a cold and can't go out."

Janet was fingering the curtains.

"Did she design these figures as well as applique them on?"

Iris danced over to her.

"Yes, every single one. Her and me sat together and she asked me what to draw an' I chose, and sometimes it was a person like Goldilocks, an' sometimes an animal like this." She pointed to a whale cut out of black sateen. "That's the one that sicked up Jonah."

Janet looked, at Gladys.

"She was an artist?"

Gladys gave a slight shrug of her shoulders.

"She did a little of everything." She turned away, her manner suggesting, "I could, tell you more if I would, and if the child were not here."

"Well, I must get on with my work, and I should think it's time you started, isn't it?"

All Janet's irritation was back, but she controlled herself this time. She nodded and told Iris to show her where she kept her books.

The morning passed quickly. Janet discovered that Iris had practically nothing to learn from. There was no atlas, there were two exercise books full of her early efforts at letter making. There were three or four Beatrix Potter's, and one *Babar*, which had been bought to teach her to read. There was a box of lettered bricks, and the little library of books from which her mother had read aloud to her. She and Iris made out a timetable of things that must be learned, and things which Iris wanted to learn. Things which should be done in the schoolroom, and things which could be done out of doors. They had just finished a rough list when a bell clanged. Iris jumped off her chair.

"Come on. That's my milk. Is my hair tidy?"

Janet had a comb in her bag, she ran it through the child's hair, and straightened her bows on her plaits.

"You'll do; anyway, I don't expect it matters very much just for drinking milk."

Iris led the way downstairs.

"Oh, it does," she spoke in a hoarse whisper. "It matters awf'ly to Gladys. Ben says she's so tidy she won't be able to lie quiet in her grave if her shroud don't sit sweet."

Gladys was flying round the kitchen apparently doing three jobs at once. On the table was a glass of milk and a plate with two biscuits on it.

"Sit down, Iris, and eat tidily," she said in a voice which made Janet bristle. "You can have a cup of coffee, Miss Brain."

"Thank you, I don't want anything." Janet pushed Iris' chair a little nearer the table. It was all right where it was, but in the gesture she intended to show she too had authority over the child. Evidently Gladys was not only house-proud in the way she kept a home, but over food; she was one of those women who do not like to see people in her kitchen without a cup of something in their hands. She paid no attention to what Janet said, but with a flare of colour in her cheeks, poured out a cup of coffee, and with a you-dare-not-to-drink-that look, put it in front of Janet. Janet was cross with herself for the number of times her hackles had stood up that morning. She was cross, too, with herself for the way she had pushed in Iris' chair. She was being petty, and it was foreign to her nature. She stirred the sugarless coffee and managed to smile. Gladys, who was turning back to her pots and pans, hesitated as if she would like to say something, and from the softness round her mouth something friendly. Then her mind changed, and she was back at her stove making an unnecessary clatter with a saucepan lid.

Janet thought that enough time had been spent indoors; the moment Iris had swallowed her last crumb, and had gulped her last drop of milk, she had her out of doors, and the rest of the morning was spent on what Iris grandly described as 'bot'ny', which meant that Janet picked every flower she could see and asked Iris what its name was. Dinner at the farm, Janet learned, was at one o'clock. As the time drew nearer her sandwiches became important. She could not, she told herself, face a drawn-out meal with either Gladys or Donald; she would like the time to herself sitting under a haystack. She was not going to be about at dinner-time, but if the question of where she should eat arose, she would say right out she preferred having the time to herself. She took Iris in at a quarter to one and brushed and replaited her hair, and saw her wash her hands, then she gave her a kiss.

"Read a book until you are called, darling. I'll be back to tuck you up for your lie-down after dinner."

"Where are you going to have dinner?"

"Outside, I've brought sandwiches. Look!" Janet held up her parcel.

Iris looked worried.

"It sounds awfully queer to me your sitting outside eating and us inside."

"It isn't, really; be a good girl and run down directly Gladys calls you."

In books there always seemed to be haystacks standing about under which people ate their meals. Donald's farm seemed badly laid out in this respect, there were none standing in a handy and picturesque position. Janet did not want to be seen hunting about so as to attract notice from the farm hands, so she walked quietly out of the yard and through the gate. There was some rough grass and a hedge between the garden and the cornfield; the hedge was just what Janet was looking for, handy, and screening her from the house. She sat down and undid her sandwiches, then, because it was hot, and peaceful, and the view lovely and restful, she forgot to eat, and instead fell into a daydream, a daydream in which Donald was the central figure, saying—they were on Christian name terms in the dream—"Janet, can you forgive me for being a parsimonious beast? How could I have grudged you two guineas! You are a wonderful governess and worth at least five." She was brought back to the world by a shadow which fell across her, and she looked up to see Donald with a frown between his brows glaring down at her. "What is this nonsense?"

"What nonsense?"

"Eating sandwiches out here."

"There was no mention of meals in our agreement. I don't want to sponge on you."

He looked as if he was going to shake her.

"Please come in at once, lunch is getting cold."

She was just as angry as he was.

"Thank you, I prefer to stop here."

He made a noise of utter exasperation, and before she knew what he was thinking of, had stooped down, gripped her by the arms and stood her on her feet. Then he released one arm and gave her a pull to make her walk beside him.

"Come on at once, and don't behave like a fool."

"And don't you behave like a bully. I suppose this is how you treat your farm hands and the cows and sheep, but you can't treat me in this way."

He gripped her more firmly.

"As you can imagine from my behaviour, I flog my farm hands, and as for the sheep and cows, it's pitiful the way I knock them about, so it won't surprise you when I tell you that you're either coming quietly, or I'm carrying you in."

Janet, with a supreme effort, dragged her arm free.

"You are the most insufferable man; such a way to treat a governess."

"My dear girl, I don't look upon you as a governess. Seeing how we know each other, it's hardly likely that I should, is it? I'm doing my duty, that's all. I know what's expected of me, and leaving you sitting like a tramp in a ditch is not what would be expected, is it?"

"I've no idea what you're talking about, but if, because the first time you meet a person you find them crying, you think it gives you the right to throw it in their teeth for ever more, you're quite wrong."

"Will you come on and not talk rubbish! I'm throwing nothing in your teeth, I'm asking you to lunch. It's spoiling, I should think, and I can't spare much time, but I'm not going in without you."

"You are mean, you know." She fell into step beside him. "You're taking advantage of the war, in farmers being busy, and everything. If I have lunch here I'll bring my rations."

"You can arrange that with Gladys, I expect she'll be glad of them." He opened the yard gate. "Come on."

The dining-room was hideous. It had been papered and furnished by Donald's grandfather. The walls were covered in red paper and there was some horrible heavy mahogany furniture about. On the walls were several bad oils of immensely fat cattle, under each was a glass case of medals. Gladys was sitting with an aggravatingly resigned expression at the bottom of the table. A chair with arms stood at the head of the table for Donald. Iris sat on Donald's left. Janet, as she walked in before Donald, felt like a foolish schoolgirl. She sat in the vacant chair on Gladys' right and heard, with crimson cheeks, her ring the bell, and when the door was opened by a cheerful, stout woman, listened to her saying in an exaggeratedly patient voice:

"You can bring the things in again now, Mrs. Honeywell. Miss Brain has been found."

"You were silly to go out," Iris said cheerfully. "We always have dinner and there's plenty for you."

Janet glanced down at her neat frock, and thought of her tidy hair, and of how like a governess she was looking, and pulled her pride together. It was ludicrous to feel like a badly behaved child.

"I'm sorry if I've kept you waiting," she said to Gladys, "but you see I've always worked in an office, and expect to arrange about my own lunch; if I'm to lunch here I must have a talk with you about rations."

"Where on earth were you?" Gladys asked. "I thought one call from Donald would bring you."

Mrs. Honeywell carried in a joint and put it in front of Donald. Janet took advantage of her being in the room not to answer. What on earth was she to say? Would Donald describe the scene? Donald watched Mrs. Honeywell waddle out to fetch the vegetables, then he said:

"She was only under the hedge in the home field, but you know what I am when I'm outside, always get sidetracked by something."

Janet had her eyes on the tablecloth so she could not see his face, but she listened to his words with thankfulness and exasperation. What a mixture the man was, making you like him one minute, and dislike him the next! Mean about money, odiously domineering, and yet she couldn't really hate him; she had always relied on impressions, and she could still feel the glow of companionship as they talked in the spinney, and the friendliness there had been between them when they had discussed Iris in the stable; he was two people really. Perhaps if she subdued herself to what a daily governess ought to be, she would only see the nice side; being a docile governess ought to bring all the best out of him, because then the two guineas wouldn't rankle, for he would feel he was getting his money's worth.

Gladys leant back in her chair while Mrs. Honeywell put the vegetable dishes in front of her.

"What lessons did you do this morning, Iris?"

"Nothing, really. Me and Janet had a lovely morning making plans."

Janet felt this was a deplorable picture of how two guineas' worth of governess spent her time. She turned to Donald.

"We worked out a timetable. It seems to me special hours will have to be given to arithmetic. Iris is very weak in that subject."

"Dear! Dear!" Donald's voice was so grave that it was clear he was making fun of her statement. "What a dreadful thing! I hoped to hear she was sufficiently advanced to start algebra."

"Silly Daddy!" Iris said contentedly. "Me and Janet did some bot'ny."

"Janet and I," Janet corrected.

"Is Janet making you learn the Latin names of the plants?" Donald teased.

The Christian name had fallen off his tongue with the unforced ease which means that is how the mind is normally thinking. Janet found that his using it gave her pleasure; she was not introspective, she did not reason why, she just knew that it made her feel less ruffled. It had the exactly opposite effect on Gladys. Her deep voice broke up the intimate, happy atmosphere the lesson talk was creating.

"Sit up, and eat tidily, Iris. How often am I to tell you not to talk when you're eating!" Then with a complete change of tone: "It's your fault, Donald, you lead her on, you naughty man."

The kittenish tone of the last words went badly with her appearance. To Janet the effect was embarrassing. Donald was evidently too used to it to find it that, but he clearly felt that Gladys needed soothing.

"I'm sorry, but she's only just got her plate; I won't speak another word to her until she's finished."

Janet blazed. What was a governess for if Gladys was to order the child about? She knew that for peace and a quiet life it would be better to remain silent, but on the other hand she wanted opportunities to show Donald she intended to earn her salary. No wonder he grudged paying it if he thought Gladys Batten was going to do half her work. She had no real views on a child's behaviour at meals, but she had Maggie's upbringing to quote.

"I don't want to start new ways too soon, but I believe that no conversation leads to eating too fast, and that means indigestion later on."

"Do you?" Gladys' voice was quiet. "How interesting, but I think we won't change my methods with Iris."

Janet's chin shot up, and a biting retort was on the tip of her tongue when she felt a kick on her ankle. She looked up, and Donald gave her a slight frown and a gentle shake of the head. If ever gestures said "For goodness' sake be a pal and don't stir up trouble," his did. Once more Janet felt utterly at sea. How could a man be so rude and truculent with you one minute, and in the next take you so into his confidence! His look won her; it was a hard struggle, but she let Gladys' statement pass in silence.

The rest of the meal there was spasmodic conversation, mostly about farm and local matters, each topic started by Gladys and chosen to make Janet feel a stranger. When the suet and fruit pudding arrived there was a further small argument, but Janet had no share in it. Donald, having helped Iris, picked up the sugar-bowl and shook a heaped spoon on to her plate.

"Do be careful, Donald," Gladys said. " Iris doesn't need all that; sugar in this house should be kept for you. You're the heavy worker."

"Oh!" thought Janet. "So that's what the sugar's saved for!"

Donald was annoyed, but he almost hid it.

"Nonsense, children come first, don't they, Iris?"

Iris looked anxiously out of the corners of her eyes at Gladys. "It's on my plate now, I can't scrape it off."

Donald was back at the pudding; he pushed the spoon into it savagely.

"Once and for all I will not eat more than my share of anything. If there is anything extra in this house, it's for Iris, and if we've anything to spare it's to be given away to children. What are we fighting for except the children; it's their future which is the stake."

"You are the man who grows the food, your strength needs keeping up."

Donald's voice showed the edge of anger.

"My dear Gladys, must we go through all this in front of Janet! She can see I'm not wasting away; you'll embarrass the poor girl so that she'll eat her pudding unsweetened."

Gladys set her mouth and said no more. Janet thought of her wonderingly. She did not know much about men, but she would have thought that Donald was the last sort of man to like being fussed over, or did all men? Perhaps he was only, pretending he didn't because she was there. Well, Gladys was in love with him, she ought to know.

The telephone rang just as they finished eating. Donald answered it; he came back and grinned at Iris.

"It's Barbara, she's asked you to tea." He glanced over to Janet. "She met Sheila this morning and heard you were here; the invitation is for you too. I said I thought you could go. Is that all right? We look on Barbara as almost a relation, and Iris likes being with her; she hasn't been able to go there much for we've had no one to send, for, of course, Gladys is usually busy."

"I'll be delighted." Janet remembered the kick and turned to Gladys with what she hoped was the perfect manner. "If it's all right with you, Miss Batten."

Evidently what took Janet and Iris away from the house was more than all right with Gladys; her tone was graciousness itself.

"I don't mind at all, it's good for Iris to see more people."

While Iris was resting, Janet, who had no wish for a *tête-à-tête* with Gladys, walked through the yard and out through the back gate to a lane. Across the lane was another gate, and inside it Donald was discussing something with one of his men. The last thing Janet wanted was to be seen loitering about the farm, so she made a pretence of glancing round to get her bearings, then turned and hurried back the way she had come. She had not taken many steps when she heard Donald call her.

"Janet! Janet!" She stopped. His manner was awkward and abrupt. "I say, you were a sport to shut up when I kicked you. Gladys is simply splendid, but she's not very good with a child. I want you to change things and all that, but for goodness' sake avoid a rumpus; if you think that something different has got to be done give me warning and I'll back you, but easy does it. Got it?"

She nodded. Then, as embarrassed as he, for to reopen the subject of money was horrifying to her, she blurted out:

"I'll need some money, Iris has no books or anything."

"Right, leave a chit on my desk saying how much and I'll have it ready for you in the morning."

Janet walked across the yard in a daze. "What a man!" she thought. "So mean one minute and so nice the next. Will I ever understand him?"

§

JANET and Iris walked to the Haines'. Gladys had laid out on Iris' bed the clothes into which the child was to change, and Janet, with Donald's words in her ears, had put them on her without protest. Not that she did not protest internally, she did; she thought it an insufferable position, to be only partly in charge, and for the rest under Gladys' orders. The clothes, in her opinion, were unsuitable for going out to tea in the country, and she marvelled that Gladys, who looked so *soignée* herself, could have selected them. There was a fussy organdie frock over a silk slip, silk socks, white shoes and a hat trimmed with ribbons. Iris was delighted to dress up. She pirouetted round the room, and then held out her skirt and danced a few steps.

"I feel like Cinderella when I put this on. I should think she wore something very like this to go to the ball, wouldn't you?"

Janet's mind was on the dancing steps and pirouettes.

"Have you been to a dancing class?"

Iris pirouetted again.

"Not since Mummy died; she taught me. Every day we practised since I was three. 'Course when I was very little I just did a polka, but at my last lessons I was doing real exercises."

It was lovely out. Janet was almost dazzled by the intense green of the fields, and fascinated as the wind ruffled the surface, and shadow and sunlight made an ever-changing picture. To her town eye Donald's fields were just grass, but Iris put her wise.

"Daddy's got strong wheat, hasn't he?"

"Has he?" Janet studied the young green on her left. Then she looked to the right and, not wishing to seem ignorant, said admiringly, "Magnificent wheat."

Iris pealed with laughter.

"That isn't wheat, that's oats."

Janet could see no difference whatsoever, stare as she would. There were fields of corn on each side of the path. When they came level with the second fields, Iris, enchanted to show off, called out:

"What's that, Janet? What's that?"

Janet stared blankly at two more fields of incredibly brilliant green. The obvious answer was grass, but that plainly was wrong.

"Corn?"

"'Course. What sort?"

Janet gave in.

"I haven't the faintest idea, I'm a silly Londoner, you'll have to teach me."

Iris flung herself at her.

"You're not, you couldn't be silly. I'll teach you what everything is." She lowered her voice. "Should you think, as we're out of sight of the house, I could take off my hat?" It was on the tip of Janet's tongue to say, "Of course, take the wretched thing off," but she stopped herself just in time. She was for a moment outside herself, and saw, not the Janet Brain that had so far existed, but the new Janet Brain, governess to a child. A person whose least word and action were important because they could influence the moulding of a character. If she said, "Yes, take the wretched thing off," it was established in Iris' mind that she approved of the principle of doing things behind a person's back that you would not do to their face. The moment when she saw herself objectively passed in a flash, but her temporary clearness of vision left a thought on which she brooded for the rest of the walk. She took off the hat, merely saying, "You need never have worn it if you'd asked me when I was dressing you."

"My goodness me, you don't know how fussy Gladys is about going out to tea." Janet said nothing. After a moment Iris shook her arm. "Did you hear what I was saying?"

Janet blinked.

"Not a word. Hop along, darling, I'm thinking something important."

Iris entirely understood.

"I won't say another word, I'll sing instead."

The Haines' house would always be beautiful, but it was essentially a house to enchant on a summer day. The high wall and iron gates, which Janet had seen on her drive through the village, hid much of the charm of the place. Now, as she and Iris passed inside, she found it was like moving into another generation. The garden wall was old, and had wallflowers and stone-crops in its crevasses. There was a small lawn of the velvet quality, which can only come with age and loving care. There were old-fashioned flowers in the long beds under the windows. Pinks, stocks, forget-me-nots, and more wallflowers.

Barbara had seen them coming; she threw the front door open and Iris tore to meet her.

"Hullo, darling!" Barbara hugged her. "Your overall's on my bed; for goodness' sake hang that frock up carefully!" She turned apologetically to Janet. "How do you do! I'm so sorry, you must think me awfully interfering, but Gladys always makes Iris so grand to come here, I make her take her clothes straight off and put on an overall, or else we can't play at anything for fear of getting her messed up."

Janet watched Iris disappear into the house.

"I'm thankful. It's an idiotic way to dress a child, I think."

"Oh, well, it pleases Gladys, and Iris adores it, and nobody's any the worse. She doesn't really like children, so she tries much harder with Iris than she needs to." Barbara linked her arm through Janet's. "Come and meet Daddy."

The colonel was in the garden on the other side of the house. Barbara led the way through the hall and drawing-room, and out through the french windows. Janet had a fleeting impression of oak and what appeared to be family portraits, and a long, low, white drawing-room with leaf-green curtains and chair covers, and great bowls of flowers everywhere.

The colonel was bent over a border. He had a thin, intelligent face, iron-grey hair, and an air of distinction. He did not look up as the girls came towards him, but he evidently heard footsteps.

"Come here, Barbara. Look at that lupin, some damn thing's been at it."

"Well, leave it a minute, this is Janet Brain."

The colonel straightened himself and Janet found he was over six foot. He held out his hand, and gave her a searching glance accompanied by a most charming smile.

"I beg your pardon, my dear, I thought Barbara was alone. So, you're the friend she made on the train!"

Janet was not used to meeting colonels, in fact she could not remember meeting one before, but she felt entirely at ease with him.

"Wasn't it queer we found we were going to the same place!"

"Very glad of it. Hope you two girls will be friends. Bit lonely for Barbara trading round after her old father. I've been laid up, you know, Miss Brain, can't get used to bein' an invalid. Never had a day's illness in my life."

"He's worse than a child," said Barbara. She pointed to a deck chair. "And where are you supposed to be now? Kennel, sir!"

The colonel smiled at Janet.

"You see, treats me like a dog!" He walked slowly towards his chair. "Do I hear you're bear-leadin' young Iris?"

"Unless she bear-leads me."

"Shouldn't wonder at that either. Her mother was a looker, with a will of her own, the child takes after her. We don't see much of Sheldon these days; these farmers are busy, you know. Young Dick was our pal, and gave us all the news, didn't he, Barbara? You haven't met him, of course, he's overseas."

"No, I've heard of him."

Barbara pushed her father into his chair, and put a cushion behind his back. She looked in a puzzled way at Janet.

"Funny, I thought you knew him, I can't think why."

The colonel glared at his daughter.

"Take that damn cushion away. How often am I to tell you that I'll rest if I must, but I won't be poodled about. Talkin' of dogs, where's Hoover? You better go and have a look, Barbara; if that blasted dog is diggin' up my seeds I'll have the hide off him."

Iris, dressed in a striped linen overall, came bounding out of the house. The colonel held out a hand. "Hullo, twopence!"

Iris hugged him.

"How's your poor ulcer?"

"Tiresome; you don't know how much milk I'm made to drink. Shockin' stuff!"

Iris leant affectionately against him.

"When you've had your rest would you like me to help you move the flags on your maps? Last time we did that you drank a whole glass and never noticed."

Barbara touched Janet. She spoke in a whisper.

"Come and help me find Hoover. Those two will be perfectly happy together."

Almost the entire garden, and it was far larger than it looked, was given up to vegetables. Barbara led the way and talked to Janet over her shoulder.

"Daddy simply adores Iris, he thinks she's so intelligent."

"So she is. What was her mother like, not in face, I mean, but as a person?"

"Oh, she was lovely! She had been a dancer . . ."

"A dancer! Then that explains Iris. She danced when I put her frock on this afternoon, and I thought she put more to it than you'd expect from an ordinary child."

"Anna, that was her mother's name, was more than a dancer, she had trained for the ballet since she was a child, and she danced for some seasons with the Russians, and had travelled everywhere, but what she wanted to do was design, scenery and everything."

"Fancy her marrying a farmer!"

Barbara stopped to examine some tomato plants. "Donald met her in London and they fell in love with each other. I don't think she ever thought about how it would be living on a farm. You wouldn't, if you were in love, would you?"

"No, I suppose not, but it must have been difficult to throw everything up like that."

"You've never been in love," said Barbara decidedly. "If you're in love you don't care where you live, or what you have to live on, it's just being with the one person that matters . . ." She broke off, conscious she was showing more of herself than she intended. "At least, that's what I should think."

"I've never been in love," Janet admitted, "so I wouldn't know. And she was quite happy on her farm?"

Barbara was a little reluctant to continue her story.

"To begin with she was, but at the end she missed things awfully, I think. It was partly her illness, perhaps, it was tuberculosis; it seems to make you awfully gay and alive in between bring very ill."

"Did Mr. Sheldon know she was missing things?"

Barbara stood still, then turned impulsively.

"I'll tell you something I've not talked about to anybody, not even to Dick, that's Donald's half-brother. I think he did. I think he knew that even if she hadn't died she wasn't going to be happy. Of course Iris was an interest, but . . ." Her voice trailed away, then she added vigorously: "That's where Gladys came in. She came when Anna was ill, and she did everything for her and was supposed to be marvellous to her and all that, but I don't believe she was more marvellous than anybody else would have been, anyway not so marvellous that Donald need feel he's got to marry her."

"She's in love with him."

"I suppose she is, but as I told you in the train, I don't like her, and I'm mean about her." Shrill, excited barks came from the end of the garden. "There's Hoover, come on."

Hoover was a dachshund, orange brown, thin and long as a walking-stick, and shiny as a seal. He had decided that something that would be better dead had taken refuge under a marrow bed, and he had set out on an excavation scheme on a vast scale. Only the back half of him was visible. Barbara clutched at it, and brought out the earthy, wriggling, barking front end. She held the dog in her arms and introduced him to Janet.

"Hoover, Janet. Janet, Hoover." Hoover licked her face. "You dirty boy, look at the earth on your nose. Let Mother brush you!"

"Isn't he heavenly!"

"You ought to talk about him to Donald. He doesn't think a dog's a dog at all unless it's useful, looking after sheep, or for shooting or something. You are the most exquisite beast, aren't you, my sweet, but I couldn't pretend you are useful. Come on!" She put Hoover down. "Walk quietly back to the house and try and pretend you've been good."

They had tea on the lawn. It was served by an elderly, old-fashioned-looking parlour-maid. She put a silver tray, with a silver tea-pot, kettle and jugs, and frail, lovely china, in front of Barbara. To Janet both the parlour-maid and the tea-service showed a new world. The colonel saw from her face that something had pleased her.

"Wonderin' at our luck, my dear? They tell me servants are gettin' scarce these days, but old Miller has been with me nearly thirty years, so's the cook, and they were no chickens when they came."

Barbara handed Janet a cup of tea.

"Miller and the cook came when Daddy was married, but Jennings, the housemaid, only came when I was little, that's about eighteen years ago, but she's still spoken of as 'the new girl' by the other two."

The colonel offered Janet a sandwich.

"Mincin', the cook, is quite a character; you must have a talk with her sometime."

Barbara got up to put a mug of milk beside Iris' plate.

"She and Daddy see spooks together."

"Ladies and gentlemen in lovely clothes," said Iris.

Janet turned to the colonel expecting to see a twinkle in his eye, but he answered perfectly seriously.

"Barbara laughs at us, but it's true enough. I don't see them like Mincing does, but I hear them, and I know when they're about. They're particularly fond of the back stairs and the servants' rooms; I said to Mincing one day, 'There's a lot of these people about, aren't there, Mincin'?' and she said, 'Yes indeed, sir, I had to undress last night with the light out because of the gentlemen in the room.'"

Barbara was watching Janet's face.

"Marvellous, isn't it? You wouldn't think a colonel could be so silly, would you? He and Mincing just lead each other on."

The colonel did not mind his daughter's teasing.

"She cooks all right, though, ghosts or no ghosts, you can't deny that." He turned back to Janet. "I'm afraid you're havin' trouble gettin' help. Barbara brought that little sister of yours to see me, and she was tellin' me."

Janet laughed.

"She's a bad girl! What she meant was that she wanted somebody to do her work for her. She hates housework, for she's never had to do any; my mother has always managed alone, except for occasional help, but now she ought not to be doing so much, she's not strong enough, and Sheila was getting worried it was all going to come on her."

The colonel cut the cake.

"Good looker, that little girl, but I shouldn't think work of any kind is much in her line, is it?"

Janet spread some jam on Iris' piece of bread and butter.

"She's going to take a war job. She's going to the Labour Exchange to see what's going; she's trained as a shorthand-typist, so I expect she'll go into something in that line."

The colonel passed Janet the cake.

"Then what's happenin' to your mother if you're teachin' twopence here?"

Her anxiety about her mother showed in Janet's face, but since Iris had receptive ears, and probably an indiscreet tongue, she managed to make her voice light.

"I'd like to ask you afterwards about doctors; she's bad about obeying her daughter."

Iris looked up from her bread and jam.

"When I was ill Dr. Nelson gave me a rabbit made of white fur." Her voice rose at the memory of an old injury. "Gladys burned it because it wouldn't wash, which I thought was very mean."

The colonel ruffled the child's hair.

"You get on with your tea, young woman, I'm wantin' your help with my maps."

Tea over, Barbara took Iris in to wash. The colonel lit a cigarette.

"You can trust your mother with Nelson, our local sawbones. He's got a damned interferin' wife, and a couple of daughters with faces like sheep, but he's all right at his doctorin'."

"Thank you very much, but the trouble is going to be getting my mother to see him." Janet had taken to the colonel and knew she could trust him. "As a matter of fact, her heart's not good, but she doesn't know it. You see, we've always been poor, and she's worked like a slave at housework and all the rest of it, and our doctor in London advised me not to tell her it was her heart; he said she was like a kid who thought she could swim, and perhaps if she found she couldn't she would sink."

Once more her anxiety showed. The colonel patted her hand.

"You mustn't worry, my dear, that never did anybody any good. Tell you what, suppose we set a little trap. You won't be teachin' young Iris on Sunday, I suppose? Well, you bring your mother along to tea, and I'll get Nelson to meet her. I'll put him wise, of course, and we'll see if we can get your mother to take to him. Then before you go you say right out in front of us all, that you want him to give the old lady an overhaul, and we'll have things tied up and sealed before she's got time to argue."

"It's awfully kind of you, but . . ."

"Now . . . no arguin', it's settled." Barbara came out of the house with Iris. The colonel raised his voice. "I've been tellin' Janet here that she's to bring her mother to tea on Sunday." He turned back to Janet with his really charming smile. "You don't mind my usin' your Christian name, do you, my dear? May as well start as we mean to go on, for I can feel we're goin' to be friends."

Village life was new to Janet. Iris, back in her organdie frock, insisted on a route home that took her up the main street. To Cockney Janet there was rest even in watching Worsingfold. The slow but methodical country way in which everything does get done in its proper season, but very much at the countryman's own tempo, was new to her, and enthralling. Cows came down the road escorted by a small boy. The cows strolled, apparently aimlessly, the boy whooped and called "Get along up, Daisy," a suggestion in which none of the cows appeared to take any interest, and yet somehow the procession disappeared with no trouble through the proper gate, which, to Janet, was nothing less than miraculous. The small boy, who had passed them without a sign he had seen them, turned at the gate and made a horrible face at Iris, to which Iris retorted by an even worse one, and by putting out her tongue.

"Iris!" Janet said, shocked. "What a way to behave!" Iris skipped in a pleased way.

"I put out my tongue. He's a nasty boy."

"Why? When did you know him?"

"I don't exactly know him, but he sings in the choir and we look at each other. He's a foreigner."

"Is he? He looks very English, but if he's foreign all the more reason to be polite."

Iris spoke as if to a child.

"I don't mean he's not English. I mean he doesn't belong to Worsingfold. He's a 'vacuee."

Janet glanced back through the gate where the boy and cows had disappeared. Her voice was overflowing with admiration.

"Do you mean to tell me that he comes from a town and can lead cows about like that?"

Iris had no idea what Janet was admiring.

"'Course. Look, there's Tom, his grandson's a sailor. He's got a mermaid tattooed on his chest, and a heart on his arm with an arrow through it and his young lady's name. It's Violet."

Janet had already seen Tom. He was leaning on his gate smoking. She waved to him.

"How's the taxi?"

"Actin' up. Give me a 'oss."

"This is Janet, she's my governess," said Iris.

"So I knows." Tom considered Janet ruminatively. "Your Ma'll be glad havin' you. She doesn't look so good."

"She isn't so good. She does too much."

Tom nodded.

"I hear you are making her put her feet up. She'll want feeding too. Don't you forget to be along for those chops when I kill my pig. Give you two, one for you and one for your Ma."

"Tom doesn't like Sheila," Iris unnecessarily pointed out.

Tom spat into his garden. Janet thought the best thing to do was to move on. She gave one of her radiant smiles.

"It's grand of you to spare the chops. Good night."

Iris was, of course, known to all the village, but, being motherless, she was something more. Everybody popped out of their cottages to have a word with her, and they obviously knew her foibles.

"Aren't you dressed up fine today, Miss Iris dearie!" "Been out to tea with the colonel, Miss Iris dear?" And all eyes studied Janet, and behind them she could read the anxious queries. Is she going to be good to her?

Iris sighed when they left the village behind.

"I do simply hate nobody seeing me in this frock."

Janet was doubtful if she ought to let that pass.

"I expect your friends like you whatever you wear."

"I expect they like me better when I'm dressed like this instead of my awful check cottons. My mother never wore check cotton, nor, as a matter fac', organdie either."

"What did she wear?"

Iris stopped to pull up her socks.

"She looked the very most opposite of you. She never looked all tidy and neat exactly. She wore things very soft; she had a lot of blue frocks, and there was a lovely one that was grey. I called it her Cloud frock. She never plaited my hair for lessons like Gladys does."

"You were smaller then, perhaps your hair was too short to plait."

"I could have had little ones, but Mummy wasn't a plaiting person. Do you know what we used to do sometimes? We used to go out and we would stop where nobody was looking, and Mummy used to take off her shoes and stockings and dance for me. Then, when she had finished, she would stand with her arms stretched out like as if she was getting up after lying down, and she said, 'That's better! Now we'll go home and behave properly.'"

"Come on," said Janet gently, and opened the gate to the farm road.

Iris caught her arm.

"I know I'm not dressed right, but could you swing me?"

Janet laughed.

"Don't you dare tear your frock or I shall be spanked!" Iris climbed to the top of the gate and sat astride it, her skirts spread round her. Janet gave the gate a push. It swung easily. Iris squealed with pleasure.

"Let's sing," she shouted.

"What?" Janet called back.

"Something like swinging. Girls and boys come out to play."

Janet knew that one, and together they made a gay, if not very tuneful noise, and in Janet's case, towards the end, it was rather breathless.

"There," she said as the song finished. "Come down, darling."

Donald startled them both.

"I should say so!" He lifted his daughter off the gate. "What a way to treat my hinges!"

Iris put her hand in her father's and held out the other to Janet.

"We've had a lovely time. The colonel's ulcer is still there."

Donald looked across the child to Janet.

"Pretty tiring for you."

She shook her head.

"No. You saw the only energetic bit."

He smiled down at Iris.

"We ought to find somebody of your own age to play with you, young lady."

Iris' voice was contented.

"I don't want anybody but Janet."

"I dare say, but what about poor Janet? She's not used to swinging gates." He turned back to Janet. "I hope you see a lot of Barbara. We feel her rather a special charge, but I expect you know as much about that as I do."

Janet was puzzled. As it happened she knew about Barbara and his half-brother from her mother, otherwise all she had to go on was his statement at luncheon that they looked on Barbara almost as a relation. They must, she thought amusedly, rely a great deal on local gossip in the country. It would be queer in London if everybody was expected to know the ins and outs of people's lives by what news they could pick up, but she said nothing on the subject for they were at the field path leading to the cottage; instead she had a look at Iris. The swinging on the gate had tossed the child's hair about. Hers was evidently a personality which lit like a match when there was anything whatsoever to be gay about. Her cheeks were pink, her eyes sparkled and she looked what is known in the nursery world as 'above herself'. Janet got her comb out of her bag.

"Stand still," she said firmly, "and you've to put on your hat. I can't have Miss Batten saying I sent you back looking like a rag-bag."

Iris pulled away from the comb, and pirouetted, chanting:

"Rag-bag! Rag-bag!"

Donald gave Janet an understanding grin.

"It's all right. I shall get blamed. I'm renowned for my bad effect."

Janet gave him Iris' hat.

"We didn't do anything to excite her, really."

Iris danced back. She flung herself on Janet.

"Good night, darling, darling Janet. Every single day is going to be nice now you've come. Isn't it, Daddy?"

Donald held out his hand.

"Come on, young woman. Bed-time."

"But don't you think it'll be nice, Daddy?"

Janet kissed the child.

"Good night, goose."

Iris took her father's hand.

"But you do see her being here will make everything diff rent, don't you?"

Donald gave Janet an enigmatic nod, which might mean good night, or, more likely, "You see what I'm forced to say."

"All the difference," and he led the dancing Iris up the road.

Janet walked home, not consciously noticing what she was about. It was only when she was in sight of the cottage that she found she was singing.

§

Maggie was against the tea-party from the moment she heard of it.

"They're not my sort, darling. I've never been used to people with big houses and a lot of servants."

"How can you be so silly!" Janet protested. "You'll like them awfully, and they'll love you."

"I like Miss Haines very much already, but I was brought up only to eat with people I could ask back without feeling uncomfortable."

"Well, you can ask Barbara Haines here; you could ask the colonel, only I don't think he goes out yet."

Maggie looked stubborn.

"All the same, I'm not going, and that's flat."

They were talking in the kitchen. Janet pretended to dust a shelf in order to turn her face from Maggie.

"All right, I'll let them know. I don't see why you should bother if you don't feel like it, but I'm sorry for them. Barbara Haines is young and inexperienced, and I don't think she's clever about all that milk the colonel has to drink. I think it's given him just as it is, or perhaps hot one time and cold the next, and he hates it. I don't suppose there is any better way of serving it, but I just thought you might be able to help. Still, it's unimportant." Maggie was mixing a pudding. She stopped and leant on the wooden spoon in her hands. Her voice was indignant.

"Of course there's a better way. It's duodenal, isn't it? Mrs. Rose's husband, he was a bus conductor, you remember, and the jolting upset him, well, he had one. When Mrs. Rose was working in the house with me she told me a lot about it. She told me at first she got so that she dreamed about milk, from the fuss he made taking it you would have thought it was poison. Then she got clever, flavoured it with this and flavoured it with that, and made milk puddings, milk soups and junkets. She told me she had got so milk-minded that she reckoned he never had it served twice alike in any week."

Janet went on dusting.

"Barbara Haines is young, and I don't suppose she can cook, and it's left to the maids to fix, and I don't expect they have ideas. Still, I suppose it doesn't matter if it bores him. Drinking pure milk is probably the best way to take it."

"Nonsense! I'll have a talk with Miss Haines. I can put her up to a lot of little tips. Come to that, I could make one of my milk jellies with the cinnamon, and take it along. Things often go down easier when they're made in somebody else's kitchen."

Sunday afternoon was hot and thundery. Janet, with Maggie carrying the milk jelly, walked slowly down to the farm road. Janet had put on a flowered linen frock. Her hair, as it was not a school day, was free of pins. Maggie, walking behind her, thought how charming she looked. Already the country air was doing her good; there was a faint golden tan over her face, and the dawning of pink in her cheeks. "She's not a patch on Sheila, of course," decided Maggie, "but she does look nice, bless her!"

Janet glanced back at her mother.

"Do you think Sheila really didn't mind not being asked? The colonel gave the invitation and it was really to you. I'm only a make-weight. I never thought about Sheila."

"She doesn't like being out of anything, and she particularly dislikes the Haines cultivating us, because she thinks they are stuck up, but except for that she's far happier reading a film paper."

Janet felt her heart give a thump.

"Oh, bother! Look, there's Mr. Sheldon and Iris."

"Really, dear, what a tone to take! I think he's such a nice man, and she's a dear little girl."

"I know, but I see them all the week, and I don't want to run into them every five minutes when I've got a day off."

Iris, who had been skipping down the farm road beside her father, had seen Janet and Maggie and came tearing up the field track towards them, shouting unintelligibly as she ran. She flung herself panting at Janet.

"Janet, me and Daddy were just going our Sunday walk. Usually Gladys comes, but today she's got a sick headick; at least that's what she says it is, but when I told Ben he said that her trouble was that her eyes were fuming green." She broke off and held out her hand to Maggie. "Good afternoon, Mrs. Brain. Very pleasant weather we're having for the time of year."

Maggie kissed the child.

"Well, I don't know about that. I rather expect it to be nice in June."

Iris led the way along the track towards her father.

"Mrs. Honeywell says that it's a good thing when passing the time of day to refer to the weather, as it's not a subject where offence can be taken where none's intended." She raised her voice and shouted to her father. "I was just telling Janet about Gladys' sick headick . . ."

"Headache," Janet corrected.

Iris shook her head.

"Not what she's got isn't. Everybody calls it a headick. Me and Daddy are quite pleased, really. We like it when we can walk alone."

Donald did not answer this, but smiled at Maggie. He was in a flannel suit, and Janet thought how nice he looked out of working clothes, and what easy manners he had. It was queer that somebody who could be such a nice person, so often spoilt himself by being unpleasant without reason.

"Good afternoon, Mrs. Brain," he said. "How are you getting on? Is your daughter taking you for a walk?"

Maggie explained their errand.

"And then we're going to the evening service," she added. "I really like the morning best, but as we were coming down to the village this afternoon we're saving ourselves the second walk."

Donald looked worried.

"I'm afraid I don't get to church much these days. We do as little work as we can on Sundays, but in times like these we can't lay off altogether. There's a service for the children at ten o'clock on Sunday mornings, but I can seldom manage the time to take Iris, and Gladys doesn't have Mrs. Honeywell on Sunday, so it's a hopeless day for her."

"I don't mind," said Iris. "On Sundays we do our big walk, and Ben says you can do all the praying you need out of doors, and there's no need to go to God's House to pray. He can hear you just as well in a field."

"Ben's an old heathen." Donald turned back to Maggie. "Were you very strict about church when Janet and Sheila were Iris' age?"

"Yes. They went to children's service in the afternoon when they were tots. Some people say forcing church on a child puts them off going when they grow up; but I say they'll have heard a lot that's good, and maybe a help to them, you never know."

"I rather like God," said Iris. "He's got a nice face."

"But we don't know what He's like," Janet objected.

Iris held Janet's hand.

"You will if you look in my drawing book" She fingered Janet's frock. "Daddy, doesn't Janet look nice today? Not all buttoned up like she is when we do lessons."

Donald's eyes ran over Janet.

"Very nice, but we mustn't expect her to waste her pretty things on us."

Janet's cheeks flamed.

"That's a horrid thing to say. This is only cheap linen; the dress I wear to come to the farm cost more, if you want to know."

Donald gazed at her with hurt surprise. Iris stared at her with her mouth open.

"Why are you angry, Janet? Don't you like me and Daddy to think you look nice?"

Donald caught hold of the child.

"Come on, young woman, if we are going to have a look at that drain in Lower Bend we must be stepping. Goodbye, Mrs. Brain. Have a nice tea-party."

"Well, really, Janet!" said Maggie as the Sheldons disappeared out of sight over the turn of the field. "Whatever's the matter with you? It's high time I saw something of you. You've picked up the manners of a bear living by yourself in London."

"You don't understand . . . He's funny about money . . . I thought he said that about my frock to get a sort of kick at me."

"Bless me, child, your liver must be out of order. I think you'd better have a glass of salts each morning for a day or two."

Janet, wretchedly conscious that this time Donald had not meant anything except niceness by what he said, walked on in silence. "I just don't know what's happening to me," she thought miserably. "I seem to care so much what he says; it's that makes me behave like an ass."

The colonel was lying in his chaise-longue reading a Sunday paper when Miller showed Maggie and Janet into the garden. He did not see them until they were beside his chair. He threw down his paper and made a move to get up, but Maggie put out her hand to stop him.

"Don't get up. I know what those chairs are like to get out of. I haven't one myself, but Janet makes me put my feet up, and I tell her it keeps me in a constant state of jump in case someone knocks on our door, for you can't get up quickly however you try." She pulled a basket chair towards her and sat down. "It's hot today. I'm glad to get off my feet."

The colonel settled back against his cushions. His eyes twinkled at Janet.

"Your mother's a person who gets her own way, I can see. If you go down to the bottom of the garden you'll find Barbara and the doctor." He turned to Maggie. "Our doctor feller, because he can cut insides about, thinks he knows everything. I've a very special loganberry, did very well last year, but the doctor wanted to prune it, and keeps lookin' at it now hopin' it will go wrong because I wouldn't let him."

Maggie held out her parcel.

"I've made you one of my milk jellies. Janet was telling me how much you disliked milk." She lowered her voice. "There's just a drop of sherry in this, not enough to hurt you, but it makes all the difference."

The colonel looked at the parcel without enthusiasm.

"It's very good of you to bother. Disgustin' stuff, milk. That damn cook of mine, Mincin', takes all our sawbones says as gospel. I know all he says about milk, I tell her, but forget some of it. But will she? Nor every hour or two there's Miller standing beside me bleating like an old sheep, 'Here's your milk, sir.'"

Maggie took her knitting out of her bag.

"At our age we hate being ordered about, don't we? Janet's been dictating to me, I mustn't do this and I mustn't do that, and bless the child, I find it very annoying."

The colonel remembered the main object of Maggie's visit. He wondered guiltily if he had said anything about the doctor to put her off.

"Nice girl that of yours. My Barbara's taken no end of a fancy to her. Glad of that; bit lonely for her lookin' after an old feller like me. Comes hard now, you know, when other girls are off in uniform doin' this, that and the other. I wouldn't keep her, mind you, but she says she'd only worry if she was away. 'Course it makes all the difference her bein' about. Between you and me my heart sinks a bit at the thought of being alone. It would be damned lonely. Still, as I say, I wouldn't stand in her way."

"You're in just the same position as I am. I'm perfectly willing to stay alone and let both my girls go, but Janet won't hear of it."

"I should think not. That cottage of Sheldon's is no place for a woman on her own. Why, it's miles from anywhere."

"That's true, but I've kept Janet from joining the W.R.N.S., and she's just the type to do well in the services."

"Well, what about little Sheila stayin'? She's not the cut for service life."

Maggie chuckled.

"She certainly isn't, but she slacks at home and I spoil her. She could be useful, she's quite a smart little shorthand-typist. I gave her a week to make up her mind what she'd do, and it's nearly up. She's off to the Labour Exchange in a couple of days. I can put down my foot when I want to."

The colonel looked at her. She had on a black straw hat at which her daughters laughed, but he saw only that she had on something sensible and suitable. He liked, too, for the same reasons, her grey dress, and low-heeled black shoes. What he did not like was the transparency of the skin of her face and hands. It looked so thin that it was a wonder her bones did not cut through it. "Somethin' very wrong there," he thought. "We'll see what Nelson says. Maybe we could help. We'll certainly do what we can." Barbara introduced Janet to Dr. Nelson and left them to talk together. Janet looked at him shyly. He was round and chubby, rather like a bear with grey hair, she thought, but the moment he spoke she forgot her shyness, and what he looked like. Years as a G.P. doctoring bodies and souls alike, scolding here, cajoling there, bringing his patients into the world, and helping them when the time came for them to leave it, had given him an ease of manner which was utterly disarming.

"So you're worried about your mother, my dear?"

Janet told him what their own doctor had said.

"I know what I'm asking you to do is very difficult, but if you could make Mother rest without telling her why—" The doctor patted her shoulder.

"Take that anxious look off your face, my dear. The world is so full of sorrow these days that keeping cheerful is a duty. I don't suppose I can cure your mother, but I've no doubt that I can help. I've bullied patients for years, I've kept farmers in their beds from fear of me, and believe me it's no mean job keeping a farmer on his back when he hears stirring in his yard and his milk pails clattering. I'll get round your mother, you'll see."

Miller had laid tea on the lawn. The colonel looked up as Barbara brought Janet and the doctor to the table.

"Ah, Nelson! This is a new acquisition to the village. Mrs. Brain. I believe you haven't met yet."

The doctor shook Maggie's hand and sat down beside her.

"I know Mrs. Brain by sight, and, of course, we all know young Sheila. I said that all the men's temperatures went up the first time she walked down the village street."

Miller stood beside the colonel's chair.

"Your milk, sir."

The colonel scowled.

"Take that damned stuff away. I told you at luncheon I was havin' a cup of tea this afternoon."

Miller looked at the doctor.

"It's your orders, sir."

The doctor was offering Maggie a sandwich.

"The colonel's got a certain amount of milk to get down every day and he knows it, Miller. If he won't drink it and likes to be ill instead that's his business. You can't do any more than put it by him."

The colonel bristled.

"I never said I wouldn't drink the stuff. I only said I wasn't takin' it at tea-time. I'm allowed a cup of tea, you said so yourself."

Maggie beamed sympathetically at Miller.

"I've made him a milk jelly. He's eating that for his tea."

Miller was surprised as she carried the milk back into the house to find she had not taken offence at Maggie's interference.

"She spoke ever so nicely," she told Mincing. "She's only homely, you know. You could hear she sympathized with us, knowing how difficult men are when they're ill."

The doctor believed in hobbies. Many was the person he had persuaded into the cottage hospital while poring over a stamp collection, or admiring a piece of patchwork. The jelly gave him his line on Maggie. Happily they discussed herbs, home-made wines, cake-making and recipes for jams. At a wink from the colonel Janet interrupted them.

"I'm sorry to break in on this kitchen-front talk, but if Dr. Nelson will forgive my talking shop at tea-time, I want him to give you an appointment to overhaul you. She's too thin, isn't she, doctor? I want you to order her to rest."

The colonel, who had been playing with Maggie's jelly, took advantage of the attention being on Maggie to put the glass containing it under his chair. He clicked his fingers to draw Hoover's attention to what was waiting for him.

"That's right, Janet, my dear," he said. "You make the doctor bully your mother; it might give him less time for bullying me."

The doctor smiled at Maggie.

"I shall like to see you. I'll bring you over a sprig of dill, when I come. If you take to it I can let you have some for your herb garden."

Maggie's heart thumped. Fear, in spite of the heat, turned her hands cold. Her forehead was clammy. Tell herself as she would that nothing was wrong, she did not want to submit to a test. Suppose the suspicion which crawled like a worm at the back of her mind should prove to be more than a suspicion! It was easy to carry on as long as you did not know, but suppose you were told an unpleasant truth, what was to happen then to all the "Nonsense, of course you aren't too tired to do that."

"All this suffocating feeling when you lie down is imagination." The phrases with which she got herself through the daily round.

Barbara saw her face. She sprang to her feet and hung over Maggie's chair.

"Mrs. Brain, darling, do let Dr. Nelson see you. You are too thin, and perhaps he'll order you milk, and then I can hold your example up to Daddy, for I know you'd drink it like a martyr."

The colonel looked under his chair and saw the empty glass dish. He slipped it back on to the table and gave Hoover a grateful pat.

"You wait, Mrs. Brain. I'll bet at the end of a fortnight you find it as difficult to get it down as I do."

Maggie felt the blood flowing back into her hands. Barbara's arm lay near her, she gave it a grateful pat. Of course the child was right. Milk, and perhaps a tonic, was what she needed. She turned to the doctor.

"I suppose I must give in to my daughter or I shall have no peace. I am a little thinner. Overhauling is a ridiculous waste of your time, I'm afraid, but you've daughters of your own and you know what bullies daughters are."

The doctor took out his notebook.

"I'll be along tomorrow morning, bringing the dill with me, and unless I'm very much mistaken it's a herb you'll be very glad to have got to know."

The doctor had to get off after tea, and the two girls went indoors, for Barbara wanted Janet's advice about a frock. The colonel looked contentedly at their arms linked in each other's.

"That's just what Barbara needs, a friend to talk frocks and things with."

Maggie was still taut at the thought of the doctor's visit; she was glad to chat and distract her mind.

"Very nice for Janet too, though actually Sheila's the one to advise on frocks. It's queer, but now I come to think of it Janet's never had a close friend. You know how it is in London. A girl goes to an office miles from where she lives, and the friends she makes may live an hour's journey away."

"Do you miss London? Always thought it a noisy hole myself, but I know Londoners see it differently."

Maggie smiled; she lay back in her chair, her eyes on the colonel's lovely twisted chimneys and mellowed roof.

"I came to London as a bride. My husband hadn't much money. He had rented a little house—just three bedrooms, two at the back and a big one in front. We had a laburnum and a may tree in the garden. Both my babies were born in that front bedroom, and my husband died there. That little house and that street is all London to me."

The colonel's voice was so gentle it was no more disturbing to Maggie's thoughts than the twittering of the birds, or the buzz of a passing bee.

"You been without him long?"

"I only had him until Sheila was nine months. They have been long years." Perhaps it was the garden, or perhaps the feeling which the colonel exuded that whatever was said to him he would regard as a confidence, but Maggie found herself speaking of things which before she had clamped down in her heart. "Of course, nobody seeing me now could imagine me as I was in those days. Such a silly little thing, never able to make a decision for myself, running to my husband about everything."

"Must have been a bit hard to take the other line, and I suppose you weren't left too well off."

"No, there was hardly any money at all. That was what pulled me together. I think if we had been rich I should just have settled down wrapped in self-pity; you can, you know, but there were the children, needing education and nourishing food. Janet was at school, but I put Sheila in her pram, and together we cadged round and got sewing to do." She laughed. "I got quite famous in my little way, and I thought no end of myself, and then one day when I was fitting a frock for one of my richest clients, she said: I've made a secret of you. People think I go up to the West End for my things; they would have a shock if they knew I just went to a little woman round the corner.'"

"Damned cheek, and not fit to clean your boots, shouldn't wonder! What happened about the girls' schoolin' fees?"

"Well, thanks to the dressmaking, I was able to manage the High School. It was rather wasted on Sheila, but Janet did very well. She could have had a scholarship for a university, but she wouldn't hear of it; right down angry she was. 'I'm going out to work,' she said, 'and with what you save on my school fees, and what I give you, that's the end of your dressmaking. The day I bring home my first pay envelope you take no more orders, or I'll take a hammer to your sewing machine.'"

The colonel chuckled.

"Good girl, and did she have to?"

"No. I know my Janet. She would have done it. Often I wanted to work so the girls could have a little more fun, and some nice frocks, but I didn't dare, and I had no excuse, for any time Sheila wanted something special Janet paid for it."

The colonel clicked his fingers at Hoover, who was snuffling by. He picked him up and sat him on his knee.

"Hear that, old man? And we think we're bullied." He shook his head. "Shockin' to think of all the comfort I've had while there are people like you strugglin' alone. You happy in that cottage of Sheldon's?"

"Yes. I came to it for Sheila's sake, and even when she's got a job I shall stop on. It will do Janet good and, you know, I don't think people like myself ought to be in the big towns, if we can reasonably move out. There was a friend of mine buried under her home before I left London; the rescue-party were working for hours before they got her out, and they looked so dirty and tired, and all the time they were working I thought to myself that she could have gone to her daughter in Devonshire, and what a lot of unnecessary work she was making."

The colonel roared. He was still laughing when Janet and Barbara came out of the house. Barbara kissed the top of his head.

"What's the joke? I haven't heard you laugh like that for ages."

"It wasn't me," said Maggie. "I wasn't being funny."

The colonel turned to Janet.

"Bring your mother again. She's better than fifty glasses of milk."

Janet held out her hands to Maggie.

"Up you get if you want to go to church."

The colonel stroked Hoover.

"One of the good turns my ulcer's done me is keepin' me from hearin' another of the vicar's sermons. Shockin' bore." He lifted Hoover's muzzle. "We do a nice bit of psalm singin' out here, don't we, old man?"

"Daddy's an old heathen," Barbara apologized to Maggie. "For years he had to go to church parades, and now he's got lazy. I go."

Maggie laid a hand on the colonel, for he was getting up.

"No, sit still. If I'm going to be allowed to count myself a friend, and pop in when I'm passing, I don't want any formalities. There'll be none when you're well enough to come and see me."

"Do you like them?" Janet asked her mother directly they were outside the house.

"Now don't hustle me. You know I'm slow at making friends."

"Still, you got on all right with the colonel."

Maggie considered the point.

"I should think he's a very difficult person not to like."

Janet put her arm through her mother's and hugged it to her side.

"You cautious old woman you!"

Worsingfold church was beautiful. It was Norman, and though it had been repaired here and there, it was very much as the worshippers had seen it in the twelfth century. Janet, used to a modern church built to accommodate villadom, was conscious at once of the prayers of over eight hundred years clustering in the stones and woodwork. It was all very simple. On the altar, flanked by two candles, were garden roses. The choir had only five men, and four of those had the boots and gaiters of the Home Guard showing beneath their cassocks. The boys had the shiny-cheeked, rather wooden faces of country children. Amongst them, looking like an angel, Janet spotted Iris' 'vacuee.

Worsingfold liked evening church, and when, because of the black-out, evening church was at half-past three, there was very little church-going in the village, for it considered church at any other time than evening meant for gentry. Having come to church, Worsingfold liked to sing. 'Sun of my soul' in the burred local accent echoed round the roof, through the open windows and down the road. The vicar was old. Maggie's description, at least sixty-five, had been generous, but age had not spoilt a beautiful speaking voice; in fact it had mellowed it. Prayer could never be spoken parrot-wise by him, for he was an old saint. The words could not be ignored as he spoke them. "And that the rest of our lives hereafter may be pure and holy, so that at the last we may come to His eternal joy, through Jesus Christ our Lord, Amen." Janet had to raise her head from her hands to look at him, so calm and reassuring he sounded. Maggie half lifted her head and glanced at Janet. "Bless the child," she thought; "if the rest of her life is one half as good as the first twenty-five years she'll do all right."

It was during the singing of the Nunc Dimittis that Maggie recollected tomorrow. "Lord, lettest thou thy servant depart in peace, according to thy word." Of course, if she must depart, she prayed it would be in peace, but fear gripped her again. She shivered. Janet felt the movement and frowned at her.

"Sit down," she whispered, and then, as Maggie hesitated, she gave her a little push. "Sit down and don't swing your legs."

Maggie sat and a faint smile twisted her lips. How often had she said that, particularly to Sheila, a hand on the child's knees. Sheila no longer swung her legs, but she needed just as much looking after. A new anxiety passed through Maggie's mind. Was she right to turn anything as lovely and as silly out into the world? But conscription for girls must come. Sheila would have to go then; she would be just one of thousands of mothers who had a daughter whom they thought pretty and silly. She got up for the Creed and, though her lips said the words, her mind was forming its own prayer. "Oh, Lord, do stop me fussing. Let there be nothing the matter with me, and let Sheila settle all right, and in Your own good time please let Janet fall in love."

"He is a bad preacher," said Janet as they came out of church, "but he's got a lovely voice."

"Was he dull?"

Maggie was surprised.

Janet laughed.

"You're a bad old woman. I don't believe you heard a word he said. You were thinking of something else, weren't you?"

Maggie looked at the sky.

"Yes, darling, and I have a feeling God understands."

NOBODY likes Mondays. This Monday in the Brains' cottage started particularly badly. Maggie had scarcely slept. She had woken with a jump, short of breath, and with the sinking feeling she so dreaded. She had sat up. She would have been glad of a light, but before she had got into bed she had pulled back the black-out to let in the air. The wind flapped the curtains, somewhere an owl hooted, a dog barked. The sky was inky black. Then suddenly a fork of light slit the darkness and distant thunder rumbled. Maggie hated storms; they frayed her nerves, added to her fears and gave her a feeling of foreboding. Why had she agreed to see the doctor? Was she being selfish in allowing Janet to stay with her? Ought she to insist on both girls doing war work? If she had got to see the doctor she must get Sheila out of the house first. Oh, dear! Why had she given in to Janet! She wouldn't have the energy to have a row with Sheila after a night like this.

Anxiety made Janet cross. She came down to breakfast meaning to be nice, but so worried at the thought of what the doctor would find wrong with Maggie's heart that she could not help sounding snappy.

Sheila had been far more annoyed about the tea-party at the Haines' than she would admit. She told herself that the Haines were stuffy, or they would obviously like her better than Janet, and that they were boring and she did not want to go to their house; but the truth was that she disliked Barbara Haines because she made her feel inferior. The colonel she did not mind quite as much. He wasn't bad, she thought, only he didn't appreciate people properly. He treated her as if, just because she was pretty, she was less use than other people. Besides, he had been unsympathetic about her going into pictures. Dismissing the subject as if it wasn't worth talking about. All the same, it was not the colonel but that awful stuck-up Barbara she couldn't bear. There was, too, her innermost private reason for hating Barbara. It was very annoying that her mother and Janet should take up with her. If they knew everything, which, of course, they couldn't, they wouldn't see Barbara, because they would have to be on her side; relations always stood together.

It was natural that breakfast should be a stormy meal. Maggie looked so worn that Janet said in an angry voice: "You didn't sleep."

Maggie was on the defensive at once.

"Don't keep picking on my appearance."

Sheila poured milk on to her cereal.

"Your own isn't too good. I can't think why you make more of a fright of yourself than you are naturally to go and teach that kid."

Janet had taken particular pains to look prim and tidy; she wanted to look exactly as she had looked last week to give Iris no possible chance to comment, in front of her father, on her looks. She stared at Sheila as though she could have bitten her.

"I'm suitably dressed for my job, which is more than you are in that pink thing, if you're going to the Labour Exchange today. Nobody would think of you for a good job dressed like that."

"Who said I was going to the Labour Exchange today?" Maggie seized her chance.

"I do, and you're starting the moment you've eaten your breakfast."

Sheila looked sulky.

"It was agreed I'd go when I liked."

"It was not. It was agreed you'd go within a week. You've been shilly-shallying for days. It's fine today, and not too hot. The bus leaves the corner at twenty past nine and you'll catch it."

Sheila sighed wearily.

"I didn't sleep very well, the thunder made me nervous; you know how it does. I've rather a headache; I thought I'd stay quiet this morning."

Maggie glanced at Sheila's clear, wild-rose skin, and unwillingly hardened her heart, but her voice softened; too well she knew what thunder could do to the nerves.

"You go along, dearie, the Labour Exchange won't take long, and then you can get those stockings you want. I'll give you my margarine coupons."

"If you're going into the town would you look at an art shop, which I hear is near the Town Hall, and see if you can get some things I want for Iris?"

Sheila swallowed her coffee. She looked sourly at Janet. "I shan't have time." She got up. "If I'm being pushed off like this I'll have to go hungry." At the staircase she looked over her shoulder at Janet. "If you want to go to the town ask your friend Barbara to drive you in. She's often there; petrol never seems to worry her."

"There!" said Maggie remorsefully. "I've driven the poor child out without any food in her. Perhaps she shouldn't go today as she has a headache."

Janet cut herself a slice of bread.

"I don't believe in her headache, and if she's hungry she can have a cup of something and a bun in the town." Maggie was too tired after her night to be fair.

"I wish you wouldn't be so hard, Janet. She's a frail little thing; you shouldn't judge everybody by yourself."

Janet flushed, and was about to retort when her heart contracted. Oh, God! How ill Maggie looked! She got up and leant over the back of her mother's chair and pressed her cheek close to hers.

"Darling, I'm a cross-patch, but you're a silly old woman. You know in your inside that Sheila hasn't a headache, and that she's only at her old game of stalling for time. But don't mind me; I've got a black dog on my shoulder this morning."

Maggie patted Janet's cheek.

"Did you take those salts this morning?" Janet shook her head. "Bad girl; I'll bring it in to you tomorrow. Nothing like salts for black dogs."

When Janet reached the farm she found Iris in bed.

"It's a little tummy upset," said Gladys. "Bed for twenty-four hours and castor-oil. That's my cure."

Janet looked pityingly at Iris. It was a warm morning and the child had on not only a woollen jersey, but Gladys had brought back the winter eiderdown and tucked it firmly round her, and given her two hot-water bottles, "What would you like to do?" Janet asked Iris as the door closed behind Gladys. "Would you like me to read to you?" Iris, who had been looking sorry for herself, had brightened since Janet had arrived.

"No, I'd like to do something. It was a very, very little chill I had, only feeling sick, but I'm much worse since Gladys has done me good. I think castor-oil is a real illness, don't you? Could I draw?"

Janet considered Gladys' clean sheets.

"With a pencil; it would be so awful if we upset things on the bed."

Iris giggled.

"And made all the sheets striped with paint. I have some chalks. The clean sort with proper outsides like a pencil. Could I use those?"

Janet fetched a drawing-book and the chalks.

"What are you going to draw?"

Iris bounced in her bed.

"I've had a beautiful idea. You get another drawing-book and we'll both draw. I'll tell you what to draw and you tell me."

Janet fetched the second book.

"You draw a tiger."

Iris selected a brown chalk.

"And you draw the Holy Ghost."

"I can't. I've no idea how to start."

Iris found a yellow chalk and rapidly striped something dimly reminiscent of a tiger.

"I'm not very certain of his face myself, but I know he wears gold boots."

"Does he?"

"Yes, once me and Mummy went to a church where they acted a play about the Virgin Mary and Bible people. When we came in the play wasn't ready, and there was a man lying half under some straw that was going to be the stable, and somebody asked what he was going to be, and somebody else said the Holy Ghost. So then I looked very carefully because I've often wondered what the Holy Ghost looked like, but all I could see was gold boots. Have you finished? I have!"

"Nowhere near."

"Then I'll put in some jungle for my tiger. I was only little when I saw that play, and I went to sleep in the middle, so I never did see the Holy Ghost, for it was all over when I woke up."

Janet was drawing hard when Donald came in.

"Good morning, Janet. Hullo, invalid, how are you getting on?"

Iris ran a hand over her stomach.

"I'm moving about round here. You know what castor-oil does?"

"I do." He looked at Iris' drawing. "A very handsome beast."

Iris pointed to Janet's book.

"Let's see hers. She's drawn the Holy Ghost."

Donald's eyes crinkled at the corners.

"Iris' choice, I take it."

Janet held out her page.

"I've only drawn a sort of sunset. He's behind that."

Iris considered the effort.

"I think that's rather good. Now draw a water-can with water coming out of it. What shall I draw?"

Donald sat down on the bed, and put an arm round Iris.

"Your mind is like a see-saw, old lady. A water-can indeed! What a come-down! Is the castor-oil going to keep you in bed all day?"

"Yes. What shall I draw, Janet?"

Janet searched her mind for a subject which would take some time.

"A church full of people."

Donald turned to her.

"I have to go into the town this afternoon for a meeting; I had thought that you might have come to get the stuff you want for Iris."

The 'you' clearly meant herself and Iris. Janet looked regretful.

"What a shame we can't go; it would have been convenient."

Iris examined the drawing with her head on one side.

"It's no good hoping. Gladys always says twenty-four hours in bed about everything."

Janet felt puzzlingly disappointed. She knew she ought to be glad to be spared the drive with Donald, who would probably be rude, but instead she felt like a child who watches its mother refusing on its behalf an invitation to a party.

"It would have been awfully handy," she said. "I want such a lot of things."

"And there might have been time to go to the toy department and have tea in a shop." Iris' voice was resigned. "But these things are sent to try our spirit."

Donald laughed.

"I recognize Mrs. Honeywell's quotation, but it's trying Janet's spirit more than yours, I believe."

"It's tiresome having nothing in the way of books and things," Janet explained.

"Well . . ." Donald started, and then broke off as Gladys, carrying a glass of barley water, came in.

"You here, Donald! I should have thought you'd be too busy to sit about in the morning."

Donald got up.

"I am, too, but I had to see how Iris was. Besides, I have to go into town this afternoon, and I thought I'd take Janet and Iris along with me."

Gladys put down the glass on the table by the bed.

"Out of the question. Iris will stop where she is for twenty-four hours at least. I've nursed her through one bad illness and I don't want to nurse her through another, thank you."

"As a matter of fact, Gladys," Iris broke in, "I'm not feeling at all like measles. It was only a little sick I felt, and I wouldn't have told you except I had to have the basin in case. I don't feel so well since you did me good, but that'll be better when it's worked. It's going round and round just now."

Gladys tidied the child's sheets and pillow.

"Anyway, you're staying where you are."

"I don't see why Janet shouldn't go and get my lesson things with Daddy," Iris suggested. "I'll miss her, of course, but I'll read a book."

Gladys spoke sharply.

"I've no time to wait on you this afternoon. I'm rushed off my feet."

"Nobody doesn't have to wait on me. I'll read a book. Mrs. Honeywell will look in; she always does if I'm in bed."

"Mrs. Honeywell's leaving early this afternoon." Gladys turned to Donald. "It's out of the question."

"Now he'll crawl," thought Janet, "and agree with her at once." But Donald did not seem to notice Gladys' tone.

"I don't see that it's out of the question. The car is going in; it's only sense to use it. I won't be going again for days and Janet wants the books and things."

Gladys patted and pulled at Iris' bed things, then she seemed to come to a decision.

"You're quite right, Donald; as a matter of fact, I think I'll take advantage of the car going in and come with you too."

Iris did not lift her head from her drawing, but her voice was reproachful.

"Who's going to give me my tea?"

"Mrs. Honeywell, of course."

Iris raised her eyes.

"You said she was leaving early."

Gladys flushed; she was behaving like a fool, but she could not stop herself.

"Surely you can wait for tea until we come back."

Iris looked anxious.

"But I'd be all alone up here. Nobody wouldn't hear if I called; burglars might come, or a German."

Donald kissed her.

"You shan't be left, twopence."

"No, I'll stay," said Janet.

Donald looked exasperated.

"What's the point of that? It's you who want to get her lesson things."

"And you did say you were rushed off your feet," Iris reminded Gladys, "so I don't see how you can go."

A dull crimson flooded Gladys' face. She said nothing, but as she moved to the door she gave Janet a look which said as clearly as if she had spoken, "So that's your game, is it? Very well then, we're enemies from now on."

Janet turned impulsively to Donald.

"I'd really rather stop . . ."

His voice rang with impatience.

"You're coming. Never in my life did I hear such a fuss about a simple shopping expedition."

§

"Is there only one town in these parts?" Janet asked Donald.

Donald slowed his car for some cows to be driven through a gate.

"To us there is. It's our market town." He smiled. "You think it a one-horse little place, I expect, but in Worsingfold we think it a metropolis, and a bit alarming."

"Alarming!"

He turned to her, his eyes twinkling.

"We look on it as a den of vice. It's got a dance-hall! You want to watch your step in a place that goes in for things like that."

Janet leant back in her seat; she felt easy and relaxed. She forgot that she and Donald were ever at cross purposes. He was speaking in a gentle, laughing way which fitted in with the purr of the car, and the white dust of the road, and the passing hedges starred with early dog-roses.

"Does Worsingfold go and dance there?"

Donald grinned.

"We like people to think we do; makes us feel rather dogs, you know. If anybody comes on leave it's taken for granted they'll go there. We dig our elbows into their ribs and we wink and we say, 'You'll be goin' into town dancin', shouldn't wonder!' We don't say that because we necessarily think they'll be doing anything of the sort, but we're paying their manhood a compliment. They may have left Worsingfold mere boys, but now they're in the Army or the Navy or the Air Force they're men."

There was a wealth of understanding and sympathy for the village point of view in his tone, and as well an allying of himself with it. Janet felt her town background.

"I've always lived in London, and in a suburban district at that. I don't understand country people; it's a pity, I'd like to."

"You will, they're easy. If you listen and watch you'll soon pick up our ways and thoughts. We're a bit careful to begin with when we meet London folk. We know you for a lot of wasteful people, who eat out of tins, and throw half of everything away, and we know you're clever and know a lot of what's going on behind the scenes. You might have met the Prime Minister, and like as not you've got friends in the ministries. I've not mixed with the village much lately, I've been too busy, but I'd take a bet that your family have been the cause of a lot of head wagging."

"Not if they expect waste, or tins. Mother hates both."

Donald laughed.

"Very suspicious in a Londoner; we probably think she's a German. Excepting that young Sheila runs true to form, that may have saved your bacon." He sounded his horn to move a woman with a perambulator off the crown of the road. "Anna, my wife, belonged to the Women's Institute, and she used to say they treated her as if she had been grown in a greenhouse, to be admired, but never planted in the back garden."

Janet felt it was unusual for him to talk of Anna, and perhaps good for him.

"Iris is always talking about her. She must have been an interesting person."

Donald's face set in grim, sad lines. He seemed to have forgotten Janet, but to be speaking his memories out loud.

"She was the loveliest thing. I was staying in town with my half-brother, and he knew a girl who was in a show, and he took me along to see it. It was a revue, usual stuff, half-dressed girls and all that, and then came a ballet. It was something to do with the spring, all green. Anna was so light a little thing, she reminded me of a fallen leaf blowing around the place. After the show we went to the back to see the girl Dick knew. Anna shared a room with her."

His voice tailed away.

Janet, to make him talk, said gently:

"And that's how you met her."

"That's how I met her." He seemed to remember her. "This is boring for you." He hesitated. "I don't know what made me talk of her."

"I'm interested; you see, knowing about her helps me over Iris."

"Funny little cuss, isn't she?"

"Will you mind if she wants to follow in her mother's footsteps, dances or something like that?"

"I don't mind owning I hope she won't, but I shan't stop her. You can't make plants grow in soil that doesn't suit them."

Janet watched the muscles round his jaw-bone contract. Her heart bled, for she could feel he blamed himself for transplanting Anna.

"Iris isn't likely to want a stage life; after all, she's country bred."

"If it's in her blood it will come out, I dare say."

"She's not getting a chance to take to anything artistic with me. I've no parlour tricks."

He spoke with a warmth at the back of his voice.

"She's happy with you, and you're dead right with her. Gladys was a bit inclined to train her too much, tie her up to sticks, as it were, to shape her. With you she'll shape naturally."

"You hardly know yet, I've been with you such a short time."

"I knew the moment I set eyes on you.'"

"Did you?" thought Janet. Then she remembered their meeting in the wood. Yes, it was probably true. He had asked her then about Iris, and had seemed keen. He probably had felt she would be right, but what about afterwards? What about that queer scene over paying her? The afternoon was so beautiful, she did not want to ruin it with worrying thoughts; she felt what for want of a better word she called to herself 'contentment'.

"Oh, goodness!" she said out loud. "It is a nice day!"

"What I used to call a chocolate biscuit day when I was small."

Janet wanted, so badly that she could hardly remember when she had wanted anything so much, to know what he had been like as a little boy. She was not naturally inquisitive, but now she surged with prying thoughts. What had he looked like? What had he worn? She almost said, "Tell me about yourself," and only stopped when remembering that she and Donald were almost strangers.

"Chocolate biscuit day! Why?"

He grinned.

"My father wasn't a farmer, though his father was. The farm went to my uncle. Father started in shipping. Then my uncle died and left him the farm. Farming was, of course, in his blood, for somehow he persuaded my mother she would like a country life, and he persuaded himself that he could risk throwing up the shipping business, and risk a new career. So he up-anchored, and came home."

"How old were you?"

"Oh, tiny, two or three. The first thing I remember is a sunflower. It was miles taller than I was, and I thought it was the most terrific thing I'd ever seen. I suppose a sunflower is pretty impressive to a town kid."

Janet saw a little figure on the lawn in front of the farm, staring up at the giant golden daisy.

"Had you curls?"

He looked puzzled.

"I shouldn't wonder, we all had curls as kids. Why?" The question had slipped out. She flushed.

"I just wondered. Tell me about the chocolate biscuits."

"My mother was town bred, and though anything my father did was all right with her, she didn't really take to country ways. So whenever she had an excuse, a fine day or anything like that, she used to say, 'Let's ask some people in.' Then we kids, my sisters and I, would chime in, 'We'll open a box of chocolate biscuits.' It was just a joke. I don't know where it started."

"Did she ever get to like the country?"

"Never had a chance. She decided to learn to ride, and she was thrown and killed."

"Oh, and your father married again. So that's why you've a half-brother."

His face changed, it was as if the sky had clouded.

"Yes, that's where old Dick comes into the story, but you know all about that."

Janet had no idea what he was talking about. It was on the tip of her tongue to say, "No, I don't, tell me about him," but she stopped herself. He was being so nice and for some reason the thought of Dick annoyed him. They were running out of the country into an area of streets and shops.

"This, I suppose, is our town?"

He liked the 'our'.

"Yes. Pity we're all so busy these days or I'd show you round. Can you get your shopping done in an hour and a half? I don't think my meeting will be longer." She nodded. "I put the car in the garage at The Crown. I'll pick you up again there."

Janet did her shopping. It was a charming little town, with some fine old buildings. In the ordinary way she would have been enchanted to look round, but, of course, the things she wanted for Iris were hard to come by, many of them unobtainable, and as well she kept looking at her watch. An hour and a half was too short for all she had to do, but the time seemed to crawl.

Donald was not at The Crown when Janet, with an armload of parcels, came and stood by the car. There was only a soldier waiting by a lorry. He was a chatty man, and thought himself lucky to run into something as nice as Janet to talk to. They had gone through his home life, which included a history of his mother's operations, his father's allotment and how well he had done with a crop of onions, and had just reached his girl, who was making munitions, and they were bending together over her photograph, when Donald came into the inn yard. Janet did not see him until he had unlocked the car doors. She gave the soldier a brilliant smile.

"Good-bye, and good luck."

The soldier put his girl's photograph back into his pocket. "Hope we run into each other again."

"Hope so."

Donald drove out of the yard in silence. Janet thought he was engrossed in the traffic, then she happened to glance at him, and saw his profile, and it looked angry. "Bother!" she thought. "He's had a beast of a meeting, and it will spoil our drive home."

"Was the meeting a success?"

He made an impatient growl, and slowed the car for a flock of sheep which were being driven out of the town.

"What meeting ever is? A lot of talk and nothing done." He had to stop the car, for the sheep were almost under the wheels. "You seemed to be enjoying yourself."

"Me!" Janet sounded surprised. "What, shopping? As a matter of fact it was a bit of a bore. I couldn't get any of the things I specially wanted."

"I didn't mean your shopping. I meant your meeting with your boy-friend."

Janet laughed.

"That wasn't a boy-friend, he was just a soldier who was waiting. We got talking; you know how one does."

"I don't. I didn't know it was the fashion for girls to pick up strange men."

She found this too silly to be annoying.

"What a way to talk! This is 1941, you know, not 1900. He was telling me about his mother's abscesses, and his father's allotment, and Millie, his girl. She works in munitions, but she ought to be a crooner."

Donald realized he had made a fool of himself.

"I couldn't know. You looked thick as thieves. I didn't like to interrupt you."

The shepherd and his dog had got the sheep into some sort of order. Donald moved the car forward slowly. Janet watched him out of the corner of her eye. What a funny man he was, so changeable! Why should he be so disagreeable? He was like a sulky little boy! It was hot in the car. The sun had blazed on it while it stood in the inn yard. She felt sticky and uncomfortable. Her discomfort seemed to transmit itself to Donald.

"Hot, isn't it? Wish this old rattler had a sunshine roof." She felt he was sorry for his surliness and was looking for an olive branch. It touched her. She wanted to say something nice, but as she was thinking what to say, she found her hand sliding over the hot leather of the seat towards Donald. She pulled it back to her with a jerk, flushing. She turned her head from him and stared out of the window. They were free of the town, back amongst the fields and hedges. Whatever was the matter with her?

Hot weather was supposed to do funny things to you, but to want to pat the knee of a man you hardly knew, and who was your employer, was going a bit far!

Donald, as if aware of her need for control, began a running commentary on the country through which they were passing.

"That barley's showing well, very well indeed. Not much amiss with that wheat, good strong bit that is."

Perhaps he was not looking too carefully at the road, and Janet certainly did not see what happened, but as they turned a corner the brakes screamed, the car bucketed and shot into the bank, and, unscathed, a motor-cyclist drew up beside them.

The motor-cyclist and Donald accepted with very few words that neither of them knew exactly what had happened, and walked round the car to examine the damage. After a short discussion the cyclist got on his bicycle and roared off up the road. Donald came back to Janet with a gloomy face.

"He's gone to get us a tow." He held out his cigarette-case. "I'm awfully sorry. I hope you weren't frightened."

"Of course not. I'm sorry about the car."

They smoked in companionable silence. The sun was hot, but they left a door open. Now and again a dispatch-rider or an army lorry dashed by, otherwise they had the road to themselves. Janet stubbed out her cigarette. She would have liked to have lolled and let the time pass drowsily by, but she was on her guard. She was liking this time with Donald too well, and was scared of herself. Donald finished his cigarette and tossed it out of the window. He moved restlessly, and ran a finger round his collar to let out the heat. Then, suddenly, without saying a word, he had her in his arms and they were kissing.

Neither of them knew how long they clung together; a particularly noisy lorry made itself heard and they dragged themselves apart. The lorry was the head of a convoy, and as it rolled by Donald gave her another cigarette.

"That was bad of me." He lit it for her. "I can't blame myself. Obviously, any man would want to kiss you, but I never meant to let myself do it; it's awkward placed as we are."

Janet stared out of the window.

"We needn't let it make any difference."

His eyes crinkled with amusement.

"Except that I shall never see you without wanting to do it again; in fact only the soldiers are stopping me now."

She shook her head.

"No, we mustn't do it again. I mean, I don't know why I kissed you then. I'm not a bit the sort of person who . . ."

He laid a hand over one of hers.

"My dear, don't let's dictate to ourselves, nor make a mountain out of this. You are young and pretty, and it's summer, and I kissed you. Is that a crime? Is it a crime that I want most desperately to kiss you again?"

She did not move her hand.

"Of course not, and it's not all you. Only I don't think we can go on doing it. It's awkward, as I'm Iris' governess. Besides, to be quite honest, I think just kissing because we're young and it's summer is lovely for once, but it would be messy if it became a habit."

He squeezed her hand and took his away.

"I see." He puffed at his cigarette. "Life's complicated, isn't it?"

She tapped her ash out of the window. She said a vague "yes", but she was not feeling at all vague, she was throbbing and alive, and radiant, and yet unhappy. "I'm in love," she thought. "This is what being in love feels like!" The dusty road with lorries rushing by suddenly became so beautiful that she spoke of it.

"What a lovely spot this is!"

Donald's thoughts were evidently miles away. He came back to her with a start.

"What spot?"

"This."

He looked at her to see if she was being sarcastic. Then, amused, he started an inventory.

"Charming. Two ditches. Two nice grass banks, one with a very handsome crop of cow-parsley, and one with a good gash made by my car. Two badly kept hedges. A long road in need of repair, and full of dust kicked up by army traffic. One . . ."

Janet stopped him. She was laughing, but rather awkwardly. Now he was describing the scene her description 'lovely spot' did seem idiotic, but all the same he could not spoil its charm for her. Did all places look different, she wondered, because of the person you saw them with? Probably yes. She had seen girls meeting men under the clock at Charing Cross or in Piccadilly Tube Station, and had caught an expression on their faces which had remained with her, but until now unidentified. Now she knew what it was. Charing Cross was not the Charing Cross the hurrying crowd saw. Piccadilly Tube was not a swarming mass pushing their way on to the escalators. Each was a rarefied and lovely world born for lovers' meetings. She could not tell Donald what she had learnt. Instead she said:

"You are looking at the ground. I was looking at the sky. Listen to that lark. Anyway, to a Cockney all the country is lovely. I think that cow-parsley that you speak of so rudely is gorgeous. So would you if the only flowers you were used to having cost good money and then weren't fresh."

He nodded.

"Mind you, I'm fond of every inch of this part. I loved it as a kid, and since I've had the farm, I've the feeling of belonging. There's a very strong hold between a farmer and the land, you know. I've had fights with it, and sometimes it's beaten me, and sometimes I've beaten it. As far as that battle goes we've broken about square." He was silent a moment, and then went on. "On other counts I've got a bit owing, though. You can't help mixing backgrounds with the things which happen on them. When the time comes for me to be boxed and pulled in one of my carts to the churchyard, I should like people to say that the land had treated me well. I'd like them to say, 'He was happy here.'"

He was miles away in his thoughts, almost unconscious of her. Janet did not interrupt him. She could see Anna so clearly; that frail little creature must haunt the countryside for him. Donald was no fool; he would have known how far she was from happiness. Wrapped in their private musings they were startled by the sound of a horn. The cyclist had stopped another farmer who was red-faced with delight at the thought of towing Donald and his governess. A proper old tale he would have to tell.

Janet got the farmer to stop in the village. She made the doctor her excuse; she told Donald she wanted news of Maggie, which, of course, was true, but only in part. She did not want to be towed up to the farm and face Gladys' prying eyes; she did not want to explain why she had been so distrait that she had not seen the collision with the motor-cycle. She wanted the walk home alone to collect her thoughts.

The Old Oast House, where the doctor lived, lay in a lane which ran up beside the Haines' house. As Janet reached the Haines' front gate Barbara came out with Hoover.

"Hullo!" She slipped her arm through Janet's. "We're taking a constitutional, as Daddy calls it. I have to make Hoover walk or he gets disgustingly fat. I suspect Daddy slips him some of his milk now and then. Where are you off to?" Janet explained. "Where have you come from? The farm?"

Janet was unwilling to talk about her afternoon. Her voice was exaggeratedly off-hand.

"No, shopping. Donald, Mr. Sheldon I mean, was going in for a meeting. He wanted Iris to come too, but she has a chill."

Barbara glanced at Janet, hearing something elusive in her voice. Janet dropped her eyes, and Barbara made a little amused face, but she could see Janet did not want to be teased.

"Hoover and I will come with you as far as The Oast House." She looked down at Hoover. "But don't imagine, my boy, we're stopping there for you to have a row with the grey cat, because we're not; we're going for a brisk walk to the top of the hill."

The doctor was in his surgery mixing medicines. He nodded at Janet.

"Sit down, my dear. Don't mind my going on with my work, do you?"

"How is Mother?"

He poured some powder on to his scales.

"Know anything about hearts?"

"No."

"Well then, let's take something you do know. You were a secretary in London, weren't you?" She nodded. "Then you understand typewriters. What would happen if you used a typewriter year in year out, never sent it away for an overhaul?"

"After a time it wouldn't work."

"Quite. Well, for overhaul take holiday. Your mother's like the typewriter, worn right out." Janet eyed him in frightened silence. He wagged a finger at her. "Now don't look scared; I've told you the worst first. With care she's going to get a whole lot better."

"But she won't take care."

"Oh, yes, she will! Did you ever hear of Tirdoutum?"

"No."

"Nor did I till this morning. It's a new disease discovered by me. Speak it slowly and you have tired-out-um. I asked your mother if she had certain symptoms, and then I examined her back, patted her spine a bit, looked grave, and said that was where the trouble lay. I told her that she'd have to rest for six months, and take certain drugs. You know, I think, she had suspected her heart, and when she heard it was a tired spine she was like a two-year-old. Anyway, she's agreed to let me try and put her straight."

"Has she really promised to rest?"

"Yes. Of course, there was a lot of 'if this' and 'if that', and 'I must talk to Janet.'"

"I can arrange everything."

"Of course you can. You take young Iris to the cottage while you straighten the place. She'll like to help. Do her good; get her away from Gladys. Very good, competent creature, and well-meaning, but no good with a child."

Janet got up.

"Thank you awfully."

He waved a friendly hand.

"That's all right, my dear. I'll be up again to see your mother in a day or two. Tirdoutum. Spine trouble, and don't you forget it."

Janet strolled home. The sun was setting in a glory of pink and gold. It was a breath-catchingly beautiful evening, and she was in the mood to see loveliness so acutely that it hurt. The buzzing, home-going bee, the delicate grasses, the trees against the sky, all caught at the strings of her heart. She tried to think coherently of the afternoon. Was today the first moment she had fallen in love? Did love just show itself in the rather primitive wish for contact? Was that why her hand had tried to touch him? She remembered the feel of his arms and his mouth. She might have said that there was to be no more kissing, but the very memory made her sway, and everything dance before her eyes. How silly she was! Of course today was not the beginning. The beginning must have been the time they first met; that was why she cared so terribly about his moods and what he said. What of him? Did he care at all? Janet was a realist and her common sense cried 'no'. He said he wanted to kiss you, but he said we mustn't make a mountain out of it. That meant don't think of a summer's day flirtation as love. But he had said life was complicated. What did he mean by that? And he had minded her talking to that soldier, with what followed; that little scene looked like jealousy. She had reached the last stile and the cottage was in sight. She sat down for a second. She spoke in a whisper, and then louder, and then in her full voice, for there were only some birds and two rabbits to hear. "I love Donald. I love Donald." She raised her eyes to the setting sun. "Please God, do let him love me." A night breeze coming suddenly across the fields made her shiver. What had she prayed? What about Gladys? She turned. The farm lay in the shadow of the gathering night, and as she looked towards it, a coldness gripped her. Oh, heavens! What a muddle life was! She jumped off the stile and, to escape from her thoughts, ran the rest of the way home.

§

Being in love is the hardest thing to hide. Janet looked different when she came home that night. Her eyes shone, her lips glowed, there was more colour in her cheeks, and a vividness about the whole of her, so that as she opened the front door it was as if a lamp came into the house.

Maggie was lying on the sofa in the sitting-room; she had a book in her hand. She was trying to read, but she had not taken a word in.

"Janet"—she held out a hand—"I don't know how we're going to manage, darling, but I've overtired my spine, and it means rest to get it right. It's nothing serious; it's called Tire . . . something, but it means rest and medicines for six months. How are we going to get along?"

Janet sat on the floor.

"You funny old woman, do you know you look better already!"

Maggie flushed as if caught out in a crime.

"As a matter of fact, I was worrying a little; so stupid of me, but you kept saying I was getting thin, and I didn't see how I could manage a real illness."

Janet held one of her mother's hands.

"Old silly, aren't you! You talk of being ill as if it were a fur coat that you either could or couldn't afford."

"Well, so it is when you've little money and do your own work. But this isn't a real illness, this just means being careful."

"I'll find out how careful; if it means taking care for six months and then a cure, it's worth taking a lot of trouble about. I can manage. I'll bring Iris along here in the morning while I get the house done, and we'll have our main meal in the evening after I'm home, or I might find a Mrs. Honeywell like they have at the farm."

Maggie was watching Janet's face.

"You were late back, what have you been doing?"

"Went into the town shopping with Mr. Sheldon. I walked back from the village."

Janet's voice was so deliberately off-hand that Maggie, pretending not to, studied her even more carefully.

"Have tea in the town?"

Janet did not want to talk about the afternoon. She got up.

"No. I'll go and see to supper; I take it Sheila isn't doing anything about it?"

Janet went up the stairs singing. Sheila's bedroom door was open; she was sitting at her dressing-table doing her hair.

"You sound cheerful."

Janet came in and sat on the bed.

"I am. Mother's been ordered to rest, and she's going to."

"I shouldn't have thought that was anything to sing about."

"I think it is. It's stood out a mile she needed a rest, and now, thank goodness, she's going to take it. If you'd ever looked at her you'd have seen how thin she's been getting."

"We've neither of us been very strong. I'd have liked to have done more to help, only I thought I ought to get my strength back."

Janet laughed.

"Don't try putting that stuff over me! How did you get on at the Labour Exchange?"

"I think I'm going to join N.A.A.F.I."

"Are you!" Janet pictured Sheila in a canteen. "I think that's a very good idea, definitely under the heading of 'comforts for the forces'. I'll bet there'll be some pay squandered."

Sheila opened her eyes.

"What d'you mean?"

"Oh, come off it! Are you going to help me get supper?"

"I suppose I must, but I do think I ought to be spared domestic work as much as possible, seeing I'm going to do nothing else for the rest of the war. I was altering my hair. We wear uniform and I'm afraid they won't let me wear it long." She looked at herself in the glass, and Janet came in her line of vision. She swung round and stared at her. "What have you been doing?"

"Nothing."

"Did you just teach Iris all day?"

Janet felt awkward under Sheila's searching eyes.

"No, as a matter of fact I went with Mr. Sheldon to the town this afternoon to buy Iris' lesson books and things."

"By car, I suppose, while I had to go to the Labour Exchange on a bus."

"I'd take a bet you got a lift both ways."

"Well, actually I did, but that doesn't alter it that I was meant to go on a bus. D'you like Donald?"

Janet, to her annoyance, felt her cheeks flushing.

"He's all right, I suppose."

Sheila glued her eyes on her.

"You better watch your step, if you're going to fall in love with him, because Gladys means to marry him."

"How can you be such an idiot!"

"I'm not an idiot. I'd be an idiot if I didn't see that you look quite different to how you looked this morning. Actually, I think it's a very good thing; you needed to fall in love. You were beginning to look like somebody who's never been kissed. You don't now."

Janet got up. She gave Sheila a half-embarrassed, half-playful shake.

"Shut up! I hardly know Mr. Sheldon."

Janet gave her arm a pull.

"Come on and get supper. I tell you he's almost a stranger, but if I had been kissing him, I can promise you that you'd be the last person I'd tell about it."

"You don't need to, I've eyes in my head, but you take my advice and be careful. I like Gladys, but she's the sort to be an awful cat if she got jealous. She was frightful to me when she first saw me, and when she thought I was coming to teach Iris, but actually Donald isn't my type. I simply can't be bothered with him. She saw that, of course, and she's been all right ever since."

Janet's heart seemed to her to give a bounce. She did not want to be small-minded, but it was good news that Donald had not been interested in Sheila, for that was how the story went when translated. Sheila had never been known not to be interested in any man, especially a man with a car. It dismissed the idea that he kissed every girl he met.

"Poor Gladys," she said casually. "I don't blame her for being anxious with you about."

Sheila turned back to the glass.

"Actually she won't worry unless she needs to. She isn't at all stupid."

The family were at supper when there was a knock on the cottage door. Janet found Ben outside with a note.

"It's Miss Iris. Master do be wholly worried."

"What's the matter with her?"

"Like as not nothing, save all the dosing done her by that besom, but maybe it's worser."

Janet tore open the envelope. The note was scribbled on a half-sheet.

> "DEAR JANET,—Iris is upset. I don't think it's anything much, but she's cried herself into hysteria. Could you come over for half an hour?—DONALD."

"Donald!" thought Janet. So she was to use his Christian name! "Thank you, Ben, I'll be along."

"I'll wait for you. Master he said to wait. 'Miss Brain isn't used to fields same as us,' he says, 'maybe she'll fall into a ditch. You stay alongside of her.'"

Janet's smile could not be seen in the dark doorway. He had thought of her. It was nice, even if you were independent and modern, used not only to getting about by yourself, but getting about while bombs were falling, to be treated as a frail thing that needed looking after.

"I've got to go up to the farm for half an hour. Iris isn't well," she explained to Maggie.

"Poor little thing! Is there anything we can send her?"

"Or is it Iris' daddy who wants company?" Sheila asked.

Janet was pulling on a coat. She stopped half in and half out of it and managed a very credible laugh.

"Silly idiot! You're altogether too romantic, my girl." She kissed her mother. "Good night, Mum. Early bed, mind. So long, Queen of the Naafi's!"

Maggie looked tenderly after Janet, then she shook her head at Sheila.

"You're a naughty girl to tease her. I don't say she is interested in Mr. Sheldon, but if she is, it's a very good thing, and you mustn't tease her about it."

Sheila sighed.

"I do hope the N.A.A.F.I. people don't want me too soon." Then she added apparently irrelevantly, "I rather like watching rows."

Iris, flushed and swollen, was lying on her face amongst her tangled and crumpled sheets. Gladys was sitting by her and Donald leaning over the end of the bed. Janet peered round the door.

"Iris is a naughty girl," Gladys explained in a loud voice intended to carry over Iris' sobs. "She's been having one of her tempers."

Donald gave Janet a grateful nod. He came to the door and drew her back into the passage.

"She's had some row with Gladys, I think. She asked for you. See if you can do anything with her. I rang the doctor and he said he'd come up if you didn't soothe her."

"Is she often like this?"

"If she gets in a state it's difficult to get her out of it. Anna was given to something of the same sort." They came back into the bedroom. Donald laid a hand on Iris' heaving shoulders.

"Here's Janet, old lady."

Iris raised her head, then sprang up and held out her arms.

"Janet! Janet! Janet! Gladsayougoawaybutyouwon'twill-you!" Janet sat down on the bed and took Iris in her arms.

"I can't hear a word if you make a noise like that." She glanced at Donald. "Do you think we could be left to our heart-to-heart?" She waited until the door was shut and then said firmly, "Now tell me slowly what this hullabaloo is about."

Iris struggled with her sobs, and gradually, in a broken, hiccoughing way, she told her story.

"It was when I was going to bed, I said to Gladys I did hope I could get up tomorrow to do lessons with the things you'd bought, and she said she thought you wouldn't buy many because you were going away . . ."

Janet waited for the spasm of crying to stop.

"Going where?"

"To be a sailor for the war."

Janet could not remember telling Gladys of her W.R.N.S. ambitions, but the news had no doubt travelled.

"I did mean to be a sailor, but that was before I met you, and the reason I can't go is because I have to look after my mother."

"But if you look after her you won't come here any more."

"Oh, yes, I will! As a matter of fact, I was going to talk to you about it in the morning. Now I'm going to wash your face and settle you for the night, and while I do it I'm going to tell you the plan I'm working out to teach you, as well as do the work at home. It's very important you should know all about it because I want you to help me."

Half an hour later Janet came downstairs. There was a light under the sitting-room door and she went in. It was not a room she had been in before. Like the dining-room it had been furnished by Donald's grandfather, left as it was by the uncle who inherited the farm, then by his father and finally by himself. It was practically a museum piece, a perfect example of Victorian middle-class taste. In two massive armchairs, with antimacassars over their backs, sat Gladys and Donald. Gladys was mending, her work-basket on the table beside her, with an impressive pile of socks lying beside it. Donald was reading.

"I just looked in to say good night," said Janet. "Iris is asleep."

Donald got up.

"Do sit down. What was the trouble?"

Janet would have liked to turn on Gladys. Tell her what she thought of her, and let Donald see her clearly, but it was foreign to her nature to make trouble, and as well she felt that in a way she owed Gladys something. She had, after all, been kissed by Donald that afternoon.

"Nothing much. She's a highly strung little thing."

"But she said something about you not teaching her any more. What's at the back of that?"

Janet glanced at Gladys to see if she was going to say anything, but Gladys' head was bent over her darning.

"She had got muddled, she had heard about my idea of joining the W.R.N.S. I explained about my mother and that's cleared that up."

Donald held out his cigarette-case.

"Have a cigarette before you go."

Janet knew the sensible thing from the point of view of peace and a quiet life was to make for home, but she could not resist seeing a little more of Donald. The case reminded them both of the afternoon; over his lighter their eyes met. Neither intended by a flicker of an eyelash to show what was in their minds, but to Gladys the tie between them, and the change of feeling, was as clear as if they had told her what had happened. Her fingers grew sticky round her darning-needle, and a pulse beat in her temples. Her voice was huskier than usual, and there was bitterness behind it.

"She'd be far better at school, Donald. What that child needs is other children."

Donald turned to her nervously.

"We must see later on. The great thing is that she's settled down tonight." He looked at his watch. "What about tea? It's nearly time, and we can give Janet a cup before she goes."

Janet watched Gladys struggling with herself. Longing to refuse because she did not want to leave them alone together, and yet conscious that if she did refuse she would look ungracious before Donald. The latter consideration won; she got up. As she left the room she propped the door open.

Janet and Donald listened to her retreating steps down the passage towards the kitchen. Desperately they both tried to think of something to say, for their silence must seem to Gladys highly suspicious. They both found words at the same moment.

"Very warm evening, isn't it?" from Donald.

Janet said:

"Quite chilly tonight."

They began to giggle, hopeless, painful giggling. Janet managed to pull herself together first. She spoke in a whisper.

"Don't offer to see me home."

"I can't let you go alone."

"It'll only make for awkwardness. Please."

"But . . ."

"Please."

Very unwillingly Donald agreed, then raised his voice.

"Tell me what the doctor said about your mother."

Gladys, waiting for the kettle to boil, came to the end of the passage. "He's told her it's her spine," she heard Janet say, and Donald answer, "He's a clever fellow." Puzzled, she went back to the kitchen. Had she been mistaken? Surely not! There was something different in the atmosphere between the two. She set the cups on a tray and then stood with the three teaspoons forgotten in her hand. "I must get things settled. He's got over Anna; he wouldn't face running this place without me. Perhaps her coming is just what I needed to give me a push. It's silly to let things drift. I must think of a way to give him a push, it's all he needs."

It was rather an awkward tea-drinking, all three making painful, forced conversation. Janet was thankful when she had swallowed hers. She got up.

"Well, I must be off." She nodded to them both. "Don't get up. Good night."

Donald, feeling an ill-mannered lout, passed his cup to Gladys for some more tea. Gladys filled it in silence, but her heart was beating at double its normal speed. "There is something. I know it. They'd arranged he shouldn't see her home because of making me suspicious. He's never rude like that; he'd never let her go alone across those dark fields."

Donald felt uneasy.

"You're looking very serious."

She passed him his cup and smiled.

"Looking after you is enough to make any woman serious. Why, you can't be out of my sight one afternoon without smashing your car. You don't know what a lot of bothering goes on in my head."

If Janet had kept a diary the entries during the next weeks would have read, "Talked to Donald while I had Iris out for her walk."

"Met Donald in the clover field. He was very nice all the time, not difficult once." She was happier in a way than she had ever been, yet it was the difference between being asleep and being awake. Her life, she now saw, had been dreamed away; it wasn't living as she now knew the word living to mean. Clearness of vision had come with her awakening, and she saw everything with a sharp edge, there were no blurred outlines. The sun rose and she saw the beauty of each day so that it hurt. The rain came down, and it was no longer water pouring annoyingly out of the sky, but it made a grey world in which Donald with his energy and vigour stood out the more clearly. Sometimes when she was tired, or for a moment or two before going to sleep, she felt flickerings of fear. She loved Donald, completely and absolutely, but did he love her at all? He was interested in her, not a doubt of that. She was not stupid, and knew that all their meetings were not accidents. Iris told her this, even if she had not got on to it for herself. "Funny the way we always meet Daddy when we're out. Usually you can look an' look an' look and you can never find him." Ben, though apparently engrossed in his yard work, still had eyes for the goings-on of master. He would cast an apparently vacant glance at Iris and Janet as they went out, either on their way to the cottage, or for a walk, but once or twice he had given Janet a hint that he knew where her heart lay, and was on her side. "Master's taking a great interest in they beans below the cottage seemingly," or, "I knew 'e'd gone to the copse, shepherd tell me. So I tells master to have a look to the fence longside of that mustard." She rather liked old Ben's interest, for it showed he approved. She hoped he approved because he thought she would make Donald happy, rather than because, if Donald loved her, it would be a knock-out blow for Gladys, but she was afraid the latter was the more true. The trouble was that interest was not enough. Donald was interested, but that was passion. The kissing episode would have been only too easy to repeat. Janet was innocent, but nobody's fool; she knew they wanted each other, but what did that mean? Hot summer weather and being physically attracted. That wasn't love. Sometimes when she was thinking it seemed to her that Donald was like a dog on a lead, rushing out, full of eagerness to be brought up short by his chain, and because checked, retiring disgruntled to his kennel. But what was the chain? Was it the memory of Anna? Because his marriage with Anna had not been a success, was he afraid to tackle it again? Or was it Gladys? Was there anything between himself and Gladys to give her a claim to him? She was certainly possessive, and he was scared of her, but was there anything more than that? Any one of these reasonings seemed good, and yet Janet believed in none of them. "It's something he doesn't quite like in me," she thought. "He doesn't want to let himself get too fond of me." She would run over in her head her blemishes. "Of course, I'm not pretty, but it's not that, because obviously he likes me that way."

"I'm not artistic or particularly clever, but that ought to be a good thing after Anna."

"It can't be that he thinks I'm not domesticated, because he knows I'm running the cottage as well as teaching Iris."

"It's some fault in my character, I'm certain of that. Goodness knows I've enough faults; I only wish I knew which it was so that I could try and improve."

Apart from Donald, Janet's life was very full and happy. She got fonder of Iris every day. She laughed at herself for it.

"Do you think, darling," she asked Maggie, "I'm one of those starved-of-mother-love people you read about?" Maggie looked at her daughter with a wealth of understanding.

"Every woman wants children, and no matter what else she puts into her life, she'll have missed the greatest thing in the world if she doesn't have any, but I don't think your affection for Iris is starvation. She's a very attractive little thing. I enjoy my talks with her."

Maggie saw a lot of Iris, for Janet brought her to the cottage every morning, and left her to play in the garden while she did the housework. Sheila, to save argument and because she really was going to work at last, was let off everything except the lightest jobs, and spent the rest of her day lying under a tree reading film papers, or occasionally she would cadge a lift in a car and go into the town to see a picture. Janet had been inclined to doubt if she really had signed on with N.A.A.F.I., but she had misjudged her. In due course forms arrived from the Labour Exchange.

"I bet you thought I'd made it up, that I only said I'd joined N.A.A.F.I.," she told Janet, "but sucks to you."

Sheila had one other occupation, and it was one that puzzled Janet. She would go to the farm to talk to Gladys. She would choose the middle of the morning when Janet and Iris were at the cottage, and would lounge across the fields to drink a cup of coffee with Gladys in her kitchen. Janet at first supposed that she must have changed her mind about Donald, and decided he was worth bothering with, but no. Gladys usually told of the visit at luncheon.

"Sheila came up this morning and had some coffee with me."

Donald, to begin with, seemed as surprised as Janet. He did not say outright that visiting a woman ten years older than herself just to drink coffee hardly seemed like Sheila, but he plainly thought it.

"What did she want?"

Gladys would fix her big eyes on him.

"Just to visit me. Is it so very surprising people should want to talk to me?"

Janet went on thinking it was astounding when the visitor was Sheila. But by degrees Donald accepted news on the visits without surprise, and would merely nod, and get on with his lunch.

"What on earth do you suppose Sheila goes up to see Gladys for?" Janet asked Maggie.

"I'm sure I don't know, dear. Company, I dare say. It's dull for her here; I shall be glad when she gets away."

Maggie having agreed to rest, began to improve amazingly. Because she imagined that her discomfort when lying flat was due to her spine and not her heart, she did not aggravate her condition by getting into a panic; instead she quietly gave herself the drops the doctor had ordered, and presently, just as he had promised, her discomfort passed. She allowed herself a little light work, because it kept her from being bored, but mostly she lay in the garden, or on the sofa, reading. There was a library in the town and Barbara Haines undertook to keep her supplied with books.

"It's no bother at all," she told Janet. "I simply adore your mother, and she's been so busy all her life she's never had time to read. She's the easiest person to choose a book for."

"So long as it has a happy ending," said Maggie. "I do like things to go right in life, and since reading is meant to be a pleasure, I don't see why I should upset myself over the girl that doesn't marry her man in the end. It happens too often in real life."

Barbara gave her a scared look.

"You mean in war-time, because of people being killed?"

Maggie took her hand and patted it.

"I mean nothing of the kind, goose. I mean peace or war because foolish boys and girls let opportunities for happiness slide. All those complexes they talk about today! When I was a girl a man came courting and everybody knew he was courting, and after a bit he popped the question, and you said 'yes'."

"And you lived happily ever after," said Barbara.

Maggie sighed.

"It's the 'ever after' bit that belongs mostly to fairy-tales." Then her voice grew in vigour. "But ever after doesn't matter, it's having known happiness that counts. It's like an extra skin, it stays with you always, and keeps out the cold."

Sometimes Barbara would fetch Maggie in her car and take her to her house for the day.

"I wish she'd come more often," she told Janet. "She's a Godsend to me; Daddy's so good with her. I put them out on the lawn side by side, and they tell each other their life histories, and admire each other's children. Then, presently, milk comes out for them both, and your mother says, 'After you, Colonel,' and believe me, he swallows every drop without a word of complaint. In the afternoon they both have a snooze, and after tea they go round the garden, and your mother says the right things about every plant."

"We seem so happy here, and Mum's getting better, and . . . and everything," Janet said, "that sometimes I get in a fuss that everything's going to smash up. Do you ever feel like that when things go nicely?"

Barbara was convinced that Janet was in love with Donald, but her father kept her busy and she had no time to go up to the farm, and had never seen them together. Only intuition, and sometimes an unwillingness in Janet's manner to talk of Donald, made her sure. She worried over her quite a lot. From what she gathered from Iris and Maggie, Donald never came to the cottage. Was Janet wasting herself on loving a man who didn't care for her? Barbara, radiant with the knowledge of how much her Dick cared, hated that Janet shouldn't be equally happy.

She did hope she wasn't making a mistake. She knew nothing about any love except hers for Dick, and Dick's for herself, but there were, she had heard, people who did love without getting it back, and anyone who knew Janet would know she wouldn't suffer casually. If Donald did what it was locally supposed he was going to do, which was marry Gladys, would it break Janet's heart?

"I think it's a good thing," she suggested, "not to be too sure of . . . of things." She flushed. "I always make myself know that Dick mightn't come back."

"You mean because feeling that now would make it easier if . . ."

"Yes."

Janet turned the conversation into herself. Suppose Donald never cared for her. Suppose, worst of all, he married Gladys. She shivered and tucked her arm through Barbara's.

"Aren't we gloomy? Mum would say we needed salts!"

§

SHEILA sat in a rocking-chair by the open kitchen window. Gladys was at the table making a pie. For once Sheila was not thinking of her appearance, but Gladys had to pause in her work to gape. "My word, she is a picture!" she thought. The sky outside was radiant blue. The yellow roses, now full bloom, made a flower-frame for Sheila's golden head and delicate profile. Sheila's eyes slid round to Gladys. Her voice was elaborately casual.

"Any news?"

Gladys rolled out her paste.

"Funny child, you always ask that. What news should there be up here?"

Sheila wriggled.

"You might have heard something in a letter."

"What sort of something? All that we get is reams of stuff from the Ministry of Agriculture, and a few advertisements. I hear every week or so from my mother, and Donald, once in a way, from Dick . . ."

Sheila turned her innocent blue eyes to Gladys.

"Oh, Mr. Sheldon's half-brother! How is he?"

"We haven't heard for weeks. He generally writes to Barbara; she rings through if there's any news."

"If he were getting leave or anything like that, that would be exciting for you all, wouldn't it?"

"More exciting for Barbara. It would only mean work as far as I'm concerned. If you ask me, it's you to whom the exciting things happen. Had any more lifts from officers who asked you to tea?"

"Actually, no. I did go to the pictures yesterday, but while I was waiting for the bus a woman in khaki stopped and offered to take me in. I couldn't very well say no."

Gladys smiled.

"Bad luck! Very tactless of her." She looked out of the window. "There's the postman, be a dear and get the letters, and give him those two on the dresser to post." The postman had brought only one letter. Sheila came back with it staring at it. Gladys glanced up. "Who's it for?" Sheila raised her head, but her eyes were vacant; it was obvious she did not know she had been spoken to. Gladys laid down the knife in her hand, and came round the table and took the letter. It was from overseas, and had been censored before posting by the writer; his signature was on the envelope. Richard Trent. She caught Sheila's chin in her hand and forced her face round. "You know Dick?"

Sheila heard that all right. She wriggled, but had to answer.

"Well, actually, yes."

"When did you meet him?"

Sheila looked young and childish.

"You'll think I'm mad, but I'm in love with him. It was love at first sight. It can happen. It's because of him we're here, really."

Gladys struggled to make sense of this.

"You're here because Janet worked in his office. He sent..."

Sheila shook her head.

"He didn't. Janet doesn't know that Dick is her Richard Trent."

Gladys went back to her work.

"I'm getting hopelessly muddled. Suppose you tell me the story from the beginning."

Sheila sat on the table.

"Well, Janet lost two pounds, and went to work in an awful flap. After she'd gone Mum found her note-case in a pocket. It was when there was bombing, and I'd left my office, and you couldn't get through on the telephone to Janet, so Mum made me go and tell her. I oughtn't to have gone really, for I wasn't strong enough and might have fainted dead away at any minute."

Gladys tried to keep her to the story.

"And you met Dick there?"

"Sort of. I was just getting to Janet's office door when he came out into the street. 'Gosh!' I thought, 'that's a good-looking man!' He reminds me a bit of Gary Cooper. He looks lovely in his officer's uniform, doesn't he? You know, Gladys, something happened to me as I looked at him, and I thought, 'Who is that gorgeous man?' and I knew I'd never love anybody else."

"How did you find out who he was?"

"Well, another man came along and said in a surprised, pleased way, 'Richard Trent! You got leave?' Then Dick said yes, it was embarkation leave, and the man said he wasn't spending it working, was he, and he said no, he'd only been in for an hour or two, and that he was starting then to his half-brother's place, and then he said it was here."

"What did you do then?"

"Followed him, and he did exactly what I thought he'd do, he took a taxi. Well of course, that was my chance. He got in at one door and I got in at the other, and he was awfully polite and said he'd find another, and I said perhaps we could share it because I was going to Waterloo. So we did."

"And what happened in the taxi?" Sheila took a deep breath. Gladys laughed. "No need to invent fairy stories for me; he's completely in love with Barbara."

Sheila lowered her voice.

"Do you believe that? I believe that anybody can get a man if they absolutely mean to."

Gladys picked up her pie to put it in the oven. Then she paused.

"Did you come to Donald with that cock-and-bull story about Janet having been sent by Dick, so that if he got leave . . . but it's ridiculous!"

Sheila's eyes narrowed.

"Not so ridiculous as you letting Janet take Donald away from you without doing anything about it at all."

There was silence. During it little sounds became important. The ticking of the clock. The cackle of the hens. Ben shouting across the yard. From deep jealousy, which had sucked at her and held her down, like reeds under water sucking round a body, Gladys pulled free. Sheila was, in her opinion, a silly little thing, but like many frail, lovely girls she was curiously powerful when it came to getting her own way. She saw her wishes like a silver path in a grey world, so had no difficulty in finding her way. Even if temporarily pushed off it, back she would certainly come. There was something inspiring in her belief in herself.

"But I thought you wanted to go on the pictures?"

"So I do, and so I shall. It'll be much easier when I'm married. I expect a man like that knows people who could help me, and, anyway, he's got a good job, and I wouldn't have to work, so I'd have plenty of time to look."

Gladys' eyes goggled.

"But he's not the sort of man to let his wife work in films." Sheila spoke with complete confidence.

"Any man will do anything for a girl he's in love with."

"But he's in love with Barbara."

Sheila gave Gladys a sideways glance. Then she slipped off the table and came round to her.

"If I had the chance to see him I'd soon have him. Barbara's pretty, but she'd never try about a man. She thinks she's just got to be herself and that'll be enough. I don't know, of course, but I've got an idea it's never enough with any man." She put an arm round Gladys. "Why don't we help each other?"

Gladys was hypnotized and fascinated by Sheila's confidence in herself, and by the relief of hearing her love for Donald spoken of. As a secret in her own heart, it seemed less real than now when Sheila, as it were, pulled it out and laid it on the table as a visible object.

"How?"

Sheila was still holding the letter. She shook it.

"Well, what's inside this? You see, I've got to know when he's getting leave. Somehow I've got to meet him, and that's going to take some arranging."

"How can you help me?"

"Well, as a matter of fact, I could probably do quite a lot about you. I could tell you something you haven't thought of."

Gladys thought of the expression, 'a thieves' agreement', and was revolted, but at the same time a voice in her said, 'Why not? Why not snatch at any help you can get? It's for happiness for all your life.'

"What could you tell me?"

Sheila lolled against the table, and spun a plate.

"If I help you, will you help me, let me know every bit of news, and all that?"

"Yes."

"Swear."

Gladys gave an impatient shrug of her shoulders.

"I'm not a child, I've promised. Go on."

"Well, if Janet thought that Donald belonged to you . . . you know, had made you think he was fond of you, she'd never look at him again. She's that sort."

Gladys gazed fascinated at Sheila's back. Her entire lack of conscience was almost frightening.

"How could I make her think that?"

"We could easily work it out. I think if she saw him kissing you . . ." She turned round and caught Gladys' expression. "Oh, doesn't he? Well, you could make him; anybody can make a man. The thing is, Janet must be here and watching. I'd have to arrange that."

"That would mean you being here when Janet is. You never are, and Donald being about and all that."

"How about a Sunday? Couldn't you ask us to tea or something?"

"It would look a bit queer when she's here all the week." She thought a moment, then an idea lit her face. "Iris has a birthday soon."

Sheila turned round.

"That's the idea! A party, and you'll fix the kissing, and I'll fix that Janet's watching."

"I suppose I will." Gladys' voice was doubtful.

Sheila stretched herself.

"'Course you will." She laid the letter on the table. "I'll be up tomorrow to know what's in that."

"He doesn't always tell me."

"Well, you've eyes, read it." Sheila lounged towards the door. "Actually, plotting things is rather fun. I'm looking forward to Iris' birthday."

Janet had never before spent a whole summer in the country. Every day it seemed to her there was a new and lovely change. The fields round the cottage flamed into flower. The scent of the beans was intoxicating.

"And it's ludicrous, darling," she said to Maggie, "to think that for years we've lived in a pokey house in a smug little street, paying more rent than we can afford, and now, for ten shillings a week, we've every luxury, and you lie in a deck-chair laid out like a lettuce, with a field of golden mustard one side of you, and crimson clover the other."

"Ten shillings!" Maggie agreed with a satisfied sigh. "As long as I live here I shall go on marvelling at the cheapness of rents in the country."

Because the world was flaunting colour Janet abandoned her severe frock. It was ridiculous, she decided, to wander about in dark blue stuffiness. Out came her short-sleeved linens and cottons. She had always been fond of dressmaking, and in the days before the war she had prepared each year for her fortnight's summer holiday by making herself at least two new dresses. In peacetime a lot of these she would have considered shabby, but now, when old clothes showed patriotism, they looked downright smart. They needed altering, of course. Like practically everybody else, she had got thinner since the war started, and as well the length was wrong. Every evening when she got back from the farm she was either stitching or pressing something to wear tomorrow. Sheila eyed these activities with amusement, but she could not resist taking an interest. She might have made a bargain with Gladys, but that did not stop her helping Janet; after all, the hotter the fight the more fun to watch, and if there was a way in which she could help Janet it was over clothes. Sheila was no needlewoman, but a most expert buyer. Her eye grasped in a second where a lift would improve a line, where a coloured belt would make the drab into the smart. Janet dressed with taste and charm, but she did not put line in its place of importance. Sheila studied each frock as Janet brought it out.

"Of course you must have those shoulders padded; when they aren't they look sloppy. If you took away that bloused look and made that fit it would be a different frock."

Sheila herself on hot days had discarded frocks. She had a lemon yellow sun-suit, very brief flared shorts and a brassiere top held in place by straps crossed over her back. She looked delicious, but she worried Maggie.

"I do wish you wouldn't go about naked; country people aren't used to it and I'm sure they're shocked."

"Very silly of them," Sheila retorted. "Actually, these are exactly like some that I saw Judy Garland wearing in a photograph, and I should think anyone would be glad to see anyone looking like Judy Garland."

Janet laughed.

"I don't believe anybody here has ever heard of her. Come here, Sheila, and pin this on me."

Janet's blossoming-out did not pass unnoticed at the farm. Iris, with a child's tactlessness, usually waited until mealtimes to mention her clothes.

"I think Janet looks simply lovely, don't you, Daddy? Daddy, don't you think that's the absolutely prettiest of all Janet's frocks?"

Donald would answer non-committally, but his eyes would run over Janet before he answered, and the look in them was not non-committal at all. Janet could not help feeling pleased because he so obviously enjoyed looking at her, but she wished the scrutiny need not have taken place in front of Gladys.

Gladys was queer these days. She had a look of somebody who is waiting for something. She reminded Janet of a girl with whom she had been at school, who used to waggle her head and try and look important, and say, "I know something, but I'm not telling you, Janet Brain."

Iris was improving in health because she was happy with Janet. Gladys, by her lack of understanding of her temperament, had strained the child's nerves. Janet was like a soothing dressing on a burn. Iris explained this in her own way to her father one

Sunday when she was as usual accompanying him on that farmer's function, the Sunday afternoon walk. It was a fine day, but there was a sharp wind, which had kept Gladys indoors, for she loathed being blown about. Donald strode along in his Sunday clothes of grey flannel trousers and a sweater, with a stick under his arm. He had on no hat and the wind had made his thatch of brown hair look as though a hen had been scratching in it. Four well-trained dogs followed at his heels. Iris, with a navy jersey over her white Sunday frock, and a blue beret on the side of her head, trotted and sometimes ran to keep up with him.

"It's not that I learn an awful lot from Janet, not like I did from Mummy, but she's kind of comfortable, like a teddy bear in bed. Do you know that feeling, Daddy?"

"I don't take teddy bears to bed much, but I know just what you mean about Janet."

Iris gave a hop and a skip to catch up with him.

"She doesn't really know very much at all, you know, except things like Mrs. Honeywell and Gladys do, cleaning and cooking and sewing. All them plaguey things that make a woman wholly tired."

Donald laughed.

"She doesn't seem to have cured you of quoting Mrs. Honeywell."

Iris dismissed this criticism as of no importance.

"Do you suppose, Daddy, that she'll ever have to go away?"

"Would you like her to stop with us always?"

"Awfully I would. She isn't going away to be a sailor, but likely she'll want to better herself."

Donald had been smiling, but the smile left his face at Iris' last words, and his brown eyes were hard.

"What makes you, or perhaps I should say Mrs. Honeywell, say that?"

"I don't know; I think it must have been something that Janet said to Mrs. Honeywell, that's what makes me frightened. Do you feel funny inside when you think of her going away? I do, Daddy."

Donald beheaded a thistle with his stick.

"You'll lay up trouble for yourself, young woman, if you love people too much. Some idols when you come to look at them closely have clay feet."

"What's an idol?"

"Something you worship."

"Is it all made of clay or only its feet?"

Donald gave a half laugh.

"Certainly not all of it, and the more you look at it the more you forget you ever saw the clay feet."

He walked more quickly. Iris galloped to keep up.

"Silly Daddy, you sound sad, and it's only a story, isn't it? I mean nothing doesn't really have clay feet, and if it did I don't see why it would matter. I mean if I worshipped an idol I wouldn't mind, I'd put boots on it so I wouldn't see."

"Boots, my child, won't help. The trouble with clay feet is that they may snap off and then your idol would topple to the ground."

"Is this going to be Humpty Dumpty now? All the King's horses and all the King's men bit?"

"It's a very good ending to the story."

"Oh, look!" Iris caught at his coat. "There is Janet, just as we were talking about her."

Janet was on the edge of the wheat field picking poppies. She did not hear them until they were almost beside her, for the wind was blowing the other way. Iris flung herself on her.

"Janet! We've been talking about you all our walk."

"What were you saying?"

"Well, mostly, Daddy was talking about idols, and them having bad feet, but do you know what we decided, that you were like a teddy bear to take to bed."

Janet's cheeks flamed. Donald spoke quickly.

"I need hardly say the definition was Iris'. What are the poppies for?"

"Tom's grandson's wedding tomorrow. Tom thinks that as he's a sailor there ought to be red, white and blue flowers on the altar. Red's hard to find at this time of year."

Donald was surprised.

"I didn't know you knew Tom."

"He's the first person I met. He drove me up from the station. He promised me a piece of the next pig he killed that doesn't have to go Wooltoning. The pig's been killed for the wedding, and I've had some chops, so I'm trying to return his kindness by helping over the wedding."

"They'll die," said Donald. "Poppies are frail, you know."

"I'm taking them straight home and putting them in water. I'm doing the vases after church this evening'"

"I'll pick some, shall I?" Iris offered.

Donald and Janet were left alone. She had tied a green handkerchief peasant fashion under her chin, and was wearing a yellow linen frock. Her arms were golden against it and the wind had whipped colour into her cheeks. He eyed her uncritically, just pleased with the picture she made standing there with the crimson poppies in her hand. He felt irresistibly impelled to touch her. Iris had wandered out of sight.

"Janet!" he whispered, and took her hand. She tried to resist him, but found herself powerless. She swayed and he pulled her towards him. "Darling!"

She was in his arms, the world forgotten, her mind numbed by his kisses. Then suddenly she thought of Iris and struggled free. The child was still out of sight. She faced Donald panting.

"I said we mustn't."

He nodded.

"But we had to, you see . . ."

Iris' head came in view, and he broke off. They stood awkwardly waiting for her, conscious of all the unsaid things between them.

"I've found some beautiful ones." Iris held out her poppies. Then she looked at Janet's bunch. "My goodness, what have you done with those? They're all black and broken. Did you sit on them?"

Janet glanced at Donald's coat against which they had been pressed. She distracted Iris' attention by sitting on the grass and arranging her flowers.

"I must have. I'm very bad with flowers. They always seem to die with me."

Iris sat beside her.

"That shows you are wholly a flirt."

Janet kissed her.

"It shows nothing of the sort, Mrs. Honeywell. My worst enemy couldn't accuse me of that." She got up. "Well, I must be getting on."

Janet waited until Iris and Donald were out of sight. Then she found a place out of the wind. She lay down and closed her eyes. "He kissed me. I let him. I can't stop myself." Then she sat up. "What on earth did Iris mean about idols with bad feet?" Idols with clay feet! Could that have been to do with her? What bee had he got in his bonnet? "It's silly going on like this. I must have things out with him. There's something, I'm sure of it."

Back at the farm Gladys had tea waiting.

"What have you been doing?" Donald asked.

Gladys spoke on a sigh. She wished she had Sheila's lack of conscience. There had been nothing of importance in Dick's letter, except that he had malaria, but it made her feel mean, sneaking it, and she thought about it when she was alone. She hated herself, too, for what she had to say. "I thought about Iris' birthday."

"Fancy me being nine on Saturday! I can't believe that I could ever be so old."

Donald helped himself to a sandwich.

"Poor decrepit thing!"

Iris looked at Gladys.

"What did you think about my birthday?"

"I thought we'd ask Daddy to drive us into the town to go to a cinema."

Iris bounced on her chair.

"Lovely, and we'll ask Janet."

Gladys nodded.

"And Sheila, and you shall stop up to supper, and we'll invite them to stay on for it."

Iris' face was crimson with pleasure.

"Do you know, Gladys, you're the most surprisingest person I ever knew. I wouldn't have thought you'd have thought of a lovely idea like that. Matter of fact I never did think you were really fond of Janet. Not like me and Daddy are, I mean."

Donald moved uneasily.

"Your grammar's shocking."

"Terrible," Iris agreed.

"I've lit a little log fire," Gladys said to Donald. "We can do with it while this nasty wind is blowing."

"Won't it be stuffy?"

She shook her head at him.

"No, just cosy. We like it cosy, don't we?"

He felt hot under the collar. He was grateful to Gladys; she had been splendid to Anna, and a grand housekeeper to himself, but it always embarrassed him when she talked in a possessive, intimate way, and lately, since he had known Janet, it made him feel a cad. Had he let Gladys understand that he was in love with her? Of course, after Anna died, when he had been so lonely, he had clung to her a bit, but surely he had never said a word to suggest he meant more than friendship.

Gladys took Iris upstairs to put her to bed. The child was old enough to bath herself, but apt to dream, so Gladys always sat in the bathroom to see that she really washed.

"Your hands are very dirty," she said, "scrub them well."

Iris examined her fingers.

"They got like that picking poppies. Janet's putting them in the church for Tom's grandson's wedding tomorrow. Me and Janet are going to see them married."

"Did Janet go with you on your walk?"

"No, we met her at the end of the long acre, where the poppies grow. Do you know, Gladys, when we met her she had a lovely bunch, all looking as new as new, and all in a minute they were so dead they weren't any more good. Mrs. Honeywell says that means a flirt, but Janet said her worst enemy couldn't say she was that. Who d'you suppose her worst enemy is?"

"I'm sure I don't know. Wash your ears."

Iris screwed up her face and did as she was told.

"I wish I'd seen them die. D'you suppose, if I'd watched, I could have?"

Gladys' foot tapped on the floor.

"Why didn't you watch?"

"I wasn't there, I'd gone to pick poppies."

Gladys got abruptly to her feet.

"Come on, get out."

"But only half of me's washed."

"I can't help that."

Iris' eyes slid up to Gladys' face. She was, she saw, in one of her worst moods, which meant she could be really angry all in a second without any warning. Without a word she scrambled out of the bath, wrapped herself in her towel, and almost fell over in her efforts to get dry rapidly.

Iris in bed, Gladys, with her work-basket in the crook of her arm, joined Donald in the drawing-room. He was smoking and deep in a crossword puzzle.

"Do you know your Shakespeare? 'Arrow of something fortune'? Ten letters."

"Outrageous!" Gladys spat out the word so venomously that Donald laid down his puzzle and gaped at her. She took a deep breath, trying to control herself, but failed. Sobs shook her. He had never seen her cry before. He loathed a woman to cry. He got up and patted her shoulder.

"I say, what's up? Cheer up, old thing, you must have been overdoing things. Come on, what's the trouble?"

She clutched at his hand and covered it with tears and kisses. Horrified, he tried to pull it away, but she held on the tighter.

"I love you! I love you! You can't hurt me! You can't!" Donald was disgusted with himself. He longed to explain himself, to get the situation cleared up. The last thing he wanted was to leave Gladys' declaration, lying between them, unanswered, but he was not easy with words. Everything he thought of seemed cruel. He went on patting her and making soothing sounds, then, for lack of any better way out, he said:

"You go up to bed, old thing. You're in a bit of a state. We'll have a talk about all this some other time."

Gladys went up to her room. She did not light a candle so that she could draw back the curtains. She leant out. The wind suited her mood and gradually her emotion died. "He didn't say he didn't love me," she comforted herself, "and at least now he knows. Is it awful what I'm going to do? It can't be; nothing's wrong when you love. He's all my life and I've got to fight for him. He said he'd talk about it some other time. Saturday is my chance and I've got to take it."

§

DONALD spent a sleepless night. There was more work the next day than his man could do, and he made this his excuse and lunched off bread and cheese in the fields. After tea he managed to slip down to the village to ask the advice of the shrewdest and most honest man he knew.

"Hullo, Donald!" said the colonel. "Fancy seem' you! Barbara's goin' to ring you up tonight. Young Dick's comin' home. Had you heard?"

"No, he said nothing about it in his last letter, but he said he'd had that go of malaria. Is it sick leave?" The colonel nodded. "That's good. I could do with a sight of his old mug." He drew up a chair and filled his pipe. "Barbara in?"

"No, exercisin' Hoover. I'll have the hide off that dog one day. He's smashed a delphinium. Nearly took a gun to him. Barbara's taken him out while my temper wears off."

"I rather wanted some advice. When you were younger, sir, did you ever . . . well, I mean, did a lady ever get fonder of you than you were able to be of her?"

"Pretended they did, anyway. A woman's always got to have somebody poodlin' after her. In India the weather's too hot, and the women haven't enough to do. Makes for a lot of trouble."

"But this is a busy woman, very busy, working all day and all night. The devil of it is she's been so damned good to me. I suppose I've been a blind fool."

"Gladys Batten. Do you mean to say you didn't know she was in love with you? Why, the whole village has been havin' bets on whether she'd bring it off."

"Why didn't anyone tell me? Did Dick know?"

The colonel chuckled.

"Dick's language about her wasn't at all parliamentary. Doesn't fancy her in the family."

"Why didn't he tell me?"

"Not the sort of thing you talk about unless you're asked. She said somethin'?"

"Yes. I feel the most damnable cad."

"Poor girl!"

"The thing is, what's the kindest thing I can do? She can't stop on in the house."

"Awkward managing without her."

"That's beside the point. It's her that I'm thinking of. Mrs. Honeywell will manage until I get somebody."

The colonel raised his eyebrows.

"Oh, you'll get somebody else?" Mincing, stout and grey-haired, plodded across the lawn with a glass of milk on a tray. "Put that damn poison down and bring out the whisky and a siphon for Mr. Sheldon. Miller out?"

"Yes, sir. She and Jennings have gone to the wedding."

"'Course. Sent up a couple of bottles of port for it. They'll come back rollin', shouldn't wonder."

Donald laughed.

"That's a good picture. I sent beer, a cheque, and my daughter as a spectator."

The colonel gave a disgusted look at his milk.

"Better give yourself a drink, Mincin'. Don't want to be out of things."

"Thank you, sir." Mincing turned to Donald. "Two fingers, sir?"

The colonel sat up.

"Now, none of that. You bring out the decanter."

"Not me, sir. I'm not having your death on my hands. As soon as my back's turned you'll have given the milk to that Hoover and yourself a whisky. I know you."

"You bully of a woman, you do what you're told." Mincing shook her head.

"You can't talk me into it. It's been queer round the house lately, terrible lot of the people about."

"I've heard 'em, but that's got nothin' to do with me and whisky."

"I wouldn't say that. I've always noticed that when there's a lot of them around it means changes."

"Certainly be a change if I get a whisky."

Mincing paid no attention to the interruption.

"Not good changes either. There was a lot about when Jennings' mother was taken."

"She'd been bed-ridden for years; it was a blessin'."

"And they were about when Mr. Dick got orders to go abroad."

"Well, he's comin' back all right. You're a ghoul, Mincin'."

"That's as maybe, sir, but I can read a warning as well as the next, and I'm not risking seeing your coffin come in at the door."

"Get along with you, coffin indeed!"

Mincing turned back to Donald.

"Two fingers, sir?"

"Three," said the colonel. "He needs a drink." He looked thoughtfully at Mincing's retreating back. "She's right, you know. Barbara laughs at us and says we imagine our spooks, as she calls them, but there are a lot around just now, and it does mean somethin'. Seem sensitive to change. Maybe it's Dick comin' home." He sighed. "Well, if he and Barbara want to make a match of it, God bless 'em; but I shall miss her."

Mincing brought out the whisky in a tumbler, and a siphon. She put them on the colonel's table, but she put the glass within reach of Donald's hand.

"I can trust you, sir."

Donald nodded. He poured soda into his glass.

"You can. I want the drink too badly to give it away."

The colonel watched him gloomily.

"Some people have all the luck. Now then, about this bit of bother of yours. Seems to me the only thing to do is to make a clean break."

"I can't. I'm a coward."

"Rubbish! 'Course the best plan would be to get somebody to make her a temptin' offer, that would save her face. Women like their faces saved. Lot of truth in that sayin' about a woman scorned."

"How can I get anyone to offer her a job?"

"Difficult. Pity we can't get Barbara to help, but we can't. Never talk about one woman to another, cad's trick. They don't mean to let the victim know they've heard anythin', but they can't help it. It's all over their faces." He sipped his milk. "Filthy stuff! I've got it! Old Poppy Broadstairs!"

"Mr. Broadstairs at the school?"

"That's right. It's just come to me that when he was in seein' me last week he told me he was wantin' a lady to run damn near everything in his school. Difficult for a headmaster of a big boys' school when he's a bachelor. Never the marryin' sort. Married to cricket we always said. Beautiful wicket-keep."

"But I hardly know him."

"You leave it to me. He'll lunch with you next Sunday. Miss Batten's just what he's lookin' for. I'll do him and you a good turn all with one stone."

Barbara came out of the house. Her face was radiant. She started to run at sight of Donald.

"Have you heard?"

"Yes. I'd know from your face, anyway."

He got up.

"When are we expecting him?"

"Any time. He'd left when the cable was sent off." She walked beside Donald up the street. She spoke in a kind of gasp. "I'm almost too happy to be true. I ought really to have gone to the wedding this afternoon, but I had to be alone. Do you know that feeling?"

He slipped his arm through hers.

"I hope you're going to marry him."

"So do I, but I couldn't leave Daddy while he's stuck in a chair half the day, he'd be so lonely."

"If Dick's stationed over here you could divide your time."

"No. I'd mean to, but if it was possible to be all the time with Dick I'd be with him. I expect we'll have to wait a little longer. As long as he's home and safe and I can see him sometimes I can bear it."

Donald kicked a stone out of his path.

"He's a lucky blighter; it's fine to fall in love with a girl who's solid gold all through."

"I'm not. You're making my face red. Oh, look! Old Tom blind to the world."

Donald laughed.

"My beer, your father's port, and God knows what else." Tom came rolling down the street. He had on a black suit, in his buttonhole was a large marguerite.

"Evenin', Mr. Sheldon," he roared. "Evenin', Miss Haines. You ought'r have been at my grandson's wedding. Beautiful. Miss Iris and Miss Brain were there. Miss Iris was wholly pleased with the cake." He swayed and Donald steadied him.

"The happy couple gone off on their honeymoon?"

"That's it!" Tom gave Donald a leer. "Reckon they're gettin' on all ri'. You know, Mis'er Sheldon, that's what you ought to be doin'. Gettin' married. That gir's jus' the one for you. Not her fancified baggage of a sister, she's no good. No, it's Miss Janet. That's the gir' for you."

Donald gave the old man an affectionate pat on the arm.

"I dare say. Off you go now, and you be careful how much more you swallow or you'll spend the night in a ditch."

Barbara watched Tom roll away, then she turned shyly to Donald.

"It's a good idea, you know. Now Janet is solid gold all through if ever anybody was."

He stopped and played with one of Hoover's ears.

"Is she, Barbara?"

Barbara's voice rose at his question.

"Of course she is."

He straightened his back. He seemed to be going to confide in her, then he changed his mind.

"I dare say I'm prejudiced, but there are certain faults I can't stomach, especially in a woman." He squeezed her arm. "Good night, my dear."

She was in two minds about running after him. A feeling she might do more harm than good stopped her. She whistled to Hoover and turned homewards.

"Janet!" she marvelled. "What fault can he have found in Janet? What a pity, for in some ways I'm positive he's fond of her."

§

THE day was chilly. Sheila came to the farm for her morning call looking like a chicken, with a yellow angora wool jersey over her linen frock. It was too cold at the window so she drew a chair up to the kitchen table.

"Thanks awfully for your note. What did the telegram say exactly?"

Gladys' face was paler even than usual; there were black shadows under her eyes, her big mouth drooped at the corners. Her voice was listless.

"I've not seen it. Donald went down to see the colonel, and Barbara told him. It said he was on his way home, to be treated for that malaria."

"Then he might be here any time?"

"Yes."

Sheila looked at her.

"You look awful. Are you funking Saturday?"

Gladys was unwilling to confide in anyone. She was spending her time forcibly poking Sunday night's scene into the background, and arguing with her conscience. She poured coffee and milk into two cups and added a minute quantity of sugar.

"Of course not. I've not been sleeping well, and then yesterday was awful, Mrs. Honeywell went to the wedding. So inconsiderate of people getting married on a Monday."

Sheila did not trouble to answer. She could not conceive why Monday should be an inconvenient day, they were all alike to her. Instead she thought of herself.

"When he gets leave will he come straight here?"

Gladys finished her coffee and got up to get on with her cooking.

"I should think so, as he's no office left, and as he's been ill"

"How will he come?"

"I don't know. Train, I suppose."

Sheila's face was full of calculation.

"You'll have to find out, everything. I can't. If it's a train I shall go and meet him somewhere down the line, and get in the same carriage with him." It struck her that if she wanted Gladys' most vivid help she must take a little interest in her affairs. "Have you thought how you're working Saturday?"

Gladys could not slide into shifty schemes with Sheila's casualness. She could not, as Sheila did, see herself as though taking part in a film, in which any method was fair. She flushed.

"Well, after Iris is in bed—the sun sets so ridiculously late with this double summertime—I thought you might take Janet up to the spare room to look at the sunset . . ."

Sheila giggled.

"Janet would think that awfully queer, looking at sunsets isn't a bit like me."

"Well, I can't think of anything else."

Sheila swallowed the last of her coffee.

"Can't it be something to do with Iris? I mean, can't you fix the big kissing act under Iris' window? If Janet stays to supper it would be natural for her to put Iris to bed, and I can easily go up to say good night to the kid or something; actually, I quite like her, and then I can see Janet looks out of the window."

"But Iris might look out."

"Well, if she did, there's no harm in kissing. I always wonder why there's such a fuss made about it. Anyway, if you're going to be her stepmother she'll have to get used to the idea."

"Don't you mind getting your sister to look?" Gladys asked curiously. "I mean, if she's fond of him she's going to mind."

Sheila was surprised.

"Goodness, no! I never liked her awfully. I don't see why one should like a person just because she's one's sister." She got up. "Well, thanks a lot for the coffee."

Outside in the yard she ran into Donald. He was busy, but he paused a second for a word, for she made him laugh.

"We can use you," he teased her; "we want some extra hands for harvest."

"Actually I shan't be here much longer. I'm going to work for N.A.A.F.I."

He grinned.

"That ought to popularize army life."

Sheila was delighted.

"Everybody teases me. Is Janet being a good governess?"

He became slightly on the defensive.

"Very."

"Actually you were very lucky to get her instead of me. Aren't you beginning to think that?"

He turned away.

"You're a minx, you're trying to salve your conscience."

"Oh, no, I'm not. You know people talk a lot about conscience, but I don't remember ever feeling mine."

He chuckled as he walked away.

"I shouldn't wonder if that was true. Well, have a heart and don't do too much slaughter amongst the troops."

Iris sat on a chair beside Maggie's sofa. She was hemming, her tongue held between her teeth, and her breath coming in anxious gasps. Maggie sat up and looked at the piece that was done.

"That's much better. Now rest a bit."

Iris relaxed thankfully.

"I'm not what you'd call a born needlewoman."

"No. We can't all have the same gifts."

"I'm afraid Gladys is going to give me a work-basket for my birthday. I saw something that she put away in a hurry, and it was what it looked like."

"You need a work-basket."

"If everybody has to have one I do, because I haven't got one, but if birthday presents are meant to be things people like to have, then it isn't a good idea at all."

"It's nice of Gladys to think of you."

"Do you know, I was 'traordinary surprised that she thought of having Janet to supper on my birthday night. I wasn't so surprised about Sheila, but I was about Janet."

"I expect it was your idea."

"No, it wasn't. She told me and Daddy she'd thought of it; it was specially s'prising because she doesn't love Janet, not like me and Daddy do."

Maggie's eyes twinkled.

"Daddy and I," she corrected. "I'm glad you're fond of her. So am I."

"Mothers are always fond of their children." Iris' voice was reproving. "It's different for Daddy an' me . . ."

Maggie heard Janet's step. She laid her hand on Iris' arm.

"Go on with your hemming, here's Janet. I shall get into trouble if she finds we are not working."

Janet had milk for Iris and Maggie.

"There's a letter for Sheila," she said. "It's from N.A.A.F.I." She put a table beside the sofa. "Sit up, dears. There are gingernuts this morning."

Iris took her glass in both hands.

"Goody, goody!"

"That sounds like Sheila now," said Maggie.

Sheila lounged in.

"Hullo, Iris! I hear your uncle's coming home."

Iris beamed.

"Yes. Last time he came we made a fire of bricks and mud and cooked soup."

"Do you know when he's coming?"

"No, but it's soon. Perhaps in two weeks, Daddy thinks." Janet took a letter out of her pocket.

"This has come for you, Sheila."

Sheila took it and stared at the envelope. She turned a horrified face to her mother.

"It's from N.A.A.F.I."

Maggie smiled encouragingly.

"So I see. Don't look so startled. You knew you'd hear soon."

Sheila seemed a child again.

"I can't go. Not now."

Maggie was touched; she held out a hand.

"Come here, goose, let's open it together."

Sheila came unwillingly to the sofa, she handed the envelope to Maggie. She turned a pleading face to Janet.

"I can't go."

Janet put an arm round her.

"Don't fuss; I expect it will be awful fun once you get used to it."

"You're travelling on Monday," said Maggie. "They've sent you a ticket and all."

Sheila had turned white.

"I can't go."

Maggie and Janet exchanged looks.

"Come on, darling, keep your chin up," Janet urged, and gave Sheila's shoulders a press.

This seemed to be the last straw. Sheila gulped and then sank on the floor, howling like a child.

Iris gazed at her with eyes on stalks.

"She cries worse than me," she told Maggie. "I never knew grown-ups did."

Janet sat down beside Sheila and patted her.

"Come on, pull yourself together."

Sheila's voice rose in a wail.

"I can't go, I simply can't! I've stayed and stayed in this dead and alive hole where nobody even sees me, and now when I could be happy I'm made to go."

Iris leant down.

"Would you like a ginger-nut?"

Maggie had strained to hear through Sheila's tears what she was saying.

"Going away from home is a big step, dear, but all the other girls in the country are taking it. You must do your share."

"Janet isn't taking it. She isn't being thrown out of her home."

Maggie became more severe.

"That's enough, Sheila. Janet wanted to be a Wren. She gave up the idea to stay with me."

"She's jolly glad now that she did."

Maggie glanced at Iris' interested face.

"I think you might go in the garden, Iris."

"I haven't finished my milk."

"Never mind, take it with you."

Iris got off her chair. She looked disparagingly at Sheila. "I don't want to be mean, but it isn't at all a nice day, and I'm being sent outside because of you. Little pitchers have long ears."

Janet laughed.

"All right, Mrs. Honeywell, I'll come with you."

"Now, Sheila dear," said Maggie, "what is all this?" Sheila sobbed dismally.

"I won't go."

"It's no good going on like that, you've got to go. You've signed on. I don't know what the law is, but I should think it's a police matter if you don't turn up."

Sheila sat up, her face distorted and swollen.

"Police!"

Maggie laughed.

"Don't look like that. It won't be a police matter because you'll go. Now run along and wash your face. Come on, give Mum a kiss."

A few minutes later Janet looked in at the window.

"Has she cheered up?"

"No." Maggie raised herself on her elbow. "Do you know, Janet, I've a feeling that this is something more than silliness. There can't be anything wrong, can there? I feel she's frightened to leave home."

"It isn't frightened she seemed to me; it's more as if there was something she wanted to stay for."

"What, here? In Worsingfold?"

"I know it seems queer, but that's the impression she gave me. But who or what could it be?"

Maggie shook her head.

"She's such a funny child. Somehow, although she signed on and all that, I don't believe she really saw herself going away. It's all this film nonsense, I expect. She can only imagine happy endings."

Janet leant against the window-frame.

"I could imagine a very good film written around Sheila in war work."

Maggie frowned.

"This isn't a laughing matter. We must get into a more sensible frame of mind before she leaves. I shouldn't have a moment's peace if I sent her away looking as she looked just now. In any case, I'm bound to worry about her."

"You mustn't. I'm certain she's very much able to take care of herself. Honestly, in lots of ways more than I am." Maggie smiled.

"If that's meant to comfort me, it doesn't. I worry about you."

Janet raised her head to ask why, but Iris came up and, lolling against the window-ledge, looked wistfully into the room.

"One would think now Sheila had gone that other people needn't stop in the garden."

Maggie held out her arms.

"Lift her in, Janet."

Janet lifted Iris over the sill and climbed in after her. Iris came to Maggie and leant against her chair.

"Do you know, I was thinking in the garden that I believe Gladys cries sometimes."

Janet's reply shot out.

"Rubbish!"

Maggie turned thoughtful eyes on her daughter.

"I dare say it's quite true. It would be queer if a woman never cried."

"Would it?" Iris turned to Janet. "Do you cry?"

Janet spoke quickly.

"Oh, sometimes, when I've a black dog on my shoulder. What makes you think Gladys cries?"

"Her face. It gets puffed up like Sheila's was just now. What do you suppose she cries about? Would it be a black dog?"

Maggie put her arm round the child.

"I expect she thinks it's a cat."

Iris was immensely interested.

"A black one. I never knew you could get them on your shoulders."

"Oh, yes. You can think they are anywhere, but it's imagination, both dogs and cats. Anyway, the polite thing for you to do is not to notice, and certainly not to talk about it"

Iris heaved a deep sigh.

"Grown-ups are very puzzling."

Maggie hugged her again, but her eyes were on Janet.

"Very. Even their own mothers don't always understand them."

SATURDAY was fine. Iris awoke early, and at first could not think why she felt so queer inside, and then she remembered. Birthday! The curtains in her bedroom were never drawn. She pulled herself up slowly, holding on to her excitement. Somewhere hidden in the room would be Daddy's present. It was a custom started by Anna. It was a very special present, and during Anna's lifetime had been cleverly hidden. Iris knew the parcel would be easy to find, Daddy was not clever at hiding things. With that shrewdness which a child has while still utterly a child, she pretended it was well-hidden; it put her father in the light in which she wanted him. Almost before she was upright she saw the parcel; it was lying on the top of the picture facing her bed. It was a picture of a spray of apple blossom framed in fumed oak; it had a slight frame and anything laid on it caught the eye at once. Iris, as she clambered out of bed, thought "silly Daddy", but she thought it with delight, his foolishness made her feel motherly and superior. It needed a chair to reach the top of the frame. Iris held the parcel delicately, her mother had taught her that. "Don't snatch at things, darling, however much you want them. Things are more exciting if you wait for them." It took very careful handling to wait for that parcel, for there was a little box inside, she could feel its shiny leather surface under her fingers. When her mother had been alive she had often played with such little leather boxes. Almost breathless with excitement she got back into bed. "Jew'ry," she murmured. "I absolutely know it's jew'ry." Carefully she undid the tissue-paper.

The box was navy blue and was familiar. Iris could not go slow any longer; she knew what was there, she knew how to open the box. Inside was a white velvet hill, and lying round it was a wristwatch.

No present in after life gives exactly the same thrill as a first watch. It is not a present which is a passion for a few days, or something which is enjoyed on special occasions; it is a thing which is a growing pleasure, from the first day when its glory is brought to public notice by endless requests "Please ask me the time", to the gradual realization that time is no longer a fugitive;

it is not a wild thing which can suddenly telescope so that what was a long morning becomes dinner-time, but can, by the watch, be checked at regular intervals to see exactly how it is behaving.

Janet, coming across the field with a parcel under her arm, saw Iris running to join her. The child's words fell over each other.

"Oh, Janet, jus' imagine! It's Mummy's watch, look! Would you like to know the time?"

It was a tiny watch. Janet looked at it doubtfully. "Can you tell it?"

Iris concentrated, frowning. "Five minutes to nine."

Janet kissed her.

"Good, but I shouldn't wonder if you guessed." She held out her parcel. "Many happy returns."

Janet had bought a book, a long children's novel. Iris was delighted and danced along talking in gay, excited bursts.

"It was a work-basket Gladys gave me. Mrs. Honeywell has brought me a vase; it's bright blue with a frog on it. Daddy said the watch was not really a present because it was my mother's and was only waiting for me to be old enough to have it, so as well what d'you think I've got? A bicycle! Do you think you could learn me to ride it this morning?"

Donald and Gladys were in the yard talking to Ben. Gladys was complaining about a bucket. Ben had the stubborn look of an animal determined not to be 'druv'.

"It's absolute nonsense," said Gladys, "any bucket that leaves my kitchen leaves it clean, you can be sure of that."

"What would I be doin' messin' up bucket?" Ben asked Donald. "Her buckets do be a plaguey nuisance."

Donald turned with relief to Janet and Iris.

"Morning, Janet. Has Iris told you what I've let you in for? Can you bike?"

Janet smiled a good morning all round.

"I never had one of my own, but I used to ride a friend's at school."

Gladys looked pleased.

"Good. There's that bicycle you got for Anna put away, isn't there, Donald? You better have it overhauled and then Janet and Iris can go careering round the countryside."

Janet laughed.

"I'm not quite careering-round-the-countryside form at the moment. I should see most of the countryside from a ditch."

Gladys took on an 'England expects' tone.

"Nonsense, it's only a matter of concentration."

Donald spoke so sharply he startled them all.

"I won't hear of it. Neither Janet nor Iris bicycle outside the farm until I'm satisfied they are safe."

Janet glowed; she was surprised to find that she liked that sort of ordering about. Gladys struggled with jealousy, but it rang in her voice.

"I don't think Janet will like being dictated to like that. We women don't, you know."

"Oh, don't we!" thought Janet. Out loud she said, "As a matter of fact I don't mind, for I don't want to go alone, and I certainly wouldn't trust myself as an escort for Iris until I'm fairly good."

"But we will be good, won't we, Janet?" Iris broke in. "We will go careering."

Janet smiled and held out her hand.

"Of course we will. Come and show me the bicycle." Donald looked after them, then, conscious of Gladys' eyes on him, he turned awkwardly away. He hated to feel awkward on his own land, it seemed so foolish. He hated the reason for it too; he was fairly sure he had nothing to reproach himself with. Yet he felt a cad; he wished the wretched business of getting Gladys out of the house was over. He felt he was living on the edge of a scene.

Gladys was annoyed with herself. Stupid on this day of days, when every word she said in front of Donald was important, to let jealousy get hold of her. For want of any other way to express her feelings, she turned back to Ben and the subject of the bucket. Ben heard her in silence, then when she paused for breath he picked up the offending bucket and turned to the stables.

"Talk, talk," he muttered. "Women need a piece off of their tongues." But as he went about his work he chuckled. "She'm properly got her nose out of joint. It riled 'er proper to hear master actin' so concerned about that Janet." He went on chuckling until another thought struck him. "Maybe we'll see another mistress." As the idea came to him he saw quite distinctly a figure with a white, eager face, and a clinging frock. He thought it natural she should be there. He nodded to her. "And you wouldn't mind neither, my poor dear."

It is odd how fast enjoyed time goes. To Iris her birthday melted. The morning with no lessons, and a lot of surprises from Maggie, who was a great birthday keeper. Birthday luncheon with her own specially chosen food. The afternoon at the cinema, the birthday cake, supper, it all rolled into one happiness and disappeared at the fatal word 'bedtime'.

Janet found the day short too. Iris' happiness was catching; Donald's concern for her safety a lingering pleasure. A day given to making a child's birthday like a brightly coloured bead, so that it would stand out radiantly in memory, was a new experience for her, and she loved it.

But time not enjoyed can equally drag to three or four times its length. To Gladys the day was endless. She could talk to herself how she would, but she could not talk herself out of thinking that what she was going to do was cheap and dirty.

Donald was too busy to take any particular notice of how time was passing, but he did think it was taking the hell of a while to reach Sunday. At the back of all he did was tomorrow's luncheon. The colonel had assured him the thing was as good as done, that Gladys was the answer to the schoolmaster's prayer, but he wished the affair was settled. He wished more than he could say that he was carrying Gladys' boxes down the stairs. He racked his brain for one thing he had said or done that could have given the impression he was getting fond of her. Always he found nothing, but that did not help him. He saw again Gladys' shaking shoulders and felt a beast. Ghastly to feel you had hurt a woman, and Gladys had been so good. If he thought that he had done or said one thing to give the wrong idea, much as he would hate it, he would marry her. At this thought which he kept reaching, his whole body revolted. Never. That brought him to Janet. But Janet was another thought; she must be given all his mind when Gladys had gone. Could so much that was good outweigh faults? From that thought he scurried like a rabbit. Everybody has certain qualities that turn them from people. Donald could not force himself into liking that which he loathed.

While Gladys was clearing the supper-table, and Janet putting Iris to bed, Sheila beguiled Donald into the garden. It was not difficult, it was a beautiful evening, and he never thought a pipe tasted half as good indoors. She and Gladys had chosen the best spot. It was at the side of the small lawn, hidden by the hedge from the yard, but in full view of Iris' window. Sheila led the way as aimlessly as if any spot on the farm would suit her equally well.

"It's lucky it's fine," she said, answering her own thought.

Donald's eyes twinkled.

"Don't know what good a beautiful day was to all of you shut up in a stuffy cinema."

Sheila turned her blue eyes up to his.

"I feel I ought to get all the pleasure I can, it may be the last cinema I'll ever see."

He laughed.

"Oh, come! N.A.A.F.I. can't be as hard as all that. I dare say you'll get a half-day now and again, and where you're going there'll be every sort of fun, dancing and all that."

Sheila, uncertain as yet of how she was going to get out of taking her job, did not want to discuss it any further. She looked impatiently at her wrist-watch. What a time Gladys was being! Iris would be in bed and tucked up, and Janet joining them if she didn't hurry. She saw a bird and it gave her an idea as to how to prolong the conversation.

"You ought to keep pigeons. The sort with pretty tails that walk on walls."

"All right in a gentleman's garden, but no good on a farm cluttering the gutters." He saw Gladys. Ever since Sunday night he had been thankful for any straw of conversation, however feeble. He turned to her with a smile. "Sheila thinks we ought to keep pigeons."

Gladys was no actress.

"Pigeons?"

"Yes," said Sheila, "the white sort with tails." Seeing no brightening on Gladys' face she came at once to her cue. "Oh, Gladys, did you see my bag in the dining-room?"

Gladys shook her head.

"Then I'll get it."

Donald moved to fetch it for her, but Gladys, not acting but only feeling what had been burning her since Sunday, laid her hand on his arm.

"No, don't go. I want to talk to you and you keep avoiding me."

He was terrified.

"There's nothing I can say."

Her hand on his arm tightened.

"Yes, there is. I don't ask for love. I quite see that perhaps you can't give me that, but I want you to marry me. It's only fair. Anna expected it. She often talked to me about it. She said that after she was dead she hoped I'd marry you, because I could give you the comfort that she'd never been able to manage. The people here expect it, I'm laughed at . . ."

"Oh, my dear, you make me sound such a brute, but I can't . . . you see . . ."

She read what he was going to say in his face and began to cry, heart-rending, tearing sobs. Awkwardly he put an arm round her, and with a gasp she had hers round his neck, and her head on his breast.

Upstairs Janet was sitting on Iris' bed while the child nestled against her.

"I feel rather sorry for Pop-eye. He tried so hard to be nice," Iris explained.

Janet laughed.

"Have you had a lovely birthday?"

"Absolutely perfect. I hope I won't be sick."

"So do I. You ate enough supper to be."

Iris rubbed her cheek on Janet's sleeve.

"Silly Janet. I was only teasing. I've got an inside can take tin-tacks, same as an ostrich seemingly."

Janet laid the child down and kissed her.

"Good night, Mrs. Honeywell."

Iris held up a battered old teddy bear.

"Say good night to teddy. He had a birthday to-day too, he's five. He loves you as much as I do."

Sheila came in.

"Hullo! I just came to say good night."

Iris held up her face politely.

"Do you know where my Daddy is? He hasn't been up to kiss me yet."

"I believe he's in the garden. Have a look, Janet. He said he was going out to smoke."

Janet leant on the window-ledge. She could not hear what was said, but she could see. With her hands turning cold and a lump in her throat she watched Gladys' hand lie on Donald's arm, then she saw his arm go round her, and saw her head drop forward.

Sheila watched Janet's back. She saw it stiffen.

"Well?" she asked triumphantly. "Is he there?"

Janet, shocked though she was, thought of Iris. She tried to speak normally, but her voice was only a whisper.

"I'll go and call him."

Sheila, charmed at the way her scheme had worked, skipped to the door.

"No, let me."

Janet sat down again beside Iris.

"Sing something," Iris demanded.

Janet swallowed. "What?"

"'Over the Rainbow.'"

"It's difficult," Janet suggested, unwilling to refuse Iris anything on her birthday, but almost sure she couldn't sing.

"I'll help you. 'Somewhere over the rainbow, way up high . . .' Now go on."

Janet managed somehow. Iris was half asleep before she had finished. Donald stood in the doorway, listening and watching. It was soothing to his ears and eyes after Gladys' ravaged face and her tearing sobs.

"Very nice too," he said as Janet's voice wavered into silence. She started. He was the last person she wanted to see.

Iris opened her eyes.

"It was a pity you couldn't come to the cinema. I like going in a motor-car better than on a bus."

He walked on tiptoe across the room.

"Is that the only reason I was missed?"

Iris sat up and held out her arms.

"Come here, Daddy. Of course it wasn't. Why are you whispering and walking soft like a cat? Don't you want Gladys to know you've come in here?"

He sat on the edge of the bed.

"She thinks, quite rightly, you ought to be asleep."

"It was a shame you couldn't come an' see Pop-eye," said Iris drowsily. "An' Gladys couldn't come neither because of old Poppy Broadstairs."

"Iris!" Donald's voice was shocked. "You mustn't call him that when he lunches tomorrow. He's Mr. Broadstairs, head of a public school."

Iris yawned.

"Colonel Haines calls him that damned old fool, Poppy Broadstairs. I heard him say so to Dr. Nelson."

Donald spoke severely.

"The colonel can call him what he likes, but to you he's Mr. Broadstairs. You understand?"

Iris held up her bear.

"Give teddy a kiss."

"And give Iris one." Janet made an effort. "She's half asleep. But first, Iris, you'll tell Daddy you were sorry for talking in a rude, silly way about Mr. Broadstairs, and promise him you'll make up for it by behaving beautifully tomorrow."

Iris had her eyes half shut. She opened them to twinkle at Janet.

"'Course I'm sorry, and 'course I'll be polite. You know that, Janet."

Janet tried to slip away before Donald, but he walked beside her down the passage. Below they heard Gladys' step. He caught his breath and held her arm.

"You go on. I don't want her upset by seeing us together."

She snatched her arm away as though his touch burned it. Scornful words seared her tongue, but before she had time to say them Gladys called her. She went up the passage and hung over the banisters. She could scarcely speak there was such a lump in her throat.

"Yes?"

Gladys seemed confused.

"I just wondered where you were. Iris asleep?"

"Just about."

Gladys' voice was elaborately casual.

"Oh!"

Janet clung to the banisters.

"Do you know where Sheila is? I've got a bit of a headache. The cinema, I expect. I shall go home."

"She's outside somewhere. I'll call her."

"Don't bother."

"Wait and have a cup of tea," Gladys suggested.

Janet could not resist one bitter sentence.

"No. I've trespassed on your and Donald's hospitality long enough." She walked steadily down the stairs. She even managed to smile at Gladys as she went out.

Donald, in the shadows of the passage, had made one involuntary movement to stop her. Then he steadied himself.

What was the good? With Gladys about he had no chance to be alone with her, which was what he was longing for. Besides, there was something about her tonight which he could not place. She had been aloof somehow in Iris' room, and when he touched her arm she had seemed to resent it. Of course it might only have been a quick movement and meant nothing, but it had seemed like resentment. He waited until the front door shut, and Gladys' feet had clicked along the passage to the kitchen, then he went to his room. He leant out of the window. He could see Janet hurrying down the farm road. She stumbled and then broke into a fumbling run. "Her head must be bad," he thought with concern. "It's as if she couldn't see properly."

In the kitchen Gladys found Sheila. Sheila's voice was full of pride.

"We've brought it off."

Gladys stood in the doorway and looked at her in disgust. "I shouldn't sound so pleased."

"Why? She saw. I could see she did."

"So could I see she had. She said she had a headache and has gone home. She smiled as she went out. I don't like to think I made anyone smile like that."

"What rot! She'll get over it."

Gladys put on a kettle to make the evening tea.

"I wonder. It's not a thing you'll ever know anything about."

"Why not? You've no idea how much I love Richard Trent. Sometimes I can't go to sleep for thinking about him."

"Love!" It was only one word, but it dismissed all Sheilas and her like.

Sheila wriggled.

"All right, sour-puss, but it's no good going on like this just because Janet looks cross. What did you think she was going to be? I hope you aren't going to get in a flap about Barbara. After all, we made a bargain, and you can't say I haven't done my share."

Gladys gave her shoulders a shake as if throwing off her discomfort.

"No, of course not. I'm behaving like an idiot." Her face lit up. "I asked him to marry me, and he won't understand why Janet's stand-offish. His feelings are sure to be hurt." She gave a sudden radiant smile. "With any luck at all I've got a real chance now."

§

"Janet's in bed," said Sheila. "She's got a bilious attack." Gladys had a look inside her oven.

"I do wish Donald wouldn't ask important people to meals in wartime, and on a Sunday, too. I never know if the meat we get will roast properly." She looked at Sheila. "What's the matter with you? Have you got a bilious attack too?"

Sheila was sorry for herself.

"I couldn't sleep for thinking how I can get out of going tomorrow."

Gladys' eyes opened.

"Do you mean to say you haven't fixed that yet? What's the good of all this planning about Dick if you've got to go?"

"I'm not going. It's only I haven't thought how I'm not. I can always be ill if the worst comes to the worst. I don't want to be, though, as my bedroom's hot in this weather."

"But your mother will send for Dr. Nelson. He'll have to send a certificate or something to N.A.A.F.I. You can't fool a doctor."

"Oh, yes, I can. I look ill awfully easily. If the worst comes to the worst, I'll take castor-oil. It always makes me sick, and he'll think it's food poisoning."

"Well, you can't do that every day."

"No, but I could twice, and with convalescence it will keep me here for quite a long time: I can easily see it does until Richard Trent gets leave."

"Funny the way you call him Richard Trent."

"That's how I think of him. Dick is short, and not so dignified. Richard Trent sounds lovely, like Clark Gable." The telephone bell rang. Gladys shut her oven door. "Drat the thing! I only hope it's Mr. Broadstairs to say he can't lunch." She was gone some time;

she came back and gave Sheila a mysterious smile. "You're in luck." Sheila, who was sprawling in a chair, jumped up.

"He's here?"

"Better than that. It was the colonel. He says that Dick will be here this afternoon, and he can't get hold of Barbara to tell her because she's gone to a troops do." Sheila looked a different person, all her lethargy gone. "How's he coming?"

"By car; he's borrowed a friend's."

"Well, that's a lot of use. He'll drive straight to the Haines'."

"Don't be in such a hurry, I haven't told you the best bit. There's a tea-garden called 'The Old Tudor'. It's up that turning to the left where the holly bushes are, halfway to the town. You know, where the bus stops." Sheila nodded. "Well, it seems it's a haunt of his and Barbara's, and he told Miller, who took the message, he'd be there about half-past three, and that he'd wait there until four on the chance they could let Barbara know. The colonel says Miller's a damn fool not to have told him to come straight on, as there's not a chance of getting hold of Barbara. He doesn't even know exactly where she's gone, and she's not expected back until about six. They've tried to telephone The Old Tudor, but the line's out of order."

"Why'd he tell you all this?"

"Just talking, you know the way he does. He rang up to tell us, of course, so that we can get his room ready." Sheila's eyes were shining.

"How simply marvellous! I shall wear white. I think all men like young girls in white, don't you?"

"I don't know, I was never the type for white."

"I must go. There's a lot to plan. I shall use that new flower scent. I think I'll carry my hat; film people always do in a garden." She widened her eyes. "Everything's turning out gloriously. You know, I think things do, if only one has faith and courage, and is willing to try."

At the cottage Janet was in bed. She had announced a sick headache, but it was a headache brought on by tears; but her first reaction to what she had seen had not been grief, it had been rage and disgust. She was fastidious, almost to the point of aloofness. Love had swept her off her feet and she had allowed Donald to kiss her, but it had never for a second been a light matter with her. That he should think she was one of a string of women whom he could hold in his arms revolted her, and bruised her spirit. The first thing she did on getting back to the cottage was to have a hot bath, and into it she tipped handfuls of soda. "Dirty beast," she thought. "I'll wash him out of my mind." But in the night it had not been so simple. All the answers to all the questions that had troubled her seethed in her mind. "Of course Donald had to placate Gladys!" "Of course Gladys could tell him she wouldn't have a resident governess!" "Of course Donald was like a dog on a chain. Gladys was the chain." "Goodness knows how far the business between Gladys and Donald had gone. Quite a way if he could hold her in his arms in the garden in full view of the windows. No wonder he had not been able to mention the word love; even he would hardly dare to talk about love to his governess, while he was still in the thick of an affair with his housekeeper." She writhed and broke into a perspiration. How he must have been laughing at her! The way she had given in to him! A pretty picture she had cut! He must have said to himself: "Just like the rest! I can get any girl to kiss me if I want them to." She had sat up in bed on that thought. "But he's got a shock coming if he tries it again. There's one woman who'll never give in to him again, and that's me, and if he asks me why I shall tell him the truth. 'You go back to Gladys, and if you've a spark of decency in you, you'll marry her.'" The twitter of the first waking birds had found her with swollen cheeks and a throbbing head. She had kept her face from Maggie's prying eyes by turning to the wall and begging to be left alone. Maggie had brought her a cup of tea and put it on the table by the bed, and tiptoed out.

The Old Tudor Tea House had nothing old or Tudor about it. It was a modern bungalow with would-be oak beams, but it was popular. It provided a very good tea, and the garden, where in the summer tea was served, was full of arbours and corners hidden behind hedges of Dorothy Perkins roses.

Richard Trent, very brown from the desert, came striding into the tea-garden. He looked rather outsize for it somehow, as if he could knock the whole place over if he had a mind to. He looked into the main tea-room; it was early for tea and the waitress, in a flowered green overall, was still putting the teaspoons in the saucers.

"Good afternoon. Have you seen a young lady with red hair? She'd have a dachshund with her."

The girl smiled. He looked so pleased with life, so obviously at the beginning of some leave.

"No. Will you wait here? Or if you like to pick a table in the garden I'll send her out to you."

"That's the idea. She knows where she'll find me."

He went outside. There were two or three couples already at tables, but none had taken the one he wanted. It was in a little summer-house with its back to the garden. He sat down with a pleased sigh. How often in the last months had he pictured this?

Sheila, in the white she had planned, with a big hat in her hand trimmed with cheery-coloured ribbons, stood in the doorway of the teashop and looked round. She would have been charmed if she had known that the waitress, eyeing her in admiration, thought she must be a film star.

"Has—has an officer been in asking for anyone?"

The waitress looked at Sheila's golden head.

"Not for you."

"For somebody with red hair?"

"That's right. With a dog."

"Yes, a dachshund."

"You'll find him in the garden."

Sheila searched the garden. The few couples looked up. The men thought to themselves that somebody was going to be lucky. She came to the summer-house. It had a cobweb-covered window. She peered through it. Then she took out her handkerchief.

Dick looked at his watch. Quarter to four. If Barbara wasn't here by four he'd give her up and make for the village; Miller had said she was doubtful if she'd get back. A girl came through the garden. She didn't see him. There were a few fruit trees in front of the summer-house; she leant against one crying bitterly. Dick was so happy himself with his leave and the thought of Barbara at his journey's end, that he couldn't bear to see somebody else suffer, especially something as young as Sheila. He got up. "I say, is anything wrong? Can I help?"

She raised her face from her handkerchief, but her head was turned away from him.

"I'm desperate."

"My dear, I'm sure things can't be as bad as all that."

"I dare say you wouldn't think them bad. It's just that I'm being sent away tomorrow to work on a canteen. It isn't that I don't want to work, I do. I've worked like a slave all the war, but I'm scared to go away from home. I've never been away from home before."

Sheila at all times induced a wish to pat in people who looked at her. Dick had the strongest wish to pat now. "Poor little kid," he thought, "this war is tough on these nervous, home-loving girls."

"Perhaps it won't be so bad when you get there."

"I expect you're right, everybody says that. I think perhaps I hate going more than most people would. I was always shy, and then we had a very bad time when London was bombed. I've been extra nervous since then." His face was frill of pity. That was the sort of story he hated to hear. War was a man's job, women and children should have no place in it. The thought of bombs on frail little things like this girl made him sick.

"That was tough. I haven't seen London yet. I'm only just home from abroad. My office was bombed out, and my poor old partner killed."

"Oh, I know my story isn't any worse than anybody else's. I just seem to be sillier than other people. Actually, I dare say you're right and I shan't mind it so much when I get there; it's just being scared at going." She dabbed her eyes. "Don't think me an awful cry baby; I think I'm crying because I'm hungry. I went out just after breakfast and I missed my lunch."

Dick looked at his watch. He grudged any minute that could be spent with Barbara wasted away from her. But he did not know if she was home yet, and she would be the first to say he was a brute if he left this little girl crying and hungry, and didn't offer her tea. He patted Sheila's shoulder.

"We'll soon put that straight. I'll go and order tea. You dry those tears and put that face right."

Sheila watched him out of the corner of her eye, then, as he disappeared behind the roses, she gave a pleased wriggle and took her powder out of her bag.

The entanglements of Sheila, though queer to more simple characters, were clear and even sensibly reasoned to Sheila. She honestly believed that any girl could get any man if she really went out for him, and had the proper opportunities to see him. She naturally counted on her face to help her, but that did not alter her line of thought; a face was a help, but it was opportunity and going all out that really mattered. All her life she had resented the family's position, but still more Maggie's and Janet's satisfied acceptance of it. She wanted money and big houses, and to be waited on. She began to want these things from the moment she heard the story of Cinderella, but from the day she went to her first film she knew that these things did not only come to a girl in fairy-tales, but could happen in real life. Through her childhood years she fixed her mind on the prince, or his equivalent, who would give her one kiss and then she would be dripping with mink and lolling in a rich car. It was with adolescence that the dream became less clear. She began to go to little dances and parties, and she had a thoughtful look at the boys. The sons of people very like her mother, respectable, hardworking, but on the whole unambitious. Where was the prince coming from out of that collection, and yet, as things were, they would be all the men she would know. She toyed with the vision of going into business and marrying the owner; she had seen that in a lot of films, but it seemed a dim chance, the owner would probably be old, and married, and the girls in the office possibly never saw him, anyway.

It was about this time that admiring boys, and her friends at school, began to say she ought to go into pictures. Sheila took her time to think this out. She read film papers too carefully to have any illusion about the film road being an easy one, and she detested hard work. On the other hand, with her face, it did seem likely she would succeed; and if she did succeed there was the mink, the cars, the houses and the servants, and eventually she would pick and choose until she found a rich husband to keep her in the way to which, by then, she was accustomed. Sheila, at about fifteen and a half, definitely decided on a film career. Maggie's unexpected stubbornness about having her trained as a secretary was a blow, but only a small stumbling-block; the training and six months in an office, what was that in a star's life? The war coming when it did seemed to Sheila deliberately planned to upset her life. She could not at first believe that it had trapped her in her office. She could not believe that she was not to follow the path that she saw so clearly. She cried, she sulked, she made herself quite ill, but Maggie was adamant, she could not take up a film career when the country was at war. She would have defied Maggie, but the film industry itself seemed to be agreeing with her. Studios, her film papers told her, were making little or nothing, everybody was waiting, saying, "What happens next?" When the bombing of London started she had no courage for it; she was glad of any excuse to get out, and still more, of an excuse to leave the office. She was planning some place near, or at least within bussing distance of a film studio, when the morning came on which Janet mislaid her two pounds. Seeing Richard Trent was Sheila's childhood dream come true. He was good-looking, he was a partner in the firm, he was the answer to the Prince and Cinderella story, and then and there Sheila decided to get him. The films could wait, perhaps they would come later, in the meantime he was exactly what she wanted and every sacrifice she thought worthwhile in pursuit of him. That she could sit patiently in Worsingfold month after month waiting for the leave of a man that she did not know, incomprehensible to anyone else, seemed common sense to her. He would turn up eventually, and when he did she would be waiting, and then, after a little hard work, there would be her wedding.

The summer-house was perfect from Sheila's point of view. There was a honeysuckle climbing over it, and the table and basket chairs inside were practically identical to those she had seen used in a dozen films. She thought regretfully that it would have been nice if Richard had arrived on horseback. She always thought men looked their very best on horses. Still, he was good-looking enough to satisfy anybody. The tan he had picked up in the desert suited him. Sheila did not start her big effort with him until the waitress had brought the tea. Then she gave him a carefully planned shy smile.

"Would you like me to pour out? If you've been abroad I don't expect you got much waiting on, did you?"

"Not feminine waiting. I've been in the Near East." Sheila raised eyes rounded with admiration.

"Fancy! Riding on camels and all that?"

Richard looked at her with amused tolerance. He took his cup from her.

"Camels are a bit out of date; but look, you mustn't talk. You eat all there is on the table."

Sheila looked at a large plate of bread and, presumably, margarine, and another of the sort of cake that is bought by the yard. She wondered if she dared say she had got past eating, but discarded the thought immediately, seeing the risk of the party coming to an end. A girl who could be bored for months in Worsingfold was not going to see a lot of food, however unpalatable, standing between her and her chances. Metaphorically she threw back her shoulders; actually she moved the muscles of her stomach as if to warn it of what was coming. Systematically she began on what was on the table.

Richard was a most unsatisfactory player in the scene. He was friendly and kind like an elder brother taking a schoolgirl sister out to tea. Not for a second was her plate empty, but not for a second did she hold his interest. His head kept turning to peer out of the cobwebby window; his mind was obviously somewhere else. Sheila, chewing away, decided that she must change her tactics, this hungry schoolgirl act was getting her nowhere. She got her chance when Richard surreptitiously looked at his watch under the table. She laid down what she was eating and half got up.

"Oh, I am sorry . . . I . . . I'm keeping you. I've really had quite enough—I'm not a bit hungry now."

Richard was disgusted with himself. What a bore and a cad he had become! This poor little kid couldn't know that every second that was not at least travelling towards Barbara seemed time wasted. He gently pushed her back into her seat.

"Go on with your tea. I'm in no hurry." He smiled as she doubtfully took up her slice of bread. "Tell me about the canteen you're off to."

"It's N.A.A.F.I."

He eyed her with an amused twinkle, picturing her effect on the troops.

"I expect you'll have a royal time." Then he gave her a closer look. "Do you know, I think I've seen you before somewhere."

She gave him one of her shyest glances.

"I don't think so. I expect actually it's that I'm very ordinary looking."

What a nice, unaffected little thing she was, Richard thought. Good to meet a girl with a face like that who did not know she was pretty. On the word pretty he studied her more closely. My word, she was pretty! Quite startling, really. Of course she was not his type; he did not care for that chocolate-box sort of face. All the same, surely she was outstanding. Of course he had been abroad and got his eye out a bit, but she did seem unusually lush. He was certain he had seen her before, but he could not place where, and had a feeling, anyway, it had only been a case of seeing and not knowing. Most likely in a bus or train. He certainly was not going to spoil the little creature by telling her she was pretty if she did not know it. That would come soon enough.

"We sat opposite each other somewhere, I expect. Did you lose everything when you were bombed?"

Sheila tried to remember stories she had read, but she only skimmed newspapers.

"Nearly. I was"—suddenly the right phrase came to her "pinned under the wreck."

"Good Lord! Were you injured?"

"I was shocked, but I hadn't much time to think of myself; you see, I had my mother, she needed help so much more than I did."

"Was she injured?"

"I thought she was dead. There she lay, her face as white as a sheet."

"Didn't the lights go?"

Sheila never batted an eyelash.

"I still held my torch. And oh, I forgot, actually one of my arms was free."

"What had happened to your mother?"

"Concussion. Presently, after what seemed like hours, I heard hammering, and then the rescue men came. They tried to release me, but of course I said, 'No, take Mother first.'"

"What a time you women have had! Is your mother all right now?"

"Yes, that's why I'm able to leave her." She paused to think how she was to reconcile her original story, that she was being sent to work on a canteen, with her present role of war heroine. "That's one reason why I was crying. I do want to work for the country, of course, but I feel Mother needs me."

"I dare say it will pull her together to manage on her own," he suggested consolingly. "I hope it won't be too much for you though. I mean, what you've been through is a pretty good shock. Where are you living now?"

Sheila filled her mouth to give herself time before she answered. Somewhere near enough for meetings, but indefinite enough to put off the day of his finding out exactly who she was as long as possible.

"A cottage, a new one, just outside Worsingfold."

"Worsingfold! My word! It's a small world. I'm going there. Staying with my half-brother. I expect . . ."

She broke in quickly.

"We hardly know anybody. We didn't want to, really. We just wanted time to get strong again."

He watched her admiringly. Plucky little thing! Buried in a cottage, no wonder nobody had told her how lovely she was. He was glad she was making a good tea. Not much money perhaps, though it seemed a pretty smart rig-out she had on. She still looked a bit frail. He hoped she would not have too tough a time.

"If you live near Worsingfold I can give you a lift." She smiled at him gratefully.

"How kind you are," she sighed. "Honestly, I didn't know anybody could be so kind. I wish I could think of something I could do for you."

Nice little thing though she was, he wished she would hurry up. He gave a friendly nod.

"You get on with your tea." He got up. "I'm going to find the waitress and pay her. I'll be back in a few minutes and I expect to find every plate empty."

Sheila peered out of the window to be sure he had gone. Then she quickly shovelled the last of the bread and margarine and all the cake under one of the basket chairs. She let out a deep breath. "Gosh!" she said out loud, "am I full!" Then she got out her mirror and touched up her face. While she was working she was thinking hard. She had not made much progress, but she had awakened his interest. What came next? In the car going home she must charm him. Be very feminine. Make herself so attractive that when Barbara saw him she had got a tremendous lot to live up to. When Richard came back she looked up at him with obvious adoration.

"You can't think what an exciting day this is for me. It's so wonderful to be looked after. I shall remember you all my life."

§

Barbara got away from her troop party earlier than she had expected. She had not gone out in her own car but had been given a lift. She was dropped off outside the village, having said she would enjoy the walk home. It was nice with the breeze in her face after the stuffy canteen. "I hope," she thought, "the country doesn't dry up before Dick gets home. It's so green and full of flowers just now." Dick! She hugged herself at the thought of him. They would have a gorgeous time; they wouldn't waste a minute. Thinking of Dick somehow switched her mind to Donald and Janet. What had Donald meant? "Certain faults I can't stomach, especially in women." Janet was an angel. What faults?

Wondering about her friend made Barbara feel mean; it was as if she didn't trust her. She was as near the cottage as she was home. She turned to the cottage.

Maggie was in her chair on the lawn. She was delighted to see Barbara. With Janet in bed, and Sheila out, she was feeling lonely.

"Where's Hoover?"

Barbara explained what she had been doing.

"So I had to leave him with Daddy for the day, and by now he'll have drunk all Daddy's milk, and dug up several pet plants. I bet I'm going home to trouble. Where's Janet?"

Maggie's face clouded.

"In bed with a sick headache. They went to the cinema yesterday for little Iris' birthday. I never knew her to have a bad head like this before, I hope it's not a germ. I always say cinemas are dirty places."

"Would she see me?"

"I expect she'd like to. She's bad company, though, poor darling, just lying there with the blinds down."

Barbara knocked on Janet's door. The listlessness of the "Come in" shocked her. The cretonne curtains were drawn, but not the black-out. Janet was lying facing the wall. She turned her head as Barbara came in and sat up.

"Barbara!"

Barbara was horrified at Janet's appearance. 'Drained' was the word that came to her. It seemed as if all vivacity and colour had poured out of her. She sat down at the end of the bed.

"Sorry your head's bad."

Janet made an obvious effort to appear herself.

"Where's Hoover?"

Barbara again explained what she had been doing. Janet seemed to listen, but her eyes wandered. Barbara broke off.

"You do look ill. Is there anything I can get you?"

Janet clasped her hands and gripped them together so tightly the flesh turned white under the pressure of her fingers.

"Don't be nice to me, please. I can't stand it."

There is nothing more moving to watch than somebody's fight for self-control. Barbara sprang up and knelt by the bed. She put her arms round Janet.

"What's wrong?"

Janet's head sank into her hands, her body shook.

"I didn't mean to tell anybody, but you'll understand because you love Dick. I love Donald. I can't help it, but I do."

"And doesn't he love you?"

"I thought he was beginning to, but he was up and downish. One minute I'd think he's starting to, then the next minute he was being stand-offish again, at least that's what I thought; but now I know he's in love with Gladys."

Barbara sat up on her haunches.

"That's not true!"

"It is. I saw him kissing her. I expect he's made love to her ever since Anna died; anyway, if it's not love he's made her think it is."

Barbara gasped.

"Goodness! When did you see them kissing?"

"Sheila and I stayed there to supper last night and . . ."

Barbara stopped her.

"All right, don't tell me. I can guess. How hateful of him!"

"Oh, well, he was lonely, I expect."

"It's not that part I think hateful, it's . . ." Barbara broke off, no point in adding to Janet's misery by telling her that when she had talked to Donald about marriage he had excused himself on flaws in Janet's character. "It's deceiving everybody," she finished lamely. She turned back to Janet. "What are you going to do?"

Janet shrugged her shoulders.

"I don't know. My head aches so that I can't think. I don't believe I can go on working at the farm, and I can't live here doing nothing. You see, when I was working in London I sent Mum money every week. She's hardly any. She used all Dad left on bringing us up. Sheila will only earn money for herself."

Barbara got up.

"Gosh! It is a mess!" She kissed Janet. "Don't worry, we'll think of something, I promise you we will, and, after all, Donald isn't the only man in the world."

Janet looked at her.

"Would you say that if it were Dick?"

Barbara was at the door. She turned. It was as if her smile was a lamp it shone so brightly.

"No. I was a fool to say that. For everybody, however many second bests they may find, there'll always be only one man that really matters."

Barbara slipped down the side of the clover and bean fields to the main road. She did not want to risk running into Donald. In her present mood she felt she might give him a piece of her mind. There was a hedge between the main road and the bean field. There was no way through it, and she had to follow it until it joined the farm road. She was nearly at the end of the hedge when a car stopped on the other side. She had her breath taken away at the sound of Dick's voice.

"Are you sure this is where you want to be put down?"

"Quite sure." There was a pause, and then Sheila's cooing voice. "Thanks awfully for tea and everything." There was another pause and the sound of the car door opening and shutting. "Well, good-bye. You've been simply marvellous to me."

Dick's answer was lost in the noise of the engine as the car moved on.

Barbara crouched back against the hedge. She watched Sheila, her frock gleaming in the sunlight, walk up the farm road and turn off at the track to the cottage. She had not known jealousy before. Now it racked and tore at her. Dick home and picking up Sheila for an afternoon's fun! How could he! Simply marvellous to her! Well, two could play at that game. He probably thought she would be out and wouldn't see him. Well, he'd soon find he'd made a mistake. She wasn't going to be slighted. If he thought he was coming home to open arms, he had a big surprise coming.

Sheila slipped into the cottage unnoticed. Maggie was on the lawn and Janet in bed. On tiptoe she crept up the stairs and into her room, softly she shut the door. She studied herself in the glass and saw that she looked lovely.

"Goodness," she said to her reflection, "it does seem mean to make myself ill after an afternoon like that." She felt in the back of a drawer and got out a bottle of castor-oil. The sight of it made her retch. "Still, for a man like that any sacrifice is worth while," she told herself severely. "I wish he'd tried to kiss me. He treated me like a stranger. I suppose that sort of man doesn't like to be friendly too soon. I suppose he'd think it familiar, and he holds himself back however keen he is." She gave another look at the bottle. "He said he'd got three weeks' leave. If I take a really good dose and manage to keep it down, I bet I could get the doctor to say I oughtn't to work for another three weeks at least." She picked up her tooth-glass and gloomily poured out a large measure of the oil. "Gosh, it does look disgusting! What a girl has to do when she's in love!" She put the cork back in the bottle and replaced the bottle out of sight in her drawer. Then she held her nose and tilted the castor-oil down her throat.

Maggie, knitting on the lawn, had her mind busy. Where it was showed in her movements, she kept raising her head and looking in a worried way at Janet's drawn curtains. She had hoped that Barbara's visit might have cheered her, but Barbara had called out good-bye some while ago and Janet's curtains remained drawn. "I don't like it," Maggie said to herself. "I never knew her to give way like this, not even when she had influenza so badly. I think I'll get the doctor. Anyway, I'll take her temperature."

Maggie had not seen Janet's face; it had been carefully turned from her when she brought her morning tea, and some soup at midday. It would have been turned from her now if Janet could have managed it.

"I haven't got a temperature," she protested.

"I dare say not," Maggie agreed, "but I'd like to take it just in case. Anyway, your bed is a mess and I'm going to tidy it."

Janet unwillingly turned and stretched out her hand for the thermometer. Maggie looked at her. Then laid the thermometer down and held out her arms.

"My lamb, what is it?"

Janet knew she could not fool her mother, and knew that if she did not tell her the truth she would worry, and it would be bad for her heart. It was no easier for Janet than for any other girl to make a confidante of her mother. She prefaced her story with: "You won't understand," and, since her face was against Maggie's shoulder, she did not see the half-tragic, half-amused smile flick across Maggie's face, as she remembered her own lack of belief in the understanding of her mother. Had any girl in history believed her mother understood? Yet as her story, jerkily and haltingly, crept from her, Janet felt easier. Maggie said no real words, merely cosy sounds, and gentle pats, but she made the position feel less desperate.

"... and I don't want ever to see him again," Janet finished. "I'll get another job. I'll just send a note."

At that Maggie stiffened.

"You'll do nothing of the sort. Face everything in life is my motto. You can't run away from anything. Everything has got to be faced sooner or later, and the quicker you turn and look at things the easier for you."

"But writing a letter isn't running away."

"Isn't it? What about Iris, are you going to send her a letter too? No, you've got to tell Donald Sheldon something approximating to the truth. If he's got the sense that I think he has, you won't need to say much. Iris is different, you must be guided by her father what you say to her."

"I'd much rather write," Janet begged. "Going to see him will hang over me."

"Well, don't let it," said Maggie briskly. "Go up and see him now."

Janet pulled away from her mother, her eyes scared.

"I can't. What on earth could I say? I can't say, 'I saw you making love to Gladys so I won't come and teach Iris any more.'"

Maggie smiled.

"As you were telling me about yourself and Donald, you said that sometimes he seemed to be getting fond of you. You're not a sentimental girl who imagines things, you had reason to say that; in fact, though you didn't say so, you meant he's made love to you." Janet shivered. "Be your honest self, my child. Let him know the truth. You needn't say much, but you can let him understand that love-making isn't the light thing to you that it apparently is to him. Then let him know that you saw him with Gladys. That'll be enough."

Janet looked round the room as if seeking a way of escape.

"I can't go now. I feel too in bits somehow."

"You'll feel worse until you've got your talk over." Maggie got up. "I'll make you a cup of tea, and give you two aspirins. Hurry up now and get your clothes on. There's one thing you never were, Janet Brain, and that's a coward."

Janet raised her eyes to her mother.

"Can't you understand that I don't want to make the final break? You see, I love him. I keep trying to tell myself that I don't, that I hate him for what he's done, but it's not true."

Maggie's face was soft. Across the years she saw her young self. If Janet's father had made love to another woman would she have forgiven him? Like the incoming tide the answer surged over her. He never would have made love to another woman. There was unusual colour in her cheeks and her eyes flashed as she turned them on Janet.

"Get along with you, and dress. I know you, my child, I know your worth, and a man like that's not good enough for you."

As Maggie came into the passage Sheila opened her door. Her face was greenish and her forehead damp.

"I'm afraid I'm going to be sick."

There was consternation in Maggie's glance. She had been hoping that Sheila's delicacy was half imagination, but this attack looked very like a nervous crisis at the thought of tomorrow. She put her arm round her.

"Let me help you undress. I dare say you won't be sick if you lie flat. Perhaps it's the sun. You dashed out straight on top of your lunch, which might easily have upset anyone. I expect you'll be all right in an hour or two."

Sheila allowed herself to be helped to her room.

"Perhaps it's something I ate?"

"Ate! You've only eaten the same as I have. That was a very good bit of mutton."

"I had tea."

"Well, that couldn't hurt you. Where did you have tea?"

"I went for a walk and I had it in a . . ." She suddenly remembered that there were no teashops within walking distance. ". . . in a cottage."

"What cottage? Why didn't you come home?"

Sheila could not wriggle; her inside would not stand it. She looked martyred.

"I wanted to be alone. It's a big step for me tomorrow."

Maggie studied the girl's green face, and felt anxious. It would be too tiresome if Sheila were not well enough to travel. There had been so much fuss that it would be cruel on the child if she had to go through it all twice. She had seemed more or less resigned these last days, and any change of plan would probably send her into hysterics again.

"I don't think tea could have upset you," she said gently. "It's just the heat. You lie still and you'll be all right by supper-time."

Sheila laid her hands on her stomach.

"I don't feel as if I'd ever be all right again. I think I've ptomaine poisoning. It must have been that potted meat."

"Potted meat?" Maggie tried to disguise her anxiety. "What potted meat?"

"Sandwiches at tea. When I ate them I said to myself they were queer."

"Did you?" Maggie's voice was determined. "Well, I'm just getting Janet a cup of tea, and you shall have one too, but first I'll give you a big dose of castor-oil. Nothing like it for poisoning."

Sheila dragged her mind from her outraged inside. How on earth was she to explain the castor-oil bottle missing from her mother's cupboard? Thank goodness it was missing, though, for she was sure another dose just now would kill her. But her mother was no fool and would be certain to put two and two together. Desperation, helped by the fact that she really was feeling wretched, enabled her to give the best performance of illness she had ever given. She gasped and closed her eyes.

Dick, having dropped Sheila at the end of the farm path, put his foot on the accelerator and made for Worsingfold House. He was glad to be rid of Sheila, poor little thing, but a silly chatterer, and with the car heading for Barbara he did not want a chatterer at his side; he wanted silence in which to feel suspended excitement. How would she look, bless her! What were the first words she would say? He was glad he had been decent to Sheila and given her tea. The bombing of the towns at home had stirred the chivalry in him. He would have blushed if he had known it, but what he was longing for was a sword, a bright flashing sword defending the women of the land. His kindness to Sheila had been a manifestation of this secret, unworded wish. Not that his chivalry would have allowed him to spend time on her that could have been spent with Barbara, but still, if Barbara had not turned up it was probable she was not home yet, so he could bear to give half an hour away. It had been a blow to him to find Sheila lived in Worsingfold, and his chivalry would not have taken him out of his way to drop her, but anyway, as she passed the farm gates, she had asked to be put down, which had salved his conscience.

Miller, beaming from ear to ear, greeted him on the doorstep. Miss Barbara wasn't in, wasn't expected before six, but the colonel was on the lawn. Wasn't he looking brown! She did hope the war was nearly over, did he think it was? He gave her a grin and said he would be out in the kitchen to see them all, and she was to tell Mincing to have a good-looking ghost ready to meet him.

The colonel beamed at sight of him.

"Hullo, Dick, old man! You're a sight for sore eyes. You been hangin' about that damn tea-garden? I told that old fool Miller what I thought of givin' you a message like that. She knows just as well as I do that when Barbara goes off on one of these jaunts we're lucky if we see her back by six."

"Six! Blast! It isn't five yet!"

The colonel chuckled.

"Wish I was your age. Feelin' as if the bottom had dropped out of my world because I couldn't see my special girl for an hour."

"You don't look so bad for your age."

"If you think that, keep it to yourself," said the colonel earnestly. "That damn sawbones, old Nelson, thinks he's savin' my life drinkin' milk. You ever drink milk?"

"Not since I was a kid."

"Never start it. Shockin' stuff." He lowered his voice. "It's my belief I'd be dead if it wasn't for Hoover. He's a wretched beast, but I will say he's obligin' about milk."

Dick looked round.

"Where is he?"

"Smashin' my plants, shouldn't wonder. If it wasn't for the milk he puts away on the quiet I'd have had the hide off him weeks ago. You'll stay to dinner, of course. Better tell Mincin'. There's such a hullabaloo about rations these days."

"I'll do that," Dick agreed, "and if Barbara's not getting back for an hour I'll pop up to the farm and leave my things."

Dick strolled into the kitchen, where he was a great favourite.

"Hullo, Mincing! How are the spooks?"

Mincing shook his outstretched hand, but looked grim.

"They're no subject for joking. The house is so full just now that often I have to squeeze my way up the back stairs."

Dick eyed her waistline.

"I can't believe it."

Mincing had to smile.

"You may laugh, but when they're about it means change; something's coming to this house, you'll see. And if you're smiling at my size it's not the food I eat, for what we get from the butcher wouldn't keep a mouse going."

"Dear! Dear!" he said gravely. "I can see famine written all over the three of you. I could have done with you in Libya, Miller. I've often thought of you coming towards me with the whisky and a siphon on a silver tray. You're my private mirage." He turned to Jennings. "How are the young men? Breaking any more hearts?"

This was a stock joke, for though still referred to as new, Jennings was by so few years younger than the others. The joke had its usual success, and Dick left them giggling.

Donald was in when he arrived and delighted to see him. Iris, he said, was out with Gladys. The two greeted each other in the usual brotherly, off-hand way, but both studied the other carefully. Donald was thankful to see that though Dick looked thin and fine-drawn, he seemed otherwise reasonably strong. Dick was not so pleased with Donald. There was a change in him which he could not place. He looked tired, he thought, and strained. Over drinks he mentioned it.

"Been working too hard. You're a bit green about the gills."

Donald had been wanting an opening.

"I've got that girl of yours working for me."

"Girl! What girl?"

"Janet Brain."

"Janet Brain! Well, I am glad! A friend wrote and told me about the office and poor old Horace Pringle, but I wondered what on earth had happened to Janet."

"But you knew. I must have told you in a letter."

"If you did I never got it."

"Anyway, you must have known I'd do what you asked."

Dick shook his head.

"What are you talking about? What did I ask?"

"You told Janet Brain before you went abroad that if she was in any trouble, wanting to get away from the bombing or anything, to come to me."

"She told you that?"

"No, actually she sent the younger sister to tell me."

"What did you do?"

"Let them have the cottage. The Moretons had to leave suddenly, and I hadn't fixed another let. As they were friends of yours I gave it them for ten shillings a week."

"Ten shillings! But you got a hundred a year for it even in peace-time."

Donald's eyes were bitter.

"I know. I made a bargain, though, I said I'd take the rest of the rent in service. I wanted a governess for Iris. The sister said she'd take on the job. She never got started. Then your girl turned up. She said she'd do it, and then she stung me two guineas a week."

Dick whistled.

"That was a bit steep."

"As a matter of fact she's very good, and I would have fixed a fair arrangement, but it got me, grabbing at a salary after we'd made a bargain. I can't understand it . . ."

Dick put down his glass.

"You'll understand it less in a minute. I never gave Janet Brain any message for you. In fact, as far as I know, I never mentioned you to her in my life."

A muscle twitched in Donald's cheek.

"What! Then how did she get this address?"

"She'd access to all the papers."

Donald slammed his glass down on the sideboard.

"Just a try-on, and it came off! Pretty!"

"Very. Anyway, now you know, you can get rid of them. Janet Brain! Good God! I always thought her such a nice girl. Looked on her as a real pal. How many are there in her family?"

"A mother and sister."

Donald looked so wretched Dick was puzzled.

"This has upset you. I suppose it's awkward getting a governess for Iris."

"It's damned awkward, Iris fairly dotes on her. Made all the difference to the kid."

"Well, then, why not keep her? After all, money's not everything, and the difference isn't all that much."

"It's not so easy as all that. You see, I've got fond of her. I thought I was in love with Anna. So I was, but this is different. Anna was so lovely, but Janet makes you understand that prayer-book talk, 'a help-meet'. I've fought against caring for her. I hate shifty dealings, as you know, and all that business of sending the sister to plead a hard luck story, and agreeing to work as part of the rent—well, anyhow, a bargain's a bargain. I can't explain it, but I felt there was something queer somewhere. Now I come to think of it, she never mentioned you. Small wonder!"

Dick put down his glass.

"Well, I must be going. Barbara ought to be back."

As Dick's car passed out of the yard Janet was coming in. He saw her and raised his hand, but did not stop. She was so stunned that she forgot her mission, and stood still staring after the car.

"That was Mr. Trent."

Donald was closing the gate, his tone was impatient.

"Of course it was, but you knew he was coming. Iris has spoken about nothing else for days."

"But my Mr. Trent isn't Iris' Uncle Dick."

"My dear Janet, I think it's time we had a little plain speaking."

That recalled her to what she had to do.

"Oh, yes, I came for that." Her legs felt wobbly so she leant against the gate. "I don't want to come here any more."

"I dare say you don't, but suppose I decide to keep you to our bargain."

His tone hurt her, but she was quite glad he was speaking so roughly, it made it easier for her not to cry.

"I'm to blame," she said gently. "I expect you thought I was more experienced at my age than I am. As a matter of fact I've never let any other man kiss me. I had to let you because . . ." Her voice trailed away.

Fight as he would, tenderness was overmastering his anger.

"But it means something to me too, only in my case I'm wanting everything. Fineness of character as well as charm."

She ran a finger disconsolately along the top of the gate.

"I quite see that, and I do awfully hope you've found it, and will be happy. I do really think she's an awfully fine woman, and ought to make you a good wife."

"What on earth are you talking about?"

She did not hear him.

"I suppose everybody saw it except me, but you do understand that, feeling as I do, I can't come here any more. Perhaps Iris could come to me until you've made some other arrangement. Don't think I'm bitter, or angry, or anything like that; I was at first, but afterwards I saw that we just had different standards, that was all."

His eyes blazed.

"Different standards! Look here, I've had enough of this play-acting. How dare you stand there and talk to me of standards, you little cheat!"

Her cheeks flamed.

"Donald!"

"What else are you? You get into my household, and a cottage cheap, on false pretences, and then, when you hear that the one person who can show you up has arrived, you come up here and say you can't teach Iris, or come to the house again because you have different standards to mine. Then, to crown everything, you add please will I not think you're bitter or angry. Now, listen to this, it's I who am bitter and angry. I wouldn't have you teach Iris if you were the last woman on earth. You can get out, and stay out, and you and your family are to be out of that cottage at the end of the month." He went into the house and slammed the door.

Janet held her mouth with both hands. It was not that there was any sound coming from it, for all sound had been struck out of her. Ben had come up to the yard to get things ready for milking. He had watched Donald and Janet from a shed. His eyes might be old, but he had read all that movement could tell him, and he had countryman's eyes, used to reading much from the way things fell. He hobbled across the yard and, with surprisingly gentle hands, moved Janet so that he could open the gate. Then he patted her arm.

"Away home, now, you do look wholly pale."

"Ben!" It was so faint a sound it might have been a murmur in the trees.

Ben had not handled sick animals for nothing.

"You go home now," he repeated, and then, in the encouraging voice he used to a sick mare, "Up, old lady, we'll have you fine and right by mornin'."

She shook her head.

"He hates me. He hates me, Ben."

He watched the tears trickle down her cheeks, then he shook his head.

"I been knockin' round this many a year, and I've learnt a parcel of thin's, and one of the first is there ain't not a blade of grass between hatin' and lovin', not between a lass an' a man there isn't."

Janet did not hear this. Ashamed of her tears, and with desperation forcing her to move, she was running to Maggie.

§

Barbara was sitting by the colonel when Dick came across the lawn. She gave him a cool little nod.

"Hullo!"

He had planned the meeting in the tea-garden just to avoid a public greeting. He wanted her in his arms. His voice showed it.

"Barbara!"

The colonel looked up, his eyes twinkling.

"Don't mind me. You take her down the garden." Barbara's voice was icy.

"No, thank you, I'm quite comfortable here."

The two men stared at her. The colonel turned to Dick. "You wouldn't think to hear her that she'd been like a mad thing ever since we knew you were coming home." He gave Barbara's knee a pat. "Get along, old thing. Here's poor Dick been kickin' his heels since three o'clock waitin' for a word from you."

Barbara played with Hoover's ears. Her voice trembled a little.

"Perhaps he hasn't been kicking his heels. Perhaps he's had company he prefers to mine."

Dick was like a dog who, expecting a pat, has been given a kick.

"I say, what on earth's getting you?"

"You know."

"I don't."

Barbara sighed.

"I don't want to be cross or anything just when you're home, and you've a perfect right to go about with any girl you like; I've not any special claim."

"Girl?" Then Dick's face lightened. "Oh, did you see me with that kid? But that was nothing. She was upset and I was just doing what I could, that was all."

Barbara raised her head.

"I always tell you everything, so I'll tell you I heard her say you'd been marvellous to her."

If Barbara had not looked so distant and unlike herself, Dick would have laughed.

"That kid! Oh, I was going to tell you about her . . ."

"You needn't bother; if you like to go out with Sheila it's your own business."

"Look here, I was waiting for you at the tea-garden, and I saw the poor kid crying because she's being packed off on a job. I gave her tea and a lift home. I didn't even know the girl's name was Sheila."

Barbara looped Hoover's ears in a knot at the back of his head. Usually his little skinned face, minus ears, made her laugh, but now she could not see him. Her eyes were dim with tears, one of which rolled off her nose.

"I don't want to quarrel on your very first day home, but you see, I know Sheila Brain, she's the sort . . ."

His voice stopped her.

"Sheila who?"

"Brain."

"That blasted family again!"

"They're not blasted, at least only Sheila is. Mrs. Brain's an angel, and a great friend of Daddy's, isn't she, Daddy, and Janet's grand."

"That's all you know. This Janet worked in my office."

"Of course! D'you know, I heard that. At least I must have, because at the back of my mind I knew there was some connection between you and Janet, but I'd forgotten it and she never mentioned it."

"She wouldn't. She seems to have taken advantage of my being abroad to search out Donald's address, and use a mythical arrangement with me to get Donald to house her beastly family for almost nix."

"It's a lie!"

"It's not, darling. She came to Donald; or rather she sent her sister, with this story, and I can promise you I never breathed Donald's name to her."

Barbara's forehead was furrowed with puzzlement.

"But it doesn't make sense. You've seen her. You know."

"I agree it's very unlike what I knew of her, but those are the facts."

"Donald must have made it up."

"Don't be a little idiot."

"Idiot nothing, I . . ."

The colonel had been listening intently. Now he sat up and took command, as he would have done in his army days. There was authority in his voice.

"Be quiet, both of you. You, Barbara, ought to be ashamed of yourself, sayin' over and over again that things aren't true, and not bringin' one fact to substantiate your claim. As for you, Dick, I don't know what manners they teach you in the Army these days, but in my time we didn't insult ladies the way you've been doin'."

Barbara shook the tears out of her eyes and crouched down beside her father.

"It's not Dick's fault. It's just some awful muddle, but Janet couldn't have cheated."

The colonel looked away from Barbara's red head to the sky, where some rooks were cawing homewards.

"Barbara's got the right of the thing, Dick. There's nothin' wrong with Janet Brain, and there's nothin' wrong with the mother." He got up. "Off you go, Dick, to the farm, and fetch that brother of yours and tell him he's to meet me at the Brains' cottage."

Barbara sat up on her haunches.

"But, Daddy, you can't. It's two fields to walk. You couldn't do it."

The colonel stiffened and straightened.

"For weeks now I've been thinkin' to meself I've had enough of that damned sawbones' mollycoddlin', but I didn't see me way to make a break. I'm goin' to the Brains' cottage, and it's not goin' to do me any harm, but there's one thing I insist on, and no arguin', mind. I'm havin' a whisky and soda before I start."

§

Because it was hot the party sat on the lawn, Maggie in one deck-chair and the colonel in another. Hoover, who had somehow got himself included in the party, lay under Maggie's chair. Barbara and Dick sat on the grass, Donald, looking stony, stood with his hands in his pockets. Janet, her face ghastly, and too feeble to stand, was half sitting on a window-ledge.

"These are the facts, Mrs. Brain," the colonel said gently, "as Donald and Dick have got hold of 'em. I wasn't havin' that kind of tale in my garden, with no one there to refute it, so we came to put the story in front of you." Maggie was looking at Donald.

"Do you mean to say I've been paying you only ten shillings a week for a house worth a hundred a year?"

"It was a fancy price the Moretons paid," Donald said awkwardly. "I dare say I'd never have got it again."

Maggie looked at Janet in pity and dismay. Of course it was understandable that she had wanted to get her mother and sister away from the bombings, and all credit to her, but it was not understandable that she should send her younger sister with the story of a faked understanding, to beg favours of her employer's brother. That was not like Janet, nor the way she had brought her up. Yet nobody could speak harshly to the crushed, broken Janet sitting on the window-seat.

"Janet, you should tell the truth, I think. In extenuation for you I can only say that a wish to get one's family away from the bombings was understandable, though, by the methods you used, unforgivable."

There was silence, then Janet raised her head; her eyes were black with suffering.

"I can't bear it that you, Mum, and you, Donald, can believe all this of me. I would never have believed such stories of either of you."

Maggie's voice was still gentle.

"But, Janet dear, here are the facts. Sheila came straight to this place, to this address; well, who gave her the address if not you?"

Donald gave a sudden quick movement and stepped to the edge of the lawn. He looked over his shoulder at Maggie.

"I thought you said Sheila was in bed with food poisoning?"

Maggie nodded.

"Potted meat at tea."

"She didn't have potted meat for tea," said Dick. "There wasn't any."

Donald gave a grunt.

"Whatever she had she's legging it across the fields now."

The colonel sat up.

"Run after her, Donald, and persuade Miss Sheila to come back here and have a word with us."

Sheila was a pitiable spectacle. She made no protest when Donald stopped her, but weakly, and with a cowed expression, returned with him to the cottage.

"Give the poor girl a chair," said the colonel. "You look very seedy, my dear. I understand it's potted meat."

Sheila fixed her eyes on Dick; her voice was so tiny that it was very difficult to hear it.

"Actually, no. It was castor-oil."

The colonel's lips twitched. He put a hand over his mouth to hide them.

"You've heard a good deal of what we've been sayin' from your bedroom, haven't you, that's why you ran? Where were you goin'?"

"To Gladys. We—we planned things together."

"Ah!" The colonel shifted his position. "Now tell me, did Janet send you down to Donald, to get this cottage?" Sheila turned hunted eyes round the party.

"I shouldn't wonder if I was sick."

"Never you mind that," the colonel said firmly. "You answer my question."

"Well, actually, no." Sheila fixed her eyes on Dick. "I was going on a message for Janet when I saw you outside her office. It was love at first sight."

Janet saw a twinkle in all the men's eyes, and she could not bear it. She got off the window-ledge and knelt beside Sheila, with a protective arm round her.

"Come on, you've been awfully silly, but let's have it all."

Slowly and painfully, struggling to make it dramatic, Sheila told her story. When she came to Gladys' share, she turned to Janet.

"I don't think she'd have ever thought of it alone. You see, he'd never kissed her and it was difficult for her, but I got her to do it, or I knew she'd never have let me know about Mr. Trent coming home."

When the story was finished the colonel was the first to speak.

"God bless my soul! Talk about female minds! You better get back into bed, my dear. If I was your mother I'd pack you off on your job in the morning whatever you felt like."

Maggie's face was grim.

"You can be sure I will."

Janet had seen an expression on Donald's face which made her heart miss a beat.

"Come on, Sheila," she said kindly. "I'll tuck you up."

"Then will you walk with me to the farm?" asked Donald urgently, and felt a new glory in the night when she nodded.

Dick's hand was already in Barbara's, and they were disappearing together round the side of the house. The colonel looked after them all and smiled.

"They've forgotten me. I suppose Barbara will be back presently." The night breeze rustled the trees, a sleepy bird cheeped. His voice dropped. "Maggie, my dear, I'm a bit of an old crock, but you've a great deal of happiness stored up in that heart of yours that you could give me if you would: and in return I'll do everything that's in me power to make you happy."

Maggie's eyes were misty, but she managed to smile.

"Including drinking milk?"

The colonel sighed.

"Even that."

Maggie did not answer for a moment. When she did she spoke hesitantly.

"It's a big step at your age. You'll laugh at me, but I feel shy. I mean, won't people think it queer?"

"Who cares if they do? Bound to be talk; there's talk about everythin' in Worsingfold. Kindness really to give 'm somethin' to jabber about. Tell you what, we might have a threesome weddin'. Bit of labour savin' for the vicar."

Maggie sat up.

"Nonsense. All my life I've planned my girls' weddings. Times without number I've seen myself fixing the orange blossom in Janet's hair. I'm not going to be done out of my rightful place as mother of the bride, and Janet's going to have her day to herself."

"I should think Barbara and Janet might share, one party for both and all that."

"Nonsense! In the first place Donald and Janet aren't even engaged yet."

"Neither are Barbara and Dick."

Maggie chuckled.

"I shall be very surprised if you don't hear about that tonight. I mean, when Barbara knows you are going to be looked after . . ."

"Ah! So we're comin' to us at last. But you've got the wrong idea, you know. It's I that'm goin' to look after you."

Maggie flushed.

"It's people like your servants I'm thinking of. I mean, they've been with you years. They aren't going to like a new mistress, especially a mistress like myself who, however hard she tries not to, will always be poking her head into her own kitchen."

The colonel's eyes were twinkling.

"No wonder Mincin' has been seein' a change comin'. Place full of spooks, and she strainin' round planning it was my coffin that was causin' the stir. 'Stead of that it's you comin' home."

Maggie was silenced by the word 'home'. She saw the Georgian house, the high wall with its wallflowers and stone-crop, its iron gates. The low, lovely drawing-room. The garden round which she could potter. She was not old, she would soon get her strength back, and now the years ahead, instead of being lonely, would be filled with the duties which went with such a house, but above all filled to overflowing with what she loved most, someone to care for and to make happy.

"Oh, my goodness!" she said at last. "I am a lucky woman!"

The colonel had been watching her face; he stretched out a hand.

"Can't kiss you here, bit public. There's life in us two warhorses yet, you know. We may be crocked for the time bein', but I shouldn't wonder if we managed to have the devil of a time when the children aren't lookin'. Thank you, my dear, you've made me very happy."

Barbara drew herself out of Dick's arms.

"You're an angel to forgive me. I'm not usually the jealous sort, but Sheila is the sort of girl that, if anyone was going to be jealous, it's about her they would be."

He kissed her again.

"What an involved sentence! I couldn't make out all that rubbish the kid was talking. I mean, some people don't plan to marry people they don't know. Anyway, why me?"

Barbara rubbed her face against his shoulder.

"That's the one thing I do understand. I imagine she lives in a fancy world where anything is possible."

"I'll take a bet, with her face, that in a couple of years she won't know us, she'll have climbed so high."

Barbara stepped away from him.

"Don't say 'us' in that positive way. You know I still can't marry you. Daddy's better, but this walk to the cottage is the first decent one he's taken for months. If I go he'll die of boredom and loneliness, cooped up seeing nobody."

"Well, couldn't we marry and live with him for a bit? I might get a decent slice of sick leave. Won't be the same thing as being on our own, but it'll be a lot better than nothing."

"If only we could, but you'll be stationed somewhere sooner or later, and then Daddy would make me join you."

"Might go East again."

"You are only saying that to weaken me. You know it's unlikely after malaria. Anyway, you'll have to spend a good deal of your leave in London, won't you? What about your business?"

"Yes, that wants disentangling. Easier now Janet's here, but I could go up and down, I suppose."

Barbara's voice had tears at the back of it.

"Don't go on. I want you all to myself so terribly. Don't weaken me. I simply can't leave Daddy alone. I've made up my mind to it."

Dick put his arms round her.

"Don't worry, little sweet. I can wait. Let's go and fetch your father. It's time we were toddling home."

At the side of the house Barbara stooped and picked up Hoover. She clutched Dick's arm and whispered "Ssh." Together they stared at the colonel and Maggie.

Dick put his lips against Barbara's ear.

"Jiminy Cricket! I never thought of that."

Donald and Janet had walked to the copse where they had first met. As Janet joined him he had pulled her arm through his.

"You are going to marry me, aren't you? In spite of all I thought about you."

"Well, I thought some things about you too. You know I love you." Walking across the fields she said: "But don't let's be engaged until after Gladys is out of your house."

"Oh, mercy! I'd forgotten her. I could strangle the wretched woman."

"Sheila's the one to strangle. Gladys really loves you. Poor Gladys!"

"She's got a job, anyway. Broadstairs is crazy to have her. He's sending her a letter tonight making her a very decent offer."

Janet paused, struck by an idea.

"Wouldn't it be simply glorious if they married? I mean she'd be marvellous as a headmaster's wife."

"Doesn't deserve anything. She's made you unhappy, blast her!"

"I'm only sorry. I know what her sort of unhappiness is like. You'll have to talk to her, you know, or she'll refuse Mr. Broadstairs' offer."

"I say, couldn't you?"

"Me! I'm the last person. Poor beast. You'll have to be frightfully nice and, if absolutely necessary, you can kiss her."

"Brute! I suppose you'll rub my nose in that as long as I live."

"Shouldn't wonder."

They had reached the copse. Donald had her in his arms. The minutes slid away, they had starved for one another, and now they were sure of each other time ceased to exist. They were dragged back to earth by a moan. Staring at them, her face greenish-white, was Gladys. She spoke on one dead note like a sleep-walker.

"I saw you go across the fields. Iris is all right. I said I shouldn't be long. Oh, God! Donald! Oh, Donald!"

Janet came to her.

"I'm sorry. Donald and I love each other. I know just how you feel. There isn't anything I can say."

Gladys seemed hardly conscious Janet had spoken.

"Ever since Anna died I've hoped and hoped. Even before she died I was planning. She knew. She used to tease me. 'No harm in trying,' she used to say, 'but you're not his sort, you know.' But Anna was fond of me, and I was good to her, and I have been good to Iris. I knew ever since you came it was all up. I tried not to believe it, but you can't fool yourself, can you? I'm not Sheila believing fairy-tales. It's a cruel world for lots of women."

Donald spoke gently.

"There's a good job being offered you. Mr. Broadstairs is writing to you to ask you to housekeeper the school."

"I think you'd like it," Janet added.

Gladys nodded.

"I dare say. One job will be the same as another now. I don't care where I go."

Trying desperately to help, Janet remembered the one source of comfort she knew. She took hold of Gladys' arm.

"You come to my mother. You can have my room, and I'll manage on the sofa. You won't want to go back to the farm tonight." She glanced at Donald over her shoulder. "Go on and look after Iris." She did not add, "And I'll be up later on," but Donald knew what she meant.

Maggie was bursting for Janet's return. She was longing to tell her the news, and yet shy. Still, if there was one person who would understand, it was her Jan. She busied herself after the colonel, Dick and Barbara had left, packing Sheila's things.

"It's no good moaning, dear," she said firmly. "This once you'll get no sympathy from me. A lot of sentimental twaddle you've been dreaming, and perhaps the best cure is castor-oil, and you've taken that."

"Even Janet's nicer than you are," Sheila sobbed.

"You don't deserve that she should be. Letting us all live here under false pretences. I should think it's an offence against the law."

Sheila gave a hiccoughing moan.

"I'd as soon go to prison as be driven away to live in a canteen." Maggie folded some cami-knickers.

"You won't live in a canteen. I wish I thought you wouldn't get the best of what's going, but I know you will."

"I wish I was dead." Maggie set her mouth and went on folding. "Nobody knows what love scorned feels like but me. A broken heart is a most awfully painful thing. It's an illness, really. Actually I think I shall take the veil and go into a monastery."

Maggie's lips twitched; she struggled with herself, then she began to laugh. She sat down on the bed and took Sheila in her arms.

"My silly goose! If you did take the veil I can quite believe you'd try and enter a monastery instead of a convent. Now stop crying; it's no good my telling you what I think of you, for one thing I shouldn't have time to get through it all before your train leaves. I'll just tell you one thing, and you'll have to take my word for it; however you feel at this minute, life hasn't finished for you." She patted the pillows, and gave Sheila a kiss. There was a twinkle in her eye. "In fact I think we can say about to-day that it was only the end of chapter one."

Maggie was in the kitchen getting Sheila a drink when Janet brought Gladys in. Her call of, "Come here, Jan," was on her lips. At sight of Gladys' face all thought of herself disappeared; here was suffering and she knew all about that.

"Make a pot of tea, Jan," she said lightly. "Miss Batten and I will have it in the sitting-room and take a cup up to Sheila." She led the apparently stunned Gladys to an armchair. "There's nothing like a cup of tea. It's a national joke saying so, but it's true, you know, and in my life I've had occasion to find out."

It was half an hour later before Maggie came out of the sitting-room. Janet was leaning against the lintel of the open back door.

"How is she?"

"She's had a good cry. She's better for it. Poor woman!"

"I knew you wouldn't mind my bringing her to you. She looked so awful I had to do something. You always comfort somehow. Besides, it's been a bit of a day, and I seemed used up."

"From what I gathered from Gladys it's had a good end though."

"Glorious! It's not over yet either. I'm going up to the farm just to say good night." Janet turned and hugged Maggie. "Oh, gosh! I'm so happy. You must think me a mean beast with Gladys crying in one room and Sheila howling in another. Not that I really mind about Sheila. Poor lamb! Fancy believing in fairy-tales!"

Maggie flushed and then gave a positively childish giggle.

"It runs in the family, darling, even the bit about living happily ever after. You see, I'm going to marry the colonel."

The country can look enchanted in the half light, and Janet ran through fields dimmed by an evening mist, under a sky crimsoned by the setting sun. "It can't be true," she thought. "This can't be me. Nobody on earth can really be so happy. Everything can't be as lovely as I see it."

Iris' excited squeak greeted Janet as she came into the farm.

"Janet, Janet! Come and say good night."

Janet ran up the stairs. Donald was sitting on Iris' bed. Janet looked at them with mock disapproval.

"Why aren't you asleep, Iris?"

"We've been playing blow feather. Daddy's got a bigger blow than me." The feather fluttered off the bed. Iris made a clucking sound with her tongue. "Drat the plaguey thing."

Donald picked it up.

"Here it is, Mrs. Honeywell." He stuck it on Janet's face.

"Excuse me, Miss Brain, you've a bit of moss on your chin."

They laughed. Iris looked puzzled.

"Why do you call a feather moss? An' why are you laughing?"

Janet hugged her, and tucked in her sheet.

"Just for happiness, darling."

THE END

FURROWED MIDDLEBROW

FM1. *A Footman for the Peacock* (1940) . . . . Rachel Ferguson
FM2. *Evenfield* (1942) . . . . Rachel Ferguson
FM3. *A Harp in Lowndes Square* (1936) . . . . Rachel Ferguson
FM4. *A Chelsea Concerto* (1959) . . . . Frances Faviell
FM5. *The Dancing Bear* (1954) . . . . Frances Faviell
FM6. *A House on the Rhine* (1955) . . . . Frances Faviell
FM7. *Thalia* (1957) . . . . Frances Faviell
FM8. *The Fledgeling* (1958) . . . . Frances Faviell
FM9. *Bewildering Cares* (1940) . . . . Winifred Peck
FM10. *Tom Tiddler's Ground* (1941) . . . . Ursula Orange
FM11. *Begin Again* (1936) . . . . Ursula Orange
FM12. *Company in the Evening* (1944) . . . . Ursula Orange
FM13. *The Late Mrs. Prioleau* (1946) . . . . Monica Tindall
FM14. *Bramton Wick* (1952) . . . . Elizabeth Fair
FM15. *Landscape in Sunlight* (1953) . . . . Elizabeth Fair
FM16. *The Native Heath* (1954) . . . . Elizabeth Fair
FM17. *Seaview House* (1955) . . . . Elizabeth Fair
FM18. *A Winter Away* (1957) . . . . Elizabeth Fair
FM19. *The Mingham Air* (1960) . . . . Elizabeth Fair
FM20. *The Lark* (1922) . . . . E. Nesbit
FM21. *Smouldering Fire* (1935) . . . . D.E. Stevenson
FM22. *Spring Magic* (1942) . . . . D.E. Stevenson
FM23. *Mrs. Tim Carries On* (1941) . . . . D.E. Stevenson
FM24. *Mrs. Tim Gets a Job* (1947) . . . . D.E. Stevenson
FM25. *Mrs. Tim Flies Home* (1952) . . . . D.E. Stevenson
FM26. *Alice* (1949) . . . . Elizabeth Eliot
FM27. *Henry* (1950) . . . . Elizabeth Eliot
FM28. *Mrs. Martell* (1953) . . . . Elizabeth Eliot
FM29. *Cecil* (1962) . . . . Elizabeth Eliot
FM30. *Nothing to Report* (1940) . . . . Carola Oman
FM31. *Somewhere in England* (1943) . . . . Carola Oman

FM32. *Spam Tomorrow* (1956) . . . . Verily Anderson
FM33. *Peace, Perfect Peace* (1947) . . . . Josephine Kamm
FM34. *Beneath the Visiting Moon* (1940) . . . . Romilly Cavan
FM35. *Table Two* (1942) . . . . Marjorie Wilenski
FM36. *The House Opposite* (1943) . . . . Barbara Noble
FM37. *Miss Carter and the Ifrit* (1945) . . . . Susan Alice Kerby
FM38. *Wine of Honour* (1945) . . . . Barbara Beauchamp
FM39. *A Game of Snakes and Ladders* (1938, 1955) . . . .
. . . . Doris Langley Moore
FM40. *Not at Home* (1948) . . . . Doris Langley Moore
FM41. *All Done by Kindness* (1951) . . . . Doris Langley Moore
FM42. *My Caravaggio Style* (1959) . . . . Doris Langley Moore
FM43. *Vittoria Cottage* (1949) . . . . D.E. Stevenson
FM44. *Music in the Hills* (1950) . . . . D.E. Stevenson
FM45. *Winter and Rough Weather* (1951) . . . . . . D.E. Stevenson
FM46. *Fresh from the Country* (1960) . . . . Miss Read
FM47. *Miss Mole* (1930) . . . . E.H. Young
FM48. *A House in the Country* (1957) . . . . Ruth Adam
FM49. *Much Dithering* (1937) . . . . Dorothy Lambert
FM50. *Miss Plum and Miss Penny* (1959) . Dorothy Evelyn Smith
FM51. *Village Story* (1951) . . . . Celia Buckmaster
FM52. *Family Ties* (1952) . . . . Celia Buckmaster
FM53. *Rhododendron Pie* (1930) . . . . Margery Sharp
FM54. *Fanfare for Tin Trumpets* (1932) . . . . Margery Sharp
FM55. *Four Gardens* (1935) . . . . Margery Sharp
FM56. *Harlequin House* (1939) . . . . Margery Sharp
FM57. *The Stone of Chastity* (1940) . . . . Margery Sharp
FM58. *The Foolish Gentlewoman* (1948) . . . . Margery Sharp
FM59. *The Swiss Summer* (1951) . . . . Stella Gibbons
FM60. *A Pink Front Door* (1959) . . . . Stella Gibbons
FM61. *The Weather at Tregulla* (1962) . . . . Stella Gibbons
FM62. *The Snow-Woman* (1969) . . . . Stella Gibbons
FM63. *The Woods in Winter* (1970) . . . . Stella Gibbons
FM64. *Apricot Sky* (1952) . . . . Ruby Ferguson
FM65. *Susan Settles Down* (1936) . . . . Molly Clavering
FM66. *Yoked with a Lamb* (1938) . . . . Molly Clavering
FM67. *Loves Comes Home* (1938) . . . . Molly Clavering

FM68. *Touch not the Nettle* (1939) .... MOLLY CLAVERING
FM69. *Mrs. Lorimer's Quiet Summer* (1953) ... MOLLY CLAVERING
FM70. *Because of Sam* (1953) .... MOLLY CLAVERING
FM71. *Dear Hugo* (1955) .... MOLLY CLAVERING
FM72. *Near Neighbours* (1956) .... MOLLY CLAVERING
FM73. *The Fair Miss Fortune* (1938) .... D.E. STEVENSON
FM74. *Green Money* (1939) .... D.E. STEVENSON
FM75. *The English Air* (1940)* .... D.E. STEVENSON
FM76. *Kate Hardy* (1947) .... D.E. STEVENSON
FM77. *Young Mrs. Savage* (1948) .... D.E. STEVENSON
FM78. *Five Windows* (1953)* .... D.E. STEVENSON
FM79. *Charlotte Fairlie* (1954) .... D.E. STEVENSON
FM80. *The Tall Stranger* (1957)* .... D.E. STEVENSON
FM81. *Anna and Her Daughters* (1958)* .... D.E. STEVENSON
FM82. *The Musgraves* (1960) .... D.E. STEVENSON
FM83. *The Blue Sapphire* (1963)* .... D.E. STEVENSON
FM84. *The Marble Staircase* (c.1960) .... ELIZABETH FAIR
FM85. *Clothes-Pegs* (1939) .... SUSAN SCARLETT**
FM86. *Sally-Ann* (1939) .... SUSAN SCARLETT**
FM87. *Peter and Paul* (1940) .... SUSAN SCARLETT**
FM88. *Ten Way Street* (1940) .... SUSAN SCARLETT**
FM89. *The Man in the Dark* (1939) .... SUSAN SCARLETT**
FM90. *Babbacombe's* (1941) .... SUSAN SCARLETT**
FM91. *Under the Rainbow* (1942) .... SUSAN SCARLETT**
FM92. *Summer Pudding* (1943) .... SUSAN SCARLETT**
FM93. *Murder While You Work* (1944) .... SUSAN SCARLETT**
FM94. *Poppies for England* (1948) .... SUSAN SCARLETT**
FM95. *Pirouette* (1948) .... SUSAN SCARLETT**
FM96. *Love in a Mist* (1951) .... SUSAN SCARLETT**

*titles available in paperback only
**pseudonym of Noel Streatfeild

Lightning Source UK Ltd.
Milton Keynes UK
UKHW041921010822
406672UK00012B/290